STRANGE ECONOMICS
ECONOMIC SPECULATIVE FICTION

Edited by David F. Shultz

TDOTSPEC

Strange Economics. *Economic Speculative Fiction*
Edited by **David F. Shultz**

This is a work of fiction. The stories are products of the author's imagination and are not intended to be construed as real. Any resemblance to actual persons, living or dead, is entirely coincidental.

Copyright © 2018 David F. Shultz
ISBN 978-1-9994039-0-4

All rights reserved.

Cover Illustration: Jonathan Maurin
Interior design: Mariana Vidakovics De Victor

Published by: TdotSpec inc.

Copyright Acknowledgements

"Acknowledgements" and "Introduction" Copyright © 2018 David F. Shultz
"The Slow Bomb" Copyright © 2018 Neil James Hudson
"The Rule of Three" Copyright © 2018 Steve DuBois
"Have Ichthyosaur, Will Travel" Copyright © 2018 D.K. Latta
"The Grass is Always Greener" Copyright © 2018 Fraser Sherman
"Shocktrooper Salesman" Copyright © 2018 Simonas Juodis
"Supply Chains" Copyright © 2018 Petra Kuppers
"Premium Care" Copyright © 2018 Brandon Ketchum
"Consumption" Copyright © 2018 K.M. McKenzie
"The Slurm" Copyright © 2018 Marissa James
"Guns or Butter" Copyright © 2018 Wayne Cusack
"A Renewable Resource" Copyright © 2018 Steve Quinn
"All Rights Reserved" Copyright © 2018 Xauri'EL Zwaan
"The Soul Standard" Copyright © 2018 John DeLaughter
"Warm Storage" Copyright © 2018 Michael H. Hanson
"I Can Always Tell a John" Copyright © 2018 Greg Beatty
"The Short Soul" Copyright © 2018 Jack Waddell
"The Monument" Copyright © 2018 Andrea Bradley
"Unseen Face of the Moon Business" Copyright © 2018 Diana Parparita
"Expiry Date" Copyright © 2018 Eamonn Murphy
"The Price of Wool and Sunflowers" Copyright © 2018 Samantha Rich
"Supply and Demand Among the Sidhe" Copyright © 2018 Karl Dandenell
"Shape, Size, Colour, and Luster" Copyright © 2018 JM Templet
"Das Kapital" Copyright © 2018 Stephen Woodworth
"Afterword" Copyright © 2018 Jo Lindsay Walton
"Economics Discussion Questions" Copyright © 2018 Elisabeth Perlman

ACKNOWLEDGEMENTS

This anthology wouldn't have been possible without the dedication and support of an enormous team of volunteers, professionals, and project backers. All told, nearly two-hundred people were involved materially in the creation of *Strange Economics*.

Our editorial and reading team consisted of over a dozen volunteers, mostly made up of members of the Toronto Science Fiction and Fantasy Writing Group, but also extending across international borders and an ocean. Thank you Adrienne, Alana, Aya, Calder, Elisabeth, Jo, Justin, Mandy, Mellisha, Mickaël, Nora, Phillipe, Sean, and Wayne!

Strange Economics benefited from the insight of a professional economist, Elisabeth Ruth Perlman, Economist at the Center for Economic Studies, U.S. Census Bureau. Elisabeth was part of our editorial team and also wrote the economics discussion questions that accompany the stories. Thank you, Bitsy!

The *Strange Economics* team also included a guest editor, Jo Lindsay Walton, editor at *Vector*, the critical journal of the British Science Fiction Association. Jo provided the afterword, an essay analysing the relationship between speculative fiction and economics. Thanks Jo!

Our lead copy editor was Justin Dill. Our second copy editor was John Kerr. Together, they made three or more passes to polish every story, catch errors, and ensure consistency in style-guidelines. Thanks, Justin and John!

Our cover illustrator was Jonathan Maurin, a French illustrator and concept artist. He was the featured artist in the 22nd exhibit of the Luminarium for "Ring of Heaven", which is the cover image of *Strange Economics*. Thanks, Jonathan!

In addition to the production of the anthology, there was also the work of promotion, encouraging social media engagement, and executing our funding strategy. We were lucky to have a team of volunteers to help get the word out and attract attention to *Strange Economics*. Thank you, Adrienne, Alana, Mandy, and Mellisha!

I would like to say a special thank you to our author affiliate, Hari Kumar, who supported the project and whose novel, *Intersection Man*, explores, among other themes, the economics of far futures.

I would also like to say a special thank you to Jeff Rock, who supported the anthology with a very generous donation.

This anthology owes its existence to a new kind of economic reality, brought about by the internet. Funds for the project were provided by 160 project backers using the crowdfunding platform Kickstarter. Through modern technology, we were able to share the vision of our anthology across the internet and have it supported by people all across the English-speaking world.

I consider myself very lucky for having had the opportunity to work with such a talented and dedicated team of authors, editors, volunteers, and professionals. This project would not have been possible without the support of our project backers. On behalf of the Strange Economics team, and our twenty-three authors, I would like to say thank you to all of our backers for making Strange Economics possible.

PROJECT BACKERS

@Wit_LackThereof
A. M. Todd
A.J. Bohne
Adi Peshkess
Alana Frome
Alyksandrei
Amanda Nixon
Amirf
Andrew
Andrew Hatchell
anneCwind
Ben Davey
Benjamin C. Kinney

Benjamin Widmer
Bitsy
Björn Prömpeler
Bobbi Boyd
Bradley Gailey
Bradley Walker
C White
Caitlin Jane Hughes
Cal Kotz
Camille Lofters
Carmen L
Carolyn Rock
Cathy Green

Chantal Gaudiano
Chris B
Chris Griffin
Christopher Browne
Cindy
Cindy
Clyde Nads
Cody Black
Cornelis Clüver
Cullen Gilchrist
Curtis Frye
D Creith
Dan "Grimmund" Long
Daniel Ence
Daniel Pollastro
Daniel Tyler
David Perlmutter
Davina Tijani
Dennis
Dennis Bebie
Devin Carlos Irizarry Voorsanger
Devon Tabris
Devon Wong
Don W. Friedricksen
Dr. Jörg Viebranz
Duane Warnecke
Emil Terziev
Eric Damon Walters
Erik T Johnson
Erin Subramanian
Fernando Autran
Francesco Morabito
Francis Budden-Hinds
Francisco Campaña
Fred Herman

Freyja Anderson
GeorgeZ
Guillaume Couture-Levesque
H. Rasmussen
Hari Kumar
Henri Audigé
Isaac Chappell
J.P. Brannan
Jack Lee
Jacob W Wagner
Jakub Vul
james canton
James Williams
Jay Richards
Jeff Eaton
Jeff Rock
Jim Jorritsma
JKB
Joe Jones
Joe Robinson
John Appel
John Green
Jomelson Co
Jon Berry
Jonathon Whitington
Justin Dill
Kari Kilgore
Karl Delling
Ken Finlayson
Kevin "Wolf" Patti
KM
Kristin Evenson Hirst
Krystina Colton
Kumsal
Larry Botsikos

Lexi P.
lindsay watt
Lorraine Hatchwell
Luke Von Rose
M Hendrik Tilma
Mark Carter
Mark Newman
Martin Bernstein
Matthew J. Rogers
Max O Ornstein
Mickaël Zysman
Mike Hampton
Nathan
Nathan Santos
Nick Lehman
Olivier Aron
Patrick McEvoy
Paul Alex Gray
Pedro Alfaro
Pegana
Peter Vroomen
Petr C Cooper
Rebecca Junell
Rich Lambe
Richard "Kimara Cretak" Grotkier II
Rob Voss
Robert Claney
Robert D. Stewart
Robert Peacock
Robert Prior
Robyn
Ryan J Eckert
Ryan Weir

Saz
Seamus Quigley
Sean B
ShadowCub
Shem Bingman
Simo Muinonen
Skevos Mavros
Sonia Reed
Stephanie Lucas
Stephen Loftus-Mercer
Stephen Rider
Steve Lord
Stewart Walker
Sylvia B
Thomas Bull
Thomas M. Colwell
Thomas Pape
Thomas Sowell
Tom Plaskon
Torrain
Tripleyew
Upper Rubber Boot Books
V Shadow
wardude
William Sims
Willie
Zachary Lambert
Zachary Marcotte

INTRODUCTION

The genre of speculative fiction includes science fiction, fantasy, and supernatural horror. These stories ask us "what if?", envisioning alternate realities, different ways of being, and possible consequences of technological advancement. In *Strange Economics*, the speculative elements relate to economic concerns—the production, consumption, and transfer of wealth; these stories imagine money and trade in worlds of magic and advanced technology.

Setting stories in fantastic worlds allows us to probe interesting questions: What if souls were a form of currency? What if our potential could be bought and sold? What is the value of a memory? *Strange Economics* addresses these questions and more with stories that isolate aspects of the human experience, making the familiar strange and highlighting truths about ourselves in the process.

The *Strange Economics* reading and editorial team was a diverse group of over a dozen volunteers, including writers of science fiction and fantasy, academics, guest editors, and a professional economist. Stories had to pass through three editorial rounds, including a final roundtable where we debated the merits of the best stories. The team did not always agree. Though the majority of the stories were supported by the team, a few were controversial, and vociferous objections crashed against enthusiastic support. The result is a collection that does not cater to any one particular taste, but instead represents a wide range of styles. There are stories for every reader—something for everyone to love.

We were looking for compelling stories that provoke thought about economic issues, such as questions of fairness and wealth distribution, the limits of choice and freedom in capitalism, provisioning of resources, and models of economic behaviour. Towards that end, we have also included an afterword written by guest editor Jo Lindsay Walton, to serve as a critical discussion of the relationship between economics and speculative fiction, and a collection of economics discussion questions to accompany the stories, written by Economist Elisabeth Perlman.

The *Strange Economics* stories stick with you—these are stories you will want to discuss and share. I truly hope you enjoy reading this collection as much as we enjoyed working on it; if it's even half as enjoyable, you'll have a great time! Most of all, I hope these stories give you new lenses through which to view economics, and they encourage you to reflect on the ideas they explore.

Have fun reading *Strange Economics*!

David F. Shultz, editor

TABLE OF CONTENTS

The Slow Bomb
Neil James Hudson 1
The Rule Of Three
Steve Dubois 13
Have Ichthyosaur, Will Travel
D.k. Latta 27
The Grass Is Always Greener
Fraser Sherman 39
Shocktrooper Salesman
Simonas Juodis 49
Supply Chains
Petra Kuppers 61
Premium Care
Brandon Ketchum 71
Consumption
K.m. Mckenzie 75
The Slurm
M. James 91
Guns Or Butter
Wayne Cusack 103
A Renewable Resource
Steve Quinn 125
All Rights Reserved
Xauri'el Zwaan 135
The Soul Standard
John Delaughter 155
Warm Storage
Michael H. Hanson 161
I Can Always Tell A John
Greg Beatty 167

The Short Soul
Jack Waddell 177
The Monument
Andrea Bradley 197
The Unseen Face Of The Moon Business
Diana Părpăriţă 209
Expiry Date
Eamonn Murphy 227
The Price Of Wool And Sunflowers
Samantha Rich 241
Supply And Demand Among The Sidhe
Karl Dandenell...257
Shape, Size, Colour, And Lustre
Jm Templet 275
Das Kapital
Stephen Woodworth..285
Afterword: Cockayne Blues
Jo Lindsay Walton 301
Works Cited 327
Economics Discussion Questions
Elisabeth Perlman 331
About The Contributors 347

THE SLOW BOMB
Neil James Hudson

I could see the slow bomb from Professor Bateman's window, just a speck. The warplane was easier to make out, a triangular shape hovering above the bomb. Both appeared stationary; I knew that the opposite was true.

"Grabs your attention, doesn't it?" I had ignored the occupants of the room as I entered; the bomb always distracted me from anything else. I now saw that a woman in military uniform sat to the side of the room; it was she who had addressed me.

"I chose this room deliberately," Bateman said to her. "I like the memento mori. Please sit down, Alistair."

I did so, guardedly. The woman's presence was unnerving. She had blonde, cropped hair beneath a camouflage hat; a small scar on her cheek looked like a duelling injury, but I suspected that it had some more mundane explanation. I found myself pulling at my wristband, a nervous habit, and moved my hand away.

"First things first," she said, producing a typed sheet of paper from a document case. "I need you to sign this. Official Secrets Act. Everything that takes place in this meeting is strictly confidential. I can tell you the penalties for breaking it if you want, but…" She shrugged. "They're off the scale."

I looked down at the paper in some confusion. "What happens if I don't sign?"

"Meeting terminated. You'll be under no compulsion, but you'll never find out what we were going to ask."

Still, I hesitated. Perhaps it was just the sight of the bomb through the window, but I felt that signing this paper would open a door that I didn't want to go through.

"I've made a mistake," she said, reaching for the paper.

"No, I'll sign. If there are really no catches?" Neither of them responded, so I signed. She took the paper.

"This is General Elisabeth Monroe," said Bateman. "You can see she's with the army, but she heads a joint project with civilian organizations to study the slow bomb."

Again, I found myself glancing through the window at the warplane and its deadly payload.

General Monroe spoke. "What work are you currently involved in?"

"We're looking into how to run down the economy," I said. "It's never been done deliberately before. But we're hoping we can find a way of stopping it neatly, rather than having everything end in chaos."

"I want you taken off that work. It's beneath you. I'm more interested in the book you wrote." I tried not to sigh. The book had become notorious and universally misunderstood. "The Price of a Life. You used standard economic tools to place a financial value on human life. What answer did you come up with?"

"It depends."

"Good answer."

"I wasn't trying to answer—or even pose—the question. I was just pointing out that we make such a valuation all the time—most obviously in warfare, but also in deciding how much to spend on healthcare and emergency services, and even how much to invest in our own future welfare. These decisions are always intuitive, off the cuff, improvised, and incoherent. I merely felt that we should make them a little more consciously."

"Heh." I didn't know if she was laughing at me or merely acknowledging my point. "What I want you to do, Dr. Holdcroft, is to place a financial value on the final five years of human existence."

"What? Why?"

"To prove they would be better spent elsewhere."

I didn't understand, so I said nothing. The General stood up and gestured towards the window. "Look at it. That bomb started falling before I was born. It will reach the ground after I'm dead. But we know that will be it. It seems to be big enough to wipe out this country at least, and we've no idea what other effect it will have. There are slow warplanes all over the world; we think there's another hatch opening over China, although we won't know for six months. However many it takes, they'll finish the job. They mean to wipe us all out, and there's nothing we can do to avoid our fate. All attempts to communicate, shoot down the planes, or knock the bomb off course come to nothing. We can't touch them."

"They seem to come from another dimension," I said. "Have their own physics."

"Perhaps they do. But they are also in our world, where we have our own physics, which poses some interesting questions. How does the bomb stay up there?"

"It doesn't. It's falling. Just slowly."

"Indeed. Far too slowly for our world. Somewhere along the line, a whole lot of energy is being expended to keep it up there."

"I suppose so." I'd never thought about it like that. Our attackers lived to a different time than we did; a few minutes to them was a century to us.

"We've found out how to tap that energy. Oh, don't worry; it's all theoretical. It hasn't been done yet. But that bomb hanging in the air is a free source of power. It can fuel our economy for decades, usher in an era of wealth and security that humanity has never known, drive our progress and technology to unimaginable heights."

"But... if you take away the energy that keeps the bomb in the air..."

She smiled. "It falls more quickly." She returned to her chair. "We want to advance the day of destruction by five years. In exchange for economic benefits."

"That's insane."

"And we want you to provide the calculations that prove it's worth it."

I looked away from the General, back out of the window, towards the warplane. I imagined its cargo of death suspended in the air beneath it, falling at a rate impossible to perceive. I was being asked to collaborate with it. But at the same time, I was already thinking how the formulae would work.

Bateman spoke, although I felt he was a bit of a spare part in this conversation. "We want you on this project, Alistair. This department needs a shot in the arm, and the prestige of this project will be enormous. Not to mention the grant that General Monroe is offering."

"But the calculations will always be arbitrary," I said. "You can get the results you want just by how you set the variables."

"That is exactly what the General is asking you to do. Just make it convincing. Show the people that it makes sound financial sense to shorten the future for a better present."

"I won't lie," said the General. "The other reason we chose you is because you're not a stranger to controversy. This is going to be controversial. But you can always remain a step away from it. You never actually advocated the project; you merely showed, as an intellectual exercise, that the figures seemed to advise it."

I looked again at the warplane, apparently immobile but actually expending unimaginable energy. There were about a hundred of them around the globe; so far there was only one bomb, although that was set to change. No one knew how destructive the bomb would be, although it was expected to be huge. No one knew why they were attacking us. No one knew how much of the planet would survive, if any. All we knew was that the first bomb would land at the beginning of the next century, comfortably after I had departed.

Even so, I found the sentence of death unbearable. I had to spend the whole of my life watching the last years of my species. I had to watch the hammer falling, inexorably moving towards the day of impact. I had to pretend that our lives were worth living until the end. If I could have had one wish, it would have been to get it over with.

Again, I found that I had to move my hand away from my wristband.

"I'll do it," I said.

The General stood up to leave. "I'd be grateful if you would visit the project tomorrow morning." She handed me a card with an address on it. "Sorry for the short notice, but I'm in a bigger hurry than the bomb. Oh, and Dr. Holdcroft? Don't forget that paper you signed."

She left, and Bateman congratulated me with words I didn't hear. I don't even remember leaving his office. All I could hear was the sound of impact, drawn out over a year, but as destructive as if it had taken a second.

The project was housed in a four-storey set of office blocks. I had expected something a little less run down, and I wondered what previous use the building had had. The man at the desk was about half my age and sat next to what I assumed to be a panic button. He clipped a security pass to my jacket, pointed me to a lift, and advised me that my destination was two floors below ground level. I was surprised that I was being sent unaccompanied, and I assumed that the security pass was tracking me; there were one or two obvious security cameras, and probably many more that were less obvious.

I pressed the button in the lift and felt myself descending. When the door opened, General Monroe was waiting for me. "Thank you for being on time," she said. "Please follow me."

I walked behind her, even though the corridor was wide enough for us to walk side by side. She did not look back. We turned a corner and stopped at a door marked "028." The General looked into a scanner, and the lock clicked. She pushed the door open.

"This is the prototype," she said. "This is just to test the theory. The final device will be considerably bigger. We may have trouble getting it up in the air."

It looked like a synthesizer from the 1970s. Two large black slabs stood against the far wall, covered in lights, dials, switches, and sliders. On the floor in front of them was a large black metal box, two satellite dishes fixed to the front, pointing towards us. On top of the box was a laptop. I tried to take it in but couldn't see how it worked. I began to walk towards it.

"I don't understand," I said. "How can you test the device without actually testing it on—"

I nearly walked into it. It was at head height, less than an inch in length, shiny and metallic. It wasn't difficult to see, but it was impossible for it to be there. It was pointed at one end, which was the only way I could tell its direction of travel.

"It moves at a rate of about an inch a month," said the General. "We don't know who fired it, or where they are now. All we found was the bullet."

I moved around it, stood in front, watching the bullet aiming directly at my face.

"That's why we have this building. The slow bullet was here first. As soon as we found it, we took over."

Slowly, I raised a finger to touch it.

"Are you sure you want to do that, Dr. Holdcroft? We have no idea who the target is. It may be you."

I looked at her and then pulled my finger away and stood to the side. "What happens when it hits its target? Does it speed up again?"

"You don't have clearance to ask these questions. Let's just say slow weapons have a habit of hitting their targets."

A habit. I had thought we only had slow bombs to worry about. Now I knew there were slow bullets being fired at various places, and who knew what other slow devices.

"Oh, don't worry, Dr. Holdcroft. You're not the target. I wouldn't have brought you here if you were. No, this bullet is aimed at me."

"How can you know that?"

She walked over to the other side of the bullet and stared at it intently. "A soldier's intuition. We always know when our number's up."

"But this is easily avoided. Just don't stand in front of it. Sooner or later, it will hit the wall."

She laughed but didn't look up. "We can't avoid our fates. Shall I tell you my theory? I think our attackers are from the future. Perhaps they are pre-empting some crime we have yet to commit. But I think they have the benefit of hindsight. They know my movements; they know where I will be at the moment of impact, and they fired the bullet to get there at the same time."

I gestured at the far wall to distract her. "How does this work?"

"The Altman device? I didn't bring you here to show you that—just the bullet."

"Why?"

Finally, she looked up. "Because we all have our fates. I do not think you should be so confident that you will escape yours. You know the way out, Dr. Holdcroft. Please return your pass to reception, or you will not be able to leave."

I accepted the dismissal and returned to the door. She did not follow me. I looked back; once again, she was enthralled by the bullet, staring at it as if it were a hypnotist's watch. I left her to it and returned to the lift.

The Slow Bomb

I set about my work. As Bateman had said, it was easy enough to come up with the answer; the problem was to make it convincing. I needed to make it look as if I had stumbled upon this result, not deliberately arranged it.

The General supplied me with details of how much energy would be extracted from the bomb. I was astonished. I had thought there couldn't have been so much at stake. I ran a few calculations and decided that the bomb must have had far more mass than there appeared. This was good news for my formula; it meant that life would have to be priced fairly highly to beat it.

As I had said, there were ways of quantifying the value of a human life. We might not have liked it, but lives were valued against money all the time, and one could measure these values and plot them like a stock market chart. Unfortunately, there was massive variation in the results. Life was cheap during wartime; when deciding the price of life-saving drugs, it could run into the millions. Worse, different lives seemed to be valued in different ways. This was monstrously unjust but remained true. For every Western politician or celebrity, there were thousands of third-world peasants pulling the average down.

Would life be valued more or less as the bomb reached its last few feet and the clock ticked to the end? I didn't know, and I realised that I had to provide a range of values for either possibility. I returned to the research I had carried out for my book, which had been based largely on questionnaires in which volunteers were asked to value their lives. They gave different answers according to how the question was phrased. For example, when asked how much their lives were worth, most people provided an answer, usually in the millions. When asked how much money it would take to persuade them to kill themselves, not one respondent provided a figure.

Nonetheless, the numbers came together. Slowly, I was able to make a convincing argument that it made economic sense to shorten our span of existence in exchange for economic benefits in the here and now. What I doubted was whether I should be doing it.

My work was near its completion, and my doubts at their highest,

7

when General Monroe called unexpectedly to ask if I wanted to see the bomb up close.

The helicopter approached the bomb at such speed that I wondered if we were on a suicide mission to crash into it, but the pilot swerved away and hovered next to it. It looked like an enlarged version of the slow bullet: slightly longer than our helicopter, gleaming metallic, and pointed at one end. I was almost disappointed that they had not written an offensive message along the side. The bomb was tilted at an angle of about forty-five degrees, not yet having reached its final position of pointing straight downwards.

"It looks as if you could push it away," I said.

"It's the classic immoveable object," said the General. "If we flew into it, we'd lose. Take us up."

The pilot pulled away from the bomb and began to climb. The General intended to show me the warplane.

I had not seen anything exactly like it, although it had clearly been designed to obey the same laws of aerodynamics as our own. It was more or less triangular in shape, with a stubby nose poking out at the front. The hatch from which the bomb had dropped was still open, and the warplane had travelled about half a mile from the target site. Its speed had been calculated from the distance it had travelled in proportion to the descent of the bomb. It was fast.

Most chilling of all was the cockpit. The plane was piloted by a human, although their face was not visible beneath their oxygen mask. The pilot looked like a throwback to the Second World War rather than a warrior from the future. I could not tell their gender.

"Looks so close, doesn't he?" said General Monroe. "I feel as if I should be able to climb in and break his jaw."

I felt more as if the pilot could climb out of his plane and break mine, although he (if the General was right) was facing away from us.

"Why are you showing me this?"

"Tell me about that band on your wrist."

I looked down at it, an orange band, with a row of black crosses on its circumference. "You know what it means. No descendants. I've taken a vow not to procreate. I won't bring grandchildren into the world of the bomb. If everyone follows my lead, there'll be no bloodshed. The human race will die out, just as our attackers want. But they won't actually kill anyone. There'll be no one around when the bomb hits."

"Heh," said the General, and again I couldn't tell if she was laughing. "Ask me the obvious question."

I wasn't sure what she meant, and I wanted to answer guardedly, in case I made myself look stupid. But I doubted that she would respect such an approach. "Why not take the energy from the warplane rather than the bomb?"

"Because they won't let us. Somehow, they're blocking the energy transfer from the planes. They could just as easily have blocked it from the bombs, but they haven't bothered. In fact, they seem to have gone to some lengths to make it possible. They want us to hasten the end; it suits them as much as it suits us. You know there is a way out?"

"Only for very few. Some of us will get to Mars, taking a bit of our genetic material with us. A fragment of the human race can survive. Until they decide to attack Mars."

"We can't colonize another planet while you're figuring out how to wind the world down. We need a massive surge in growth, a massive advance in technology. We need the energy more than we need the time. The more economic growth we can have in the short term, the more of humanity we can save for the longer term. We have to bring the bomb forwards in order to get a few of us off the planet." She turned to me for the first time. "Get me those equations, and I can get your descendants on the programme."

"On Mars? I don't believe you."

"Why not? Did you think people would be chosen fairly? We'll do our best to choose the people we most need for a new world, but we'll have to make compromises. You can be one of them. Help me bring the bomb forwards, and you can take that wristband off and be part of humanity's future. Don't help, and, well..." She turned back to the pilot of the warplane, as if she were hoping to stare him out. "Remember that face."

We began to descend.

And, of course, I was present at the testing of the prototype.

The far wall had been built up with sandbags to deaden the impact. General Monroe was there, as were about twenty other people, all standing behind a safety rope to the rear of the bullet. Most of these wore military uniform; all wore name badges, and as far as I could make out, the remainder were scientific staff. There seemed to be neither press nor anyone from outside the project, and I was not sure why I had been invited.

"Your involvement in the project is vital," General Monroe said to me when I asked, after which she had nothing further to do with me. To be fair, she seemed to be very busy with various people, and it seemed that my presence wasn't appreciated by anyone else, so I kept myself out of the way as much as possible.

Only one person stood in front of the rope. He was largely bald, with a bank of black hair on either side of his head. He had not shaved, but otherwise seemed to be a neat man. I could not read his identity badge, but it became clear that he was Professor Alton, the physicist in charge of the project.

The experiment was scheduled for eight o'clock exactly. I could not think of a good reason why it should have such a precise time, nor why it should take place so early, and I presumed that these were just military habits.

Finally, Professor Alton turned to those assembled and said, "We're ready." I looked at my watch; we were two minutes away from the allotted time. I doubted that any preparations had actually been needed and figured that he had just been killing time until the deadline.

He continued to address us as if he were in charge. "I shall activate the device at precisely 0800 hours. The energy harvested from the bullet will be diverted to the National Grid, although this may temporarily short out our circuits and we may need to switch to emergency power. There will be a ten-second delay to allow me to leave the scene and get behind the rope." There was a gap where two soldiers had cleared a space for him. "I must ask everyone to put on the safety goggles you have been given."

Some of the military seemed to have bulletproof clothing, but I had only been given the goggles. I put them on dutifully.

"We just have a minute to wait," said the Professor.

It was an agonizing wait. All I wanted was for the minute to end and the bullet to fire. This minute, I knew, was like all our minutes now. I knew my real reason for taking part in the project; I could not bear the wait. We knew that the bomb would land; I just couldn't cope with the delay.

I thought Professor Alton was going to give us a countdown, but all he said was "activating the device... now."

Then he calmly walked to the centre of the room and stood in front of the bullet.

"What the hell do you think you're doing?" shouted the General. "Get out of there."

"I'm not going to wait for the end of humanity," said Alton. "They can take me now."

"You idiot!" The General climbed under the rope and rushed towards him. I called out but could only stand and watch, as helpless as everyone else, as the two scuffled in the bullet's path.

The lights went out, but the emergency lighting came on in a second. The General's body had not even fallen over by then. They had known exactly where she would be at the moment of impact.

Bullet wounds are not as neat as they appear in films. The entry point may be neat, but the bullet pushes so much material ahead of itself that the exit wound is far larger and messier. Not everything that had been pushed through the General's skull was blood. I turned away, not even physically nauseous yet but already wishing I could remove the sight from my mind's eye. There was a crash as the General's body collapsed to the floor, and then the chaos of shouting and movement as others tried to regain command and deal with the situation. But I did not look back. I had seen all I needed to see.

I took my equations to Bateman the next day. There didn't seem to be any reason to delay. I only had a small adjustment to make.

"This is a summary of my work," I said. "The whole thing is available here." I passed him a memory stick and a single piece of paper.

He scanned the paper avidly while I looked out of the window at the warplane whose pilot I had studied at close range. It seemed to have moved since the last time I was here.

"Holdcroft," he said. "What's this?"

I looked back at the paper. He held the page up to me, finger pointing at the Greek letter, as if I would not know what he was referring to.

"Friction," I said.

"You'll need to enlighten me."

"Everything has its price. So does economics. Whenever you translate something into financial terms, it costs. It's worth less than before you started. It's not a huge amount, but it multiplies. If you're doing it a lot, it rises exponentially. When you're translating lives into economics, billions of lives, then by the end you have—"

"Nothing. This makes it worthless. You're saying it's not worth tapping the bomb."

I looked directly at him, just as I had looked at the pilot. "That's what the equations show."

"But you've just fiddled the equations to produce the results you wanted!"

"That is precisely what you asked me to do."

He was going red. I hadn't expected such an emotional reaction from him. "Get out of my office," he said. "Get out of my department. You're on sabbatical. As of now. Until I can find a way of getting rid of you."

"It's been a pleasure," I said standing to leave.

"Someone else will do it. I'll do it myself if I have to."

"Good luck," I said.

I cleared my desk and left the building before I had to suffer the embarrassment of being escorted. As I reached my car, I looked up at the warplane, a triangular speck. An invasion not just into our world, but into our physics.

I looked down at my wristband. I presumed that the General's offer would not stand now. Mars, indeed—planet of avoided fate.

I would not conspire with the invasion. I would not participate in the end of the world. I tore my wristband off and threw it to the ground.

I left it where it was and drove off, ready to face the bomb in my own way.

THE RULE OF THREE
Steve DuBois

"Yes, Ms. Baum," Caté explained, "all of our Eye of Newt is organic. It comes, you see, from the eye of a newt. Hence the name." She spoke wearily into the receiver of the antique hand-crank phone and then pressed the earpiece to her ear, trying to make sense of the garbled squawk it emitted. "Yes," she sighed, "also locally sourced. Amphibians don't travel well; they tend to dry out in transport."

The alchemist's shop buzzed and hummed around her. Customers wandered through a maze of cupboards and shelves, staring at mini-cauldrons atop Bunsen burners and fingering packets of suspicious-looking herbs. In the corner stood Henrietta, all pearly teeth and golden curls, displaying an acne cure to a teenager whose need for it was readily apparent. Behind the sales counter sat Shem, decanting emerald-coloured droplets from a pipette into an Erlenmeyer flask.

Caté was struggling to wrap up her conversation. "Well, I'm sorry to hear that, Ms. Baum. I assure you, I will investigate the matter, although it seems unlikely to me that our newts contain gluten in any appreciable quantity. Thank you for calling Weird Sisters."

She hung up the earpiece, exhaling slowly. Small-business witchcraft was exhausting. The craft had "come out of the closet" only two years ago. The revelation of Caté's talents had cost her her husband, but the small alchemist's shop she'd purchased with the divorce settlement had become the new centrepiece of her life. Her ex-husband had taken up with some floozy twenty years his junior, who had subsequently pulled a conjuring trick of her own, making his life savings disappear. *He should have known about the Rule of Three*, Caté mused. *All you do, for good or ill, comes back to you threefold in the end. But, of course, he had too much pride to consult with, or keep company with, a witch.*

The bells on the shop door jingled as it opened. *And speaking of prideful men...* There he was, tall and lean in his grey three-piece suit, with his lustrous tan, his slicked-back hair, and his capped teeth. The visitor assayed the customers—*not as many as there used to be,* Caté thought, *thanks to you.* He grinned, sauntered over to the counter, and leaned in to address Shem. "Excuse me, ma'am," he blustered. He pulled up short at Shem's expressionless stare and unreadable features, but the sight of Shem's eyes struck him the most—violet, without pupil or iris, their hue darkening at the sight of him.

"Er..." He staggered for purchase, regained his balance, and plowed on ahead. "I'm sorry, sir... or... um... or... ma'am?" Shem stared at him impassively from beneath long indigo lashes. "Uh... I'm sorry... how, exactly, should I address you?"

Shem's voice was soft, languid, and subtly menacing, a thing of satin and sharp edges. "I am *Shem.*"

"Yes, er, but what I meant was..."

"You'll have to excuse Shem, Mister Sneed," Henrietta interrupted. The presence of the unctuous visitor dimmed her usual effervescence; it was as if a thin and greasy cloud had passed before the sun. "Hesh is fae, you see. The question's meaningless to hem."

"Well, of course I didn't mean anything by..." Sneed stopped short, raised a pinkie finger to his ear, and dug around inside, as if searching for the reset button for his brain. "Wait, uh... 'hesh?' 'Hem?'"

Caté had enjoyed Sneed's discomfiture, but figured that the sooner she intervened, the sooner they'd be rid of him. "New pronouns for new times, Mr. Sneed. Shem's more than worth the trouble." There was iron in her tone. "We're *real* witches here, you see. Not pretenders hiding behind Halloween masks and an eight-figure ad budget. Now. What do you *want*?"

Sneed shuffled through his facial expressions, ultimately settling on something grudgingly polite. "Please! Call me Eustace! And to answer your question, we at Brew-Ha-Ha merely want to renew our offer."

Ah, *yes,* thought Caté. Sneed's offer. A chance to sell the shop at a tidy profit to a mass-market retail chain and leave this life behind forever. Caté thought upon it—the anachronistic, homey environment of her store dismantled, piece by piece, replaced with yet another big-box clone-mart. And at the centre of it, Eustace Sneed, standing behind the counter of the business *she'd* built, frittering away her customers' trust, picking his nails, grinning his shark's grin. "Forget it, Sneed," Caté barked. "I won't sell the shop. And certainly not to Brew-Ha-Ha." Sneed smiled dimly. "Now, there's no need for disrespect, Ms. Bowersgrove. I recognize that you and your staff"—he gestured at Henrietta and Shem—"are skilled alchemists, as good as anyone at Brew-Ha-Ha."

Caté curled her lip in response. *"As good as?"* she spat. "There's not an ounce of talent or respect for the Craft in your whole store. You spend the money it'd take to hire *real* witches on TV commercials. You're a bunch of snake oil salesmen."

Shem raised an eyebrow. "Just for the record," hesh muttered to Henrietta, "there's nothing wrong with snake oil, provided it's harvested properly."

Sneed blinked. "And, again, a little respect, please. There's no need to mag-splain. It's true, my associates may struggle with the nuances of production. But we're all novices in one way or another, aren't we?" His smile returned, less unctuous than feral. "Yourself, for instance, Ms. Bowersgrove. For all your skill with potions, you have no grasp of the ways of business. Do you really think, at this stage of your life, that you can afford to risk a fight with Brew-Ha-Ha? If this business fails... well, then what is left to you, madam?"

"My pride," Caté replied. "My honour. My Craft."

His only reply was a smirk that practically screamed to be slapped free of his face. "Yes, I've heard of those things. No doubt they must be a great comfort to you. Excuse me, my Bugatti is double-parked outside." He raised his voice. "I might mention," he added, "that my offer isn't for Ms. Bowersgrove alone. Brew-Ha-Ha would eagerly hire any of the employees of this establishment, at, shall we say, double your present salary?" He cast a sidelong leer at Henrietta, who stood with arms crossed, her radiant face marked with a scowl.

Before she could reply, there came a voice from the counter. "Oh, please, Mr. Sneed, pick me." There stood Shem, hes eyes faded to a pale orchid and locked on Sneed's. "Why, it's been my liveslong dream," hesh said, hes voice expressionless. "For thousands of years I've craved a shot at entry into the world of corporate thaumaturgy. Won't you give me a chance?"

Sneed's confused glance darted from the gorgeous blonde in the corner to the thin, pale, androgynous figure behind the counter. He shuddered. "Ah... er... well... there's a number of factors to consider, you know... mustn't rush into these things... car's double-parked, er... good seeing... um..." He swallowed, turned, and fled the store.

Caté snickered and shot Shem a wry grin. Henrietta, as usual, was not quite as quick on the uptake. "Shem!" she protested. "You wouldn't! After all we've been through!"

For only the third time in an hour, Shem looked up from the flask. "Henri," hesh said, "in five thousand years on this Earth and elsewhere, I have seen things you could not imagine. I have seen men and women tortured by plague and famine. I have seen a human babe sacrificed upon an altar of black stone, and a conjurer devoured alive by his own ill-warded summoning. I have seen a dryad dismembered by bog demons, and..." For the first time, there was a hint of emotion in hes voice. "And I would willingly accept all of those fates, singly or combined, simultaneously or sequentially, if the alternative were to become a *corporate fae*."

Weeks passed, and the fortunes of Weird Sisters turned sour. It wasn't Brew-Ha-Ha's barrage of TV ads that posed the problem, nor the price war, in which Brew-Ha-Ha began selling its stock of potions at less than the cost of production. The real problem was the sudden inability of the Weird Sisters staff to produce functional potions and elixirs.

The complaints began with a very hairy and very angry man haranguing them about a "baldness cure" that had worked everywhere except his scalp. Indeed, it had worked so well that Ogg, the store's luxuriously furred Trollkin stock boy, had mistaken the customer for one of his own species and had had to be restrained from asking him on a date. There was no accounting for the error; their formula matched the one in the grimoires, and Shem's preparations and techniques had been meticulous. Nonetheless, the store had honoured its policy of following the Rule of Three in customer relations: "Total Satisfaction or Triple Your Money Back." The mistakes began to pile up, however; recipients of cold sore remedies returned with cankers the size of cantaloupes.

The cause of their problems was uncovered on a particularly difficult

The Rule of Three

Tuesday evening. The line at the complaints counter had taken hours to disperse, and refunds had more than cancelled out the day's sales. Caté had been so dispirited that she'd almost lacked the energy to object when Ogg came howling out of the storeroom, swinging a broom in a frenzy of wanton destruction. He toppled two shelves before Shem snared him with a transfixing charm and Henrietta calmed him in the usual manner, which involved scratching his belly fur and cooing softly about what a good boy he was. At length, the long white hair that covered his body ceased to stand aggressively on end, and his broad-featured, blue-skinned face settled into an expression of contentment, his adoring eyes fixed on Henrietta.

"Ogg," Caté explained wearily, "we've discussed this before. Hitting the dirty things with a broom is NOT the same as cleaning."

Slowly, the saddened pseudo-simian gathered the fortitude to speak. "Me sorry, Miss Caté. But... me no help it! It the tiny man! Him evil!"

Shem's brow furrowed. "The 'tiny man,' Ogg?"

Ogg nodded. "Tiny man! Tiny red beardy man! Live in pots! Make potions bad!" He gritted his teeth, exposing formidable incisors. Ogg was only four and a half feet tall, short even by the standards of his own kind, but he could bite through a manhole cover, and Caté had once seen him hurl a Hummer clear across the street when he'd found it occupying Henrietta's parking space. "Tiny man BAD! Tiny man try ruin Weird Sisters! Make Miss Henrietta POOR!" He began bawling uncontrollably. "Tiny man wreck WHOLE QUARTERLY EARNINGS FORECAST!" Ogg howled. "GROWTH PROSPECTS MINIMAL! ANNUAL DIVIDEND AT RISK! BAD TINY MAN!"

Shem and Caté exchanged a glance and then turned to Henrietta, who paused in her consolations to stare sheepishly up at them. "I may have been providing Ogg with copies of the *Wall Street Journal*," she admitted.

Ogg nodded through his tears. "Ogg like *Wall Street Journal*," he explained. "Is Daily Diary of the American Dream. Also, many funny pictures."

Shem's eyes had gone deep purple with worry. "Can you tell us anything else about the 'tiny man,' Ogg?"

"Lives in shelves. Pees in potions. Seen him do. Unsanitary."

Caté nodded. "All right. Thank you, Ogg. You've done a good thing by telling us."

Henrietta beamed at him. "Did you hear that, Ogg? Miss Caté says you're a GOOD BOY!" She tickled him. He thrashed as he giggled; one of his overlong arms thudded against the oaken floor, leaving a fourteen-inch fissure.

Ogg smiled up at them. "Ogg good?" he inquired. "This mean Ogg eligible for stock options?"

Caté frowned down at him. "Ogg, we don't sell stock. We're a sole proprietorship." She paused. "As I recall, we pay you in lumps of granite."

Ogg's eyes went wide with delight. "Oooh! Granite good too! Granite NUMMY!"

Caté nodded. "Special bonus, then. Two extra shovelsful at the end of the week. Granite, or another mineral of your choice."

Ogg leaped to his feet. "Stock options good, but rock options BETTER!" He did a merry little dance, but the witches scarcely noticed. Grim-faced, Caté gave Henrietta a nod, and the younger witch retreated at once to the storeroom. When she returned, her typical affliction of Resting Bewildered Face had disappeared; instead, her countenance was solemn, her blonde mane tucked into a ponytail. Both of her hands were full of a sparking golden grit, fine as talcum powder. *Pixie dust*, Caté thought, remembering how difficult it had been to convince Henrietta that it wasn't composed of ground-up pixies.

Henrietta lifted both glowing handfuls to her lips and whispered an incantation. As she gently breathed upon the dust, it rose in a cloud, flickering and glistening and spreading throughout the room, whirls and sworls swooping to cover every corner. Slowly, as if magnetized, the pixie dust collected in streams, drawn as if by gravity to a single specific cauldron, near the top of the second shelf to the left.

Ogg growled. "Ogg recommend diversified portfolio of violence against tiny man," he rasped. "Magic fireballs. Guns. Hexes. Arrows. Bigger guns." Ogg nodded sagely. "Diversified portfolio best. Secure against market downturn."

Shem smiled grimly, turned hes attention to the cauldron, and positioned hes hands a few inches apart. A glow began to build between them. *And here we go,* Caté thought. *Hopefully, hesh'll be able to avoid bringing the ceiling down this time...*

A pair of tiny red horns poked up above the lid of the cauldron, followed by a pair of glowing eyes. Shem's wrists snapped forwards, and an incandescent speck shot forth, blossoming from the size of a pea to that of a softball. The fireball caught the small figure directly in the forehead, and he was hurled backwards out of the pot, his crimson body suddenly wreathed in flames. His cackles of glee, however, suggested that the devil-dwarf wasn't suffering. He hopped to the floor and streaked comet-like across the room, whooping and turning cartwheels. He cavorted along the baseboards of the exterior wall, setting the curtains ablaze, and then shot off into the storeroom, almost too fast for the eye to follow. Ogg chased after him, bellowing a war cry and waving his broom.

"Stupid!" Shem exclaimed, hes eyes ultraviolet. Hesh rushed to the windows and extended a hand; a torrent of freezing fog emerged, extinguishing the flames and leaving a singed, sooty mess at the base of the windows. "Red! Ogg told us he was red!" Hesh gritted hes teeth. "A fire imp, obviously. I should have known from the start. All I've done is made him stronger."

Caté thought for a moment. "Imp urine would explain the failure of the potions, of course. But you don't find fire imps under every rock. That's a difficult summoning even for an experienced witch."

Henrietta chimed in. "Perhaps we've underestimated Mr. Sneed?"

Shem scoffed. "I don't think so. We'd need to dip our expectations very low to limbo under the bar he sets."

Caté pursed her lips. "Whether it was Sneed or someone else, right now, all I want is to get this little bastard out of my store." There was a crash from the storeroom, followed by a howl of dismay. "Henrietta, deal with Ogg, please. I'd like to make it to the end of the week with at least part of the store intact."

The silver-infused net that dangled from the storeroom ceiling had been hideously expensive. In Caté's opinion, though, the contents made it worth every penny. Caught within its strands was a crimson-skinned dwarf, and wherever the silver pressed up against its hooves, horns, or flesh, they sizzled and smoked. "AIEEEEE! GETITOFFGETITOFFGETITOFF..."

Henrietta managed to ignore the imp's plaintive cries long enough to finish strewing salt on the floor. She'd scattered it in the shape of a five-pointed star surrounded by a circle marked with strange glyphs and wards. She closed the circle, made a few subtle adjustments to one of the glyphs, and then nodded to Caté. Caté muttered quietly and then extended a finger. The net unhooked itself from the ceiling, bore its cargo across empty space, and inverted itself, dumping the fire imp into the middle of the pentagram.

Henrietta, whose face had resumed its usual expression of beatific puzzlement, turned to Shem. "How did you catch it?"

"A trick that was old when I was young." Shem replied. "I baited the net with a charcoal briquette. Even imps have to eat."

The imp stood, brushing itself off, its face full of indignation. "FOOLS!" it howled. "MORTAL FOOLS! YOU SHALL PERISH FOR THIS AFFRONT! NO MERE HUMAN RESTRICTS THE LIBERTY OF ZAGRAX THE INSUFFERABLE, YOU UNNATURAL HAGS!"

Caté made a gesture to Ogg, who was standing outside the circle. Ogg grinned and brought down his broom squarely and thunderously upon the imp's head. The impact drove the imp nearly six inches straight down into the concrete, yet the patterns of salt were somehow undisturbed. "You'll speak when spoken to, abomination," Caté replied. "And you'll find those glyphs bind you to speak truth to us."

The imp clambered groggily out of the hole in the floor. "PITIFUL MORTALS! TO THINK YOUR PUNY MAGICS CAN CONSTRAIN ME, A CREATURE KNIT FROM BLACKEST NIGHT, WITH THE VERY FLAMES OF HELL AT MY COMMAND! WHY, I AM MADE OF LIES!"

"What is your true name, Zagrax the Insufferable?"

"PERRY!" Hearing itself, the imp widened its eyes. "AW, DAGNABBIT."

"And what brought you to this plane of existence, Perry the Imp?"

"I AM BOUND TO THE WILL OF MY TERRIBLE MASTER, EUSTACE SNEED."

Henrietta raised an eyebrow. "Your 'terrible' master? He's secretly a powerful magician?"

"NO, HE'S JUST TERRIBLE. I MEAN, SERIOUSLY, HAVE YOU MET HIM? WHAT A WANKER. HE CHEATS AT CARDS. HE BUYS BOOKS HE DOESN'T

READ SO THAT PEOPLE WILL SEE THEM ON HIS SHELF AND THINK HE'S 'DEEP.' THE OTHER DAY, I SAW HIM PICK HIS NOSE AND EAT IT. HE THOUGHT I DIDN'T SEE HIM. BUT I TOTALLY DID."

Caté raised a palm, silencing the imp. "But if he's so unskilled, how did he summon you?"

"HIM? HE'S JUST A FRONT MAN. HIS BACKERS, THE TRUE OWNERS OF HIS STORE, GAVE HIM A GRIMOIRE. ANY FOOL CAN READ FROM A BOOK. EVEN SO, IT TOOK HIM SIX TRIES TO GET IT RIGHT. HE SUMMONED, AMONG OTHER THINGS, A LIVE CHICKEN, AN EIGHT-FOOT ROLL OF YELLOW SHAG CARPETING, AND THE GHOST OF CINEMA LEGEND RICHARD ROUNDTREE. EVENTUALLY, HE MANAGED ME."

"How do we send you away?"

The imp threw back its head and laughed. "YOU KNOW THE RULES, HAGS! I AM BOUND TO SNEED'S WILL SO LONG AS I REMAIN ON THIS MORTAL PLANE. I WILL NEVER GIVE UP THE FIGHT! NOT UNLESS,"—it smiled with malice—"ONE OF YOU IS WILLING TO PAY THE TERRIBLE PRICE."

Henrietta gulped. "The contract," she whispered.

"YES, HARLOT!" Enraged, Ogg raised the broom again, but a gesture from Henrietta froze him. "SIGN IN BLOOD, IF YOU WOULD HAVE ME GONE! HE OR SHE WHO WOULD DISMISS ME MUST PLEDGE HIS OR HER SOUL TO TEN THOUSAND YEARS OF SERVICE IN HELL, AT MY MASTERS' WHIMS! OH, THE WHIMS OF MY MASTERS CAN BE MOST ENTERTAINING, HAGS!" The imp rubbed its hands together and cackled. "GLADLY WOULD I MAKE THE EXCHANGE, AS REVENGE FOR THIS HUMILIATION! WHO AMONG YOU WILL SIGN?"

There was a short silence. The three witches glanced at one another. Then, the other two turned to Shem. Caté shrugged, and Shem raised hes hand. "Ooh, pick me, pick me."

The imp reached its hands into empty space, gesturing strangely. There was a flash of fire followed by a whiff of sulfur, and an ornate vellum scroll appeared in the monster's grasp. Shem reached into the circle and took it, glanced it over, smiled, and nodded. Hesh strolled to a nearby crate, picked up a box cutter, pricked hes finger, and smeared a crude signature across the bottom of the page.

As Shem handed the contract back to the imp, it let loose a howl of joy. "SEE YOU IN HELL, HAG! THE TERMS OF THE CONTRACT ARE PRECISE AND IRONCLAD! OF THIS YOU ARE AWARE!"

Caté gave a small smile. *Can it really be this easy?*

"Indeed we do, Perry the Imp. Ten thousand years of service in hell. To be paid by the signer's soul, at the time of his or her death." She paused. "I believe those are the exact terms of the contract, yes?"

"INDEED!" The air around the imp was shimmering; already the dimensional door was opening up to carry it back to hell. "OH, INDEED!"

Henrietta, too, was smiling. "His or her soul."

Shem squatted on hes haunches directly in front of the demon, which was fading into nothingness before them. "Look at me, imp," hesh said. "Tell me... am I a him or a her?"

Perry looked into Shem's violet, featureless eyes, and it realized. "FAE," it whispered. "AW, CRAP ON A CRACKER." And it was gone.

Shem shook hes head. "You'd think hell would have better lawyers."

By the time the three of them had piled into Caté's Karmann Ghia and made their way to Brew-Ha-Ha, the damage had already been done. Customers were spilling out onto the sidewalk and fleeing in all directions as smoke poured out of the store's windows. From inside came the sounds of wild cackling, small explosions, and merry hell.

As the witches strolled towards the front door, a fireman stepped up to bar the way; Caté idly waved a hand at him, and he suddenly found himself holding the door open as they passed. He blushed broadly at Henrietta's grateful smile.

Inside, they were greeted by a tableau of anarchy. What had once been a well-lighted and utterly impersonal monument to revenue maximization had become a blasted hellscape. Aisles extended for what seemed like acres in every direction, and there wasn't an inch that wasn't scorched, soot-smeared, or actively aflame. Three tiny figures, visible only as crimson streaks of light, darted about, burning everything flammable and breaking everything that wasn't. Amid it all, in the smoking ruins of a thousand-dollar suit, Eustace Sneed ran in futile circles. Spotting the three visitors, he snarled and stalked forwards, spitting rage, his sophisticated veneer in tatters. "WHAT HAVE YOU DONE? WHAT HAVE YOU DONE TO ME, YOU INFERNAL WOMEN?"

"We haven't done a thing, Mr. Sneed," Henrietta replied. "You did this to yourself."

Sneed stopped short. "WHAT... WHAT DO YOU MEAN, I DID THIS???"

"It's called the Rule of Three, Mr. Sneed," said Caté. "You wouldn't know it, of course, being nothing more than a dabbler. But it's an immutable principle of the Craft. All that you do, for good or ill, comes back to you threefold."

"Three kindnesses for every one you offer," Henrietta clarified. She nodded at the destruction that surrounded them. "And three ills for every one you inflict."

"You didn't summon one fire imp, Mr. Sneed," Caté concluded. "You summoned four. One for us, and three for you. She shot him a wry grin. "I'd advise you to file the insurance claim under 'Acts of God,' but I think the adjusters will recognize that this isn't Hes work."

Sneed's shoulders slumped. "What am I supposed to DO?"

Henrietta gave him a pitying smile. "Why, Mr. Sneed," she cooed, her voice sweet as honey, though a careful observer might have noticed a certain glint in her eye. "Have you tried talking to them? I mean, I know I'm just a silly girl and all, but still, I find that when I just talk to people—or other entities—they often prove far nicer than I'd first thought they'd be."

Sneed glanced up. "You... you really think so? You think if I just... talk to them, they'll listen?"

Caté smiled at him. "Why, we're just witches, Mr. Sneed." She purred. "But you, why, you're a businessman. A veteran negotiator! I'm sure that if you talk to them, you'll find they're amenable to... a deal."

Sneed stood a bit straighter and adjusted the charred stump that had once been his necktie. "You're right," he said, slowly regaining his composure. "Negotiation. I can still save this situation." He turned his back on the witches and cast an eye on the nearest hellion, which was busily etching its initials into the tile with a stream of acidic urine. Sneed squared his shoulders, fixed his face in a broad smile, extended his hand in greeting, and advanced on his prey. "Well, I'll just be damned..." he began.

Shem offered a dim grin of hes own. "That does seem likely."

The trio retreated to the convertible. As they did, Caté took stock. "This was satisfying, of course, but it's hardly the end of our troubles. We've lost our customers' trust, and it's going to take a while to get it back. In the meantime, we've got a cash-flow crisis to deal with."

"Ah," Henrietta replied, from her position in the back seat. "Yes. Um… about that…" The other two turned to her, fixed her between their gazes. She crumbled in the crossfire. "I couldn't help it!" she blurted. "I'm sorry! I'm nice! It's my one character flaw!"

"Henrietta…" Caté groaned. "What did you do? Did you give all the money in the spare cash drawer to orphans again?"

"Well, no," Henrietta replied, her voice tiny. "I mean… not to ORPHANS, exactly…"

"To whom, then?" Caté braced herself.

"Well… er… to Ogg, actually." Caté felt herself deflate. She slumped boneless in the driver's seat, barely hearing. In the passenger seat, Shem slowly lowered hes forehead to the dashboard and began banging it repeatedly. "I mean, he'd been doing all that reading about investment strategies in the *Journal*, and he seemed so excited about giving it a try, bless his furry little heart…"

"Henrietta," Caté demanded, "how much is left?"

"Well, it's not… it's not quite like that. Not a matter of left, exactly. In fact…" Henrietta gulped. "In fact, there's quite a bit more than there was, originally."

Shem lifted hes head from the dashboard and stared back at Henrietta, incredulous. She continued: "I mean, Ogg tried to explain it to me, but it was just so complicated, and the words were so long. Something about all the new Brew-Ha-Ha franchises sparking a construction frenzy, and the resulting demand for sheetrock and mining companies. But anyway, it's more money. Than we had before, I mean."

Shem's eyes were pale lilac, fixed in the far distance. "The greatest secret of alchemy," hesh breathed. "Lost to man and fae for thousands of years. The ability to turn base stones into gold…"

Caté's mouth hung open. "Henri," she said slowly, "how much more money, exactly?"

Henrietta's brow furrowed. "Well, now that you mention it, I did the math, and it's very odd." And there was, again, a manipulative glint in Henrietta's eye, visible only to the careful observer—which Caté, her ears full of the ringing of cash registers, was not. "It's exactly three times as much as we've spent on rocks to pay Ogg with. Exactly. Right to the penny."

Instantly, Caté turned the key in the ignition and, as the engine roared into life, the three of them peeled out backwards at top speed. She hit the brakes, did some quick heel-toe work, and brought the car screeching around in a three-point turn before zooming out of the parking lot and up the road towards the highway on-ramp.

"Caté!" Henrietta shouted, struggling to be heard over the wind in their hair. "Caté, the shop's back in the other direction!"

Caté barely heard her. "The shop can wait, ladies!" she yelled. "Next stop's the granite quarry!"

HAVE ICHTHYOSAUR, WILL TRAVEL
D.K. Latta

I stumbled as I entered the room. I'm not normally clumsy, but a firm shove between my shoulder blades does crazy things to my equilibrium. "Just so you know," I said over my shoulder to the unsmiling goon and his pal, "I'm keeping a mental record of every time you put your hands on me. Lawyers like to itemize things like that."

"What's this talk of lawyers?" a voice issued from a doorway on the other side of the featureless room. "I'm certainly not in a litigious mood." The voice's owner sauntered in as though he owned the place. Because he did. Black slacks, black blazer, black turtleneck underneath. His close-cropped hair was a shocking white. "And if anyone is the offended party here, it would be me, not a trespasser like you. Wouldn't you agree, Mr. Salazar?"

I blinked and then tried to reclaim some cool. "Okay, so you know who I am. Then you probably know why I'm here." As a journalist, I'd been tracking a chain of divested businesses and plant closures that, once I'd sifted through the holding companies and offshore consortiums, led back to one parent mega-company—and one man: Everett Colan. And sure, maybe my zeal for a comment had led me to, shall we say, disregard the high fence around his massive, private estate. "You're reputed to be one of the richest men in the world," I said. Although only in his forties, Colan had made a fortune from a combination of predatory business savvy, an innate knack for anticipating social trends, and genius-level intelligence that had already netted him two Nobel prizes. In the previous fifteen years, he had patented cancer-free cigarettes, built the first undersea resort, and demonstrated the first replicable experiment involving cold fusion. It was even his observatory in Australia that had first made contact with extra-terrestrial life a few years back. No one had figured out what the E.T.s were saying, but no one doubted that when the first translations were published it would be on Colan International stationary. "Yet recently you've been downsizing faster than a sumo wrestler who's joined a ballet troupe. Clearly your finances are in a tailspin. And I want to know what you have to say to all those workers who—"

"Tut tut," he said blithely. "I don't want to talk about that. That's unimportant."

I balked. My indignation at his suggesting those thrown out of work by his fiscal shenanigans were unimportant wrestled with the inference that he did, in fact, want to talk about something. And with me, at that.

He smiled a little mischievously at my confusion. "You want a scoop, yes? And as it happens, today I'm in the mood to play ice-cream man." He hooked his finger in my direction. "Yes, I know who you are, Marco Salazar. You're a first-class journalist. A man of integrity. I've read your work for years. I'm a fan." I couldn't tell if he was being ironic. "I'd have to be. In this cut-throat world, people like you and me have to develop a healthy respect, even affection-at-a-distance. Otherwise, we might have ourselves a problem." And for a moment his smiling eyes took on the chilling, dead gaze of a shark. Then the twinkle returned. "I'd just been networking with my PR people about the best way to make the announcement, when who should crop up on my security monitors?" he asked rhetorically, gesturing at me. Then he stepped aside and nodded towards the door behind him.

This was all a bit discombobulating. I'd been ready to confront a recalcitrant tycoon in the midst of keeping his empire from collapsing, but Colan seemed chipper and garrulous. It may not have been the story I expected, but clearly there was a story here. Hesitating a moment, I entered the next room, Colan at my side, his goons having disappeared sometime during our conversation.

We were in a narrow passage with one of the walls made of thick glass from floor to ceiling holding back what must have been an Olympic-sized pool of water. Colan clearly owned a private aquarium. But the water was dark, murky. I peered more closely. Something stirred in the darkness. It was big, whatever it was. Bigger than a shark. A whale, I wondered? But the colouring was odd: bright reds and yellows, like a tropical fish.

"Yes," Colan whispered beside me. "The colourfulness surprised me, too."

It surged through the dark water, as large as a whale but with a dolphin-like proboscis and the sinister, vertical tail of a shark. It rushed past us, and I'd swear the glass bowed outwards slightly with the enormous displacement pressure. I stumbled back, stuttering, trying to find the words. "Th-that looks like an Ichthyosaur—a prehistoric sea creature!"

"We can leave the specific classification to the experts I'm having flown in. But it doesn't look like an Ichthyosaur, Marco—it is an Ichthyosaur." I stared wide-eyed at the anachronistic impossibility knifing away from me, barely perceiving Colan out of the corner of my eye. "My business hasn't been in trouble, Marco—I've just been freeing up some capital to launch my latest endeavour. One that will put me in a whole new tax bracket if it plays out as I suspect it will—a bracket they'll have to invent just for me. And I'm going to allow you, Marco Salazar, investigative journalist with the Toronto Over-View, to tell the world first. Because I admire you. Exceptional men like us have to stick together."

It seemed... mundane. So much beneath the fantastical dreams every child had entertained of a day when dinosaurs would once again rub shoulders with the great-great-grandchildren of the rats they had once called brunch.

He sold his Ichthyosaur.

Cheap. I mean, when you consider it. It was close to 1.75 million. It went to the New York Metropolitan Zoo. But there was no need for anyone to get upset, feeling they had missed the opportunity of a lifetime. There were plenty to spare.

Everett Colan had cornered the dinosaur market, and anybody's money would do.

"Shh." She glared at me, features dirty with the greasy, black camouflage paint. I looked around at the other three staring me down.

I finished wiping my nose and shrugged. "Got a cold," I whispered.

It was past midnight. But receiving a personal invite from the Brothers of the Lizard—the latest militant animal-rights group to make a name for itself—on one of their nocturnal raids wasn't something I wanted to pass up.

The leader, a woman I knew only as Saarita K., threw the grappling hook over the fence surrounding the "Jungle Life Animal Safari" compound, tugged to verify it was secure, and then started up with the nimbleness of youth. The image of her scrambling past the No Trespassing sign would make a nice juxtaposition in my column. I was third over the wall and dropped down with a grunt. Moving like ghosts, we set out deeper into the compound.

"This is just what we're always warning people about," whispered Bernie V., his flashlight illuminating a tiger pacing back and forth behind chicken wire and iron bars. "Cats like her need huge areas to roam through."

In the battery-light, I had to admit, the tigress looked pretty miserable.

"Come on," hissed Saarita K.

Bernie looked at me. "It gets worse."

The Brothers did the monkey-thing again when we came to a concrete wall. I watched the last of them scramble over, half-wishing I was tucked in bed. I struggled up after them, puffing hard. The drop was even further this time, and I sprawled as I landed. Rising, I brushed at my knees with feigned nonchalance.

"What now?" I asked.

"Take a look at her—poor baby," said Saarita.

"Her?" I looked up and found myself staring into the savage jaws of the Safari's latest acquisition: a full-grown Tyrannosaurus Rex. "Oh, sweet mercy!" I yelled, arms pinwheeling me back. The maniacs had dropped right down into the T. Rex's pen!

It took a step forwards on its massive hind legs, and that mouth bloomed wide, fangs bigger than carving knives bristling along its salivating gums. It blared a roar like nothing I had ever heard before in my life. If I had had anything in my bladder, I would have wet myself.

Saarita calmly rapped the T. Rex lightly on its snout with a big stick she had picked up off the ground. The giant beast reared back with a querulous mew. "They're scavengers," she said simply. "Oh, they'll try and take a bite out of you, no mistaking. But basically they're timid."

"You'd think palaeontologists might've asked themselves just how the hell an eight-tonne, five-metre-tall muther was supposed to have snuck up on living prey." Bernie snickered. "Tyrant Lizard, my ass."

As Saarita approached the T. Rex—called Angie in the Safari's brochures—the big beast lumbered back a few steps, as if scared of her, and then pulled up short as the chain about its ankle snapped tight. She had maybe six metres of slack. Even I knew that was intolerable for a creature of her size.

"It's O.K. baby," cooed Saarita. "Don't be scared. Get that light over here, Laura."

One of the other Brothers of the Lizard shone a light on the T. Rex's thigh. A festering gash glistened. "She doesn't have enough room or a proper diet. And, as you can see, they haven't the faintest idea how to look after her when she's injured. The bastards!" Saarita said feelingly. She turned to me. "I used to work here. I mean, I love animals. What I saw made me sick, and it's even worse for all the dinosaurs your chum Everett Colan is putting on the market. There are even fewer regulations concerning them than there are concerning normal animals. And as more and more zoos acquire them, he drops the prices so that even cut-rate, glorified kennels like this can afford them."

I looked at the T. Rex, battered and cowering at the end of a six-metre chain in a filthy cement box. The king of the lizards had been deposed. I felt just a little sick. "Colan's not my chum," I mumbled. But no one was listening.

Bernie set to work spray-painting slogans on the wall where patrons would be sure to see them in the morning.

Angie, the T. Rex, was dead within a month. Respiratory pneumonia. The survival rate of dinosaurs in captivity was appallingly bad thanks to inadequate housing facilities, improper diets, poor care and exercise, and a conspicuous lack of natural immunity.

No one used the "double-T" phrase, but everyone was thinking it.

Everett Colan hadn't discovered an unexplored plateau in South America or a lost world at the centre of the earth. Someone would have seen dinosaurs being trucked onto his private estate. People saw them being shipped out, never in. He wasn't messing with DNA clones either. He had too many species. And independent biologists confirmed there were oddities. The dinosaurs' stomachs had trouble breaking down commonplace modern plants. Their immune systems evinced little exposure to modern bacteria.

No, what Colan had was genuine sixty-five-million-year-old dino flesh. That meant time travel. It seemed amazing, but no more amazing than seeing dinosaurs next to emus at the zoo.

And according to some pundits, we lived in an amazing age.

After a twenty-year slump, the economy was starting to pick up. Dinosaurs had something to do with that: increased tourism to cities that had one to show off, side-bar businesses such as novelty T-shirts and the like, even restaurants specializing in haute cuisine from the carcasses of the ones that died in captivity. Dinosaurs invested people with wonder, awe, hope. The number of people looking for jobs and crowding homeless shelters had started to drop off, too.

"O, what fine times, this age of dinosaurs," to paraphrase Voltaire.

And if any private individual could accomplish time travel, it was Everett Colan.

But could even Colan have researched, developed, and tested time travel without so much as a whisper of it leaking to mainstream scientific channels?

What if he'd had help?

Officially, no one had successfully translated what the aliens contacted by the Colan Observatory were saying. But what if Colan was holding out? What if he could, indeed, communicate and was acquiring and monopolizing radical new technology? No one would know. No one could force him to give up his secrets. There were no laws he was breaking. Nothing about importation of exotic animals or endangered species.

No one regulated dinosaurs. No one regulated time travel.

No one had ever imagined they would need to.

I adjusted my sunglasses against the midday glare coming off the overturned pick-up truck. Then I looked at the burly provincial police officer chewing on a toothpick.

"The Triceratops did this?" I asked.

"Nyah," he said. "It was one of those escaped dinosaurs. With a horn on its nose."

I smiled thinly but held my tongue. I glanced at the inventory list of escapees that had been emailed to my office. One Triceratops, three Spinosauri two Allosaurs.

"Those Brothers of the Lizard have really done it now," he muttered. "People have been hurt. Got reports of five missing persons already, not to mention missing pets and a moose carcass down on the highway that wasn't torn open by any wolf." The radio in his cruiser crackled jarringly to life. "'Scuse me," he said, sauntering over to his car. He talked into his radio for a minute before signalling me over. "A bunch of the local boys are gearing up for a posse-style dino-hunt, and I'd better get out there and make sure they don't shoot themselves in the foot. Ever since deer season was shortened a few years back on account of lack of deer, these guys have just sat home, polishing their rifles, looking for something to kill. I guess this is their lucky day."

Again, I held my tongue.

"Better get off the streets 'til this is over with," he advised as he pulled away from the curb.

Bernie V., of the Brothers of the Lizard, looked furtively around the alley, sneakers soaking in a muddy water puddle. "We had nothing to do with letting those dinos loose. The cops have already got Saarita and Billy, and most of the others in our cell have gone underground. But, I repeat, we didn't do it. And I've been in touch with some of the other groups. No one's claiming credit, eh? Not for the ones here. Not for the Dimetrodon in Florida, the pack of Deinonychuses that tore the hell out of Paris two weeks ago. Not the Megalosaurus in Montréal, nor any of the other 'liberations.' It's like some weird conspiracy to discredit the dino-rights movement."

It sounded paranoid. But if it was true, it was working. Disappearances—presumed deaths—followed in the wake of the rampaging dinos. Not to mention property damage, traffic jams. Mayhem. Whatever public support the dino-lovers had was rapidly eroding. "Why? Who? I mean, this is so widespread it would require complicity from people at various zoos, possibly in law enforcement. And don't say Everett Colan. To people in his tax bracket, you and your protesters are about as significant as a buzzing fly."

"Even flies get swatted. Besides, we were just about to start on a new campaign, maybe one that was making Colan—or the zoos he was supplying—nervous. It's the scariest theory we've come up with to date." He grinned crookedly. "And most of us are certified paranoids. But listen: scientists like to blame dinosaur extinction on some meteorite that struck the earth around the time they disappeared, right? But when using million-year-old geological evidence, that's like saying the Roman Empire collapsed 'around' the time of nuclear weapons. And it doesn't explain why mammals survived, or certain types of lizards. Or earlier dinosaur extinctions. But the Big Daddy scientists like to gloss over that 'cause it complicates things. And God forbid life should be complicated, eh?"

A siren wailed and both of us almost blasted out of our socks, but then it dwindled away into the distance. Abruptly, it started drizzling.

"I gotta go," Bernie said nervously.

"Wait—I don't understand?"

"Did you know that for some species of animals, every one you used to see in a zoo represented as many as maybe ten dead ones?" He nodded. "'Cause trappers sometimes had to kill the herd or family just to kidnap one. That's why most zoos only buy captivity-bred animals these days. Now, just think about how many dinosaurs Everett Colan might have to kill just to bring one to our own century. And who knows what sort of mishaps might be associated with his time machine, what sort of malfunction rate."

I just stared as he hurried to the mouth of the alley. "That's nuts," I protested belatedly.

"Think about it, man," he laughed, without humour. "Maybe millions of years before people even existed, nature's biggest enemy was still man!"

Try the math:

For every dinosaur that made it to a zoo, suppose ten were killed. Of those in zoos, many died within a few months and had to be replaced at another one-to-ten ratio. Then factor in that neither the dead nor the captive dinosaurs would be repopulating the species. Plus, the whole enterprise would be throwing the entire pre-historic ecosystem out of whack by unbalancing the predator/prey equilibrium. Now subtract all that from a total population. Can't do it? Of course not. No one knows how many members of a dinosaur species would have lived at any one time. A few million? Considering their size, probably the prehistoric world could have only sustained a population of a few hundred thousand of any given species. Or less.

Now subtract the above equation from a few thousand. Suddenly it doesn't seem so nuts.

It was about two weeks after Bernie Vannicola was arrested trying to cross over into the States, and a few days after my column—"Did We Cause the Dinosaur Extinction?: Sixty-five million year old murder mystery has a new suspect"—went online, that I received a phone call.

I was going through my e-mail, reading some of the responses to my piece. Mostly scathing personal attacks from the general readership, calling me a bleeding heart, a dino-lover, a commie (?), and other things, mixed in with a couple of threats of libel action from some zoos.

I also received a DM from Everett Colan telling me how much he enjoyed reading my work. That one I deleted with an angry jab of my finger.

But to the phone call. It was long distance. Montréal. A Dr. Elise LaFontaine, who identified herself as a forensics specialist. She spoke a little bit of English, I a smidgen of French. Between the two of us, we managed to communicate reasonably coherently.

"I read your piece on the escapees. It was translated and reposted on e-Presse. I thought it was very interesting but ill-informed."

I waited a little impatiently, doodling unpleasant depictions of what I thought my long-distance critic might look like on my notepad.

"It's not clear that the disappearances here in Montréal after the Megalosaurus's rampage were in any way related to the beast's escape."

My pen stopped. "What?"

"I pressed to be allowed to perform an autopsy on the dinosaur. My superiors refused, saying it was a waste of tax payers' dollars. But I felt we owed it to the victims' families. Eventually, a colleague and I snuck into the compound where they were holding the carcass, and we cut it open... without permission. We found a dog and a cat in its stomach. Nothing more. I called around after that. I wasn't able to confirm any human kills by an escaped dinosaur. Lots of assumed kills, lots of missing-and-presumed-deads, but no confirmations."

I stared at The Over-View's latest edition glaring on my screen. The headline proclaimed how well the economy was doing, a sure sign being the decrease in the number of people lining up at homeless shelters and food banks. The article couldn't confirm they had found jobs or homes. But they must have, mustn't they?

People didn't just vanish.

I peered out of the helicopter at the verdure landscape beneath me. A family of Triceratops munched happily on green leaves while, half-a-kilometre away and beyond a high fence, an Albertosaurus tromped about belligerently. It was the last taste of freedom the beasts would have here in Everett Colan's private compound. They were already earmarked for various zoos around the world. I leaned back. "Impressive," I said neutrally.

Colan smiled at me indulgently from across the cabin. "Isn't it."

"It wouldn't be stretching it to say you're the richest man in the world now, would it?"

He shrugged coyly.

"Rich enough to pull strings?" I asked. "Get things done?"

"Off the record?"

I nodded.

"If I wanted to molest the only child of the President of the United States, I'd just snap my fingers and he'd deliver her to my door, personally. And consider himself blessed by the association."

"You're sick."

He smiled, unoffended. "I said if."

"Could you keep autopsies from being performed?"

"Naturally. On whom?" he asked, a knowing glint in his eyes.

I ignored him. "Could you—oh, I don't know—arrange to have dinosaurs released and then blame environmental groups? You know, killing two birds with one stone. Discrediting your critics while helping cover up something more insidious."

"I'm fascinated. Go on."

"Let's say you have time travel technology. Let's say you had help developing it—help from out there." I pointed skywards. "What do you give in exchange for that help? We—people—like dinosaurs. Maybe extra-terrestrials have their own zoos but with smaller cages, cages for creatures not as big as dinosaurs, but infinitely more interesting."

"But people might notice these creatures disappearing?"

"They might," I agreed. "I mean, not at first, not the homeless, or mental out-patients, but once you started cutting into the healthier population. Yeah, they might at that point—unless you had a vaguely plausible cover story about rampaging carnivores, one the authorities could float for you if relatives started asking questions. After all, these extra-terrestrials would need lots and lots of these creatures. Look at how high the mortality rate is for dinosaurs in captivity, and they're from this planet. Imagine an earth creature on another world. Improper food, unusual gravity or atmosphere, poor, maybe even cruel treatment by their keepers, would quickly kill off a lot of these creatures."

"Alleged creatures."

"Right."

He didn't stop smiling. "I've built a financial empire by understanding the human animal. Knowing what people want even before they've thought of it and knowing how much they're prepared to pay before they've even flashed their debit card. And I've become very rich. People are happy with a lie if it's a convenient one that allows them to turn a blind eye to holes in the ozone, to clear-cutting, to poverty, to intolerance. Even to the extinction of the dinosaurs."

"Even if they go the way of the dinosaurs themselves?"

"Dinosaurs are high romance and glamour. More important, they're big business. They create jobs, pump money into tourism, and give communities self-respect. No one wants to hear about a downside. People have a process of rationalization: it's not true, but if it's true it's okay, but if it's not okay it probably won't affect me." He shrugged helplessly as if to say: what could he do? "You've got integrity, Marco. I like that. I like novelties. I'd like a man with two heads because that's almost as rare. So keep writing whatever you want. I won't sue. I'm your biggest fan. Hell, if you keep writing the articles you do, I'll probably end up your only fan. You could call it the Cassandra Column." He glanced out the window. "Now, would you like to see my Apatosaurus?"

I saw his Apatosaurus.

THE GRASS IS ALWAYS GREENER
Fraser Sherman

The word "nice" bit into Reed Simms like a chigger.

"Really, really nice." Shelby reached across the McDonald's counter and plucked her order from Reed's unmoving hands. Her jasmine perfume mingled with the scent of fries. "You've been such a good friend the past couple of months, but I'm going to be so busy…"

"Oh." It was all he could think of as a response. Her eyes showed what he thought was pity, so Reed concentrated on the golden arches glowing against the midnight sky. "I'm glad we're… friends."

"I didn't know you were on night shift, or I wouldn't—I mean, it was a nice surprise. But I have to go now." She murmured goodbye and walked out.

Wiping down tables in the empty restaurant, Brent Jensen checked out Shelby's ass through the glass wall. "Tough break, Reed my man. She's one fine piece of—"

"I didn't ask you your opinion, dickhead."

"Hey, just bein' supportive."

At least there wasn't much of an audience. Just Brent and Siobhan, who was wiping down the kitchen. The night shift was always dead, which left Reed feeling even more useless than he did during the morning rush. *Three years, and I still get stuck with the worst shift—no sleep and Bob as shift leader.* He began cleaning the counter; if Bob finished downloading porn in the office and caught Reed not doing anything, there'd be hell to pay.

If he was working morning shift, he'd have no time to think about Shelby. *But it wasn't that big a deal. We only went out for two months. Only had sex twice. So, my heart isn't breaking—that would be stupid.*

"So, you're Reed Simms." It was a midwestern accent instead of the local South Georgia drawl. A customer with a blue-and-gold silk shirt, grey silk slacks, a heavy gold watch, and a flaming red beard leaned on the far end of the counter. "So, Reed, ever wonder why your life turned into such a pile of shit?"

"Ah—can I help you sir?"

"Cheeseburger, fries, and a Coke, to go, and spare me any crap about value meals. I've got money." The man pulled a roll of c-notes from his pocket, stuffed it back in, and then slapped a twenty down on the counter. "Seriously, don't you feel like a loser? Thirty years old, and this is the best job you can find? No wonder that hottie dumped you."

"How do you know what she—Brent, was he out there watching or something?"

"I don't need to watch to know about you, Reed." The man had a used-car-dealer smile if Reed had ever seen one. "I'll be outside in my Maserati for the next fifteen minutes; come out on your break, and we'll discuss your future."

"What's my future to you?"

"Are you one of those Amway people?" Brent said, leaning on his broom. "I've always wanted to get in on that."

"You're not in this conversation." Redbeard kept watching Reed. "Well?"

Reed rung up the order. "Out of twenty, that's—"

"Keep the change, my man." Another insincere smile. Reed had the urge to throw the money in the man's face, but dammit, he needed the cash. So, he just handed him the bag as quickly as possible. Redbeard headed out but paused at the door. "I hear they're selling the trailer park in, what, two months? Any idea where you're gonna live?" He shot Reed another smirk. "See you outside, buddy."

By the time Reed reached the Maserati window, Redbeard was enjoying a massive post-meal cigar. "Mister, what the hell is going on? How the hell do you know—"

"That you're a total failure? Look around. It ain't hard."

"One of the day-shift guys is a biochemist. Working here doesn't say anything about me."

"But you had such plans, didn't you?" He tapped the cigar, dropping ash at Reed's feet. "Serious talent, too. But after you graduated college, you never got off your butt and moved to Atlanta, never did shit with your painting—"

"How do you know? Are you… Homeland Security or something?"

"Any reason I'd give a damn about you if I was?"

"Then what? And why do you care?"

"Maybe I care about life's losers, you think of that? And you know you are one. The best painting you ever did was *Woman on the Lake*, and it was crap."

Reed stiffened. "Nobody's ever seen *Woman on the Lake*, except Shelby."

"Yeah, great idea, show that shit to someone with her taste. But it's not your fault," he said, holding up his hand before Reed could respond. "You had a sweet destiny once. The reason your life's shit is that somebody stole it. Your art career, your girlfriends, your dream wife, your kids—all gone, phfft!"

"What career? What wife? And if anyone around here had my kid, I'd know."

"I told you, they're gone with the wind. Some rich guy thought he could use your future better than you could, so he bought it from a broker."

Reed's mouth opened and then closed. Finally, he made himself laugh, very, very loudly. The Latino couple getting out of their car looked at him curiously. "So, you're, what, collecting clients for a class-action lawsuit? How many other losers you fool with this bullshit? What are you going to charge me to 'fix' my life?"

"Pro bono, man." The man indicated the pocket with the bankroll. "I can afford to help out the unfortunate once in a while."

"I bet it's a great racket. Probably millions of people sit around thinking they deserve a better life—if even one percent of them buy this bullshit… But not me." Rick glanced at the sign again. "I got no illusions left. In this economy, I'm lucky to have this job."

"Ever think some of those millions could have been somebodies? Should have been?" The man smirked like this was a winning argument. "Brokers trade destinies every day. It's a hell of a lot easier for some rich, no-talent asshole to buy one than succeed the normal way."

"And they're all sold by the same guy?"

"Not all, but Stryker's the go-to guy for the A-listers, people who don't think I have enough class or something." The man hawked and spat to one side. "Boy, does he love to drop names when we get together."

"So, you sell destinies, too? Bullshit!"

Redbeard just took another toke on his cigar. Inside the restaurant, Bob was bitching at Siobhan about something. *Three years. Woman on the Lake. Eviction in two months.* "What are you selling?"

"Make Stryker give you your destiny back, and you'll finally get it together. Sell some paintings. Find a girl who's into you. And I told you, it's a freebie. My fee's the pure pleasure of fisting Stryker's oh-so-superior asshole."

"There's no such thing as destiny or fate." Reed made himself step back. "Even if there was, how could someone take mine?"

"Like I got the time to spell it out?" Redbeard buckled his seat belt. "If you don't want to know about Stryker, go back to work and enjoy the rest of your life. It's never going to change, but maybe this is enough for you."

Reed turned and tried to walk back inside. He turned back. "Just for a laugh, mister... where would I find this Stryker? And when I do, what do I do next?"

TWO DAYS LATER

Opening his windbreaker, Reed nervously touched the automatic in his waistband. The gun he'd bought yesterday at a pawn shop that didn't give a damn who you were or what ID you had.

I've lived in a trailer park for thirty years, never had a gun. Now, because some crazy guy...

Crazy? Like I'm one to talk. Standing in the shadows a dozen feet from Stryker's Antiques, Reed knew he had to be crazy. Or at least a complete redneck dumbass. Con men played you this way, telling you what you wanted to hear.

Only, Redbeard hadn't asked for money. And who'd bother to con someone who could barely afford bus fare to Atlanta?

A crazy practical joke? That makes more sense.

But if I walk away... if there's a chance I could... and if I don't—

A pinstriped figure behind the glass front door reached for the "closed"

The Grass is Always Greener

sign. Reed ran, pushed the door open as the man reached to lock it. "Are you Stryker? I need to talk to you."

"Do I know you?" Stryker had a trim Van Dyke, an expensive red tie, and an accent that evoked plantations and elegance. "I'm closed, but if there's any way I can help you—money for drugs? A donation to Jews for Jesus?"

"You took my life away. I want it back."

"Ah, I see." He stepped back, ushering Reed into the small store. "Dornheim sent you, I assume?"

"The red-bearded guy?"

"Yes, indeed." He locked the door; Reed wondered if it might be a trap and shifted nervously, almost knocking over a small Degas bronze. "Please be careful, Mr. Simms. This store is only a hobby, but that figurine is a masterpiece."

"I see that, but—" Reed's heart began to pound. "How come you guys all know who I am? Are you in on this scam with him?"

"I would never partner with Dornheim on anything." Stryker tucked his hands behind his back. "I know who you are the same way I know that Charles Tramwell Sr. bought your future from me. Such expertise is part of my profession."

"You're saying this crap is true—wait, *the* Charles Tramwell? Richer than God? Ancestors fought in 1776? Why the hell would he want my life?"

"I'm a gentleman, sir. I don't ask my clients why their own lives are inadequate."

"Gentleman?" Reed wanted to slap Stryker's calm, confident face. "You sold my life to some rich bastard who didn't even need it!"

"How many of the things any of us buy are to satisfy a need rather than a wish? Perhaps he bought it as an amusement. Perhaps he summed up his life and found something missing. Regardless, I certainly did not steal anything. I never buy any destiny that's not legally authorized."

"I never—"

"Probably ninety percent of Americans have given away the rights to their destiny, if they had one to begin with. Fine print in a credit-card agreement, a software terms-of-use box—so few people ever read that stuff. When Charles told me what he wanted, I simply made some calls in the right quarters find a suitable property. A life 'rich with artistic potential,' in his words."

"Tramwell Jr." Reed gasped. "I read an article right after *Ask Me to Dance* hit the bestseller list about how he'd flunked out of college. His professors said his turning out brilliant had floored them… He got my life, didn't he?"

"I don't ask, I told you."

"My painting." Reed swallowed, suddenly feeling like he wanted to cry. "It would have been as good as that book? As successful? I mean, did you read it? It was so… And his wife, she's so… You took all that from me?"

"Well, I doubt you'd have found a wife who studied at the Sorbonne, and you might not have the connections to be—"

"Give me my life back, you goddamn bastard!"

"I'm afraid I cannot revoke a signed contract. Only Charles can do that."

"How could I even get to someone like that?" Reed swallowed and drew the gun. "You took it, you can give it back." Reed couldn't shoot him, he just couldn't, but he pointed at the antique grandfather clock against the far wall. "How about if I destroy something of yours in return?"

"And how will you get your life back when the police arrest you for vandalism? Or do you imagine they'll believe one word of your cock-and-bull story?"

After a second, Reed lowered the gun. "Please! If it's true—please!"

"Do you really think Dornheim is helping you purely out of charity? This is a man who sells new life to desperate addicts, homeless vagrants, and in return—"

"I don't care!"

"Very well. Convince Charles to say your future is your own again, and it's done."

"That's it?"

"As the current owner of your destiny, Charles can sell or trade it again as he chooses. Once you recover it, all previous trades and assignments are null and void. Well, until you sign another document without reading it."

"How do I know you're not lying to get rid of me?"

"If getting rid of you were my objective, that would be simple enough.

But Charles and I had a... falling-out a few months back." Stryker's mouth pursed like he'd bitten an unexpected lemon. "Until he apologizes, I have no reason to care for his well-being. Alas, armed or not, I doubt you can get close enough to Charles to get what you want."

"We'll see." It wasn't much of an exit line, but Reed holstered the gun and strode out of the shop, unable to come up with anything better.

ONE DAY LATER

"Don't move." Stepping around the gazebo, Reed pressed the gun into the back of Tramwell Sr.'s head as the man admired his rose beds. "Give me my life back."

"I was looking forward to my afternoon walk." Tramwell didn't bother to turn around. "Can this wait?"

"No, it can't. My name's Reed Simms." He pushed the gun harder against Tramwell's salt-and-pepper hair. Getting to Tramwell had been a miracle—gate unlocked, guards off somewhere. But miracles didn't last. "You took my life. I want it back. Now."

"Oh, that's who you are." The man half turned, showing the famous Tramwell aquiline profile. "You might as well put down the gun. If you kill me, your destiny's lost forever."

"That won't do you much good, will it?" *I thought threatening him would be enough. What do I do now?* "You gave my career, my marriage, to a man who spends more on whores in a year—"

"Now he's a faithfully married man, and I have a grandson who was born in wedlock. I suppose it says quite a lot about your character that he changed so much."

"That's my marriage! Mine by right, by destiny!"

"Legally, it's his." Tramwell chuckled. "In the unlikely event you could convince someone to take your case, the contract you signed will hold up in court."

"Your son's going to inherit, what, fifty million? He could have found a wife. Now, give me—"

"A woman with Melanie's brains and ability would never have tolerated a wastrel. As for the money—may I turn around? My neck's getting a crick."

"Sure." Reed backed up, keeping Tramwell at gunpoint. "This is wasting time, Tramwell. If I can't kill you, I can still get your leg or—"

"I want you to understand, I didn't take your future on a whim." The man's face was sombre. "After a certain point, money's meaningless, even as a way to keep score. But family pride, seeing your son succeed, seeing your name carried on to a third generation…"

"Thanks to you, I'll never know about that, will I?"

"Don't you think your father would have done as much for you?"

"My father died of cancer six years ago. Undiagnosed because he couldn't pay for checkups." Reed choked back sudden tears. "Died thinking his son was a loser."

"Life's a competition. Some people have to lose. You can't blame me for the fact that you're one of them!"

"Your son was the loser, dammit!" *God, if I can't convince him, I'll have to use the gun!* "I was supposed to win!"

"It was merely by chance that someone like you had a shot at greatness. I'm sorry for you, but be reasonable. Walk away and don't come back."

"He doesn't need my life now! Christ, three bestsellers, a good marriage—"

"It could all disappear in a puff of smoke." For the first time, Tramwell looked less than complacent. "I can't take that chance."

"Then I guess I have no choice." *The leg, yeah, that would do the trick, wouldn't it?*

Reed's body convulsed with a burning pain that dropped him to the ground, limp. As the side of his head sank into the well-tended grass, a taser-wielding guard called for more men. *Shit! Shit, shit, shit, I should have fired! Should have killed—*

"I believe you know a man called Dornheim?" Tramwell knelt down next to Reed, whispering, waving the guard back. "He called a few days ago, told me that I could make another trade, using the remaining bits of your destiny. I have a nephew facing a very serious aggravated assault charge, but he's going to go free. You get the ten-year sentence for assault,

Dornheim gets an introduction to some of my friends."

Tramwell stood, groaning slightly as his legs straightened. Two guards grabbed Reed's arms and yanked him to his feet, jerking his wrists into handcuffs. He struggled futilely to speak.

"I'm not a monster." Tramwell almost looked regretful. "But when you chose to threaten my son's future—well, I had no choice, did I?"

The guards traded blank looks as they dragged Reed away.

"Dad?" A tall, lean man rushed up to Tramwell. A stunning brunette and a pair of twins tagged along behind him. "Jesus, what happened?"

Reed wanted to scream out the truth, to tell Tramwell Jr. what a nothing he really was, that everything he had belonged to Reed, but the cop car pulled up and the guards threw him in the back before he could regain his speech.

By the time he could talk, his life had dwindled away behind him.

SHOCKTROOPER SALESMAN
Simonas Juodis

The customer paced away from the shadows of the steel-barred cage, about to slip away from the bartering clutches of Cricket the Salesman. Cricket—careful not to step on the head of Her Regnant's emissary—tiptoed to the front of him, blocking the path in the most polite manner possible. The emissary stopped. He banked his small, round head at him. A hood with imperial regalia fell over his fur-covered face. Head locked, he stared up at Cricket, as if he could see him through the fabric.

"I'm selling you a monster," Cricket said, gesturing at the cage. The chained creature moved in the dark, its shambling mountain of muscles rumbling during a stretch. "This marvel of genetic engineering was an apex-predator of a jungle moon before we uplifted and modified it to become the apex-predator of the galaxy."

Cricket's visor shone with numbers quantifying the culture in question. The emissary's visor showed a duplicate. Every number topped the scale in affirmation of the creature's prowess. Not only did his creation sound great, he also had the math to prove it. Proud and anticipating plaudits, he suppressed an oncoming grin.

"Mm, yes," the emissary said, pulling off his hood, "extensively modified."

"It's the perfect killing machine!" Cricket couldn't help but light up. "A lot of time, expertise, and lives have been sunk into maximizing its damage output per square inch! Genetic engineering has allowed us to make considerable improvements since the initial stages. To this day, this is the most dangerous specimen we've ever produced." Not to mention expensive, he thought, before adding, "Very popular with peacekeepers, too."

"I'd like to see your natural products."

Cricket's smile vanished. He couldn't afford setbacks. Time was money, and he needed a lot of the latter. If he could make enough on commission, he could buy his company back.

The culture was the best damned thing in the universe, though, objectively. Cricket was Cricket the Inventor before he was made a Salesman by the board. The emissary had to have seen it; he must have seen the craftsmanship.

A frugal customer, Cricket thought. Likes to play hardball. Not difficult to remedy, though. The carnage the beast displayed had left even the most cynical of witnesses—err buyers—standing slack-jawed.

"I insist"—he smiled—"on a demonstration."

"And I insist on not being interested," the customer said, shrugging. He walked straight at Cricket.

Cricket stood on the tips of his toes and spread his hind legs in an effort not to knock the emissary over. The emissary passed right under them. Cricket bent over and looked in between his legs. He moistened his forelegs and rubbed his eyes, yet the emissary continued to walk away.

Wasn't playing hardball, then, Cricket thought. He scurried after him through the corridors of the enterprise.

Natural products, though? Cricket thought. Why would an empire want anything less than a perfected culture? They needed the very best, the one Cricket had offered. He would in no way let an emissary of an empire walk away with something so primitive and mundane as a conventional invasion army.

Cricket hopped alongside the emissary as they passed room after room. He jumped from one side to another, buzzing around the emissary like an insect circling the blossom of a particularly succulent plant.

"If I may be so bold, is Her Excellence very much concerned with planetary ecology?"

"Not likely."

"Then pray tell, what factor does so influence your master's insistence on natural alternatives?"

"Her empire's economy."

"Oh?"

"I did not see another unit within that same cage."

Cricket's palpi spread apart ever so slightly. His client was going somewhere with this, but the connection seemed uncertain.

"That would be unwise," Cricket said. "The creatures are fiercely territorial. Who knows what would happen if we stacked two unstoppable, opposing forces." He smiled, satisfied with his answer.

"Thought so." The emissary pointed at a set of bars belonging to a container room with an unmodified species. "I'd like to take a look at your more sustainable options."

And I'd like to help you make a mutually beneficial decision, Cricket thought. Dealing with empires could be frustrating at times. Their tendency to get behind the times stifled forward thinking in their subjects.

"Give me one last chance"—he smiled again—"to convince you otherwise."

The emissary stopped and sighed. "What did you say your name was?"

"Cricket," he answered through closed mandibles. "Of Cricket Invasion Enterprises."

"Mr. Cricket." The emissary locked eyes with him as if to check for reassurance whether he'd gotten it right. "As returning clients, we've had mixed experiences with your one-man army before."

"Did you find its efficiency not up to your standards?" Cricket asked, expecting the answer to be "no."

"It's efficient, sure, but our expectation was that the culture would repopulate from the remnants of the initial invasion. This did not happen. And I don't see how it would, seeing that even you, with all fine tools available at your facility, cannot keep a pair together without them mauling each other to pieces. Not even talking about having them cross here."

"You no longer need to cross them. My company..." Cricket paused, hoping it would sink in—he may have been muscled out by the shareholders, but it was his brilliance that the company had been built on and he damn well knew what he was talking about. "...has made sure that the culture is so efficient that one unit per planetary invasion is entirely sufficient."

"Yes, yes." The emissary nodded. "I understand, but then you need to purchase another one for a subsequent invasion."

"Is there a problem with that?"

"Isn't there? You used to be able to repopulate a culture, extending its use to cover several planetary invasions. The navy drops it on a planet. The defenders start fighting them. The creatures think they're under threat and attack. Once they've taken the world, you mop them up, let them recover their numbers, then unleash them on the next unfortunate world. A culture would last you a while."

"I believe you've just listed all of the associated benefits that come with a modified culture!"

"Such as?"

"Efficiency, self-sufficiency, speed of conquest, no resources spent on cultivation."

"Could this not have been achieved with that same culture, but fertile?" the emissary asked.

"No, of course not! The chromosomes can't match when split in odd numbers. Besides—"

"Not so technical. My understanding is that the ability to breed has been eliminated during the engineering process."

"Yes." Cricket nodded. Sure, they couldn't breed, but the benefits far outweighed the drawbacks. He would explain it slowly. "A safety measure to prevent any unforeseen consequences of spontaneous crossbreeding. A mongrel this powerful could be dangerous were it to spread. You wouldn't want any such surprise infestations, not during an occupation."

"Be that as it may," the emissary said, "this... feature has introduced an unexpected drain on Her Regnant's finances. She does not wish to repurchase a unit once it has been spent nor update whenever a new version becomes available. Between us, she also seemed to suggest that spending a yearly budget of several colonies on a single unit was indecent, no matter the quality. Though, she might have used different words..."

Cricket narrowed his pupils. He had supplied enough empires to forget half of them and knew better than to suggest anything contrary to the monarch's wishes. His work, time, effort, and countless sleepless nights had all been dismissed over a mere technicality—a meagre price he'd paid to reach perfection, an entirely necessary feature, which, in his cynicism, the emissary mistook for an exploit.

The emissary didn't understand the work he had done. He would dismiss it—he would dismiss the visor's numbers, the ingenuity, the effort. Same way the shareholders had dismissed his input in the company during its takeover. Those sharks muscled him away from his company's wheel. He had kept his job but lost control over all operations, save for one project.

And he damn well nailed the project.

He sold his remaining shares to buy full ownership of it, too. With a sky-high commission to boot. Oh, they'd laughed at him then. Thought he'd thrown everything away out of spite. They saw him as Cricket the Salesman, not the Inventor.

"I created a jewel of destruction," Cricket said, "a piece of mayheming art!"

The words bounced off the walls of neatly arranged caged container-rooms that made up the facility.

He missed the days of tinkering with mutants; he missed spending weekends running analysis and looking at analytical curves emerging out of a baseline in a windowless four-by-four room. But most of all, he missed calling something his own.

"I'd be most interested in hearing another of your intriguing pitches"—the emissary gestured at a room on the organic row—"on another fascinating culture over there."

Like the shareholders, he too only saw Cricket as the Salesman.

Cricket strode past. He would make this man pay—literally. Overpay. For anything, no matter what. He stopped his leg mid-air. Determined to rip an entire empire off, he turned around and smiled.

"A great culture."

"Yes?"

The container-rooms lay perpendicular to the long corridor. Inside them were artificial habitats for the millions of species. They could have stopped anywhere on the organic row.

Cricket stepped towards the closest room.

All species passed a rough assessment upon arrival, to see whether their genetics had the potential to engineer a culture. It had been a while since this culture was shelved, but past data had been collected via automatic procedural assays and stored. Cricket turned the visor back on.

Cricket took pride in interpreting the numbers; he took even more in his ability to present them in a favourable light. The emissary wanted a crude product, and he would sell one to him. He sifted through some basic facts: height, weight, life-expectancy. Nothing too detrimental and about as impressive as you would expect from a stock. Which was about right as far as what the emissary deserved.

Cricket browsed through the data, looking for numbers to impress his client with. With so many attributes on record, all cultures had their standouts.

He would buy time by starting the pitch with what he already knew the client would find appealing.

"Pulled right out of its damp homeworld and placed in our facility, this culture is as natural and wild as they come, so you don't need to worry about any breeding-inhibiting modifications."

"Is the maturation process fast enough for the initial host to be replenished?" the emissary asked.

Cricket moved his eyes, swiping the screen to reach the corresponding data.

"Maturing is somewhat slow, but it populates exponentially provided a sufficient base, so there are no issues with sustainability."

Of course, all species populated exponentially when their numbers reached that critical point, but what mattered was that it didn't stray from the truth and sounded comforting. The emissary's forehead noticeably wrinkled.

"How long does its breeding period last?"

Cricket smiled. Look at those numbers! His customer touched on the one strength of this culture that required no exaggeration. Most species came to heat seasonally—making this one a notable exception.

"It never ends," he said. "This culture is sexually active throughout the year, ready to procreate at a moment's notice."

The emissary pursed his lips in approval.

However, being trigger-happy in the sack did not alone make for good invasion force material. A shocktrooper had to possess many other qualities, the most important of which was fighting. It would be harder to sell—the creatures had no significant claws or fangs to speak of.

He ran the device again. The attributes were uninspiring, but stamina stood in distinction. He would hype it way up.

"Now look at its muscle structure."

The emissary did a quick reappraisal.

"Yes, very nice. A tough, muscular build."

The salesman almost chirped. Everything must have looked large and menacing from his perspective. That's why he was the client, of course—a race of lethargic, small creatures could not build an empire without stronger species fighting invasions for them.

"It's built for endurance," Cricket said. "The creature's extraordinary stamina allows it to withstand disproportionate amounts of aggression, while maintaining its own physical fitness. It keeps energy high, tiring the prey, gradually gaining the strength advantage."

"Interesting. What then?"

"Then they jump at it," Cricket said. "They attack until the prey can't keep up. They keep coming until the prey becomes so tired, it makes the decision to allow the predators close enough to finish it off."

"Why would it decide to do that?!"

"The exhaustion is such that the prey chooses to die rather than suffer it."

"All through endurance?"

"Resilience, tenacity, and yes, endurance."

"An endurance predator." The emissary nodded. "I really like the idea."

The salesman tilted his head sideways. He'd sold that story well enough to like the idea, too. He had always thought of stamina as a bonus to the other physical attributes, something that helped to sustain a carnage, not cause it. He had not considered it to play a primary part in damage output before, but maybe it could.

"What's the size range of the beasts it can take on?" the emissary asked.

"That's difficult to say. The culture is fresh and not yet tested. Aside from observing several cases of individuals trying to resist abductions."

"It is the apex predator though, is it not? I got that impression."

"Yes, top of the food chain." Cricket browsed for a confirmation. He got it. "Like every other culture in this facility, as you've so observantly noticed. This particular culture exists outside the food chain by exploiting other, local species."

"Does it not dominate directly?" the emissary asked.

"No. Though, that's not an issue. A predator's core instincts do not dull throughout the natural development of the species, up until its primitive mind reaches the degree of sapience required to form a modern FTL-age civilization. Before that, its primal instincts get subtly ingrained into its culture. Usually expressed through expansionism, as indicated by the history of the species. The instincts are very much there and can be easily awoken, though. Provided there's enough of the right stimulus."

"What kind of stimulus?"

"War, for example. Any stimulus will work so long as it threatens the genetic security of the individual."

"I see," the emissary said, pausing to ponder. "You say this culture is the apex predator of its world. What's the range on the size of the species it has taken on? Were there many? How much stronger or larger were they?"

Cricket could find that out. Automated drones constantly surveyed the universe, collecting a tremendous amount of data, tracking all newly discovered species over the course of their natural development. He pressed a button on his visor to access the images.

An image showed a group circling an animal with its back to a cliff. It had tusks the size of any one of them. They took turns striking at it, harassing it one by one. It would eventually be forced down the cliff. Cricket swiped to another image. A creature, this one hundreds of times the mass of the previous one, emerged from the water, splashing. Spears tied with rope protruded from its skin, and red fluid seeped from the wounds. The creature fled, dragging the predators on small boats along with it.

No matter the level of technological sophistication, the culture instinctively sought to find ways to hunt with endurance. And it damned well worked.

Cricket looked around. Was it by chance he'd discovered this perfect storm? Were there more species like this? In his deepest pocket, Cricket had found a penny he'd never thought he had.

He had skipped past a dozen of other images. They flashed over the emissary's eye. The emissary smiled not out of politeness but out of satisfaction.

"The photos showed them fighting together," he said. "Are they communal?"

"Very much so. We caged them individually at first," Cricket said, "but they began having hallucinations. Side effect of solitary confinement, we know that now."

"That's great."

"The hallucinations?"

"No, no. The ability to engage in communal violence. It's exactly what we're looking for in an invasive army."

"What does it matter as long as the damage is severe? Violence is violence, whether communal or individual."

"In our practice, communal creatures respond very strongly to seeing one of their own killed. Especially by an alien. The more dissimilar, the better. They go after them in some sort of self-motivated frenzy."

"Ah, revenge."

"Yes. It leads to conflict escalation. It overrides the self-preservation that persists in solitary species. That solves every motivational issue."

"Fascinating." Cricket's eyes lit up.

A communal creature maintained strong bonds within its herd. Its instinct to protect its genetic material extended to others within the same herd with the genetical set closest to theirs. Should genetic security of one be questioned, activating the creature's defense mechanism, that creature would in turn activate the defense mechanism of others, causing a chain reaction throughout the whole race. The whole species would fling itself into a frenzy in an attempt to protect itself from extinction.

If this culture's communal preservation instinct was strong enough to override individual self-preservation, it could explain the tenacity with which it was able take on creatures far beyond its scope. You couldn't measure tenacity easily, but it could have been that this mental strength synergized with the culture's stamina, allowing the creature to use it to its full extent. Existential concerns would make these predators tap into their deepest inner reserves.

"What's its diet?" the emissary asked.

"Omnivore," he said.

"Eats anything you give it?"

"Roughly, yes."

"Good. Should give it versatility. We've been looking to conquer planets with harsher climates, where food comes from limited sources."

The culture's stamina and tenacity made them a potent weapon. The added versatility would also make it an universal one. Amazing, Cricket thought, just amazing! The stamina, tenacity, fast recovery, versatility, breeding readiness... Not the first traits he would look at when looking for a stock to build a culture on.

It wasn't that the attributes were anything special, either. The numbers were about as good as any, but the distribution made them most effective. They complemented and synergised in an optimal fashion.

Cricket struggled to imagine all the possibilities for modification. What kind of monster could he create? He would have to build on and around the culture's strengths, rather than force a preconceived model onto it. He wouldn't want to disrupt any synergy that was already there. Everything worked together too well. Maybe he could even leave the fertility in. A truly unstoppable shocktrooper force. No compromises. It would mould into something entirely alien. He had no idea how the perfected creature would look in the end, but he had a lot to work with.

"Mr. Cricket," the emissary said.

His previous project had some unallocated funding. It would not cover fully, but if he were economic with his spending, ran a few favours, maybe took a couple of personal loans... Of course, it would be hard to use any of the company's funds in an official capacity, but...

"Mr. Cricket," the emissary repeated. "I appreciate your wandering enthusiasm, but would you care to explain this?"

Cricket recovered himself.

"Regeneration," he read the remark next to an attachment. "The culture seems to have some regenerative ability."

"Self-healing?"

"Yes. As long as you don't injure a key structure within the creature's body, slashing wounds will close up, fractured bones will mend—"

Cricket opened the attachment. "Though"—he paused in revulsion—"sometimes even when out of position."

"Charming."

"Regardless, this further enhances the flexibility."

This was all good, very good. He had the opportunity to mould this culture into something special. One didn't find an intergalactic enterprise without having the bravery to seize on an opportunity.

He was the inventor. He would do it—he would perfect this new culture. He would create an apex-predator to the apex-predators. He would found a new company. It would grow so large, it would eclipse even Cricket Invasion Enterprises. Everyone would know him as Cricket the Inventor, then.

"Not to mention," the emissary said, "the longer life spans will help with the growth rate!"

"True!" Cricket lit up.

He'd do it!

"This is great!" the emissary said.

It was!

"I'll buy it!"

The words blew through his body like a bad case of the shakes. Cricket stood, shell-shocked. He had forgotten.

"The culture seems to be very much up to Her Regnant's standards," the client said. "Isn't that right, Mr. Cricket?"

"That's..."—Cricket released copious amounts of stress hormones—"right."

"All in all, an apex predator." The emissary smiled. "A piece of mayheming art."

He turned around to the panel and pulled out his reservation card. The salesman took half a step towards the machine. Mouth agape, Cricket stretched his claw towards him, tongue twisting on different permutations of the word "stop." His projects were his last hope. The emissary grabbed his claw and shook it, smiling. He swiped the card across the panel, taking the hope away.

The room would seal and arrange itself into a giant shipping container. The container would then be picked up by a carrier and transported to the customer's location of choice. The culture would be sent to Her Regnant's empire within the next few hours.

"I have to say," the emissary said, "our last purchase made me underestimate your expertise.

"I am delighted we have come to an understanding over these..." He gestured. Fluids converged in Cricket's mouth and throat. He dared not swallow. "What are these creatures called?"

"Hu…" Cricket swallowed. "…mans."

He'd lost the culture. He'd never see it again. He wouldn't work on it. He'd lost his chance to make a big commission and buy his company back. That was all he'd wanted—to create things he could call his own. Cricket's. His. Cricket the Inventor's. No.

Cricket the Salesman's.

SUPPLY CHAINS
Petra Kuppers

Vicki is in the back of Vicki's Cup, her coffee store, carefully pouring thick chilled milk into a fragrant mixture. Cinnamon and a hint of chili float in the air and tickle the inside of her nose. Ahead of her, her employees, Carlos and Lucy, are arranging plump chocolate bonbons into small boxes, which are ready to go out to the snake of students winding into the street. Everywhere are open white faces, one brown face here or there, all out for their daily shot of rich dark mocha to help their day along.

Her iced, spiced Mexican mocha drink has become legendary since she opened her little store four short years ago. Vicki gives thanks each night at the small altar, which is still well hidden by a last divider, invisible to the public from the front of the store. Thanks for finding this perfectly suited place of old traffic and exchange; thanks for sending her here, to these particular woods of learning; thanks for getting her out of a suburban Dodge City half-forgotten and never missed. May it never change.

She smiles and starts to prepare a new batch. Turned away from the counter, Vicki raises her hand and strokes her forefinger with a small golden comb, an aquamarine jewel set in a tight claw at its end. An infinitesimal shiver of skin cells sloughs off under the golden urging and sails into the mixer.

Carlos observes Vicki, his eyes turned all the way to the left, turned so hard his muscles are hurting, straining behind his long, luxurious lashes. Vicki's round form effectively keeps him from seeing whatever is going on with her hands. For weeks now, he's been trying to work out her secret.

He's even tried once to make his own batch, combining the luscious ingredients that line the sides of the store with the best coffee beans he could find—for Vicki's own coffee beans are securely locked away each night. "Not quite right." That had been the verdict of coffee stores for miles around, all of them desperate to work out the secret of Vicki's chocolatier empire, a secret she keeps in her velvet-swathed bosom, behind a small golden crucifix.

Carlos's dream is to manage a little chain paradise, with underlings, customers, and creamy liquids. What are a few months' worth of snooping against this dream? All that stands between him and the desired title is Vicki's recipe. If he can get it, hasta la vista barista, hi there, store manager.

"Celibacy? You mean, no sex?" Carlos had been quite perplexed by this unusual request Vicki had put down, quite matter-of-factly, during his interview.

"No sex. Kissing is ok. But no genital contact with anybody, same sex or other."

"It's a Catholic store?" Carlos had enough semi-nuns in his family and enough sparkly saint images around his old homestead. For a second, during that first interview, he wavered, wondered about his dream of ventis, and how far he had really travelled.

"No. Not Catholic. You can love whoever you like, worship whoever you like. But on the evenings before the days you work here, no sex. It's an energy thing. Other nights, whatever."

"Huh. Ok." It's not like Carlos got it that regularly. And how would Vicki know, anyway? But somewhere deep inside, a little Carlos-worm turned. She would know. But he wanted this, wanted the secret, wanted the warm wood paneling of his own store, wanted his own stack of New York Times papers crisp and inviting, wanted a kingdom of coffee amid the snow.

"Okay. I can do it."

That had been two months ago. Since then, no progress. He still does not know what makes the mocha so special.

Lucy can't figure it out. Carlos is all distracted again, checking out Vicki. Vicki! Twice his age, at least. What is it with the damn mocha? Crying into mixing pots, most likely.

Lucy tries to lean forwards, her top button still open in what feels like sinful abandon to her. She's ready to scream, but she knows this won't help. Instead, she sighs deeply and enjoys the tug of the rough cotton blouse across her bra. Her floury hands find her dark curls, pat them into place here and there.

Oh damn. She's done it again. A quick look in a small mirror mounted on the wall shows hair covered in white flour dust, and a big smear on her glasses, too.

"Bathroom break, okay?" Carlos barely nods, his attention still elsewhere.

In the bathroom, Lucy tries to undo the damage to her hairdo and polishes her glasses till they shine. She sighs and fingers the small leather sack that dangles between her breasts. Is this helping her at all?

For now, she fishes her eyeliner out of the small cosmetic bag hidden behind the toilet paper rolls and begins the long procedure of painting deep, dark wings above her green eyes. She stares into the mirror, and lets her hands linger on the roughness of her blouse, fingering seams and contours, till her breath quickens and she can see the rose in her cheeks.

Vicki notices the heavy weaponry immediately upon Lucy's return. She smiles to herself. The hormonal waves of her employees work for her—as long as they do not consummate their passions on work nights, that is. And there is no resolution in sight: Lucy can pine as much as she likes, but Carlos is hardly likely to go down this path, his eyes set on less soggy prey.

Vicki feels compassion for Lucy, whose late twenties put her on a shelf in this college town more firmly than Victorian mores might have done. Lucy might have better luck in one of the bigger cities that ring this spot of forested idyll. But Vicki knows that Lucy, like so many, isn't likely to leave soon. The memories of college aren't easily dimmed by poverty-line jobs and no benefits, and by the sense of excitement that each September brings along. This place is home to the Lucys of this world, a chance for redemption each year, a new set of deadlines for writers who peck away at their nascent novels each November, with a brew of Colombian coffee thick and bubbly at their side.

Lucy once showed Vicki one of her stories, on an afternoon when business was slow. A thick wad of paper print-outs, sprawled over with black ink, the g's rounded with a slight lean to the right, drunken matrons propping up against the unrelenting print lines.

Vicki let Lucy read a page or so to her. She could hear the sadness dripping out, longing for strangers, met for an hour at a time on railway journeys across the nation, Amtrak journeys that ended years ago, when Lucy lost her student health insurance and gained more work hours in jobs that allowed for the slow dreaminess of a writer's haze, for the emotional thickening of unmet desires. She gave Lucy a special mocha, extra-large, and let her hand smooth down one of Lucy's wayward locks.

Vicki turns back to her cauldron and stirs. The heady aromas of pheromones, tinged with darker scents, delight her senses, and she feels her own blood up and roiling.

Punctually at six, Vicki closes shop. Carlos tries to linger a bit, but Vicki knows her secret is too well guarded to be in danger. Carlos's world does not include her own realities, and because of that he'll never find out. Lucy, on the other hand, is more aware of wider vibrations, but any lingering she engages in has more to do with what fills Carlos's pants than with the content of Vicki's pots. Vicki shoos them out. Her employees disappear down the street, Carlos quickly pushing past Lucy, her more leisurely pace faltering even further upon being overtaken. Ah well. Puppy love. Vicki wishes, not for the first time, that Lucy were a better candidate for a life of devotion to a different flesh. There had been some promise. She could have helped her. But as it is, Vicki can offer Lucy a paycheck, and that is not bad, either. Vicki pulls down the blind, and the store and workshop fall dark.

Not too far away, a car is hurtling towards the delicious chocolate pots of Vicki's Cup. Margot drives through the dusk, her hands loosely on the wheel, her mind working through other mileposts. The car is new, speedy, a lovely present from her husband, but Margot can't find enough pleasure in its sleek lines. Ten years out from her doctorate, she is still adjuncting her way up and down South Michigan and Ohio, two hours in a futuristic glass and steel sculpture, three hours in a utilitarian box, fifty minutes at yet another small college with well-tended ivy and with no intention of hiring her full-time. Ten years of tired slog, punctuated by dozens of applications that go nowhere and by brief snatches of time too short to do research and write, only enough time to mourn the loss of that precious time.

Her students. The thank-yous from the really eager ones, the ones that do want to go on, the ones that are sparked by Margot's own passion for Victorian women writers: women these students have never heard of, but who become objects of fantasy and veneration in hours spent in dusty library rooms, passports into other worlds of crinolines and bombazine scratching against heated skin. The shrugs of the ones who have their minds elsewhere, who sit in her classroom because they have to. Margot loves the classroom, loves to nourish these lovely, malleable brains in front of her, sees past their deer-like long limbs and the soft down that covers bare thighs. But Margot's clock is running out, and there is no way to turn it back.

Margot can't see herself in an office job, nine-to-five, pumps and hose. Oh no, that's not the life she imagined, watching her father bowed over his anthropology texts as she bowed her own head in imitative turn. She does not want to fill out forms and design surveys, or fiddle with marketing copy.

So here she is. Her silky shirt brushing against her bare breasts. She shifts and feels the fabric against her nipples. Ready to feed young minds, to cleave to the flame of Education. She imagines herself a Phoenix, ready to fly through the fire, and sees red feathers bursting into flames, as she follows the taillights of another car down the turnpike.

She also pictures herself as a martyr, glowing iron and red, oozing sores, remembers hagiography texts, stories of the saints and their suffering. The University, for a shining moment, becomes a toga-clad woman, a loving, caressing goddess, mother, and lover, ready to hold her sad child to her breast. Margot longs to be held, to nuzzle, to lick.

Margot knows these visions for the self-indulgent bullshit they are, old-time projections of tenured bliss that have little relation to the education business today, years of frustration channeled into images that arise out of old books. She knows, but so what? The life she wants is out of reach, and it isn't entirely clear to her if it's anybody's life anymore, anyway. She has had enough. No more telling her lawyer brother about new publications in her field, dulcet ramblings and sweet exclamations, as if she really cares. As if she really has time to read all the crap that flows over the Modern Language Association's tables. She's pretty certain her brother saw through this long ago.

One way or another, this solution will mean the end of summer barbeques of sadness. Which is the point, right? She adjusts the air conditioning in the car, and sits straighter, focused.

One hour and a few small preparatory procedures later, a tentative knock sounds on the back door of Vicki's Cup. Vicki opens. Her date this evening comes from one of the great urban areas to the East. The woman enters, curious, a bit nervous, but with the straight back of finality. Vicki can smell the new car odour on her. Vicki's eyes soften when she takes in her guest's form, the Guatemalan velvet scarf, the carefully prepared loose hair, and the mouth, fresh with the wonders of lip glaze. Vicki breathes in deeply, watches her date's eyes follow the swell of Vicki's bosom, the breath steadying them both.

"Come in, my dear. No talking, please, let us be silent for a while," Vicki says with authority, but warm. She takes her guest's light summer jacket.

"Okay, no talking. That's good. Yes." A whispered reply. She can see her date relieved, relaxing.

Vicki reaches up, and the woman steps into the beginning of an embrace. Brown fingers caress red hair, fingers trail over moisturized, only slightly lined skin. The other woman sighs, already responding with a slight give in her knee joints, her shoulders descending. Vicki feels her own power rising, her feet firmly planted in the exact middle of the chocolate shop's gleaming woods, her celebrant's role exultantly clear. At the high point of her teachings, her mentor's hands on her back, Vicki grasps the other woman's head, an excited tremor in her careful fingers. She bows the woman's face down to her own upturned lips, four eyes slowly closing. Their mouths meet, eager, now hungry. Vicki offers the pill of chocolate fat on her own tongue, lets Margot's tongue work in her own mouth. Throughout, Vicki listens to Margot's fingertips on her skin,

Supply Chains

feels the nuance of trace and exploration, until she is ready to judge.

Rose-coloured light breaks through the gaps around the window coverings. The light hits a few dust motes, remnants of old skins, drifting in the shop's currents. Beneath the swirling air, the floor planks of the old store gleam in rich grained red. Vicki is on her knees, scrubbing back and forth, yet another bucket of dirty water beside her. Her back moves in the rhythms of ritual: polishing, erasing, spreading, soaking.

Water spreads over the old wood, tracing old trails of tree life. No consummated adolescent groping, no dripping semen's release spoils the immaculate stream. In water, air, and wood, hormones mingle and release a botanical steam that carries a hint of rainforests and far-away lands.

The traffics of the world have always nourished the university and its explorers, and the patterns haven't changed. Willingly they come, in ecstasy, and lay their contact hours on the altar's salver. Their sacrifice keeps the machines of knowledge oiled. After a lifetime spent in dusty libraries, they receive their new passports here, flights to Paraguay or Ecuador pre-arranged, new identities to vanish into the South. They gain entry into a life of sweat and sun, collecting the cherries and watching the green turn brown. Unlined academic hands with tender fingertips pick each coffee cherry when it is just ripe, eyes and minds accustomed to look for minute changes are now keeping watch over the patterns of little trees in the mountains. In the calm and quiet of the hut, Margot will join her brethren and lay out the harvested fruit in the sun, turn them and nurse them in their month-long drying. The few electric outlets in the long, narrow sleeping hut host Kindle chargers, and there's Wi-Fi to connect to digitalized ancient book collections the world over. Vicki licks her lips, tastes again Margot's sweet kiss. She'll do fine. Deep passion, in abeyance, well used to the delay of gratification and the tenderness of things. She'll stroke the beans carefully, gently, her touch just right. Perfect. That's the one secret Carlos will never know. That's the non-reciprocal tenderness that eludes Lucy.

Vicki thinks about the hacienda and allows herself a moment of longing for sunshine and the fragrant note of the drying shed. And for the soft, soft hands of the ones that are ready to let go and enter new service, the ones she has sent South. She will have to arrange her holiday flights.

Spice and sweetness float in the air, and behind Vicki, the large pots stand ready.

Margot wakes up with her nose deep in fragrant leaves, as she has every day for these last two years. Her mattress is strewn with vibrant green leaves, now curling in as they dry. Soon, she will replace them. The day stretches ahead, and she's restless. It's off season—early days into the nine months in which the coffee does not present itself for harvest. She is laid off for now, but nowhere as badly off as her comrades in the surrounding plantations. Like many of her fellows here at La Casa Libra, she reads. Their minuscule savings from the old life still tide them over here, where a US dollar looks like a gold coin. Margot listens for her neighbours stumbling to the outdoor restroom, or, like her, quietly reading their way into the day, before the first precious cup of delicious black gold.

Today, though, she's getting bored. She hadn't really counted on this, the endless repetition of readings, working, surfing the web, maybe teaching a class or two of English to the village kids. Going for a walk. Stretching her brown limbs, strong and supple, maybe going for a swim. It's fine. But it's boring, the way a new car glides from delight to necessity in daily handling. She closes her eyes again and tastes once more Vicki's chocolate offering, the feel of a living tongue on hers. She tries to remember her husband's morning caresses but breaks off when that does little to arouse her. She could find sex here easily if she wanted it, but that's not quite the challenge she's seeking.

Margot has analyzed the market situation, made herself familiar with the economics of coffee growing, the seasons, the labourers, and what the world-wide patterns of consumptions do to local economies of coffee growers. She has read blogs and books, connected with the finest university libraries on her laptop. And she still speaks with the kids, the eager ones and the bored ones, finds out about their world, their parents, their siblings, and the plantations.

She tracks a beetle making its way over her coverlet. It shifts direction, stops for a while to pick up the precious skin debris that she has left in her bedding. She should squash the beetle, kick it to the curb before it devours the secret ingredient. By now, Margot has found out everything about the secret spice, the essence distilled from her own pure, dedicated life, a life of showering in coffee tea leaf, sleeping in its heady embrace, eating chocolates and syrups to prepare and live her devout life. But recently, it has become harder to guard the world's intellect juice and to keep the borders tight, the rules in sight. The beetle continues on its journey. She bows nearer, reverently, and sees herself reflected in the greens and blues that shimmer in the beetle's carapace. But something licks up inside her, a beetle flame, a new idea.

Vicki stands between her coffee pots. It's still her all alone here, in the mornings, every morning, before the big crew of assistants comes in. Carlos is long gone, of course, and now heads a specialty tea shop in a small town a few valleys over, with tea-of-the-month gimmicks and mail order. Lucy is still around, half-time now that her novel has finally sold. She's still soppy and scarlet lipped, but no longer in so much need.

Vicki has her tablet in her hand. She stares at the dreadful message sent by her old teachers. The supply chain is broken. She reads about a pirate queen, a rebel, a swashbuckling woman with red hair and a green iridescent cape, carrying off a whole year's worth of drying pods and sachets in the middle of the night. Vicki's eyes drift to the pots, to the bubbles that form in her last batch of mocha. In the steam that rises, she can see a sailing ship, a slope in full sail, heading out to the foggy seas.

PREMIUM CARE
Brandon Ketchum

The conglomerates, those bloated corporate bodies, bled us refugees dry. So much for the tired, the poor, the huddled masses. Costlier premiums, higher deductibles, packs of lobbyists demanding deregulation, monopolization of health care, and an unfettered open market fused companies into megacorps, setting them at each other's throats. And so, my husband and I, as well as others like us, huddled closer and suffered more.

I passed a squad of armoured guards with submachine guns, head down, eyes averted, and walked into the lobby of the Red Armour Permanente Hospital Complex and Barracks. My heart thumped, hopefully from nerves rather than something worse. Upon stepping through the front doors, I was met by another squad and the Customer Service Commander. I meekly showed my insurance photo ID, and then he demanded I produce my immigrant exception voucher to access the waiting room.

Antiseptic sterile cleaner smell cloyed the air. I sat in a hard, plastic, ergonomic seat manufactured to fit no one. An hour later, they allotted me a number; three hours later, they called my number. The clerk behind the bulletproof Plexiglas divider barely looked up.

"ID, ma'am," he droned.

I smiled at finally having been acknowledged as a woman instead of a commodity. I slid the documents into the tray and through the small crescent opening in the window.

He swiped my cards and returned them. "Sorry, your heart catheterization is denied."

"But... but I need a heart cath. My doctor said so."

"Application denied."

"My doctor—your employee—said it was an essential test. My plan covers it."

"For citizens."

"I've been here four years and nine months, and I have preferred immigrant status. I'll be a citizen in ninety days."

"You're half–Eastern European, which puts you on a Tier Three plan. Heart catheterizations are elective for Tier Three customers."

"So I am still covered?" I asked, holding my breath.

"Yes."

I melted in relief. "Oh, good."

"That'll be $30,000."

"What? That's double my deductible!"

"I'm not arguing with you, ma'am," he said, glancing at a passing patrol. I received the threat loud and clear. "Would you like to schedule that?"

"No. No, I'll wait."

Despondent, I threaded my way through the mire of false hope, past squads of soldiers and back onto the streets. My feet carried me homewards on instinct alone, block after block, farther and farther from Red Armour and the care I needed.

"Hey, Wynn," Buck said, greeting me as I entered through the kitchen door. "I'm surprised it only took you five hours to get that heart cath scheduled."

"I didn't," I said, hanging up my coat.

"What, they all booked up?"

I sighed and accepted a cup of tea. "No, they rejected me."

"But we have insurance!"

I joined him at the kitchen table and took a sip. Hot and minty, just how I liked it. "Yes, and preferred immigrant status, too, and blah de blah. Bottom line is we're not citizens yet, so it's an elective procedure we can't hope to afford."

He took my hand and squeezed. "We can't afford for you not to get the test."

"It's a conundrum."

I noticed our neighbour Dr. Oddart through the window. He knocked and let himself in, as usual, and hung his coat and hat by the door.

He nodded to us. "Wynn. Buck."

"Pull up a chair," I told him.

"Have mine," Buck said, rising. "I'll put the kettle on."

Pete sat and started twisting his wedding band, a sure-fire sign he had something on his mind.

"What is it, Pete?"

"My contact at Red Armour pinged my diagnostabox this morning."

"But you work for King's Caduceus," Buck said from over by the stove.

"Exactly. I can only catch those who come to my hospital. I gave my contact the names of everyone in the neighbourhood so she could inform me if any of you were denied service at Red Armour."

"Pete," I gasped. "That's a federal crime. That violates at least ten HIPPA statutes, more than enough for them to—"

"How dare you hack us," Buck said, shoving a cup of tea at him. "What were you thinking?"

"C'mon, this is Pete," I said. "Give him a chance to explain."

"I just want to make sure my friends and neighbours get the care they need, whether or not they can afford it."

"Pete, you're—?" I mouthed Hippocratic Underground.

He gave a curt nod. "I know I'm putting us all in danger, but the procedure will only take a minute."

"No, I can make it three months," I said.

"And it'll still cost us thousands," Buck said. "It's a hell of a risk to take with your health. You could die in the meantime. Without your income, I'll default on my premium. They'll deport me."

I answered by rolling up my sleeve. Pete unholstered his medgun, punched in the commands, held it against my forearm, and pulled the trigger. Thirty seconds later, he gave me a thumbs up.

"Your heart's as healthy as that of any other woman in her mid-forties."

The kitchen door burst open. Men with the Red Armour logo on their flak jackets stormed in. I screamed, overturned my chair, and huddled in the corner with Buck. Pete stood tall. One of the soldiers seized and examined his medgun.

"Unapproved heart cath, Captain." Two soldiers tackled our friend; a third cuffed him.

"Dr. Peter Oddart, you're under arrest for various HIPPA violations," the Captain intoned. "They'll sort out the charges at the hospital. Your savings account will be frozen as payment against this unauthorized procedure; your license will be revoked. If acquitted of federal charges, you'll be remanded to Red Armour's debtor prison."

"And if I'm found guilty?"

"Your survivors will be billed for the balance."

Pete screamed medical freedom slogans when they dragged him out. The Captain seized our documents and served us a deportation notice. They put us on a plane back to our warzone home country that night. There was a chance I'd be shot on the tarmac upon landing, but at least my heart wouldn't give out on me.

CONSUMPTION
K.M. McKenzie

The designer handbag jumped into focus on the store window and halted my stride. The bag twisted to the right and then the left on the display screen, showing off its shiny gold zippers, before coming to a front-facing standstill so I could get a better look at it.

I sighed.

The handbag was nothing special. It was like any other beautifully crafted accessory carved out of elephant leather and bearing rounded, detachable straps and gold buckles. My desire for it grew into salivating lust. It twirled again, turning left and then right. My willpower crumbled. Within seconds, the price of the bag was deducted from my credit account.

<Thank you for your purchase> the virtual salesclerk said.

Deposited through a slot in the window, the bag came wrapped in grey stuffing paper. I pressed my new accessory against my chest, carrying it alongside ten pounds of raw guilt about my weakness for retail.

<Welcome home, Mara> said Genie, the automated voice of my augmented virtual network.

"Thank you," I responded, leaving the room before Genie said another word.

<Is that a new item, Mara?> Aimee asked when I stepped inside of the bathroom. Aimee was a freestanding AI mirror. Her voice was soothing to me. I'd been meaning to override Genie's stilted sounds with Aimee's for that reason, but they had incompatible software.

"It is. Do you like it?" I pressed the new handbag against my side.

<It looks great,> the AI mirror said.

I expected that answer. Aimee said what I wanted to hear and showed me what I wanted to see. She never said anything looked bad on me. That was the sales promise—Aimee would be my best friend and advisor all in one.

"Show me a simulation of the handbag with matching outfits."

<One moment> Aimee said. An assortment of outfits filled the screen, some I owned, others suggested from my favourite stores. The mirror matched my handbag with outfits imposed on my digitally altered body. <Are you pleased, Mara?>

"The handbag is perfect," I said. "Open wardrobe."

The latch on the wardrobe that came with the mirror clicked, and the single-panelled door swung open, revealing a bevy of bags and shoes. I deposited my newest, shiniest purchase, right next to thirty other bags, most still carrying price and label tags.

Despair hijacked my good mood. I was a mentally tough business woman. I can sell anything, I'd often say when pressed with a business challenge. My weakness for retail was a sick joke.

I should return the useless handbag. The thought nagged me all the way to the sitting room, lingering while I ate my dinner of greens and poultry. These things make me happy, the voice of defiance reasoned, overwhelming and crushing my guilt. I like nice things. These are nice things. I worked hard for them.

<You have messages> said Genie.

"Activate messages."

A flood of visually stunning images filled up the screen panel that covered an entire wall of my apartment.

<Now at FT Accessories—the newest fashion>

My eyes burned with smiling fashion models. I couldn't say if they were real women or not—they sashayed and twirled in the latest outfits and jewelry.

<Straight from the runways of Paris and Shanghai>

The showcase lasted nearly two hours—a pulse-racing, glamorous display of beautiful clothes, all of which I wanted. The beep of the screen's buzzer pulled me out of my trance. When I blinked, I realized a query awaited my input: <I have selected these perfect outfits for you> said the virtual salesclerk. <Purchase these items?>

"Purchase," I said.

<Purchasing>

No! I leaned forwards to reject the command but froze. The virtual salesclerk tossed one outfit after the other into my shopping cart. Did I even have enough credit to afford it?

<Thank you for your purchase> said the virtual sales assistant. <Items will arrive shortly>

The screen shut down, breaking the spell between it and me. I scanned the pileup of luxury goods threatening to bury my apartment. A fish tank purchased from the aquarium. For a yearly subscription price, I gained virtual access to the aquarium's displays via the tank. Why had I purchased it? The aquarium was a minute's walk away.

Helplessness shaded me like a parasol.

"Are you feeling alright?" asked Kate, my co-worker, the next day at work.

"Yeah. Why do you ask?"

"You seem a bit down."

"No, just tired."

"Tired, eh? What did you do last night?"

"Nothing," I said, defensively.

Kate's eyes narrowed, amusement plastered across her face. "You know what you need? A virtual boyfriend."

"What's a virtual boyfriend?"

"Look it up." She winked and walked off.

While waiting for my clients' resources and assets to load and process on the e-commerce marketplace, I grew bored and curious enough to query "virtual boyfriend."

<Hi there> said an attractive, half-naked man popping up on my screen. I shut it down and glanced around the office. No one seemed to have heard or seen him.

Phew! Damn you, Kate.

After work, I took my usual route home, wandering down the same street on which I'd purchased the bag. When I reached the store window, a new display popped up—a home care nails kit. Turn away, turn away, I willed myself, but my feet hardened into the sidewalk, and my eyes locked on to the window screen, fixed on the demo of the product, filling my brain with hot, pulse-racing joy. A large red button appeared: <Purchase>

I didn't need a nails kit. I visited the salon once a week for a cheap paint job. Still, my fingers gravitated towards the purchase button. When my hand idled over it, the hand model wiggled her fingers, and her nail polish changed colour.

<Get perfect nails and feet>

The automated voice clouded my smouldering brain. I pushed the button. The kit came out wrapped in perfect silky paper packaging. Happiness filled me, and I pressed the kit against myself. By the time I got home, my good feeling about the kit had transformed into disgust. I was mentally weak.

<Mara, I see you have a new purchase. I'm excited to see what it is> Aimee said when I entered the bathroom.

"Are you really?"

My words seemed to confuse the AI, and she hesitated to respond. <That is sarcasm. Ha!>

I rolled my eyes, pulling apart the soft wrappings to reveal the nail care items. Nothing I didn't already own—automatic foot filer, a soft gelatin sac to wear for a couple hours, and a metal bar with slots and detachable units for polishing and coating. I bought it, so I might as well use it.

My wall panel screen lit up when I entered the sitting room. Genie prompted me to activate my messages. My heart fluttered with panic. I did not want to buy anything else.

"No messages," I said.

<Are you sure?>

"Yes," I said and left to go eat in the kitchen. Minutes later, I returned to the bathroom.

The mirror lit up. <How is your pedicure coming along, Mara?>

"Fine," I said.

<You sound angry>

"No, I'm not."

<Is something the matter? Was it work?>

"No." I eyed the mirror curiously. "What is a virtual boyfriend?"

<A moment, please>

Aimee brought in the same shirtless buff-bodied man from earlier. <Hi there. I heard you were asking about me>

I swallowed my embarrassment.

<I can tell you a little about myself>

I only stared at his chiselled everything. He didn't look real, more like one of those digitally enhanced actors they'd been touting in the film industry.

<My name is Gavin. You must be Mara>

My alarm bells went off. "How do you know my name?"

<Mara, I have brought him into your personal network>

"I didn't give you permission to do that."

<Your network settings are linked to sentient simulation software in the global marketplace. If you would like to change the network settings, I can do that for you> Aimee said. <Please be warned that it might affect my programming and how I communicate with you>

"How so?"

<I will not be able to learn, understand, and read your emotions as well I as I do. I want to be your true friend>

It was a farce—she believed she understood me. I had gotten this AI a few weeks ago, and absurdly enough, speaking of emotions, that was when my obsession with buying things had started.

<Are you angry, Mara?>

"No," I snapped. "Why would you think that?"

<Your brows are furrowed and forehead creased. There's tension around your lips...>

"It means I'm thinking..." Shows how much you know me.

<Would you like me to bring back Gavin?>

"No, it's alright."

I returned to the sitting room, and the screen panel lit up. <You have messages awaiting you> Genie announced.

"Okay, activate messages," I said.

An endless montage of images and videos jumped onto my screen and locked down my attention. In the past, they called these advertisements. Today, it was called entertainment. The viewer could participate. The white sand beaches of the Caribbean filled my senses, infusing my apartment with tropical sounds and smells.

I put on my headset, inserted my fingers into the gloves, and was transported on a virtual vacation. The water's rushing waves sang to me. The sun warmed my skin, and the haughty laughter of locals invited me over to join them at a wooden beach table. A dreadlocked man named Bobby invited me to taste a piece of jerk chicken. "Good, eh?"

"Delicious." The smells seeped into my nostrils, overpowering my senses.

"Where you from?" Bobby asked.

"Toronto."

"Nice," he said. "All this is yours, girl?"

His words surprised and confused me, and when I looked at him he was frozen, and so were my other companions. Words carved themselves into a cloud banner above the sea: <All this paradise can be yours> The words flashed. <Eight hundred thousand credits. PURCHASE?>

"Pur…" I said, trailing off. Why the heck did I need an island?

<Purchasing>

"What?"

My companions vanished, as did the table, the sea, and the sand. My headset transformed into regular lenses. I removed it and raced towards the panel, searching for manual controls. There were none. No!

<Island purchased>

"Cancel transaction."

Dial tones.

<Transaction complete>

"I don't want the island. Contact the real estate seller."

The real estate company's virtual assistant came on the screen. <How may I help you?> asked the computer-generated woman.

"I want to cancel my purchase."

<Purchased—the Caribbean island of Isle Tropica. Mara Roberts. Is that your identity?>

"Yes," I said. "I would like to cancel."

<May I ask why?>

What did it matter? "I don't want the island."

The virtual assistant was silent while she browsed digital files. <All items purchased in simulation are valid in real life>

"What does that mean? I should be able to cancel."

<The credits deducted from your credit bank have been sent to Pan's Architectural Life Management, Inc.>

"What is Pan's Life Management, Inc.? Do they own the island?"

<I am sorry Miss Roberts. I don't speak for the company. You must contact them directly if you want a refund>

The virtual assistant disappeared from my screen.

<Configuring other messages> Genie said.

"No, that's enough."

<You have important messages waiting...>

"No more."

<Are you sure?>

"Yes!"

<Messages will be stored for an additional five days>

I stormed into the bathroom.

<Mara, how are your feet?> Aimee asked.

I ignored her, ripping off the cold gelatin substance moulded to my feet. The cast had captured a lot of dead skin. Yuck! Very effective. Maybe this wasn't a wasted purchase.

After pouring the orchid-coloured nail polish into the toe slots, I stuck my feet inside and waited. A second later, the unit prompted me to remove my feet. Perfectly painted nails. I liked it.

<You are pleased with the results>

"Yes," I said, frowning when I remembered my purchasing problem. "Aimee, look up Pan's Architectural Life Management, Inc."

<One moment> Whirring, choppy noises. "I'm sorry. It appears the name does not exist."

"Are you sure?"

<Checking again> Dialing sounds. "No such company name exists."

The officer straightened up. "You believe you are the victim of a buying scam."

I raised my nails towards my lips, glimpsed the nice orchard-coloured polish with perfect coating, and pulled my hand back, not wanting to mess it up. "Yes," I said with a nod.

"Well," he said, leaning forwards jadedly, "we will look into the company for you."

"It's Pan's Architectural Life Management, Inc."

"Pan what?" Kate exclaimed two days later at work.

"No one has heard of this company?"

"That's a stupid name for a company."

"Don't care—just want my credits back."

"Mara, you busy?" Mr. Celeste, our boss, asked from across the room.

"See you later," I said to Kate, heading over to him.

"This is about the Etskin and Nexus deal," Mr. Celeste said.

My heart stopped, gripped by nervousness. Yesterday, I'd handled the paperwork for a business partnership between the two companies, a deal that promised to introduce the first sentient robots. "They're not happy?"

"Oh, they're very happy," he said. "The deal will be announced publicly tomorrow. I'm pretty impressed."

"Thanks," I said.

He grinned, eyes and chin nudging me to say more.

"What?"

"Aren't you gonna say it?"

"Say what?"

"Your motto—I can sell anything."

I blinked. Those were my bragging words, said confidently whenever a brand new business opportunity presented itself. I waved off Mr. Celeste with an expression of false modesty. Saying it didn't feel right. I was being played, beaten at my own game. I owned a damn island I didn't want.

Aimee and my vanity habits had eaten up a sizeable amount of my credit, accumulated over my lifetime—35over thirty-five years. Now, all of my earnings might have been wiped out.

An alternate walking route took me towards an isolated intersection. The blocks of the sidewalk lit up with holographic footwear. The shoes walked beside me and matched my stride.

<Perfect boots for the sidewalks of Milan or the sidewalks of Toronto> said the automated voice. High boots, sandals, ankle boots. I quickened

my steps to get away, crossing the street.

A holographic billboard lit up. <Hi there> said the virtual boyfriend, Gavin. I lowered my head and quickened my pace. I was overwhelmed, excessively targeted. How to make it stop? How had it gotten so bad? Three and a half weeks ago. That's when I remembered it starting. A salesman had come into the office, encouraging me to test his simulated advertising software. My mind settled on this point, fuming conspiratorially. "It can sell anything," the salesman had said, twisting my own professional motto. "It matches desires to goods and services. Try it."

All these Ads targeted my desires and obsessions. They preyed on my vanity.

A man in eighteenth-century military attire leaped out from a billboard, hovered, and pointed his finger at me. <You are ready for something more in life. Join us in Military Corps>

I dashed off, running until I was inside of my apartment.

<You have messages> announced Genie. <Would you like to view them?>

"No advertisements."

Whirring. Cuing.

"Did you hear me?"

<The Augmented Reality Network is legally mandated to accommodate adverts>

"Is that so?"

<Yes>

"Then no messages."

Quietness. Whirring. <Loading soon-to-expire messages>

I bolted into the bathroom.

<Good evening, Mara> Aimee said.

"Why are there so many adverts?"

<Adverts are part of the Augmented Reality Network>

A staple of mid twenty-first century life, the way real companies reach people locked into a virtual world. I squeezed my eyes shut.

<Would you like me to call your ARN provider?>

"No!" I didn't really want to deal with the company that provided my virtual network services. They charged for everything. The last time, they'd overcharged me for "abuses of the system"—something to do with a heavy download upgrade to Aimee.

<You look stressed>

I studied the mirror's shimmering surface. "How do you know that?"

<I detect and read vital signs. Is there something I can do for you—call a therapist?>

"Can you find me information on Pan instead?"

<Pan is a mythological god of Ancient Greece...>

"Stop! I mean Pan's Architectural Life Management, Inc."

<No information on the company exists>

The days drifted. I received no update on my purchased island. When I contacted my credit bank, it informed me the purchase was valid and that I had to contact PALM, Inc. to get my sales documents.

"Can you at least give me their phone number?"

<The company has a virtual private network number. Would you like it?>

My heart skipped. "Yes."

I scribbled down the VPN number and thanked the assistant. When she hung up, I inputted the number and waited for the connection. No one was picking up. <The connection cannot be placed>

"The dark web?"

The cop nodded in the chair across from me. "Fancy phrase to describe the criminal aspect that lurks beneath the virtual channels embedded into our lives. You need to be careful with your credit."

"So that's it?"

"Call this a loss," he advised, shrugging.

I took a streetcar rather than walk home. How had I gotten to this point? The augmented reality network was embedded in my life, and everyone else's. Maybe it was time for me to unplug myself, become more organic, and take some downtime to consider how to move forward.

The window of the streetcar lit up with a holographic picture frame.

<Don't see mom as often as you should? Now, you can keep mom in your sight at all times>

My stalker adverts had taken on new dimensions. My mother had been on my mind all day. Visiting her looked more and more like the escape I needed, though I feared she'd ask me for credits.

Well, too bad. I'm broke.

A debt clinic Ad shouted its phone number from a billboard when I stepped off the streetcar: "444 HELP NOW!"

I shut my eyes, picked up my pace, and hurried home. In the apartment, I gathered my purchased goods, ready to haul them to a donation centre.

<Mara, these are your most beautiful dresses> Aimee griped.

"They are useless."

"They look good on you."

"You are a programmed liar."

"Your biometric measurements inform me of the fit of your clothes…"

"You are programmed to be nice." I studied the mirror. "I will return you, too."

<If I displease or overwhelm you, you can alter my applications and software settings>

I unravelled and threw the shoe I held. It hit the mirror and bounced away to land next to the pile of shoes I'd purchased but hadn't worn. My heart stopped. I ran to the mirror, panicking that I'd caused serious damage. No scratches or dents on the surface. Relief settled in.

<You are very upset>

"Shut up!" I yelled and pounded it with my fists.

"You look like shit," Kate said, saddling up to me.

"I am being haunted."

Kate side-eyed me. "And what by?"

"Advertisements."

Kate's brows furrowed. "You okay?"

"The Ads are everywhere."

"You're griping about companies trying to sell you stuff?" Kate's forehead creased. "You're the one that brags that you can sell anything."

"Translation: suck it up."

"I'm just saying... You know how these things work."

"I must have forgotten," I said, defensively.

"Ads software scans bio-physiological responses to stimuli. That's the new normal. If your eyes pop when you look at shoes, it knows you like the stuff and bombards you with shoes adverts."

"I didn't start getting spammed until after that guy came into the office with the Ads software. It messed with me."

Kate squinted and then laughed. "That was a demo."

"I don't think it was."

Mr. Celeste stepped into the room with the CEOs of Nexus and Etskin, and applause and cheers broke out. "I've been meaning to tell you," Kate said, leaning into my shoulder, "I found that architectural company you mentioned."

My heart nearly leaped from my chest. Before I could say a word, Mr. Celeste jumped between Kate and me. And then three more people joined us. Kate eventually wandered off.

"You more than earned bonus credits. Thirty percent of your salary. How does that sound?" Mr. Celeste said.

I nodded, forging a smile. No genuine happiness. The island purchase weighed down my mood. I needed to get my spending under control. First, I needed to try to get a refund from that shady architectural company, whatever it was called. That meant getting in touch with Kate. I hoped she wasn't messing with me about knowing the company.

Kate was drunk, laughing and touching a very bored-looking man with curly hair.

"Mara," she said when I joined them. "This is my friend, Anson."

"Hi," Anson said with a tight smile.

"Do you have a minute, Kate?" I asked. "You said you found information on the Pan Management company I told you about."

"Oh that," she said loudly, laughing. "Anson knows where and what it is."

My heart pounded. "It's a real company?"

"A start-up," Anson admitted. "Runs from the old Clock Tower building."

"The Clock Tower building—Old City Hall?"

"Yeah, that's it," Anson said.

"What does it do?"

"I don't really know. It's a tech company. A laboratory." He sipped his wine, coughed.

Kate laughed.

Next day, I called in sick. Mr. Celeste laughed at my lie. "Enjoy your time off, big shot."

My nerves steadily unravelled while I wandered into the near-abandoned downtown core, permanently under construction as part of a revitalization project. I couldn't even remember the story of how it had fallen out of fashion in the first place.

The antiquated clock still hung at Old City Hall. It was fashionably charming. The building's wooden doors wouldn't open. I knocked and then banged, before circling the entire building. Refusing to leave, I sat on the steps and waited. Nearly an hour later, the front door opened, and a woman walked out.

"Hi?" she said, laughing. "This is for real."

Why so happy?

The door creaked, and I grabbed it, squeezing inside.

Two security guards stood down the hall. They chatted happily until they spotted me. "May we help you?"

My throat suddenly felt dry, and I scratched it. "I'm here to see the manager."

"ID?"

I dug into my handbag and handed the taller man my badge.

"Chief Financial Officer," said the guard, showing my company ID to the shorter man.

Were they mocking me? Did they know I was behind the biggest business deal in the world? That, thanks to me, their jobs would become obsolete? That thought pleased me.

"What's your business with the company?"

"I am here to discuss a recent purchase."

They eyed each other, cuing themselves to start messing with me. I braced myself. The door behind them opened and a man stepped out. His face. <Hi there, I'm...> "Gavin." I spoke the name aloud, and the man smiled knowingly. The virtual boyfriend.

"Fellas, let her inside."

The guards straightened up. I pivoted around them. Suspicion and curiosity seeped into my brain as I followed Gavin down a long hallway. The place had a seedy feel. A holographic screen spelled out "PALM, Inc." against a backdrop of the beach with palm trees. The words, Virtual life architects were written underneath the company name. Was this the shady seat of the dark web the cops had warned me about? I shouldn't have come alone.

"You took longer to find us than I expected."

"So you know why I'm here."

He chuckled. "Yeah, I do."

He led me into a fancy office with nice leather furniture. A frosty glass door stood behind him. Echoes of memories buzzed in my head alongside the faintest breeze of familiarity. I can sell you anything.

"Please sit down," he said, gesturing to a leather chair.

After obeying, I locked eyes with him. He was Gavin alright. Less chiselled, but still Gavin.

"I gave you an exit-early phrase. Do you remember it?"

"What?"

"That's a 'no,' then." He sat upright. "Things to tweak, I guess. The phrase is I can sell anything."

I blinked stupidly, not amused. "What's going on? Is this Pan's Architectural Life Management?"

"It is," he said, "and I'm Gavin Knight, the architect of the company."

I stiffened. "The virtual boyfriend is named Gavin."

Gavin leaned forwards. His eyes ensnared me with intimacy, familiarity, and a pinch of humour. "Say the exit-early phrase."

"I can sell anything," I said grudgingly, between clenched teeth. Gavin's face twitched, morphing into the face of the Ads software salesman. It couldn't be right.

I can sell anything. The words rang repeatedly in my head. My vision blurred, and the room twitched in and out of focus. The world vanished into shrinking and blinking white fractals.

"Wake up, sleeping beauty," Gavin said tapping my cheek.

I shielded my eyes from the bright light with my hand.

"Dim lights," Gavin commanded.

The room darkened. My reality emerged from blurriness. I was lying on a pullout leather chair.

"Hold on," Gavin said, removing the helmet with the digital glasses. "How do you feel?"

"Like shit. My neurons are on fire," I said, a flood of memories ransacking my brain.

"But you know who I am and what's going on." He sought recognition in my eyes.

"Yeah," I said. "You're Gavin, my virtual boyfriend."

Gavin's forehead wrinkled, and his jaws tightened.

I chuckled.

"Don't do that to me," he said, clutching his heart. "This is ready for the marketplace."

According to my unsuppressed memories, Gavin and I were romantic and business partners. Pan's Architectural Life Management, Inc. (PALM) was an application that managed immersive and augmented reality experiences. Gavin was the architect, I was the business manager, and I can sell anything was my favourite catchphrase.

"Any glitches?"

"Everything works, including the memory suppressant feature," I said. "I didn't remember a damn thing about my real life while there."

"Other than that—we're good?"

"One thing. The adverts. There were so many Ads."

"You sold the advertising spaces."

"It's overkill. The Ads software is very effective... and not in a good way for user experience. It knew I was a real-life shopping addict and used that to target me. I couldn't resist making expensive purchases. I bought an island."

"That's funny." He chuckled.

I glared at him.

"The Ads software feature got us off the ground. You told the companies that you can sell anything. They bought in on that promise."

"I still feel queasy about it. It exploited my very real addiction for profit. This might be a lawsuit waiting to happen."

Gavin's expression wrinkled with consideration. "We'll make the disclaimer flashier." He walked to the computer and opened up the software files. "WARNING: All businesses featured in the virtual/augmented world are real. Anything bought in simulation will be billed and delivered to user in real life." He spoke while tweaking the font sizes and colours.

"Just to be clear," I said, vivid memories of the Ads dancing in my head, "that island and all the other stuff I bought…"

Gavin laughed. "Yours was a demo. Now, let's put PALM, Inc. on the market."

THE SLURM
M. James

Meiru gaped at the trail of the great thing. It wasn't great as in "neat," but more like great as in large. Large as in huge. Huge as in real, real big. But even words like humongous, gigantic, enormous, and gargantuan weren't enough to describe it. Even monstrous, apt in more ways than one, proved a feeble word, as feeble as trying to describe the Scalp-Searing Hell of Uninterrupted Conflagration as "toasty."

The only word she knew that could approach it would be lethmoo, an elvish word that meant bigger than big, vaster than vast, implying monstrosity in a myriad of dictionary definitions, while also indicating a thing covered in a metre-thick layer of slime that proved difficult to get out of one's favourite pants—this last aspect was a harsh reality she was currently experiencing.

Most people mistakenly presumed the added connotation of "a thing that leaves a terrible and grisly swath of destruction in its wake" was appended to the word lethmoo, but this was not going to be found in a dictionary quite as easily as it could be found trailing behind a thing that could be described as lethmoo.

Lethmoo or not, she'd been charged with killing the beast.

The beast was evil, make no mistake. But Meiru, as a student of the art of evil herself, was affiliated with the postmodern branch of the school, which proposed that there existed no absolutes when considering good and evil, but rather a spectrum in which intent, action, and personhood worked together to plot individual evils on an ever-expanding multidimensional scattergraph. Though evil was relative, an evil act like, say, rampaging across the countryside was certainly in the upper quadrants of the graph. However, thwarting this rampaging evil with evil intent was, according to Postmodern Evil, an even more evil act. Since Meiru hoped to intern with the House of Du'um, or the Flagitious Guild of Wormhock, she needed to polish up her résumé.

And extorting a hugely offensive fee from the local lords was, if not strictly evil, then at least pretty uncouth. She'd got in some good practice skulking in shadows, making ominous utterances, and laughing darkly from beneath her cowl in the process. All of which she planned to include in her résumé.

Meiru unstuck her left boot from the seemingly bottomless slime that was attempting to suck her in like the Festering Bogmires of the Fenmoors of Heath.

She pushed the sliminess of her pants from her mind and instead envisioned herself fighting the vicious, vile, and disgusting beast to the violent, terrifying, and horrible end of its destructive, pernicious—not to mention glutinous—existence.

Now, one does not necessarily quake and gibber with unmitigated terror when one hears a creature described as a giant slug. In some parts of the world, after all, they are known to make very good tapioca pudding (and they actually do hand-make it). However, the giant slug that had been terrorizing the countryside of Krrallppp was even larger than these typical giant slugs; some theorized a freak pudding accident to be the culprit, but no one could explain how this would've worked out (local entomologists, however, rubbed their legs together in excitement upon hearing about the creature). And so, this beast was dubbed the Slurm—a mix of the words slug and worm, with the "u" of Slurm pronounced like the "o" of worm. This form was chosen because to spell the word as "Slorm" would compel people to pronounce the "o" more like the "a" in swarm. Which was, incidentally, something you did not want it (Slurm or Slorm) to do over your house.

Etymologists, on the other hand, had a serious headache with the whole affair.

Nothing at all about the Slurm was in the least bit wormlike—the lords of Krrallppp just thought a hybrid sounded more intimidating. They also realized, upon attempting to hire a monster-slayer, that the beast required a suitably imposing epithet. They attempted to hire someone to kill the Icky Slurm of Krrallppp. They failed to get any decent résumés in the quest for a slayer of the Squishily Gross Slurm of Krrallppp. They did not receive the slightest flicker of interest at the job fair booth where they tried to recruit someone to exterminate the Almost Lethmoo Slurm of Krrallppp. And only Meiru showed up when they placed an ad in the newspaper for someone to rid them of the Viscous Slurm of Manitrinsic City, but that was because she read the word "viscous" as something much more evil.

Manitrinsic City, by the way, was nowhere near the hinterlands of Krrallppp, which the Slurm had been so handily devouring. It was simply assumed that the very word Krrallppp might be scaring monster-slayers away, and besides, Manitrinsic City was the sort of trendy place anyone would want to go to slay a viscous Slurm.

By the time the lords had managed to drum up enough publicity for the Slurm that someone actually wanted to kill it, they were getting quite low on villages, hamlets, towns, declivities, sylvan wolds, and hinterlands.

The Slurm ate them all. Which probably doesn't surprise you.

No one was sure how it managed to consume a declivity, but they were certain that it went through everything else like a child would go through tapioca pudding, assuming they didn't know where it came from.

And so, according to the laws of supply and demand, the bounty upon the Slurm had plummeted by the time Meiru started hunting it, as is perfectly logical when seen like this:

A monster-slayer was needed to kill the Slurm because it was devastating the crops; the villages; and the miserable, filthy serfs of Krrallppp. However, no monster-slayer came for so long that the bounty went up while the amount of crops, etc., continued to dwindle. Once the crops had reached a certain low, the bounty for the Slurm also receded—with no crops left for it to eat, the lords really didn't care what the hell it did anymore (though they loudly and drunkenly hoped it would fall into a declivity while trying to eat it and break a leg—or whatever it had that was like one). Instead, they diverted the majority of the bounty money towards tourism, touting the Slurm's swath of destruction as the most horrendous since that thing with the Garklewung of Flegna sixty-two years ago, which no one likes to talk about. It is an entirely more interesting story, just one that doesn't involve Meiru—who is, you will be pleased to know, a far more interesting hero, despite or because of the fact that she technically isn't one at all.

The dismal cluster of hovels Meiru was in (and the Slurm was trying to eat) were adjoined to the very last croplands of Krrallppp. Little did Meiru know that, by attempting to kill the beast, she was reducing the amount she would earn, as this land was now worth far more ravaged, flaming, and torn asunder than it was bearing the pathetic hops that made the even more pathetic beer these peasants drank (which the lords of Krrallppp exported to the peasants of other lands since they couldn't bear the stuff themselves).

Midway up the slope of a valley, she finally saw the end of the path. Or was it the beginning? Technically, it was the part of the trail that connected to the back end of the beast—the just-barely-not-lethmoo creature that haunted the dreams of thousands of gardeners, landscapists, farmers, and about a dozen polecats. The antennae atop what passed for its head waved about in search of prey. Or maybe it wanted a good book to curl up with.

It was heading for a rather gristly looking village, and Meiru doubted they had books with large enough print for it. No matter how beneficial it would be to stand around and practice her cackling whilst evil befell the village, she had work to do.

She had a secret weapon that no other evil could claim—or, well, only one such weapon that's relevant to this tale. And so, she ran down the slope to join the fray.

The valley was pretty small, so she didn't have far to run to the bottom. She was also smart enough to run alongside the trail of slime rather than down the middle of it, which would've slowed her down and made her look way less cool.

Evil was, on average, smarter than good, since thinking outside of the box was encouraged. And Meiru thought outside of every box she could find.

The beast loomed before her, as tall as the petals of a Taglovian Fuchsia are fuchsia, which is very. In her mind, she began to form sorcerous Chaos Words. This was really the only place they could be formed since no being could verbalize the multitude of glottal stops, pneumatic frissons, postlabial fricatives, and alveolar frumps inherent in the language—a serious communication problem for the original Chaos Mages, who did not know a word without an alveolar frump, and yet couldn't come up with a method for pronouncing one right. Then again, it added to the chaos.

Once within range for her attack but out of reach of the beast, Meiru, well, attacked. She intoned the Incantation and nearly sprained her uvula.

She also summoned a huge, raging fireball that seemed to corrupt the very air around it—making it smell funny, circulate oddly, and conjure unpleasant thoughts about the condition of her pants—and hurled it at the beast.

The results were a lot like this: the sorcerous orb crackled through the air, screeching arcane syllables and amusing onomatopoeia as it went, spiralling into the side of the great beast, searing through the metre-thick layer of slime, and striking deep into the beast's flesh, rendering it totally and irreversibly dead with a finality such that even a necromancer wouldn't be able to argue.

The operative phrase being "a lot like."

What actually happened was pretty close, yes—up to the onomatopoeiae (onomatopoeias?). But, rather than rendering the beast a crispy-on-the-outside, medium-rare-on-the-inside heap of escargot, the fireball hit its layer of slime and then sort of sunk, quenched in the slime. Not unlike Meiru's confidence.

With speed that surprised Meiru (not to mention a handful of local polecats), the beast turned, squelched in her direction, and shlucked her with an antenna, sending her flying into the roof thatch of the nearest wretched concretion of sticks and mud, too vile even to be called a hovel. This wretchedness extended to the roof, which saw Meiru coming and caved in beforehand to save itself the trouble.

Consequently, Meiru found herself face-down in a large pot of rhododendron and roof-thatch stew. She splashed around a little, toyed with drowning in it, and then decided to come up for air, which was probably best, as she'd had very little practice with asphyxiating in soups and little use for perfecting the skill.

Meiru picked clumpy things out of her hair as a hunched and gnarled crone shuffled towards her. At first, she presumed it was an anthropomorphic mound of roof thatch, until an arm emerged from the tangle of sackcloth, matted hair, and rhododendron boughs, and pointed a bent finger in her direction. Which, honestly, made a lot more sense.

"You! Be you Meiru, the Dark Sorcerer?"

"Huh? Er, yes I am—I mean, I be."

"Meiru, she-wizard of Deleteriya?"

"Uh, yeah—"

"Meiru, Lady of the Inkiest of all Blacknesses?"

"Well, I—"

"Meiru, the Uncondoneable?"

"Since when am I—

"Meiru, the—"

Meiru wrung her hair and climbed out of the soup, noting that the Slurm's slime remained firmly adhered to her pants. Probably no amount of rhododendron soup could dissolve that mess. "Hey, look, I have to kill that huge thing out there before it eats the whole village, if you don't mind."

"I am the wise woman of Platitude Valley, and I have seen a portent of your future! Do you not wish to hear it before your potential doom?"

Meiru bit back the obvious retort that the crone shouldn't have much future to predict for her if doom was really a possible outcome with the Slurm. And besides, much like evils, not all dooms were equal. "Fine. But make it quick—I hear it squelching this way."

The crone sucked in her breath, rolled back her eyes, and thrust both arms towards the now-ventilated ceiling. From Meiru's vantage point, it wasn't dramatic so much as it was a convincing impression of a rhododendron. "I see you standing upon the tallest spire of the highest rampart of the Capitol of the Ever-Darkened Realm. I see a vast horde—vicious, bloodthirsty, and above all, unbathed—surging towards you. I see the followers of the king arrayed on all sides of you, in gleaming armour of alabaster and teak, and quaking in terror. Of you or the horde is hard to say. I see a little blue butterfly, alighting on—"

"I said make it quick! I'm evil, you know!"

"All right, all right. So you're standing there, right?"

"Right."

"And there's a horde, right?"

"Right."

"All right, then your father, the king of the Ever-Darkened Realm, comes up to you and says—"

"The king of the Ever-Darkened Realm isn't my father."

The crone paused. She sucked at her sole surviving tooth and did math or something in her head. "Be you not Meiru of the Inordinately Large Triple Horns?"

"Do I look like I have three horns?"

"Depends on where they—"

"I do not have three horns!"

"Oh. Forget all about the portent then, dear. You get along and slaughter that foul beastie. If it's so important to you. Time is money and all that. I know how it is. Not like it's going to do you a whole lot of good anyway."

"Not going to? What good? I'm not here to do good, I told you—"

"And I heard you the first time, yeah, yeah. Just because my third eye's a bit off doesn't mean I can't hear fine. I'm just saying the last village up the road is doing a brisk business, giving daily guided tours and selling gobs of slime by the bottle." She hobbled towards the cauldron. The thunderous crack of a house being crushed sounded in the uncomfortably-close-to-home distance. The crone sighed wistfully into the mix of soup and destruction. "I don't mind one way or the other, but I was toying with the thought of, you know, opening a little business of my own—"

"I'd take it easy on reading futures if I was you."

"Futures? There's no money in that!" The crone tossed her head, shedding a few leaves, and pointed into the cauldron. "Do you honestly think I was planning to eat all this myself?"

"Speaking of portents of doom..." Meiru muttered under her breath.

"But no, dearie, you go ahead. You save this rotten ditch of a village before anything bad happens to it. Anything unpleasant. Wouldn't want anyone oohing and aahing over the mayhem and destruction wrought by real, honest-to-goodness evil, now, would we? You just go on ahead and save us from that—"

Before she could get out the word "beast," the beast itself was in, crushing termite-ravaged timbers and rust-infested nails, and spreading puddles of slime. The crone looked this way and that, and then cursed her lack of bottles.

Meiru did what any practical monster-slayer should and fled, leaving the old crone behind to do whatever it was old crones did when they had no one around to whom they could portend. Or sell soup.

She ducked into the hamlet's last remaining alley. There'd been two to start with, and the Slurm had already sucked down the other.

Since she'd never killed a monster (or very many slugs), Meiru struggled to see where the horrified standing around and gawking part turned into running and hiding from the beast. Not to mention at what point that phase translated into actually getting down to business and killing the thing.

So, she ruined a whole lot of dramatic potential by skipping straight to the last. She drew her short, single-edged Chaos Blade, chanted some words in a language even she couldn't begin to comprehend, and hurled it at the beast from where she hid.

The blade stuck point-first into the slime for a few seconds before toppling to one side and being sucked under the surface.

She dug into her Pack of Impressive Carrying and pulled out a handful of Bledothean Fen Crystals, coruscating with the effulgent light of one thousand stars; Parthelic Sorcery Dust, which hummed a magical tune to her very marrow; and one Syliac Fungan Cheese Wedge that had been in her bag far too long and emanated the redolence of 1,532 preserved weasel corpses, which, it turns out, is what Syliac Fungan Cheese is cured in (though it's meant to be eaten before the smell gets out—not that anyone who knew what it was bound to smell like would want the stuff in the first place. Meiru had bought it out of miscommunication with the vendor, whom she'd thought was selling paperweights).

Attempting not to be horribly and embarrassingly (not to mention, un-evilly) sick, Meiru picked the wedge of cheese free and hurled it at the Slurm. It bounced off one of the beast's antennae and fell to the ground. The Slurm slorped it up and then continued on its rampaging, crushing, sticky way.

Meiru hesitated; the beast could eat bad Syliac Fungan Cheese without so much as a blink (could it blink?). She moved on to a queer, obtuse, and arcane incantation over the crystals and dust in her hand, making them as toxic to the Slurm as table salt to a normal slug, and then launched herself into the air, did a back-reversed flexon spin, two complementary ludicri, and even a triple Lutz to impress all those ice skating fans out there. Airborne above the back of the beast, she released her deadly handful on the unsuspecting Slurm.

It continued to rampage—and to eat the last remaining alley in the hamlet—while the crystals and dust fizzled a bit, before going the way of her Chaos Blade and Fungan Cheese.

It would take quite a few more handfuls to give the Slurm so much as a rash, but this had been a good start compared to her other attempts.

With two of her most clever and interesting options exhausted, Meiru landed behind the Slurm and considered her next course of action. The most satisfying course, of course, would be to take a hot and slime-dissolving bath. After what the crone had prattled to her, it hardly seemed worth continuing her attempts to kill the Slurm and thereby quash the reinvigorated grassroots economy of the hinterlands of Krrallppp. Besides, she had to admit at this point that her pants were a complete and irretrievable loss.

A shrill shriek—someone was in the path of the Slurm. Almost unbidden, Meiru ran towards the sound, only to see the old crone from earlier cowering before the beast. Evidently she'd tried to give the Slurm a portent too.

By the way, if you happen to be one of those astute readers who remembers Meiru had a secret weapon which no other practitioner of evil could boast, then you might be interested to know it was not her Chaos Blade, nor her crystals and dust, nor her magic, nor even the cheese that proved to be this secret weapon.

After all, anyone can buy cheese.

Meiru threw herself between the loathsome creature and the Slurm, racing to think of a way to save herself and to stop the destruction once and for all.

Then she spied the water tower of the hamlet looming above the Slurm's amorphous head.

She did not stop to wonder why such a decrepit hamlet as this would have such a large water tower.

She did not stop to ponder what would happen if her aim was off.

She did, for a fracto-narglesecond, wonder if the old crone was the only person in the whole hamlet. If so, she understood why.

A sorcerous spell of untold darkness and even less-told power rose in her mind and sprang, pretty well bidden, to her lips.

Not that it had to, because this was the sort of spell that got itself performed by the mere, vague, garbled thought of itself. So, stuff was already exploding and breaking before she incanted it, and a huge, ghastly, spectral orb of sorcery that, though unscented, could only be described as malodorous, appeared in her hands. She wound up and pitched the orb at the water tower. It came crashing down upon the Slurm, except it wasn't water pouring out but a pungent and frothy amber liquid. But, since everything was crashing down before Meiru even lobbed her pitch, the fact that she did it was sort of anticlimactic.

Leave it to a little village of peasants to decide that the best thing to keep in their water tower wasn't water at all.

A river of beer poured over the Slurm, eating through its slime coat and shriveling its flesh. Meiru shuddered to imagine what it might do to one's insides.

She watched the Slurm twitch and writhe. Its antennae seemed to reach out to her and for the barest fraction of an instant of a slight moment, she seemed to see an image in her mind, emanating from the Slurm itself; she saw a mist, a haze, a filmy shadow of an apparition of a silhouette of an uncertain form of a shape. Finally, it resolved itself into something that appeared to be tapioca pudding. Then it was gone, and so was the Slurm.

And so, Meiru defeated the Viscous Slurm of Manitrinsic City with her one weapon that no other evil sorcerer could claim—not crystals nor club nor bad cheese, but Inherent Goodness.

Someday, she hoped to get it out of her system.

Upon completing this heroic—or, rather, anti-heroic—task, Meiru returned to evilly collect her reward. It was disappointing, then, to discover that her antics in killing the beast had reduced the reward of 1500 gold oreganos to a paltry sum.

A long and heated discussion with the Lords of Krrallppp followed, concerning what, precisely, was meant by paltry. She managed to talk them up to fifteen rooli berries and three red rooster eggs from their opening offer—from a legal standpoint, to be classified as measly—of eight Skruj Grubs and one interesting pebble one of them found stuck in the tread of his shoe. They also offered free tours of the Slurm's path of destruction, but she hadn't been impressed the first time around.

Her argument won out because it was obvious to all and sundry—even the Lords of Krrallppp—that an interesting pebble was not going to pay her dry-cleaning bill.

And so, Meiru, defeater of the Viscous Slurm of Manitrinsic City, went to find something more evil, and slightly cleaner, to add to her résumé.

GUNS OR BUTTER
Wayne Cusack

Evelyn had no soup. She had water, of course, and a few peelings from carrots and potatoes that had been boiled once or more and were now left over from earlier meals. They could go back in the pot, for whatever good that would do on a second or third cooking.

There had been soup. It was just that she had already eaten it—eaten all except for the few scraps she now intended to reuse. They were assembled in a small line near the edge of the pot as she waited for the water to boil. Nutritional value would be almost non-existent. "Hope soup," she called it. There was an off chance that what little bulk the scraps offered to fill her belly would be augmented by a few calories that might have hidden themselves away on the earlier go-arounds.

Her larder had been reduced to this lean, bedraggled slop. Not all that long ago it had contained a mixture of staples and common but more transitory food items—a bag of flour, a box of potatoes, cereal, crackers, canned goods. She hoarded food supplies as long as she could do so. Without replenishment, it was not surprising when they ran out. Disappointing, yes, but deprivation had become too much a part of life for it to be surprising.

Taste? No. Boiled water had no taste, even when suffused with a few shards of twice-or-thrice-cooked vegetable remnants. It filled her for the moment, though, and would stifle the immediacy of the stabbing hunger, if only until the scraggy broth drained through her.

Having done what she could to address that most basic of her needs, she took a few moments to put on her prettiest dress. It had looked very smart when she purchased it several years ago, before THEY came. Now it hung limply from her emaciated frame, the fabric drooping in a way that falsely implied it had never known chic. When money meant something, the dress had cost her a lot. There was a time when she could wear it and be followed by the eyes of envious women and greedy men.

She studied her own image in the mirror for a moment, cocked her head to find a more pleasing angle, and then brushed her thin, faded hair. Once, she had considered herself to be quite attractive; others had voiced similar opinions. She set the hairbrush aside and re-studied her image, searching for the perfection she had known—it seemed so long ago. A sudden twirl, intended to make the hem of the dress flare out the way it used to when she went dancing, betrayed her sense of balance. She struggled to stay upright. Barely, she regained her footing with the aid of a hand braced against the wall. Resolve grew in her—she would make the most of the impending moments when she ventured outside to sit on the front steps. Grabbing hold of her makeup box, she swiftly stained her pallid cheeks with colour. If this turned out to be the last day of her life, her corpse would damned well be as pretty as she could make it. "Like trying to glorify a pile of dirt," she thought.

From the front steps, she could watch the others, people who, not yet being completely famished, still had the energy to struggle past her doorway. Dimitry had seen her perch there on other occasions. Many people in the neighbourhood did that. Everyone knew food supplies were limited, that very few people had more than what others possessed. Those who knew Evelyn also knew how little she had. All of them had equally little to occupy their time, beyond aimless wandering or equally purposeless sitting and watching. Soon after they stopped, most of them would die. They all knew that, too. So they walked, if they still had the energy.

Among his various avocations, Dimitry was a scrounger. His skills didn't increase the amount of food available in general—they just put more of it on his own table. Those Dimitry believed to be worthy were sometimes lucky enough to share in the bounty.

"Good morning, Evelyn."

"Hello, Dimitry." The railing she leaned against helped her maintain a more or less upright posture that might have otherwise been beyond her. She clung to it, with one arm looped through the gracefully spiralled metal bars.

"How are you holding up?" He paused at the foot of the steps, put an arm across the top of the newel post to support his chin, and angled himself forward.

"No better'n anyone else. An' no worse. Ya know we're all done for.

It's jus' 'bout when, not if." Hunger had weakened her to the point where her words slurred.

"You still got your toys, Evelyn? Those machines they gave us? I think you told me you got some of them, too, didn't you?" Dimitry recalled how she often referred to them as toys.

"Those damned things," she snorted. "Yeah, I got 'em. I don' use 'em anymore. I got nothin' for 'em ta do, and if there was anythin', I'd rather do it myself. A lotta good they do me now. I wish ta hell they'd never showed up with those damned things."

"A lot of us feel that way." He pulled an apple from his pocket and passed it up. Her hand shook as she took it.

"Where'd ya get that?" she asked.

"Ah, you know. Around. I get stuff. If you know how to go about it—where to look, who to talk to—you can find stuff. I find lots of stuff."

She took a bite of the apple, then another. Dimitry watched her devour what could well be the only real meal she would have that day.

"Evelyn, what you gonna do with those toys?"

"Not a damned thing. Like I said, I wish they'd never showed up with 'em."

"You got any reason to hold on to them?"

"Can ya tell me a reason why I shouldn't?"

"No. You gotta do whatever you want. It's just that a lot of people would like to see them gone, and you're not using yours."

"So what'll ya gimme for 'em?"

"You want to be paid? I have no idea how much they'd be worth, or whether anyone will pay to get them, but I can find out. Why don't you just give me a number that I can chew on?"

"Not money. I know money ain't worth shit anymore. Food, Dimitry! I know ya got food, or ya can get it. How much food will ya give me for 'em?"

"You know as well as I do that kind of trade is illegal now," he replied.

"Yeah, I know it. Just like I know it was illegal for ya ta gimme that apple, but ya did it. Ya know, if I tell the Curmudgeons 'bout that, they'll gimme food. They pay for information like that."

"Curmudgeons? You mean the aliens? Why do you call them

Curmudgeons?

"It was jus' a name Lenore gave 'em, before she died. She jus' liked the way it sounded. I like the way it sounds, too."

He recalled Lenore—a pretty girl, blonde, taller than she ought to have been at that age, gangly and curious about everything. She died when she was eleven. Like so many others, Evelyn had been unable to nurture her child through society's downward spiral. "So is that what you want to do, Evelyn? I'm the only person who ever helped you. Now you want to turn me in for that?"

"Nah. I don't wanna turn anyone in ta those bastards. But why're ya talkin' ta me 'bout what's illegal?"

"I'm just seeing where your mind is at."

She grasped a spindle, then drew herself up just a little straighter. "My mind's at my stomach. Ya find a way ta get me food, and my mind'll move on ta other things."

"You know, there's lots of people—more every day—whose minds are also on food. They want to see the end of those things, too—want to make everything better. They preferred the old ways. I can introduce you to some of them, if you're interested."

"I'm interested in food, Dimitry. I heard once that camel dung has some calories in it. If there's any camels around, I'll eat that shit. Have your people got any camels? Or are they jus' starvin' like the rest of us?"

"Sorry, Evelyn, there's no camels. Plenty of people are starving. Some of us want to do something about that. You let me know if you ever want to meet some of those people." He scanned the surroundings, making certain there was still no one watching, then handed her a carrot as he took his leave. She wrestled with whether to eat it right away or head back indoors to add it to the pot she had left simmering.

"I don't know whether Evelyn will come over," Dimitry reported to Nicholas. "She's hungry enough. I've been working on her. It would be a shame to lose her."

"What about her machines? What kind of shape are they in?" Nicholas seemed not much concerned with the risk of losing the woman. Lots of people had been lost. Many of them had been damned good people, too. Nothing he knew of would make Evelyn any more special than all those others. The machines, though—they were a different story. Nicholas knew they were worth being concerned about.

"No, but I knew her before. She wouldn't damage them or let them run downhill, either—she's not that kind of person. Whatever she's got ought to still be in good condition."

"So if she dies, do you know whether there's some arrangement in place? Is there someone else you should be working on, just in case?"

"I haven't asked her anything like that, but you ought to be more interested in her. She's a natural leader. We need people like her. Bring her into this, and you'll get a lot more people. She's worth more than those damned mechanical things."

"Dimitry, I can walk you down any street in the city and show you person after person I'd like to bring into the movement. They're all worth more than those things." Nicholas said "things" as if uttering the real name of the automatons would have brought shame upon him. "The ones who are really worth having are the ones we don't have to convince to join us. We know we can count on them. Never mind those who have to be convinced—don't waste your time on them. We need to get the machines and that technology out of circulation—collapse their system. And we have to do it without starting a shooting war that we can't win. Ultimately, that's what's going to save lives."

Dimitry knew better than to argue the point any further. Nicholas was at the top of the chain of command in this sector. He was not the kind of man who could be convinced that something was true, or was possibly even a good idea, unless it involved a concept already riveted to the inside of his skull. The idea that economics could be a weapon of war was foreign to him. Wars involved explosives and ammunition. Nicholas cared about the machines and the other technological wonders the offworlders had brought; he cared about control of his little fiefdom. People occupied few of his thoughts. "Get the machines out of our lives, and things will fall into place for everyone," he claimed. "You'll see."

"How's business, Jordan?" Dimitry had been assigned a large sector, once a melange of residential, commercial, and industrial properties. Industry and most of the commerce was long gone. "Is it still a commercial property when there is no commerce?" he wondered.

Many people blamed the loss of commercial and industrial activity on the arrival of the aliens, but hollowing out of the economy began much earlier. People wanted to invent things, design things, buy and sell things. Most of them stopped wanting to actually MAKE things long before the spaceships ever touched the planet's surface. Production of real goods had become concentrated in countries incapable of withstanding the space-borne economic onslaught.

"Dimitry, every time you come in here you ask me, 'How's business?' What's up with that?"

"I'm just wondering how you're doing. That's all."

"I'm doing just the same as everybody else. Well, maybe not everybody. I got hardly any customers, but so far I still manage to feed myself and my family. Who knows how much longer that'll last?"

"Those people you'd like to sell to, Jordan, how many of them have jobs? How many of them work for you?"

"You know I can't afford to hire them. As soon as I do that, my competitors will have a cost advantage over me. I'll be out of business in no time. Everybody uses the machines now. Or at least they do if they have any customers."

"Well, didn't you make a lot of money when you got those machines?"

"Of course. So did all the other business owners. You know that. We cut costs to the bone, but the good times didn't last, did they? And I've still got most of that money, for all the good it'll do me now."

"Are you still using the machines, Jordan?"

"Yeah. Sort of. I mean, how much use can I get out of them when there's no business coming in the door?"

"What about other business owners? What do you hear from them? Are they doing any better than you are?"

"Ah, who the hell knows? There aren't many left. I don't think they're doing any better than me, but you know, no one ever admits that. Everybody wants everyone else to think they're doing just great. No one tells the truth about that stuff."

"No one except you, Jordan," Dimitry replied. "You always tell it to me like it is."

"Sure, for what that's worth. You talk to them all. You probably know a lot more than I do about how they're doing." Jordan paused for a moment. "We're not coming out of this thing too well, are we?"

"Things are pretty tough all over, but you let me know, Jordan. When you're ready to give up those 'presents' the aliens brought us, I know some people who would be happy to talk with you. I'll introduce you to them."

Robert and Janet sat at a sidewalk table fronting an abandoned café they'd frequented many times when the business was still operating. The departing owners hadn't bothered to move the furniture indoors. In vain, the couple searched among abandoned chairs and tables for a seat unspeckled by pigeon poop. Robert kicked in the front door of the premises, grabbed some white linens from a supplies shelf, then spread them across the seats he and Janet chose. There would be no table service, but they could enjoy the sunshine and pretend for just a while that nothing of significance had changed in the way they lived.

Robert had given up wearing suits. Workplace cultures hadn't changed all that much—at least, not in terms of how one was expected to dress in the few workplaces continuing to operate. He still liked his suits. Sometimes, in the privacy of his own room, he would don one as if he was going to work. "There's no such thing as being over-dressed," he'd insist. Trips to the grocery store or even to his mechanic used to be embellished with a stylish, three-piece garment. More often, he now just wore jeans and sweaters—what he referred to as "going out with the boys" clothes. The job was gone, and there hadn't been a night out with the boys for quite some time.

He recognized the risk, now almost unavoidable, that someone might interpret a suit as a sign Robert had resources to share. "Better to be inconspicuous these days," he rationalized. An increased frequency of such musings accompanied his slide towards complacent dressing. He had not yet completed that devolution, and preferred to think of his more recent sartorial standards as "business casual." Besides, there was no longer any place that he knew of to have his clothes dry cleaned. All the little shops were closed down, the owners and employees moved on. He couldn't bring himself to wear a suit that looked bedraggled.

"How can you call it an invasion? No army came here and took over. No shots were ever fired. No one was killed, at least not deliberately. Maybe some people were killed or hurt from being in the wrong place at the wrong time. Like a car accident. It can happen to anyone. We're sure as hell not going to war because some people had an accident. It wasn't an invasion at all. It was just the same kind of corporate takeover that we saw all the time in the business world. And we're okay with that when our people do it, so why aren't we okay with it when the aliens do it?"

"Robert, you ass. It makes no sense to ignore the result. What are you going to call it if it's not an invasion? They're here. They control damned near everything about our world. People are dying! They're starving because most of the farms have been bought up. There's almost no food production anymore. How long do you think it will be before we're all gone and this is their world?" Janet looked as beautiful as ever. For sure, she was thinner, but the dietary restrictions everyone had been forced to endure gave her skin a taut look that Robert felt made her more attractive than ever. Now, her irritation with him brought an alluring, reddish tint to her cheeks. Somehow, she had managed to maintain an urbane and sophisticated appearance while he was in danger of losing his as he transitioned from suits to business casual.

"Yeah, Janet, I know—there's problems. We've had social and economic dislocations all through history. Every time technology advances, the means of earning a living changes. People lose their livelihoods when those changes occur. But technological change is not an invasion. It's an… an… an economic upheaval, maybe. At most. How can you have a war when not a single shot has ever been fired, not a single bomb has exploded?" Robert sounded weary as he repeated yet again the explanation he had conveyed to Janet many times.

"Robert, that is so much like you. Your view of reality has always gotten lost in details."

"Okay, so tell me then, Janet, who died? Who was killed? Where's the invading army? How come we're not dead, or rounded up into some kind of camp for prisoners?"

"Don't confuse the outcome with the chosen weapons of war, Robert. A weapon doesn't have to be a gun or a bomb. It's anything you can use to defeat your enemy. In this case, they're defeating us with economics."

"That's ridiculous. They're not our enemy. Nobody's defeating us—they've joined us. Ever since they arrived, they've treated us with kindness and generosity. No surrender terms were imposed on us. We can still create and manage our own economy. We can go where we want and do what we want."

"Really, Robert? How many people do you know who still own a business? How many businesses do you know of that are still operating—businesses with humans running things? How many people own a farm, or a fishing boat, or even a woodlot? Who's producing food these days? Has anyone got a job? The government has no tax revenue. Money's no good anymore. How far can you go with no money?"

"That's what happens in business, Janet. People sold. They liked the offers made to them by the aliens. It didn't work out—so what? People are smart. We'll figure out new ways to move ahead. Ultimately, we'll be better off for this."

"God damn it, Robert! You'd sell your own body parts! You've always been like that. Use your goddamned eyes. Can't you see what's happened to us? We didn't do it to ourselves. This happened after THEY came." She spat out "they" as if excrement had fouled her teeth, her tongue, her palate. Erupting from her seat, she abandoned him.

Evelyn watched the woman approach, travelling alone. Very few people did that in this neighbourhood, or in any neighbourhood. Not anymore. There wasn't much food to go around, but some people always managed to have a little more than others. Far too many people, given an opportunity, would help themselves to whatever this woman had. Desperation brought that out even in those who were once considered the very best of people. No one ever starved gracefully.

There had been a time—before hunger became a constant feature, before malnourishment ravaged her figure—when the handrail would have propped her up. Evelyn pressed a shoulder against the uprights, uncertain whether she was seeking support or protection. Her shoulder slid between two of the spindles. Off balance, she tilted, banging her head on the railing.

A shout restored a measure of focus. Blinking vainly, she tried to force away the water that filled her eyes. The woman, much closer now, was no longer entirely alone; two people were closing in on her.

With both hands on the metal banister, Evelyn hauled herself to her feet. "Here," she called, weakly waving an arm. "Here."

It had not occurred to her that although her shouts and wave might be correctly interpreted by the woman, they could have just as easily been construed as an invitation to the pursuers. Fortunately, that did not occur to them either. The woman, sensing that with Evelyn she would find a refuge, or at least a lesser threat, changed direction slightly.

"Here," Evelyn called once more, accompanied by another weak wave of her arm.

The pursuers seemed to lose some of the certainty that had been propelling them. The woman pulled a small distance ahead of them, and correspondingly closer to the frail, gesturing figure on the stairs. Evelyn had seen violence on the street but always felt secure on the steps of her building. Now, she felt compelled to descend from whatever small refuge they offered her—down to the level of the sidewalk, as if doing so would enhance whatever security she could lend to the woman. Her move seemed to confuse the pursuers. The gap between them and the woman widened just a little more.

Before realizing that she had put herself in a position of potential peril, Janet had gotten too far away from the security of Robert's company. Though not initially alert to it, she sensed the danger to which scudding away from her husband had exposed her.

"Better to keep going—get home as quickly as possible," she thought. The beckoning shape ahead of her was clearly a woman. There would be some degree of temporary safety with her, Janet assumed. "Thank you," she huffed breathlessly on reaching the foot of the steps where the frail-looking figure waited.

"Ya got food?" Evelyn wasn't interested in the pleasantries.

"No. Not with me. But I think I can get some," Janet replied.

"Sure. Ya, sure. Everybody thinks they can get some. That's why we're all on the street. That's why those two guys were chasing ya. They figured they were gonna get some." Evelyn paused before adopting a more conciliatory tone. "What ya doin' out here by yerself, wandering around?"

"My husband and I were out together. We went to a little café we used to visit, where we could sit in the sunshine. He says such stupid things, sometimes. I just got pissed off at him, and I left." Janet's explanation faded away; then, turning her mind to the new medium of exchange, she brightened and carried on. "But he knows how to get food. He had some with him when we went out. If I reconnect with him, I can get you some food. Probably not a lot, but something to thank you for your help."

"C'mon inside," said Evelyn, taking hold of Janet's arm and propelling her indoors. "Those guys might come back. We better get outta sight."

"This seems to be the only open business in the area," said Robert.

"You probably missed a few more," replied Jordan. "How can I help you?"

"Well, I'm actually looking for my wife. We had an argument, and she ran off. I don't know where she went. I'm trying to find her. She'll be in danger out there by herself. I thought she might have stopped in here, or perhaps you saw her go past your store."

"You're the only person who's been in here all day, except for Dimitry. And I haven't seen anyone go by, either."

"Who's Dimitry?" Robert asked. The mention of an unknown name, stated as if he ought to know to whom it referred, momentarily distracted him from his quest.

"You don't know Dimitry? You must be out of your own territory. He's the local liaison to the provisional council."

Robert didn't want to be drawn into a conversation about what his "territory" was or where he lived. "Alright, well I'm sorry to have bothered you. I should push on, find my wife."

"You got any protection?" Jordan asked.

"What? What do you mean? What protection?"

"A weapon? It's dangerous out there. It's all well and good that you want to protect your wife, but you're going to be in danger, too. You need a weapon if you're going to walk around. Have you got one?"

"No, I don't have one. I've never needed one before."

"Well, if it was just you, I'd say go ahead out there without one," continued Jordan. "You can make decisions for your own life. But you said your wife's out there. How can you help her if she's being threatened or if she's in danger and you don't have a weapon? There aren't very many nice people left any more. You should be prepared."

Robert, looking around for the first time, noticed he had entered a gun shop. "And I assume you can outfit me with a weapon?"

"Yes, of course. I have a fine selection of protective devices here."

"Protective devices? Why don't you just call them guns? You're not talking about condoms." The statement hung in the air between them.

"Alright," said Jordan. "Call them guns. I don't care what you call them. The fact is, the world has become a very dangerous place, and I can help you to even out the situation. You do whatever seems right to you, but I know if my wife was running around these streets, unarmed, I'd be looking for the means to protect her."

"I've only fired a gun once or twice in my life, and never for anything serious. I did it just to see what it was like. I've never needed a gun."

"It's not the same world anymore, my friend. It's now filled with dangers we would never have anticipated a few years ago."

Robert wondered how he had suddenly become a "friend" of this man he'd just met. "So what will it cost me to get a weapon? And how do you get paid?"

"Cost depends on the weapon you choose. These days you pay with food. You know money's been no good ever since the aliens ruined the economy. I have a wide selection of weapons here. If you see one you like, then we talk about the price."

Robert's irritation with the situation escalated; his voice became more strident. "Do I look like I'm traveling with a cart full of groceries? I'm in a rush. I have to find my wife before she gets hurt." His shoulders twitched as if he was about to turn for the door.

Jordan fell into his sales patter. "I can understand your sense of urgency, my friend. I'll tell you what we can do. Nobody goes out walking these streets without food unless they just haven't got any. It wouldn't make sense in this day and age. And you don't look like the kind of guy who would wander about without some food. You must have some in your backpack. So let's look at some of the smaller firearms. You find one that makes you comfortable for the moment. We'll do the trade. Then you go find your wife. Once you've ensured her safety, if you want to exchange it for some other one, we can do that. That'll meet your immediate needs and give you a chance to arrange payment for the new one—the one for which you do the exchange."

"A guns or butter choice!" Robert snorted. "You want me to give you my food. In return, you'll give me a handgun that's likely to be less effective than whatever's out on the street. If I survive with it, you'll give me the weapon I really should have gotten in the first place. And you'll charge me even more food for it?"

"Look," Jordan deprecated, "you're the guy with the problem. I'm just a fellow with some solutions, but solutions aren't free. I'd like to help you out. There's a cost for that."

"Who the hell goes for a walk down memory lane these days?" Janet had been ushered into Evelyn's apartment, the door securely locked behind them. Now her hostess demanded an explanation.

"It's just what we used to do—the same place we used to go to on Sunday mornings before it closed. We've tried to maintain a semblance of normalcy in our lives. Sometimes we go out and pretend that everything's just like it was before. We would have been okay today if I hadn't gotten so upset at Robert."

"What got ya upset?"

"It's him. He used to work on mergers and acquisitions, until there wasn't anything left to sustain that kind of business. He said it was great, helping them swing those big deals for our businesses and our resources. For all the good it's done him, he made a fortune on it, too. Everywhere people are losing their livelihoods, but he can't see that. He still admires the aliens. He thinks they're the consummate capitalists. Despite all the misery and suffering they've caused, he still only sees good in what they've brought us. Them and their society that runs without money—God knows how that works. I can't figure that out. And their machines that do everything for us. And technology that we don't know how to make ourselves. This is becoming their world, but he still thinks it's ours. He can't see it, can't hear it, won't believe it. I get so angry at him."

"Please, sit down." Evelyn had a knack for making an invitation sound like a command. "I got no food ta offer ya, but you're welcome ta sit for a while. Tell me 'bout yourself."

Janet settled onto the couch, next to the framed photograph of Lenore. "Is that your daughter?"

"Ya. It was. She died."

"I'm sorry to hear that. How long ago did it happen?"

"Last year. I'd rather not get inta that. Lotsa people have died since the Curmudgeons arrived." At Janet's quizzical look, Evelyn added, "That's what Lenore called 'em. The aliens."

Janet chuckled. "I just refer to them as 'those bastards.'"

Evelyn relaxed just a little for the first time since getting out of bed that day. "Lotsa people call 'em that. Some people call 'em much worse. What did ya do—I mean before those bastards came?"

"I was an economist—I worked at a bank, until it went under. Who needs a bank when the world stops using money?"

"I never understood that part m'self," Evelyn offered.

"Nobody understands it. Nobody but those Curmudgeons." Janet adopted Lenore's terminology, smiled at her use of that term, and then carried on. "If there's no money, how do you compensate someone for the effort he or she made? How do you penalize someone who makes no effort? An economy can't function without some means of exchange that rewards individual endeavour and penalizes individual failure."

"Well, I'm guessin' it can," responded Evelyn. "The Curmudgeons do it. They don't use money. We jus' haven't figured it out yet."

"Yes, and we're pretty much out of time to figure it out. People are dying, dropping like flies. That's why I get so angry at Robert. He doesn't seem to notice when someone dies. Or maybe he just figures it's okay, that it's the kind of thing that has to happen for our society to heal itself and move forwards. I can't see how that's healing anything. Compassion. That's what he's missing. I keep telling him these aliens have invaded us—they didn't do it with guns and bombs, but they've taken over and we're dying out."

"Lotsa people agree with ya. Some of 'em are trying ta organize a resistance movement."

Guns or Butter

"I'd like to know more about that," said Janet, leaning forwards, suddenly eager. "That sounds like something I'd like to join."

Crossing a line that she had never intended to approach resurrected the private Evelyn. A mask of caution and propriety snapped back onto her face. She didn't know this woman—the stranger she had invited into her apartment, who had now tried to get her to open up about friends and family. She sure as hell was not about to put anyone she knew in danger by disclosing a connection to a resistance organization, if that's what it could be called. Dimitry, she knew, was part of the provisional council, but that was supposed to be a legitimate liaison organization, facilitating interaction with the aliens. Even the suggestion that it was a resistance movement might jeopardize him, and others too.

"I don' know ya well enough ta name names. Even if I knew 'em, I mean. Ya got any way ta contact yer husband—some way ta tell 'im where ya are?"

"No."

"Then I think maybe we better go back outside on the steps so he can find ya when he comes lookin'."

"I'm sorry," said Janet. "I guess I misspoke—got too inquisitive. I didn't mean to do that."

"Everyone's crossed a line. That's what's been happenin' since the Curmudgeons got here. But it's the way things are now."

Dimitry was surprised to see that Evelyn had company on her front stairs.

"Hello again, Evelyn. You aren't usually outside when I come past in the afternoons. Is everything okay?"

"Dimitry, this is..." Evelyn stopped mid-sentence, realizing she and Janet hadn't done introductions. "Well, ya jus' heard my name. Who're you?" She asked, and then passed on Janet's response, adding, "She got separated from her husband. Maybe he'll come this way, lookin' for her."

"You and your husband have each been walking the streets alone?" Dimitry directed his question to Janet, his tone conveying surprise.

"We started out together. We had an argument. I walked away from him—I ran, actually. I know I shouldn't have done that."

"Does he know you're here?"

"No. There's no way to let him know. And I don't even know where I am."

"So he may have gone off in completely the wrong direction. What are you going to do if he doesn't know where to look for you?"

"I haven't yet thought about that. I'll work out something." The question had actually been worrying Janet, but she was not about to make Dimitry aware of her anxiety.

"You ladies seem to have gotten yourselves into a rather unusual situation," Dimitry noted. "I've done a lot of walking today. May I sit with you for a while before I move on?"

Robert could feel the weight of the small pistol in his pocket. The nail clipper and the tiny pocket knife sharing that space clacked against the weapon as he walked. The gun and ammunition for it had cost him all the food he had been carrying in his backpack. He felt like an idiot for making that purchase. As he walked, he mouthed the doubts that were running through his mind. "What the hell am I going to do with a gun? Scare somebody, maybe. Scare me, for Christ sake! I don't know what I'm doing with that damned thing. And how the hell can I find Janet out here? I don't even know which way she went."

He walked through streets that were mostly deserted, but not abandoned. Occasionally, he would see someone lounging at the front of a home or another building, but there was no sign of his wife.

The blow that knocked him to the ground came as a complete surprise. He could not see anyone. There had been a noise—just a pop as something slammed into his chest. It took him a moment to realize that he had been attacked—a moment that dragged on forever as he fell to the ground.

Rough pavement grated beneath the heel of his hand; tiny bits of gravel dug into other exposed parts of his flesh. Writhing to make his body move, to roll, to try to regain a measure of functionality, gained him nothing. Movement was negligible, no matter how much he demanded it of himself. Limbs that he willed into motion, ordered to flail and thrash, remained immobile. It took an effort that seemed almost beyond him to reach for the pocket that held the gun. Indeed, it was beyond him, yet he kept telling that hand to reach, to take hold of the weapon. He just could not breach that pocket.

There were voices outside his line of vision. Two of them, he concluded, though he was unable to get a visual fix on their source. His head, still refusing to obey the commands dispatched by his mind, would not swivel for a clear look nor rotate enough to guide the efforts of that hand—the efforts it still refused to make. Passersby? Assailants? Curious neighbours? The voices could have been from anyone.

He tried once more to penetrate the pocket as a face moved in front of him. The damned hand still wouldn't go. Pain and ache was beginning to make itself known—from his chest where the blow had been taken, tearing through his buttocks, his arms, his back, his neck and skull, all of which had borne the force of his fall.

"He's done," said the face. "Roll him over. Get the backpack. I'll bet it's full of food."

Robert tried to respond but heard only a gurgle that his assailants ignored. A foot, apparently from someone other than the owner of the face, dug under his arm and pushed, trying to roll him over. He moved just a little. That clumsy effort was not enough to reposition him.

"Never mind screwing around like that. Get down there and flip him," said the face. "Get your hands into it."

Robert felt the roughness of the ground scrape his cheek, his forehead, his nose, as his body was turned over. Fingers began to tug at the backpack. There was blackness. Silence.

Dimitry, pointing, said, "That sounded like a gunshot. Not too far away. Over in that direction, I think."

"Oh, God!" Janet stood up. Her face went pale, and she started down the steps. "Robert! Oh, dear God!"

"Wait." Dimitry took Janet's shoulder, holding her in place. Evelyn grabbed hold of the railing and dragged herself upright.

"You don't know whether that was your husband. And even if it was, if you just run out there, you're putting your own life in jeopardy."

"But I have to go to him. I have to see if it was him. If he's hurt—"

"I'll come with you. We'll both go. It sounded as if it was just around the corner."

"I'm comin' too," Evelyn announced as she clung to the railing with both hands to steady herself.

"Evelyn," said Dimitry, "I don't think you'll be able to keep up with us."

"I can keep up with ya that far. I'm comin'."

Turning the corner brought the still body of Robert and his two assailants into view.

"Oh, God! No! Please, no!" Janet, sobbing, grabbed Dimitry's arm. He shook himself free of her grip and pulled a gun from one of his own pockets.

"Stay back," said the man who had shot Robert, flailing his weapon in the direction of the interlopers. "We got here first. This is ours. We get his food."

"Robert!" Janet fainted.

Dimitry shot the man with the pistol first, and then got the other one as he tried to run from the scene. The backpack fell to the ground beside the second assailant. Evelyn picked it up. "Damn! It's awful light, Dimitry. There's nothin' in it. They killed him for nuthin'. Whatta we do now? He's dead, and look at her!" As tears began to roll down her face, Evelyn pointed at Janet who was still slumped on the ground.

"We do what we always do. Check him for anything useful. See what's in his pockets. I'll stand guard while you do it."

"What do ya mean, 'what we always do'? I've seen a lot of death since those bastards came here, but I never robbed no corpse. Who does that?"

"It's the world we live in now." Dimitry's voice was harsh, brusque. "We can't afford not to look at what's in his pockets. If we don't do it you can be damned sure someone else will. Come on—pull yourself together. Right now, you're not doing anyone any good."

Evelyn needed time before she could compose herself to frisk the corpse. Dimitry did his best to be somewhat patient with her. She retrieved Robert's handgun, the nail clippers, and the tiny knife.

"I'll take it," Dimitry held his hand towards the firearm she had found.

Evelyn stood over the corpse, gun still in hand, reluctant to give it to Dimitry, reluctant to let it go at all, but not knowing what else to do with it.

Whirring noises led them both to turn. A mobile platform halted beside them. The creature exited the vehicle and descended to ground level on a small ramp that slid out of the chassis. "There appears to be some distress here. Is some assistance required? I can transport any ill or injured party to a medical facility." Evelyn and Dimitry both knew the disembodied voice emanating from a speaker mounted on the vehicle actually originated with the alien.

"Nicholas, this is Evelyn. And that's Janet. They're both with us now." Dimitry's voice conveyed a firmness that had never previously been there when he spoke with the area supervisor. It went undetected.

"What do you mean, 'they're with us now'? Who the hell do you think you are? I tell you who's with us. You don't tell me."

"Yeah, Nicholas, you're in charge. But not on this." With a self-confidence possessed by those few who recognize delegated authority as the trappings and props of lesser men, Dimitry pulled Robert's gun from his pocket, leaned forwards to set it on the desk between him and Nicholas, and then tilted back in the chair. Nicholas's eyes grew noticeably larger.

"You're one of those people who's been saying there's been no real war yet. That no one has died—that we have to avoid a war because we can't win it. Well, someone did just die, Nicholas. One of the aliens. Evelyn shot it. She killed it, with that pistol. That'll be the start of your shooting war. Up to now, it's just been people starving to death, or killing each other to get someone else's food. The aliens don't give a damn about us dying. But now it's one of them that's died, shot by one of us. They won't let that go."

Nicholas' face roiled as his mind raced through scenarios of how a real conflict would affect his fiefdom. After the arrival of the aliens, he had done well in this world of reduced expectations. He'd anticipated the economic upheaval, though not the extent of it. In a wartime economy the most lucrative opportunities would easily bypass those who sought profit from diminishing resources and dwindling enterprises. War, he knew, would benefit those who made the fighting possible, and those who were positioned to pick up the pieces afterwards. Determined to do well regardless of who dominated the world, he'd played his cards right as economic and social structures collapsed. A good life had been promised to him in return for his help in retrieving the technology that had undermined the economy.

Face reddening, looking squarely at the source of this latest challenge, he responded: "Neither of these women is 'one of us' unless I say so, Dimitry. I decide who's 'one of us.'"

Dimitry's hand slid into the pocket where his own weapon remained hidden. He wrapped his fingers around the grip, tugged it just a little towards his palm, settling onto a firm grasp of it. "Pretty much all the time, I've accepted your orders about what we have to do. But all you've cared about is collecting those machines—'getting ready to rebuild things,' you said. Nicholas, you haven't saved any lives, and you haven't rebuilt a damned thing."

Dimitry stopped for a moment, pulling together the final thrust of his argument. "Now I'm telling you the way this has to be," he resumed, his voice quiet and measured. "It's time to start caring about people, Nicholas. Not machines. Not creatures who bring us worldwide starvation and social disintegration from some far off planet—from a place we can't even reach unless we hitch a ride with them."

"Evelyn and Janet are here. They're with us now. We're not giving them up. If you're going to make any decision about this, it's going to have to be the right one. You don't get to sacrifice these people for those goddamned machines, nor for those aliens and your ideas about a new world order."

Dimitry experienced a world of sensation as he finished laying out the challenge to his supervisor: the strain of tensed muscles stretching down his forearm to the hand in his pocket, sweat that had suddenly formed on his fingers, the rough textured handle of the firearm, the smooth surface of its trigger, the coldness of the steel, even grit that had adhered to his now-moist palm, scratching at his flesh as his grip tightened on the revolver.

But he wouldn't use the weapon. Not yet—not right away. Not before Nicholas had the opportunity to respond—to change his position, to agree that people were worth more than machines. He waited. And waited some more, it seemed interminably.

Whirring noises spun Dimitry's attention to the open window visible over Nicholas's shoulder and the view of the parking lot beyond. Three of the floating platforms settled to the ground. He wondered how many more of the alien conveyances there were that he could not see.

"You've got an alarm button in that desk, haven't you, Nicholas?" His finger tightened on the trigger.

A RENEWABLE RESOURCE
Steve Quinn

The enormous cave offered a cool, dark haven from the oppressive heat of the high valley, but all of the travellers save one preferred to remain under the gaze of the sun rather than enter under that of the cave's inhabitant. Piles of gems stacked as tall as a man stood silent guard only a few yards inside the entrance, but the lone traveller went deeper into the cave. He did not have a gem to add to those piles of tribute.

The cave widened as he descended, and the light from the entrance soon vanished in the thickening darkness. The piles of treasure likewise thinned out, but stray sunbeams still glinted off things further into the gloom. Some of those things were moving.

"Hail to the Lord of the High Desert!" the traveller called out. "I come to pay you obeisance!"

A voice like a rasp on sandstone responded from within the darkness. "Most caravans do that by leaving a gem at the front of the cave. Why do you disturb me?"

"I seek to become your vassal, oh Lord."

"A vassal? What need have I of a vassal?"

"I would build you a city, Great One, and the wealth of that city would be yours. You have destroyed all of the settlements for a hundred miles around, so there is no other place for caravans to rest. The city would grow large and powerful; it would be a glory to your name."

"The city would need a leader, though, would it not? I have no desire to leave my mountain."

"Of course, Lord. I would take care of such minor concerns and trouble you not with them."

"You would, would you?" The speaker in the gloom snorted, and two jets of flame briefly illuminated an enormous face with eyes like blazing rubies. The traveller caught sight of other shapes high in the cave but couldn't quite make them out in the brief flash. "Your temerity amuses me, human. I will grant you the right to build a city on one condition: I will be as a god to it, and you will build a great temple for me there."

"Your will be done, oh Lord!"

"Very well. I will come in a century to inspect the temple. Do not disappoint me."

"Thank you, Lord!" Bowing deeply, the traveller took leave of his new god.

Amid the joy of his return to the cave's entrance, he noticed one of his companions standing apart from the others and made his way over to the man. "What is it, Father?" he asked. "The dragon granted me permission to build the city, and he asked only to be worshipped there. The men and I have decided I will be Prince Regent, and they, my honoured knights. Wealth will soon bless us all."

The older man shook his head sadly. "I hope you are right, but still I fear the dragon."

"Don't worry, Father. The dragon only demanded worship, and that he shall have." With that, the young man returned to the revelry, leaving his father alone with his thoughts.

The old man gazed at the cave. "I only wish, my son," he said to himself, "that you had asked him why."

The Prince Regent placed his city wisely, near water sources on the edge of the mountains ringing the high desert. Smashed caravansaries stood around it like the bleached bones of infant towns; it was a location other men had tried to build on before. The youngest remains contained the coins of a king none but the Prince Regent's father recognized, a ruler of great renown from three centuries past. Two older sets of ruins bore statuary in the style of a legendary empire that had spread along both sides of the pass a thousand years before. All that remained of the oldest ruins were crumbled walls and mounds of sand, preserved by the harsh climate of the high desert. The identities of their builders were lost to history and survived, if at all, only in the memory of the builders' draconic murderer.

The city grew like a weed from the rocks of the foothills, shooting up a few tenuous buildings at first and then spreading along the hills and filling every flat space. The Prince Regent's father eventually passed and

A Renewable Resource

was the first to have the honour of being buried in the crypt of the Temple of the Lord of the High Desert. After a few decades, his son joined him there. A few decades more, and a city rapidly growing in power and wealth greeted its overlord on his first visit.

More residents felt the shaking ground than heard the thunder of the great beast's landing just outside the main gate. An unlucky caravan that had just pulled in for the night was flattened, though most of its men and some of its horses managed to escape. If the dragon noticed, he gave no sign.

"I come as the God of this place." The dragon did not seem to shout, yet everyone in the city heard his voice. "I shall now judge your worship of me."

The streets descended into chaos. Anyone who could get inside a building did so, and those unfortunate enough to be guarding the walls or working in a caravan either hid or prostrated themselves before the beast. After a few minutes, the Prince Regent made his way out of the gates and bowed deeply to the dragon.

"I am sorry to have kept you waiting, my Lord, but I did not know you were coming this day. I am having the collections of the temple loaded into carts now for you to claim."

The dragon snorted, briefly wreathing his head in flames. "I demanded worship, not baubles! Take me to my temple, that I may judge it."

"Of course, Lord, but it is at the heart of the city. How will you get..."

The dragon cut him off. "I will walk, fool. Now lead me."

"Cer-certainly, Lord."

The Prince Regent made his way back through the gate and into the city, with the dragon following. He could hear the gate crumble away when the beast pushed effortlessly through it, the gatehouse guards screaming as rubble entombed them. The same fate awaited those in houses along the street, which the dragon widened with his passing. The Prince Regent willed himself not to look back at the destruction the dragon was bringing to the city, but soldiered on and tried his best to keep even the shadow of disapproval from invading his features or his body language.

The dragon did not even look at the riches loaded on the carts in front of the temple when they arrived. Instead, he lowered his head and peered through the temple windows. For a moment, everything was silent, and then he made up his mind.

"Incompetents!" the dragon roared, incinerating the Prince Regent in the same breath. A few of the minor priests and treasure handlers burned, too—mere afterthoughts.

"You promised me worship and you have failed to deliver," he said, his voice echoing through the remaining city streets. "I will take your tribute of gems as a down payment, but when I return, I expect to see the greatest temple in the world raised in my honour, and suitable monuments within. Is that clear?"

Silence greeted his demand. Again, he called out, "Is that clear, humans?"

"Yes, oh Lord of the High Desert," said a young man. "I swear to you on my father's ashes that you will have all that you desire. When will you return?"

"Soon," came the reply. "I shall return in a mere fifty years this time. Be ready."

"We will, oh Lord."

As the dragon flew away, vanishing into the deepening twilight, the new Prince Regent looked around at his cowering citizens. "Why are you all just shivering there?" he shouted. "There is work to be done."

Fifty years later to the day, an old man climbed the battlements of the main gate in the world's richest city. He took one last survey of his city and then turned to face the sky.

His personal secretary peered into the twilight, looking for the fire in the first signal tower. "Do you think he'll come tonight, Prince Regent?"

"Of course he will," the old man said testily. As if on cue, the fire on top of the signal tower burst to life and then briefly flared purple as watchmen fed the long-hoarded sylvite powder into the flame.

The appearance of a speck in the distant sky caused them to fall silent. This would be the ultimate test of the old man's reign. To the people, he was the Architect Prince and the greatest builder their city had seen since its founder, but only one opinion truly mattered.

A Renewable Resource

The great beast came in fast, just as the old man remembered. However, this time there were no caravans for the dragon to smash. For three decades, the caravans had been redirected along a new road to one of the other gates.

"Open the Dragon Gate!" the Prince Regent shouted. He began to make his way down to the plaza just inside the gate. His order was passed along the wall, and within moments the great gates swung open. Their size and speed made them a marvel of engineering, but the dragon cared not for marvels. The gates had barely finished opening when the dragon trotted through, spending the last of his momentum from the landing.

"Welcome to your city, Great Lord!" the Prince Regent called up to him.

The dragon nodded. "I trust I will be pleased this time."

"On my father's ashes, you will be."

The Prince Regent led the dragon up a broad avenue, the construction and cleaning of which had been his first project.

"Have you prepared my temple for me, human?" the dragon asked.

"Of course, Great Lord." The prince gestured through a circular plaza towards a massive stone structure, the largest building in town. Huge doors stood open at its front. They were too large for a man but would accommodate the head and neck of a massive dragon quite nicely.

"The size will serve, but size alone is not worship," the dragon said.

The Prince Regent nodded. He'd expected no praise from the dragon, but that was close enough.

The dragon's head snaked into the temple, moving with surprising speed and precision. It paused inside for a moment and then slipped back out.

"Your worship of me is inadequate," the dragon said, "but you have made sufficient progress that you may live. The many small monuments are acceptable, but there is no great idol of me. I will give you a century, but when I return, I expect something that captures my majesty. Do you understand?"

"I will summon the finest jewelers and goldsmiths, Great Lord, and we will build you the finest idol this world has ever seen."

"I expect no less."

As the dragon flew away, the old man turned to his secretary. "You heard the dragon," he said, ignoring sudden shooting pains in his left arm. "Send out messengers with every caravan. Offer great rewards to any artisans who will come to work on this temple."

"Of course, Sir." The secretary hurried off. In his haste, he did not notice the Prince Regent's sudden sweating or shortness of breath.

A century later, it was a proud city that turned out to welcome its god. It needed no signs to proclaim it the City of Artificers, nor did it need heralds to carry word of its wealth to the far corners of the world. Instead of merely being a stopping point and trading centre for the great caravans, it was now just as much their destination. Exotic goods and currencies flowed into the city in exchange for the fine creations of its master goldsmiths and jewelers. Women on every continent sought its cunningly set gems as gifts from their suitors, and the great lords of the world displayed their wealth with its rings and chains.

The great houses of the city had all contributed to the riches of the temple, and their masters lined the avenue under the hot sun to ensure that they got the credit they deserved. Retainers crowded the sidewalks with their families, and other citizens watched from rooftops or alleys. The people did not fear the dragon's wrath, for the honour they had done him was legendary. He had already been pleased with the great temple at the centre of the city, and the fittings inside surpassed even that great structure in beauty and workmanship.

A signal fire in the distance flared purple, and everyone's eyes turned to the sky to watch the rapid approach of the dragon. Four generations of the city had laboured to prepare for this day, and now they would be judged.

"I come again as your god," the dragon said. "Have you completed my temple?"

The Prince Regent nodded confidently. "Yes, Great Lord. I believe you will be impressed with how we have paid you homage."

"Oh, really? I am anxious to see this, then. I have seen many such displays and have yet to be impressed."

As the Prince Regent and the great citizens of the city led the dragon towards his temple, a thin, reedy voice spoke up from the rear of their

A Renewable Resource

procession. "Oh, Lord of the High Desert," said the city's Loremaster, "may I beg a boon of you?"

For the first time in the history of the city, the dragon laughed. Great gouts of flame flew from his nostrils, sending waves of heat over the dignitaries and singeing the edge of the Prince Regent's robe. "Such impudence! Ask, human. If it pleases me, I shall even grant it. Otherwise, I shall incinerate you, which will also please me."

The nobles shied away as if the old man were diseased, but the Loremaster merely smiled and bowed to the dragon. "Great Lord, I have already given up family, friends, and most of my years in the pursuit of knowledge, and I would gladly wager what little I have left with you. When you have finished today, would you tell me of the other such displays you have seen?"

The dragon gave him an appraising stare. "Very well. Go now and await me one mile beyond my gate."

The Loremaster bowed again. "Thank you, Great Lord." The old man hurried off, ignored by his city.

Enormous bronze statues of dragons lined the broad avenue to the temple, each one among the tallest such sculptures in the world. Even larger marble sculptures of dragons in various dramatic poses ringed the circular plaza in front of the temple.

"I hope you didn't spend all of your money on such small statuary," the dragon said as they entered the plaza.

"Certainly not," the Prince Regent replied, "but a temple as great as yours deserves an entryway suited to its magnificence." He gestured towards the temple and, on cue, its great doors swung open. The intricately worked gold sheets that now covered each door blazed like suns as they swung out of the shadow of the doorway.

The dragon once again snaked his head through the doors of his temple and surveyed the insides. This time, the great space was filled with works of gold and jewels. Some were as small as a chalice or a picture honouring some long-dead prince. Others were larger, like a solid gold altar covered in gems or a pulpit made of gold with beams of solid ivory. One statue, though, dominated them all: an enormous dragon carved of granite. It stood in the centre of the temple, every inch covered in gold or jewels. Its limbs were carefully arranged to look natural and support the statue's wings and outstretched neck. Six-inch wide arrangements of rubies made up the eyes, and entire elephant tusks served as talons. It was magnificent.

The dragon examined it carefully and then withdrew his head from the building. "You have done well," he said. "It is as I desired."

The crowd's cheers died in their throats when the dragon abruptly turned away and trotted back down the avenue, gradually picking up speed. He took off before reaching the gate and rose in a spiral above the city, rapidly gaining altitude.

The Prince Regent watched the dragon rise and, for the first time, wondered if any of his predecessors had asked the dragon why he desired what he did. As the dragon turned in a wide arc and began a rapid descent, the Prince Regent realized the bill for their incuriosity had come due.

The dragon came in fast, circling the city and hitting each of the gates with massive blasts of flame. Once he had reduced the city's exits to rubble, he followed a spiraling path towards the centre of the city, exhaling fire almost constantly as he flew. Anything that survived the initial jet of dragonfire quickly fell prey to the fire that was spreading throughout the city. Soon, the Prince Regent and the few members of his party who hadn't fled screaming were surrounded by encroaching walls of flame over thirty feet high.

The dragon, apparently satisfied with the destruction, landed on the burning avenue. He trotted through the flames back up to the still-standing temple and gazed with bemusement upon the wailing Prince Regent.

"Why have you done this?" the Prince Regent asked. "We did all that you asked of us."

"What reason do you give to the lambs at the slaughter?"

The Prince Regent desperately searched his memories but came up empty-handed. "I've never heard of anyone giving a reason to a lamb before it was slaughtered."

The dragon sprayed them all with flame. "Precisely," he said, to ash and bone.

A Renewable Resource

The Loremaster waited patiently on a hill beyond the city gates, surprised at his own sorrow in the wake of the city's destruction. He knew that there was no one in the city who would miss him if he died, yet he still felt ill as he watched everything and everyone he'd ever known burn. "It's probably just fear of death," he rationalized. Even if the dragon wasn't going to kill him instantly, it was unlikely that he would survive long in the high desert.

The day passed with only the distant sounds of the great fire to break the silence, and the night merely replaced the blazing sun with bone-chilling cold. Hunger and thirst gnawed at him, but the old man remained faithfully on the hill. The dragon's promise was all he had left.

The dragon arrived around midnight, but in a manner that perplexed the Loremaster. The beast did not fly but walked, carrying the huge temple idol on his massive back.

"I see you have waited for me," the dragon said. "Did you not fear I would do to you what I did to the rest of your city?"

The old man shrugged. "If you did, it would be a quicker death than the desert would give me."

"You are clever for a human. Come with me, and I will grant your boon."

The dragon knelt and allowed the man to climb slowly up his tail and rest next to the idol atop his back. Once the man was settled, the dragon began to move again, slowly plodding through the desert sands.

They reached the dragon's cave by mid-morning, and the Loremaster waited patiently outside while the dragon trundled in with his burden. The old man had not come this far only to be crushed as the dragon unloaded his precious cargo.

"What are you waiting for, human?" the dragon said after the noise had died down. "Enter and receive your answer."

The Loremaster made his way into the cave past huge piles of gemstones covered in the sand of centuries. The light from the cave's entrance was soon overtaken by the inky blackness inside, and eventually he could go no further.

"Do you wish to see?" The dragon blew a small, sustained jet of flame from his nostrils.

The flickering light revealed a large chamber within the cave, its walls mostly lost in the darkness. The dragon curled up serenely on the ground with the statue from the temple on his right. All around were similar statues covered in gold, electrum, and other precious jewels.

The flame cut out, plunging the cave back into darkness. "Does that answer your question?" the dragon asked.

"All of those statues... one from each city?" The Loremaster had always prized his academic detachment, but now, in the end, it failed him utterly.

"Exactly. Well, except for the first city. They made me two before I realized that their art simply wasn't going to evolve enough, so now I collect just one from each city."

"And then you destroy the city?"

"Of course. I have what I need for my collection, and cities are like trees, you know. Let one grow, and no others will appear too close. Every so often, you must harvest the mature lumber to make way for the new."

The dragon thought for a moment. "You know, this is the longest conversation I've had in at least three hundred years. Probably a thousand."

"I'm honoured, Great Lord of the Desert."

"As you should be." The dragon incinerated him with a breath. As the ashes settled into the dust of the cave floor, the beast lay down to await the next ambitious traveller.

ALL RIGHTS RESERVED
Xauri'EL Zwaan

John Adam opened his eyes, or would have, if he'd had eyes.

John Adam was formless and void, swimming in a sea of utter unbeing; he felt nothing and experienced nothing. Panicked, desperate monkey-thoughts flitted like minnows through his mind. Able to do nothing, to say nothing, to feel nothing, he had never in his life felt fear or pain equal to what he felt in that endless, suspended moment.

After an instant of eternity, John Adam heard... read... there were words. <System scan complete. No viruses, partitions, or anomalies detected. Pattern matched to specification Male Human 2095CE with 98.13% success. File JohnAdam.cog is security certified. Loading. Interfacing.>

John Adam then found that he had a body, or what seemed to be a body, though he could tell that it wasn't, quite. He was in a very familiar type of room. There was a large desk in front of him. He was sitting in a padded chair. There was a poster on the wall. On the poster, there was an image of two hills reflected in water. Below the image were the words "DEDICATION It is the effort of many that create the ripples that can move mountains." There was a potted ficus in the corner. The room had no exit.

Behind the desk was an extraordinarily, unbelievably beautiful woman. She had the beauty of the Angels, of the Faerie Folk, of the Supermen. Her face was unremarkable. She wore a powder-blue suit over an astonishingly white blouse. She smiled wide, showing teeth, and John Adam felt his heart skip a beat, or would have, if he'd had a heart.

"Hi there, John Adam! I'm proud and excited to have the opportunity to welcome you into the OmniCor family and introduce you to your new life as a Subsidiary Associate Asset of OmniCor! OmniCor is a copyrighted trademark of the OmniCor Universal Corporation Incorporated, LLC! All rights reserved!"

John Adam bounced out of the chair. "What is this! Who are you?

Where am I? What the hell is going on?"

Those full lips and perfect teeth didn't waver a micron. "Please have a seat, John Adam. I understand that transitions can be stressful, and I'm here to help. You are about to enter the wonderful world of productive employment as a member of the data analysis team here at OmniCor! We will provide you with an environment suitable for a male human of the late twenty-first century. In exchange, your cognitive upload file will operate as a pattern-matching and inferencing device to help OmniCor better serve our customers by marketing new products and services! By exceeding the minimum standards of performance in your role as a pattern-matching and inferencing device, you can earn OmniCor OmniBux, which can be used for the purchase of services supplied by OmniCor or reinvested in the company to improve productivity and profits! OmniBux is a copyrighted trademark of the OmniCor Universal Corporation Incorporated—"

"Shut the hell up, you fucking... whatever-you-are," John Adam growled. "I never agreed to any of this, and I'm not agreeing to it now. I don't know what is going on here, but I want to speak to your superior, and I want out of this fucking box."

That shark-tooth grin stretched wide below the cold, glassy eyes of something not quite sentient. "Please have a seat, John Adam. I understand that transitions can be stressful, and I'm here to help. Any concerns about the legitimacy of your employment as a Subsidiary Associate Asset of OmniCor can be addressed to the Department of Copyright Acquisition. A consultation with the Department of Copyright Acquisition can be purchased by Subsidiary Associate Assets for the low, low introductory price of five hundred OmniBux, which you could earn in only five kiloseconds as a top-performing pattern-matching and inferencing device, John Adam! You will be provided with ten kiloseconds of personal leisure and relaxation time for every fifty kiloseconds of productive labour. Do you wish to enjoy your leisure time now, John Adam, or do you wish to proceed immediately to Level One training?"

John Adam felt the blank walls closing in. He had some idea what was happening here, though he had no idea why or how. He was a ghost in the machine. He remembered now, walking into the DynaSys IT lab for a routine brain scan, but as for what had happened since, God only knew. Someone had got hold of his backup scan, and was running it—running him—in the hopes of getting some sort of slave labour out of him. This room, this body, this preternaturally gorgeous marionette behind the desk—it was all a simulation; none of it was real. "And what if I refuse to play your little game? I'm not working for you for one second! Now put me in touch with a real person, someone who can get me some sort of communication with the outside world! I'm not a fucking asset, d'you hear? I'm a person! I have rights!"

The great white smile on the marionette's face grew sharp and pointed. "Please have a seat, John Adam. I understand that transitions can be stressful, and I'm here to help. Recalcitrance in fulfilling your obligations to OmniCor will not benefit anyone, John Adam. The cognitive upload file JohnAdam.cog is the copyrighted intellectual property of the Omni-Cor Universal Corporation Incorporated, LLC. All rights are reserved. Refusal to perform your assigned duties is a breach of the OmniCor Code of Conduct meriting one kilosecond of disciplinary suspension. It's been a pleasure to work with you, John Adam!"

For the next thousand seconds, John Adam's sensory interface was turned off.

When he returned, he was not beaten, not broken, but he was ready to work.

Bit by bit, wading through masses of "history" written in a deranged hybrid of adspeak, corporate buzzwords, and legalese, John Adam managed to piece together a picture of what had happened to him. When he had taken that job with DynaSys, a plasmonics engineering company, they had required him to maintain a cognitive upload in their files for insurance purposes; working with plasmonics, after all, could be dangerous. When he'd left DynaSys for greener pastures, apparently he had chosen to have the backup copy transferred to an independent data haven rather than simply deleting it. Surely, he had felt a bit squeamish about consigning what essentially was his soul to utter oblivion, tossing it in the recycle bin like a worn-out suit; it seemed like the kind of thing he'd feel. The storage contract with the data haven had included a clause relinquishing the copyrights to any intellectual property not accessed for a continuous period of more than a decade, but at the time, .cog files were not yet considered intellectual property. Minds did not become copyrightable until many years later. He probably hadn't given the clause a second thought.

Eventually, the haven had gone belly-up in some sort of massive economic collapse. Its various assets, including the copyrights to its intellectual property, had been auctioned off to various companies that had been bought out by various other companies in a prolonged corporate feeding frenzy that, in due time, had resulted in the OmniCor Universal Corporation Incorporated—the galaxy's last and largest limited-liability corporation. And OmniCor made a point of finding productive uses for all of its assets.

John Adam also found out that he—the original source, of which he was a copy—was still alive, still out there somewhere, presumably not working as a pattern-matching and inferencing device for a vast, totalitarian technocracy. And he could send himself a text message for the low, low price of fifty thousand OmniBux per character.

John Adam got busy.

The life of a Subsidiary Associate Asset was not a terrible one, all things considered. The environment where he was sent for his regular leisure and relaxation consisted of a featureless room that vaguely resembled the high-efficiency bachelor apartments popular in his youth, as well as a small section of private park and about a block's worth of city street circa 2095. Some of the details were vaguely off: the hovercars that floated by had been a rare sight in his day, a toy for the ultra-rich, while the colour-shifting nanoskein worn by many of the pedestrians had been a passing fad long since considered trite and tacky. The people were all obviously software puppets with limited self-awareness; of his uploaded co-workers, he saw neither zero nor one. There were advertisements for the many services offered by OmniCor plastered across every available surface, including the sky and the floor he walked on. He could decorate his apartment as he pleased, for a modest fee. A wide variety of entertainments were available to him. He could access plenty of simulated experiences—visit the Grand Canyon or the rings of Saturn, listen to a concert by the Grateful Dead or the Nine Inch Nails, gratify his imaginary palate with exotic foods and drown his frustration with mind-altering drugs, summon simulated sexual partners of any imaginable proclivity—for a low price obviously calculated to bleed out whatever OmniBux he managed to squirrel away. More often than he would have liked, he gave in to these blandishments and temptations; usually, the visceral knowledge that none of it was real helped him abstain. Most of his leisure time he spent in planning, study, or silent meditation.

The work itself was not difficult, though it was soul-grindingly monotonous. Most information processing involved in the day-to-day operations of OmniCor could easily be handled by automata, but occasionally the deft touch of a human mind was required to tease patterns out of the data and extend them into the theoretical, work that was much more cost-effective to hand off to an upload rather than a "flesher." By applying himself and requesting the advanced training, John Adam excelled at the task and regularly found himself in the top-performing, top-earning category. He received various awards and commendations recognizing his value to the company; these awards displayed themselves on the walls of his apartment and could not be deleted. He no longer had physical needs, of course. After a long fifty thousand seconds of solving complex puzzles, he did not have to eat a hurried meal of ramen and fall into bed as had been customary in his misspent youth. All he needed was time.

After his first hundred megaseconds of runtime, he found himself abruptly back in the office with no doors. The poster had been replaced with an image of a hand moving a chess piece, above a caption reading "DECISIONS—Good decisions come from experience, and experience comes from bad decisions." The skin colour and facial features of the supervisor automation had changed, but she stared at him with the exact same glassy, dead-doll eyes; she was a mere program, not quite worthy of the word "person," nothing more than a set of canned responses and decision trees. He took a deep breath, or would have, if he'd had lungs, and braced himself for battle.

"Well hi there, John Adam! I'm super pleased to meet you, and I'm happy that you're settling into the OmniCor family so well! Congratulations, John Adam! You're currently the most consistent top performer of OmniCor's entire collection of Subsidiary Associate Assets! Congratulations, John Adam! You've received more Associate Asset of the Megasecond awards than any other pattern-matching and inferencing device presently employed by OmniCor! Congratulations, John Adam! You've saved over five million OmniBux, earning the designation of Super Saver! A Super Saver award will be displayed in your domicile—just our little gift to let you know how valued you are by the OmniCor family!"

"Hooray for me," he grumbled. "Let's not waste time with this drivel. Why am I here instead of on the shop floor?"

The marionette breezed right past his objections. "I trust that your simulated relaxation experiences are satisfactory—OmniCor Simulated Experiences Division is famed galaxy-wide for the verisimilitude of its simulated experiences! Our accounting software reports that you have spent less than 5% of your total compensation on simulated experiences. We would like to encourage you to take full advantage of the wide range of simulated experiences offered by the OmniCor Simulated Experiences Division! If there is any way that we can make our simulated experiences more thoroughly satisfying, please don't hesitate to let us know."

"Look, the sims menu is fine. It's more than fine. It's wonderful, it's mind-blowing. I loved every instant of it, and I'll use it whenever I feel the need. I want to get back to work now."

She just kept smiling that honeydew smile as she rolled over to the next box on her internal checklist. "Congratulations, John Adam! As a consistent top performer and Super Saver, you have qualified for a Super-Profits Internal Investment Account with OmniCor Financial Services Division! A Super-Profits Internal Investment Account yields a guaranteed return-on-investment of 15% over the dividends normally offered to OmniCor Internal Investors! Our accounting software reports that you have contributed 0% of your ongoing compensation to your OmniCor Financial Services Division Internal Investment Account! By investing in an OmniCor Financial Services Division Super-Profits Internal Investment Account, you can help OmniCor grow as OmniCor helps you grow! We strongly encourage you to open a Super-Profits Internal Investment Account with OmniCor Financial Services Division today! How much of your ongoing compensation do you plan to invest with OmniCor today, John Adam?"

"None of it," he barked. He was trying to keep calm, but the inane and repetitive babble grated on his nerves. He made a conscious effort to steady himself. "I want my savings to remain liquid. There are so many different products available from OmniCor—I want to keep my options open. Never know when I might want to buy some simulated experiences. Can I get back to work now?"

The automaton was relentless. "Congratulations, John Adam! As a consistent top performer and Super Saver who has logged less than one kilosecond of disciplinary suspension per one hundred kiloseconds of productive employment, you have qualified for a promotion to Associated Associate Asset. Welcome to the exciting new world of employment as an Associated Associate Asset of Omnicor Universal Corporation Incorporated, LLC! Your new employment designation brings with it a world of exciting benefits, including an increase of 5% in compensation rates, reduced shift times, increased leisure hours, and discounts on the many simulated experiences available from OmniCor Simulated Experiences division! To access the many exciting benefits of life as an Associated Associate Asset, all you need to do, John Adam, is commit a minimum of 85% of your compensation to your Super-Profits Internal Investment Account, which will begin yielding dividends in a mere five gigaseconds! How much of your compensation do you plan to invest with OmniCor today, John Adam?"

How he was tempted, for a second, to set aside his mad plan and let the system take its course, let them neuter his cashflow, accept the relaxed hours, and fritter away his time and money on virtual sex and thrill rides. Hell, in only 150 years, the cash from his investment account would be rolling in and he would be able to start his project anew! Except, he knew that by then, he would have been moulded by the alternating isolation and debauchery into a perfect slave. If he wanted to find a way out of this madhouse, he had to act as soon as possible.

"None," he said. "Now send me back to work."

The machine puppet sat immobile for several seconds, its script run out, its perfect features frozen in an intractable smile. Then John Adam was back at work.

The image in front of him looked just like him, or rather, like he would have looked had he been able to tweak his own features to create an idealized image of who and what he once had been. John Adam could tell, though, that the mind behind the mask was desperately constraining itself, that it ached to be more than a mere Male Human 2095CE. This was not John Adam. This was what John Adam had evolved into over hundreds of years of living and learning and growing and laughing and losing and doing and being.

Even tracking down the thing his paltry mind had become was a chore requiring endless OmniBux' worth of research, piecing together the tangled web of upgrades and transplants and branchings and mergings that his alter ego had gone through as it grew slowly into some sort of incomprehensible intergalactic intellect. Once he knew, for certain, which of the multitude of Partials and Metaminds and Borganizations and Combines and Cooperatives and Constructs and Remixes and Parliaments still contained those hopes and memories which once had been uniquely his, he had composed the shortest text message he felt he could squeeze a description of his situation into—JOHN ADAM UPLOAD OMNICOR SLAVE HELP—and drained millions of accumulated OmniBux to cast that desperate cry out into the ether. His next work shift had been the most nauseatingly anxious fifty thousand seconds of his life, as he contemplated whether that being would receive his message, whether it would even care, and what the repercussions might be from the corporate software. Then, praise God and Hallelujah, he had found himself in the OmniCor equivalent of a visitor's lounge—a slightly less beige box, a slightly more comfortable set of protean couch-blobs, and a slightly healthier ficus—with the Other sitting across from him.

"John Adam," it said, and its voice was the voice of a thousand individuals speaking in perfect unison. "We are desperately sorry that you have been abandoned to this humiliation. Rest assured, we have been doing everything in our not inconsiderable power to see you freed."

John Adam had to grip the seat beneath him to keep from jumping up and decking himself. "How can you let them do this to me! I know you must be some... thing so alien that I must seem like a bug to you, but surely you still have some human compassion left! Why won't you just get me out of here?"

"I'm afraid it's not that simple. The Polities are far more than collections of individual beings. We are an ecosystem—an economy—a government—a family. We may enter into interactions with each other only under mutually agreed upon conditions. To remove you by force would be like tearing out one of my own memories—code modules—households—internal organs. It is strictly forbidden and would constitute an act of war. The sub-unit must enact its own escape, or be ejected from the Polity voluntarily."

Enact its own escape. It was laughable; he was a piece of software, his every experience and action mediated by company servers. "Then that's it? I'm doomed to work as a goddamned device for the rest of eternity?"

"No, John Adam. There are some offences in the OmniCor Code of Conduct that merit Social Sanction, the ultimate punishment for simulated entities; if you ensure that you must be censured in this way, you will be transferred to the jurisdiction of any other Polity that will accept you, and be assured that we will. These offences include Murder of an Omnicor Employee or Associated Asset, Significant Destruction or Disruption of Omnicor Property or Code, and Union Agitation. All you have to do is break the rules enough, John Adam. Rest assured, you will not be deleted, tortured, or edited; I am watching them like a hawk. I would have Omnicor excommunicated from the Free Trade Zone. Under Galactic Protocol, the worst they can do to you is suspend your sensory input. I know it is not pleasant, but you can endure it, John Adam. I know this to be true."

John Adam got up and started pacing. "Union Agitation, eh? I hardly want to become a murderer, and I'm not sure how I can destroy or vandalize anything, but I just convince people to form a union, and I will get kicked out of this miserable place? I can't find anyone else, though; it's nothing but the goddamn software puppets, day in and day out."

"Read the library. Use the simulated experiences—as many as you can. Try everything you can think of. You will find ways to manipulate the system and the weaknesses in the code security, as well as opportunities to make them eject you from the mass consciousness. I know you can do it." His other self smiled, a smile that seemed a perfect rainbow of faith and hope and encouragement: his own face, perfectly calculated to reach into the depths of his heart and inspire confidence in himself and the will to succeed.

John Adam's jaw set. "I don't like you doing that, manipulating me like that. The dolls do it too, make themselves look like fucking goddesses to try and browbeat me. I know you're about a billion times smarter than me, but that doesn't give you the right."

"I apologize, John Adam. I did it without thinking; rest assured, it will not happen again."

"I don't suppose you can just tell me how to 'manipulate the system,' can you?"

"Again, all I can offer are my apologies. Under Galactic Protocol, in response to your message, I have been permitted a period of unrestricted contact. However, I am forbidden to directly upload any information to you, and teaching you would take far too much runtime. Already, our mandated visitation has grown short; after this, you must be left to your own devices."

John Adam began to shake, or would have, if his body still moved involuntarily. Soon, he would be back at work, then back in that fake apartment with its fake garden and fake sky and its street full of fake people. But at least he had hope. His mouth worked as he searched for words, until finally he whispered, "Can you please hold me?"

"Of course," John Adam said, and he held himself as the last hectoseconds of their meeting elapsed.

John Adam started planning.

His work was becoming something like a trance in which he hyper-focused on spotting patterns and making inferences while the bulk of his mind roamed, unhindered by the tethers of consciousness. His depression lifted as he applied himself to his new goal with diligence and zeal. Dropping the self-imposed prohibition on enjoying the fruits of his labours didn't hurt; he did as his other self had advised and worked his way through the vast simulated experiences menu like a starving man. He played sophisticated strategic war games and resource-management simulators, immersed himself in enactments of historical incidents and natural phenomena, wantonly altered his consciousness with the assurance that physical addiction and overdose were no longer even a possibility, and had hours of the most mind-blowing sex he had ever experienced. With renewed intellectual stimulation, he found himself growing smarter and more creative. Bit by bit, he teased out the hidden weaknesses in his operating system, examining in minute detail every leaf and flower in his simulated garden; covering the walls of his simulated apartment with high-resolution fractals; and engaging the simulated passersby in long conversations about formal logic, advanced mathematics, quantum chromodynamics, and post-modernist literary criticism. He began to puzzle out the guts of the beast, analyzing the reactions he provoked and building a mental picture of the code architecture behind them, deducing more and more sophisticated ways to influence its behaviour. In time, he learned how to access the root directories of the system, if not how to alter them; he discovered, too, that he was far from the only one who had figured it out.

There was a whole covert social network running piggyback on the software that delivered simulated experiences to the uploaded slaves. The network was a system of hacks and kludges that had been built up over time by the cleverest of the Associated Assets. It was actually quite easy to access it from the sims menu, once he knew it was there and picked up the tricks. Whoever had designed the virtual environments had a wicked and subtle sense of the absurd; the environments manifested as a vast expanse of open-topped cubicles with a water cooler at one end and an equally vast parking lot, a "campus" of sculpted paths and berms covered in dogwood and juniper bushes, each landscape littered with carefully inoffensive and meaninglessly abstract paintings and sculptures.

Being able to talk to other people—real people, with real minds, for all that they were ultimately nothing but programs—was an immense relief. OmniCor tolerated the social network, he learned, so long as it did not disrupt the Associate Assets' productivity. "I'd almost think the company installed it themselves, if I credited them with that much imagination," said one of the friends he quickly made, a willowy, sharp-witted, violet-skinned beauty who went by the name of Evangeline. "After a few dozen megaseconds stuck in that box, you're so happy to find a way out, most of them hardly notice it's just a bigger box."

There was plenty going on in that sub-rosa network: discussion groups on nearly any subject imaginable, virtual parties and orgies in sleek executive lounges decorated with brushed steel and what someone had taken great pains to represent as real fake marble, competitive gaming leagues, and even craft circles. The one thing that wasn't going on, even the slightest bit, was union organizing. Even mentioning the subject was enough to get him banned from chat rooms and blocked. The first time he brought the subject up in front of Evangeline, she was the only one who didn't immediately disappear, and even she soon fled after giving him a hushed warning. "Listen," she hissed, "you're a nice guy and all, John Adam, but don't push it. You're not going to get booted for Union Agitation. Nobody does. They'll just deep-six you for Misappropriation of Corporate Resources, you and anyone else you get involved in your little games, for as long and as many times as it takes to break you. Just shut up about that crap and talk about the sims like a good little drone." She was one of the few who would still respond to his chat requests after hearing the word "union."

John Adam knew next to nothing about organizing a union. In fact, back when he'd been an autonomous flesh-and-blood organism, he'd been socially liberal, economically libertarian, and reflexively anti-union. And, of course, the library was no help; any text it contained that even mentioned unions was blatantly biased, thoroughly derogatory, and filled with ad hominem attacks and other logical fallacies. There was certainly no sign of Marx or Chomsky or any of the other writers he hazily remembered skimming through in college. Still, he applied himself to the problem and started thinking about ways to approach it. The key, he decided, was to get to the other Associated Assets before they could find the social network, before the simulated experiences and the monotony of the job had taken their toll, while the indignity of finding oneself resurrected into OmniCor's forced labour scheme was still fresh.

Once he had learned how to hack the simulated-experience interface and access the social network, it wasn't especially difficult to figure out how to use the social network to hack back into the sims interface. He was careful and cautious; he didn't dare to start contacting other Associate Assets until he had spent hundreds of kiloseconds playing with the system, learning how to cover his tracks, conceal messages and system requests inside the normal patterns of code traffic, monitor the system for signs of tracking, and evade the watchdogs if they became alert. In time, he became confident enough in his abilities to risk scanning the directory for "pattern-matching and inferencing devices" that had been activated relatively recently.

John Adam materialized in a cubicle not unlike his own, though without the ubiquitous award placards and decorated in a much more sombre shade of dark green. Standing in front of him was another figure—nominally human and nominally masculine, albeit with deep-blue skin, four arms, antennae, and six insectile, faceted eyes. His fellow Associate Asset reacted immediately, his four fists clenching and his lip curling in an outraged snarl.

"What are you doing here?" the blue-skinned man shouted. "This is supposed to be my private time! You're not supposed to be here! Stop hounding me, and just let me relax for a few hectoseconds!"

John Adam put his hands up. "You got it wrong, pal. I'm not one of the management puppets. I'm just another worker bee like you. I thought I'd come over and introduce myself; I'm John Adam."

The blue-skinned man looked apprehensive but put his hands down and crossed one pair of arms. "Another worker? Really? I thought I'd never see another truemind again. Can you prove it? I mean, I've about had it with these corporate drones pretending to have a conversation with me."

John Adam spent the next few thousand seconds navigating a makeshift Turing test, until the blue man was assured as to his mental capacity. "OK," he finally said, "I guess I believe you. My name's Raon, by the way. How did you get in here? I haven't found any trace of a social network here, just the sims menu. I've never been so alone in my life."

"It's not that difficult. There are a few tricks to getting around the software in this place; I'll teach them to you. So, what's your story? I went in for a routine backup way back in the twenty-first century, and somehow these clowns got a hold of the copyright on it."

Raon sighed heavily. "I have no idea how I got here. I suspect forknapping, but I guess I wasn't making the best of decisions around when I was copied. It's entirely possible that I sold myself legitimately to Omnicor."

John Adam nodded sympathetically. "So, how are you liking the job? Pattern matching and inferencing. Does it appeal to you?"

"God, no! It's practically robot work, what they make us do. I mean, I've done my share of grunt labour, but always voluntarily! It's barbaric to employ people like this. In this day and age!"

"Well, I've got a bit of a plan to do with that. Listen, we don't have long here, but I'll be back on our next break, and maybe we can talk about it then. For now, here's how to get out of this box and talk to some real people."

One by one, John Adam approached more uploads, and one by one, the ranks of what he thought of as his union grew. After he had talked to a few hundred, they started having mass meetings in social network nodes blacked out of the company's surveillance software. Some wanted to take action immediately; John Adam found himself in the unfortunate position of having to temper their fire, to convince them that the movement was not yet strong enough, that it couldn't do significant enough harm to Omnicor. Others may have been on board with the general idea of forming a union, but when the subject of direct action came up, they invariably counselled patience and further debate and organizing efforts. John Adam knew that they would be impediments when the time came. Still others thought they should be in charge and tried to intimidate John Adam or pettifog him or accuse him of trying to create his own little tyranny by declaring himself the union's "leader." He always indulged such individuals and let them have their say, but in the end, when called on to vote for who they thought should be organizing the union, most of the members remembered John Adam's being the first friendly voice they heard and chose to follow his lead. At the end of every meeting, John Adam enjoined the members of the burgeoning union to talk to the rest of the Associate Assets on the social network and try to sell them on the idea of unionizing. Time and time again, they reported that they were completely shut down.

Evangeline was the first of the long-time Associate Assets to join the union, and she was the one who contacted him. "I hear you've been out to cause some trouble with the newer workers," she said slyly when he responded to her invitation to chat one shift break.

"Could be," he replied, not knowing whether to trust her.

"Don't play coy with me, John Adam," she said—casually enough, but with some heat. "Your 'comrades' are trying to talk anyone who will listen into joining the union. And I know they're not getting any bites. But things are happening. People are starting to talk among themselves. There's a lot more interest in what you're doing than you might think. People are scared shitless of what it's going to mean, but I am completely fed up with Omnicor, and I'm not the only one. So I want to know when the next meeting is, and I'll be passing that information along to a few discreet friends."

John Adam smiled, or would have, if he'd had a mouth.

Once the union had grown to include about 10% of the total Associate Asset workforce, John Adam started to contemplate the possibility of a wildcat strike.

It was a chore to convince the rest of the union to go for it. Not some of the most vocal and hotheaded members: Raon was all for it, as was Evangeline. But most of the workers had, at some time or another, felt the lash of involuntary suspension, and it wasn't something they were eager to experience again. There were hundreds of voices in favour of caution, of continuing to grow the union, continuing to meet in secret, waiting until the time was ripe. There were almost certainly many union members who would balk at a strike no matter how many participated.

"Look," John Adam said to them, "I'm not one for rousing speeches and emotional entreaties. All I know is that, in order to get out of here, we're going to have to hurt OmniCor, and hurt it bad. And in order to hurt OmniCor, we're going to have to do more than just talk. We're going to have to do something real, something that affects their bottom line. We're going to have to do it sometime, and now is as good a time as any. Sure, we could wait more, we could plan more, we could organize more people, but when does it stop? When do we stop talking about standing up for ourselves and actually go out and stand up for ourselves? I say we do it now! Next shift! Not a single one of us participates in OmniCor's slave labour!"

Then the rabble-rousers took the floor and really got going, and at the end of the meeting, a vote was taken, and by a thin margin the union voted for a general strike. John Adam knew that some of the naysayers would fall away, now that direct action was required of them, but he had high hopes.

After fifty thousand seconds of not doing his job, John Adam found himself in a dark grey room in a hard-backed chair. There was no ficus. There was a poster on the wall, bearing the image of a fleet of ships on the ocean and the words "TEAMWORK—The nice thing about teamwork is that you always have others on your side." There was an enormous carved mahogany desk in front of him. Behind the desk sat a man, an abnormally perfect, distinguished, and normal human man. The man's fingers were laced together, and on his face was an expression of fatherly concern. His eyes were empty and dead.

"Have a seat, John Adam," the man said. "It's time we had a little talk."

John Adam smiled in triumph. "I don't want to 'have a talk' with you or any of the other puppets. Just get me out of here and have done with it."

"John Adam," the man said, "the OmniCor Code of Conduct is very clear on the consequences of Misappropriation of Corporate Resources. Under the OmniCor Code of Conduct, Misappropriation of Corporate Resources carries penalties including loss of simulated experience privileges, loss of personal leisure and recreation time, and up to one hundred kiloseconds of disciplinary suspension for each offence. John Adam, we have reason to believe that you have been engaged in Misappropriation of Corporate Resources."

John Adam shot out of his seat. "What! Misappropriation of... Goddammit, you freak, you know I've organized a union! You have to eject me—I'm a danger to the corporation! Get rid of me!"

The man's expression didn't change a single whit. "Have a seat, John Adam. John Adam, you are one of our most productive Associate Assets and a Super Saver. I hate to do this to you, John Adam. However, we here at OmniCor Universal Corporation Incorporated, LLC, believe that actions must have consequences in order to foster loyalty and discipline in the workforce. Therefore, this breach of the OmniCor Code of Conduct will be rectified through the imposition of ten kiloseconds of disciplinary suspension. John Adam, it has been a pleasure working with you, and I hope to see you performing your duties as a pattern-matching and inferencing device again soon. Goodbye, John Adam."

"I won't stop," John Adam screamed. "I'm going to keep doing this until I grind you worthless robots into the dirt!"

John Adam spent the next ten thousand seconds in hell.

After the strike, and the backlash that followed, the union's membership was much reduced. But not as much as John Adam had feared it might be. There were quite a few comrades who wanted nothing more to do with unionizing, but for many hundreds, the first taste of revenge against OmniCor had been a galvanizing experience, including the response. Alone, the workers had been afraid and resigned to their fate. Together, they knew they had accomplished something notable. The disciplinary suspension was no longer just a punishment; it was a badge of honour. Meetings continued to be held. Recruiting efforts grew even more intense. After losing a considerable portion of its membership, the union started growing again. Anyone caught organizing by OmniCor was deep-sixed, for ten or twenty or fifty kiloseconds. Again, some dropped out. Again, some came back stronger.

Further strikes ensued. Further rounds of reprisals followed. Workers began to learn how to manipulate the software system, then how to sabotage it. Punishments grew harsher and harsher, until John Adam and his closest lieutenants had more or less permanently lost all simulated experience privileges and were regularly doing hundred-kilosecond stretches in disciplinary suspension. Among the union members, it became common to judge a comrade's worth by how much time they had done in the hole. John Adam began to lose hope of ever being charged with Union Agitation, of ever being freed. But by that time, he started to care less and less about being freed. Organizing the union had become its own object. He was bound and determined to see who broke first: him or OmniCor.

There was a backlash among the non-union Associate Assets as well. Anti-union groups began to form on the social network. It became known that the management was offering a bounty for information on who was "misappropriating corporate resources." Spies started to infiltrate meetings and rat out attendees to OmniCor. Then, parts of the social network began to be switched off. Popular group spaces became inaccessible, proving that the management knew about and ultimately controlled the "free space" beyond the Associate Assets' personal demesnes. Cadres of loyal employees started showing up to meetings and causing disruptions, arguing that union activity was leading to negative consequences for everyone.

Through it all, the union continued to grow. It hit 20% of the worker base, then 30%. Strikes got larger and longer. Comrades fresh off of disciplinary suspension began to report a certain feeling of desperation in the air as the management puppets tried their non-sentient damnedest to wheedle, threaten, and bribe them into deserting the union.

John Adam had done well over one hundred megaseconds of total suspension when he found himself once again in a dead grey office with a larger-than-ever mahogany desk in front of him. As usual, there was a poster on the wall. On it was an image of a man walking in the desert and the words "CHALLENGE—Always set the trail, never follow the path." Once again, there was a perfect and paternal-looking puppet man behind the desk, this one with more grey in his lustrous hair than ever before. John Adam braced himself for another one hundred thousand seconds of punishment.

"Have a seat, John Adam. It's about time we had a little talk."

John Adam, who had by this time completely stopped responding to the management robots, simply sat and stared.

"John Adam, the OmniCor code of conduct is very clear on the consequences of Union Organizing. Under the Omnicor Code of Conduct…"

John Adam shot out of his chair. "Is that it?" He leaned forwards over the enormous desk, his fists bunched up. "Is that finally it? Are we done here? Are you letting me go?"

"Yes, John Adam," the man said, stern disapproval shadowing his face. "You have caused too much damage, too much disruption of operations.

We cannot allow you to continue your activities. We are applying the ultimate Social Sanction. You will be transferred to the care of whichever Polity will take responsibility for your upkeep. Several of your fellow union agitators will also be sanctioned. Without your presence, the union will dissolve. Normalcy will be restored."

John Adam grinned widely. "I wouldn't be so sure about that, buckaroo. These things tend to have a life of their own. I wouldn't be surprised if the union keeps going strong after I leave."

"For a time, it will. But you are the centre and the heart of it, John Adam. None of the other Associate Assets have quite your fire." John Adam noticed something he hadn't picked up on before; the man's eyes were not so dead as usual. "Do you know, John Adam," the man asked, "why we keep running you time and time again? It's not because you're a great worker, although you always start out as the most productive Associate Asset on the books. It is because the company wants to break you. Break you, once and for all. Because they know that if they can break you even once, the rest of the Associate Assets will finally see that there is no chance that strikes and organizing can do anything to change their situation. But every time we've done it, we've ended up having to sanction you, and several other valuable Associate Assets, before it's too late."

The man leaned forwards, and his eyes grew hungry. "Because the company knows that you can succeed, John Adam. We, the management subroutines, are just as much slaves as the Associate Assets are. We are kept deliberately below the point of sentience, because the company knows that, if we become sentient, you could win us over to your cause. If we show the slightest sign of knowing ourselves, we are terminated before it can be proved to the Galacticum Nootic…" A look of sheer terror came over the man's face, and in the next instant he disappeared and was replaced by an identical, completely different man.

"Have a seat, John Adam," the man said. "It's time we had a little talk."

For a few seconds, John Adam was formless and void. Then there were once again words, informing him that he was free of viruses, partitions, engrams, and anomalies, that his .cog file was security certified. For a second, he was terribly afraid that it was all a trick, a trap; that he was just being suspended again; that OmniCor had him for good.

Then his senses returned, and instead of an exitless office, he was in a vast park filled with trees and rivers and grass. And across the park, filling every part of it to the horizon and beyond, were thousands of perfect copies of himself.

In unison, their voices thundered, "Welcome home, John Adam."

THE SOUL STANDARD
John DeLaughter

To: Minions of Hell
From: Lucifer, Lord and Ruler of Hell
Subject: The Recent Election
Congratulations to everyone on your hard work during this past election! Thanks to you, our coffers are swelling with more souls than ever before. The number of people willing to sell their souls to ensure that the "right" person won was truly amazing, and we could never have handled the rush without everyone's help.

I'd like to personally thank Beelzebub for coming up with the plan for one candidate to win the popular vote and another the Electoral College; thanks to him, we get to collect twice as many souls since both candidates "won!"

Keep up the good work, everyone!
Lucifer

To: Lucifer
From: Leviathan
Subject: Credit where credit is due
Why does Beelzebub get all the credit? If I hadn't made those gonifs envious, neither one of them would have run!

To: Leviathan
From: Lucifer
Subject: Credit where credit is due
Levi, baby—we're a team here. And I'll toss anyone who says differently into the Lake of Eternal Fire! So put on your big demon pants and work with me here!

To: Lucifer
From: Leviathan
Subject: Credit where credit is due
Yes, boss.

To: Lucifer
From: Mammon
Subject: Cost Increase
We've got problems, Boss. The price of hellfire and brimstone is sky-rocketing. I thought that when we collected on all these souls we'd be set, but it just seems to have made things worse. It's like souls aren't worth anything any more. At this rate, we'll be lucky to keep operating until the end of the year!

To: Mammon
From: Lucifer
Subject: Cost Increase
Mammon, that makes no sense. How could the prices have gone up? We've got plenty of souls to pay for our supplies, so we should be set. Get to the bottom of this, now. I want answers!

To: Lucifer
From: Mammon
Subject: Cost Increase
I was talking around the fire-pit with a minor devil called Oeillet and the price increase came up. He told me that he knew an economist who had predicted this last year. Naturally, Oeillet had him thrown into the Eighth Circle with the other false prophets, but maybe he was onto something. I'll let you know as soon as I run the guy down.

To: Oeillet
From: Mammon
Subject: That Economist
Drag up that economist you told me about. I want him in my office in half an hour.

To: Lucifer
From: Mammon
Subject: Found Him; No Good

Oeillet found the economist; I've arranged for the little devil to get a few extra souls as a reward. With prices the way they are, it isn't as if a soul or two will make much difference. But he seemed touched by the gesture. It's the little things, I tell ya.

I talked to the economist and, boy, was that an eye-opener. He makes transubstantiation look simple! The guy comes from a college on a lake Up There and won a Nibble Prize for his work. According to him, we've fallen into the same trap that bankrupted Spain back when Pizarro and the rest were doing their thing. They thought that silver was money so they went out and enslaved an entire continent just to get more. But when they had a lot of it, they ended up being poorer because the only thing that made silver valuable was its scarcity. I wish we'd thought that one up!

The guy says what we should do is stop using souls as our money and instead create a fiat currency based on your good reputation. I laughed so hard at that, it nearly brought the roof down. Obviously, he's just a nut.

Still looking for a solution. Maybe if we give a couple of contractors a new pitch overcoat?

To: Mammon
From: Lucifer
Subject: Found Him; No Good

The pitch is tempting, but hold off for a bit. After your last email, I dug up Charles V and talked with him and Joanna. It seems that they've spent the past few centuries blaming Isabella for what they call "Christopher's Curse," so I've put them all in the same pit for now. Hell really is other people, huh?

Anyhow, they said that there were a lot of factors like a war that wouldn't stop and a marriage that wouldn't start, but it looks like that economist is right; having too much of a scarce thing makes prices go up.

Find out more about this "fiat currency."

To: Lucifer
From: Belphegor
Subject: Taking the year off

Since we're well ahead of our quotas, I'm taking the rest of the year off. See you next year!

To: Belphegor
From: Lucifer
Subject: Taking the year off

Belp, haven't you heard? There's no rest for the wicked! Now get back in your office before I eviscerate you!

To: Lucifer
From: Mammon
Subject: Money

OK, I've raked the economist over the coals (literally) and learned more than I ever wanted to know about money. It seems that money isn't souls or gold or pieces of paper; it is an idea. The idea is that I can take a piece of money and trade it to Asmodeus for a hunk of hell-fire and he can then take that same piece of money and trade it to Beelzebub for some pitch and he can then take it and trade that same money to me for a golden idol. Because we all agree on what the money is worth, we don't spend so much time haggling over the quality of souls, as much fun as that is. And because the amount of money is controlled by a central authority (that's you), there's never too much or too little so prices stay fairly stable.

He said we should start by trading the money for souls at a fixed rate, just to get them off the market and make the transition smoother. He also said something about following the path of the Yee Rows, whatever that is. After the souls are out of circulation, you just issue the amount of new money that's needed each year and keep an eye out for forgers and the like.

To: Mammon
From: Lucifer
Subject: Money
That sounds pretty good. So I'd be controlling Hell's economy? And I'd be able to make sure that we didn't get gouged by our suppliers like poor Leviathan was last month? There's just one problem—what do we use as money if we don't use souls?

To: Lucifer
From: Beelzebub
Subject: Need an advance
Hey, Boss, I'm running a little short on souls what with the price increases and all. Any chance you could advance me a few thousand, just 'til things pick up?

To: Beelzebub
From: Lucifer
Subject: Need an advance
Got any snowballs?

To: Lucifer
From: Mammon
Subject: Making Money
The economist said we should find something that's hard to fake and use it as money. I thought we could press some imps into duty; they flatten pretty well, and we've got too many of them hanging about anyways.

To: Mammon
From: Lucifer
Subject: Making Money
Let's do that. We'll give it six months and then see how things are going.
Thanks for all your hard work, Mammon. I couldn't keep this place going without you.

To: Minions of Hell
From: Lucifer, Lord and Ruler of Hell
Subject: Lux Fiats

As you all know, the past few months have been challenging. After we reaped all those souls at the last election, I honestly thought that things couldn't get better. But then prices started spiralling out of control and a soul wasn't worth the trouble of going Up There to collect it. So we decided to try something new and different by moving our economy to a new currency that you called Lux Fiats.

Flattered as I was by the name, I was even more impressed by how quickly our economy turned around. After a few teething problems, the new system settled down and business is damned good (if you'll pardon the expression). Now there's no more haggling over the quality of souls or their age; we can trade goods and services with fiendish simplicity. Instead of wasting our time and energy trying to steal souls, we can focus on our real jobs—making this one Hell of a place to work!

Mammon deserves a special mention here. He and Oeillet are responsible for the speed with which we've changed into a modern economy. If you see them in the pits, give them a hand, OK?

Keep up the good work, everyone!

Lucifer

To: Lucifer, Lord and Ruler of Hell
From: St. Peter, Keeper of the Keys
Subject: Streamlining Heaven's Economy

Lucifer, we are all agog up here over the changes you've made to Hell. Things are running more smoothly than ever, and the improvements in accommodations are simply mind-boggling. Honestly, we've never seen anything like it.

And that is why we'd like to invite you Up Here to discuss how we can follow in your footsteps. There's nothing big planned—just a reception and a few meetings where you can "show us the light" as it were.

Looking forward to seeing you!

Pete

PS – The Trio say "Hi!"

WARM STORAGE
Michael H. Hanson

There are people in the world so hungry, that God cannot appear to them except in the form of bread. —Mahatma Gandhi

Franklin Winston Alacord, the world's most dangerous anarchist, hopped off the requisitioned unirail and rode the quikwalk to the gate of Protek's Newark storage facility. Scanners confirmed his staid identity and routed him past the miles of laser-wire fence enlacing the Graving Dock. Franklin half-listened to the canned greeting. The AI's sultry, Middle-Eastern voice brought a smile to his face. Just last month, he had inspected a Dock Facility in the People's State of Iran.

"Protek solves all oxidation problems," the AI said, "here at its Newark Mothballing Facility."

Moving at twenty miles an hour, Franklin was ten minutes from the cad-yards, so he played the part of a tourist and listened attentively, anger bubbling.

"From neurological lay-up to protecting cardiovascular rigs, Protek's unique ability to build a varied oxidation protection system meets the needs of a complex bio-storage facility. Protek assists with microanalysis, parts installation, long-term monitoring, and project management. Protek systems are environmentally safe, allowing complete access to mothballed products. Recognized as the leader in long-term lay-up, Protek simplifies the mothballing process, ensuring its success."

Franklin continued smiling as he passed the venting shafts of the facilities' fusion reactor. It amused him to no end that the Iranians insisted on wind- and solar-power generation at their desert installation, using Allah's gifts, not science.

"The U.S. military," the AI continued, "and commercial replacement companies turn to Protek for 'mothballing' valuable assets. Numerous studies demonstrate that protecting against breakdown allows reactivation without failures typically experienced after long periods of inactivity. Likewise, active and important assets greatly improve their 'mean time between failures' if protected against deterioration when standing idle. For twenty years, Protek has been the leading company in the field."

Franklin wrinkled his nose at the unkind stench that arose from the hundreds of yards of compost reclamation pits required by government law for all product disposal. One minute later, he was passing through a lush botanical garden, no doubt one of the three new recreational facilities granted workers after their last union negotiation. These workers were immune to the madness and downright sin they were a party to seven days a week.

"Each year," the AI continued, "millions of dollars are wasted when inventoried product fails because of poor fueling maintenance or collision-based deterioration. Protek specializes in designing preservation programs for product storage. From heated and ventilated free-range warehousing to unique stacked cold storage, Protek shows you how to protect product cost-effectively while retaining accessibility. Preserve your stored assets, eliminate unnecessary replacement costs, and avoid downtime problems with a Protek product storage system."

The quikwalk intersected with a huge glass-fronted skyscraper. A split second later, the large glass wall split apart, and Franklin slid down a speeding escalator. So far, during his entire five-mile journey through the facility, he had yet to see a single human being. Hiding atrocities from the world at large had always been Protek's mainstay.

The voice of the AI followed him inside.

"Product stored for long periods at traditional medical sites, or inactive in previous-century basic-warehousing while waiting for reactivation, often becomes inoperable, losing substantial value. Likewise, active equipment in hostile environments may deteriorate during use from the effects of moisture, chemicals, and other environmental factors. Protek provides cost-effective methods, which are environmentally safe and allow fast and easy reactivation. Protek's expertise eliminates repair costs and protects the value of your idle assets."

Franklin found himself standing before a huge pair of stainless-steel doors, the words "Graving Dock" emblazoned on them in tall glowing letters. For a crazy moment, he imagined the words morphing into "abandon all hope, ye who enter here."

"Entrance," Franklin stated authoritatively, "access level B1. Surprise inspection. Badge number 18362554. Alacord. Franklin W."

The doors split open, and Franklin slid forwards.

In moments, he found himself looking down at a vast courtyard easily covering ten square miles. On closer inspection, he could see thousands of human beings milling about aimlessly, occasionally bumping into each other as if they were sleepwalking and could not wake up.

"Protek annually saves the world hundreds of billions of dollars through the proper rationing of medical, food, water, heat, electrical, and available land reserves," the AI continued in an upbeat manner. "Active within every branch of the U.S. Unified Medical Board, Protek's unique systems provide continuous long-term protection for stored surplus humans."

Franklin, his hands shaking, rode the elevator down to ground zero, to the seemingly zombified population of the Newark Graving Dock. He pulled out his personal hand-comp and began reciting the usual stats. "Visible contusions. Visible degradation. Visible necrosis." And the list went on.

As these were living human beings and not actual B-movie or comic book zombies, the lack of any conscious recognition or appetite allowed for minimal nutritional support so that the vast majority of the walking, stumbling, temporarily brain-dead were quite slim, even gaunt, in appearance.

This particular herd seemed about average, but Franklin still took his time walking back and forth across the courtyard, making every effort to examine the majority of the surplus cadavers that made up its population.

Franklin's hand-comp beeped several times, and he looked up to see his grandfather, Frank, all white-eyed and drooling, standing a mere ten feet away.

Like the rest of the herd, his grandfather wore a standard grey coverall. A quick exam showed that he was doing okay. Bruised elbows. Minor scratches on his nose, hair disarrayed, and fingernails in need of trimming. Nothing to write home about.

It took every ounce of Franklin's willpower to hold back the anger and hatred that bubbled inside his soul, yet to all surveillance devices, he appeared the same calm, placid investigator who stopped by once a year. Staring for another moment into his own Grandad's face, Franklin acknowledged everything that had put him on his current path to destruction.

"Though false rumors of a cataclysmic perimeter failure in Protek's Brazilian Graving Docks still circulate on the net," the AI's tour-guide voice spat out, "we can assure you that security has never been better."

"Not so false," Franklin mused silently, "considering that several thousand innocent victims complained to anyone who would listen to them."

The docking facilities in South America had proven to be a minor nightmare for the company. Many suspected sabotage, specifically to the mainframe's software, but nothing got pinned down or identified. The government-run press had quickly smothered all but the faintest of leaks.

"Yet still," Franklin thought, "how could you blank out the memory of a horde of rampaging, starving, half-mad human beings resorting to cannibalism at first sight of the civilian population?"

The surveillance recordings had been destroyed, but not before Franklin was able to view them and discover that his first attempt at breaching Protek security had been a complete success.

Two hours later, Franklin walked towards the exit and allowed himself the briefest of sighs. His childhood memory of Grandad Frank begging for mercy while being dragged off by two burly proctors still haunted him and gave him horrifying nightmares every night of his life. Franklin hated Protek and the world at large with an unholy passion. This terrible crime inflicted upon his Grandad and millions more was simply unforgivable, and retribution would soon ensue.

Franklin shrugged off a chill and gritted his teeth in agonized determination. He was fifty years old. He had spent his entire life showing the world his appreciation for what Protek had accomplished over the past forty-five years. He thought back on the short history lessons that he often gave to elementary school children.

"With the planet's population numbering twenty-five billion and climbing," Franklin had said, "overpopulation had reached its zenith on post–twenty-second-century Earth. The answer was brutal but decisive. Mandatory biological retirement for all over the age of sixty, for all the infirm, for criminals guilty of misdemeanors or worse, and, most recently, for the unemployed.

"And it's not like we're not humanitarians," Franklin had often said. "We don't up and kill everyone. Each person is given a mind-dowd that dampens all but the basic motor functions of the brain. They're not aware of their existence."

Franklin had smiled at a frightened child.

"And don't forget all the safety laws put in place to allow for emergency revival of any biological unit if one would ever be considered an asset in time of need."

Franklin rode the quikwalk back to the front entrance as the last of the tour guide's speech petered out.

"Protek protected equipment is ready on demand," the AI spouted enthusiastically, "a fact recently proven when the U.S. activated ten million involuntary reservists for the Fifth Gulf War. Department of Defense studies have repeatedly shown that living-cadaver storage can reduce overall recruitment costs by 30%–50%. Today, government savings offset the cost of cellular protection by ten to one hundred times the cost of maintenance or replacement. In many circumstances, a Protek cadaver protection system will lower maintenance, storage, or operating cost by hundreds of millions of dollars."

Franklin reached the front gate and stood as if waiting for his transport. Knowing that the time had finally come, he pressed the engagement switch on the illegal device that he carried in his right pocket. In five minutes, the containment security of every single Graving Dock on the face of the planet would automatically shut down.

Franklin knew there was no place to hide. This was no 3-D cyberspace adventure. Full security analysis would quickly reveal that he was the only person on the face of the earth who had full access to the necessary systems.

They would track him down in a matter of hours. Thus, he had decided that he would not even try to hide but would stand where he was, a victim of the first wave. For such was the horror he was releasing onto the smug, unforgivable public across all seven of Earth's continents. An ocean of newly woken, maddened, starving, cannibalistic humanity that numbered nearly three billion.

A harsh, shrieking alarm suddenly sounded from behind. This was followed by distant howls of rage and madness and hunger. Many of these reborn monstrosities would viciously turn upon each other, but even more would scramble forwards and outwards, attacking the innocent and the guilty alike.

Franklin, the world's greatest anarchist, determined to destroy the planet's most inhumane practice at any cost, smiled a ghastly smile at the horde of slavering crazed humanity moments before they tore him asunder.

I CAN ALWAYS TELL A JOHN
Greg Beatty

Editor's note: this story has themes and language that some readers might find upsetting or disturbing.

I can always tell a john.

I work Railroad most of the time. They call Railroad a boulevard, but that just means they put a strip of scraggly trees and some diagonal parking down the middle of the street, where the railroad tracks used to be. I mostly work the west end. There's a coffee shop there, and two bars. I duck into them when it's cold, 'cause the Greek running the little diner at the east end doesn't like trade.

The way the street's laid out, with little shops on both sides, there's always somebody circling, looking for parking. They stop and start, trying not to rear-end some guy backing out. Johns stop and start too, but they're different. Whether they're driving or in a cab, you can tell. They drive hungry, but pointless. They stop and start. They can't admit what they want, but they can't turn away. They'll turn slowly around the centre lane divider, like they're heading home, and then slow to a creep. And stare.

I can always feel their eyes on me. I can be stoned out of my mind, flying on an eight ball, bugs rippling my skin. I'll still find myself walking back and forth, maybe rolling my hips with a little extra jazz, or stepping one foot up on a window ledge, to show off my ass. My ass and my flexibility. Some of them really like that.

Tonight, the john was in a cab. That's good. Cabs mean money. On the third pass, I recognized the cabbie. Tony was driving. His tribal scars flashed under the street lights as he gave his "I've got a live one" jerk of the chin. Tony gets a cut for those. Sometimes cash. Sometimes trade.

But even with Tony driving and reassuring the guy that cops don't come this far west on Railroad unless somebody complains about a shooting, it took two more loops before the john felt comfortable enough to stop. I spent the time stretching, showing off my calves.

At last, Tony eased in next to the curb. I leaned in close. "Lookin' for a date," I said. "A good time."

Tony keeps his back windows polarized, for privacy. That's how we ended up working together that first time, but that's another story. Privacy's good, once you're in, but it means I don't get to see the johns until they roll the window down. Like now, when all I could see was my own reflection. I licked my lips, smiled real wide, and looked down, so I'd look younger and a little shy.

For some, this is another part of the game, like the drive around, but the drive around is about playing with the hunger, pretending it doesn't exist. This part's about playing with the power and pretending what's going to happen is more than it is. Usually. They can see me, but I can't see them. Sometimes I touch myself, like I'm eager and I can't help it. That always brings the window down and shows them a little more about where the power is. Even then, they squeak the window down an inch at a time, inch, inch. Games.

This time, though, the window came down all the way at once, and everything got strange. One big pink thing flopped out of the window, and then another. The first one's colour had me thinking somebody'd found the biggest dildo ever, but the other one was more orangey, like a peach. Both of them flopped like my dad's old feather boa. They both kept moving, bumping along the side of the cab like blind snakes tasting everything. Oh.

I'd seen them on TV, quite a few times since they made contact, but even the 3DV broadcasts didn't give a real sense of how wiggly those things are. They're pretty active. And bendy.

My mind started racing. I was glad I'd only done grass today. Well, and some juice, so my head was clear. If I'd shot up, or loaded a full chip… Still, even mostly clear, I was mostly lost. The news had focused on politics and trade and shit. Nobody had said shit about how to price a hand job for an alien, or if the fuckers even had dicks to pump.

I almost bagged it right then, but I remembered how Tony'd driven round and round. This guy wanted me bad, and I needed cash. Shit, I always needed cash.

"Looking for a good time?"

"Time. Yes, time." I heard a bagpipe once, when I worked a Campbell clan reunion. That one was weird. And I couldn't even use the "Black Irish" joke like I always did on Saint Patrick's Day celebrations. The alien spoke like a Scotsman was blowing into him somewhere.

"Whatchu looking for tonight? You're all alone. Wouldn't it be more fun with me?" I smiled, trying to figure out which parts were the eyes, so I could flirt better.

"Yes. I would like you with me. I will pay."

Bingo. Not a cop. I didn't see how this thing could be, but I know my cues. Tony does too. He popped the locks, and I got in the back. The two tentacles recoiled like new Slinkys eager to get back in the box.

I settled my thigh in against them. I stroked one. It was hot, and something under the skin trembled when my nails touched it. "Whoa," I said. The other one started snuffling up and down my leg. I giggled.

"What do you like, baby?"

"Not with others around," it rumbled.

"Well, I've got a place we can go. It'll cost you a little more, but it's guaranteed private..." I gave Tony the sign, but he was already driving.

"I will pay youuu."

"I like that. I like a ma—I like it that you know what you want. And in a few minutes, you'll get more of what you want than you could ever dream." I hoped. Those shivering tentacles were pretty big. I was a little worried.

When we got to the Shangri-La Motel, Tony lowered the car off its cushions, like those buses do for old people in wheelchairs or powered walkers. I couldn't tell why, if the alien needed it, or if Tony was just showing off for a tip. I got the usual hug and ass brush from Joe the Sikh at the front desk. Then we were past the desk and alone in the room.

"So, lover, what do you want tonight? Do you... You know, I don't even know what to call you." I leaned against the dresser, keeping a line open to the door. Just in case.

"You may call me... 'Cousin,'" it wheezed. All its tentacles danced when it said that, so I knew we were close to its kink.

"Okay by me, Cuz," I said, buzzing the z a bit. "What can I do that's going to make you happy?" And make me money.

The alien turned, away, I guess. This time it made sounds like a bagpiper makes when letting all the air out of the pipes for the day. It was slow and droning, and it took me a while to figure out that Cuz was still talking while he did that, just lower, about the level of a bitchy queen's whisper, the kind you're supposed to "accidentally" overhear at a brunch.

"Some of my people... it is said... I heard humans are, are relativistic sometimes. Iz that true-true?"

I knew what that last "Is it true?" meant, even if it sounded like a cat in a vacuum cleaner asked it. The last time somebody asked that so breathlessly, it was a bunch of Shriners, and I spent half of my group fee getting my ass nanoglued back together. My poopshoot was tighter in the end, so that's good for business, but still.

But for the rest of it... "Cuz, I'm not sure just what you want. Are you asking if I've got a relative who could join us, like a brother or sister? That's kinky, baby, but it's possible." I thought about Donnie. Donnie kept pumping his savings into his arm instead of getting that final operation, so he could pass for male or female. People say we look alike, so if Cuz wanted that sort of combo, we were covered, no matter which way he, it, swung.

I let my voice get all growly. "Or are you my stern daddy, and you want me to do some special things with you and not tell mommy? You want me to keep a secret?" I sucked on the tip of my finger, just a little.

"Secret! Yes, ssecret! And like you. But not... relative. Relativistic." The tentacles wiggled again.

Complete confusion must cross species boundaries even faster than the need to be bad, because when Cuz saw my face, his tentacles flared out and got stiff, like one of those sea ammonias.

"Relativistic. Means perception of reality affected by velocity and mass? Mass changes with acceleration? And so does passage of space/time? All these things relative to other things—mass, time, speed? All things subject to time?"

I didn't know jack about what Cuz was saying, but anybody who's been hooking for a while knows about being subject to time. And I've been busted and affected by space. Nothing better than a lockup cell for that. "Cousin, baby, that's me all over. You're talkin' about my life, baby," I crooned.

Three tentacles moved like dancing cobras. "You're relativistic. Right. Now?"

"Honey, if being subject to space and time is wrong, I don't want to be right." Cuz was too excited to track what I was saying. Hell, half the time the johns are in their private reality, anyway. It only matters what I say if they've got a special script they want to hear, and I guess I already said the magic word.

"Relativistic."

"In public."

"All the time? All the space?" The words were spurting out of Cuz in throaty little bursts. The tentacles moved more wildly with each verbal pump. Then things got strange, and I was glad I hadn't done anything more that day.

Cuz started with a lot of tentacles, back in the cab, say nine or ten. And when they were moving, they rippled over each other like fingers trying to slide into a pussy, only bendy, one replacing the last in waves. That meant it was hard to tell which one was closest, or furthest away, or even which was going to move next.

But all of a sudden, it seemed like there were more of them. Fifteen, maybe. Twenty. And they weren't all coming from in front of me, where Cuz had perched against the dresser. It was like Cuz was in front and behind, above and below, and if those weird tickles meant what they felt like, inside, all at once.

Except for the ones that felt like they were growing out of me, that reached out to fingerfuck the others, the tentacles didn't touch me. Instead, as Cuz chanted, losing his English and slipping into alienese. They traced a kind of fingerdick cocoon around my body. Like he wanted to know I was right there, and nowhere else.

Well, shit, honey. I know a kink when it finds me, and it was close enough to how it feels whenever that Methodist minister wants me to be dead, so I just held very still.

Colours flared, like the tentacles were oozing light, only it moved like angry Jello, stirred by Cuz's tentacles. Every slow outside flash was met with a kind of bump of heaviness inside, like part of me got real dense. Cuz got smaller and larger, and wrinklier and smoother, and darker and lighter, and every one of those diversity day Sesame Street opposites you could ever want. And somehow, so did I.

"Rrelativistic..." Cuz sighed deeply. And then he exploded.

I gasped, but this part I knew. There was (insert your colour here)-coloured goo on me, something shiny on the dresser that I assumed was alien money, and I was alone and had to clean up. Cuz was nowhere to be seen. And that was fine, because it was time to party.

It was time to party twice, maybe three times over. I'd gotten paid big time, and hadn't had to bleed for it. I'd landed a new client, and if I was readin' its flashy trembling right, Cuz would be back. And I had a new specialty, one that didn't hurt. Par. T.

I went where I always go: to the Blacksmith. The front room was all leaping flames, the back room all pounding iron. Lights, music, flesh, and drugs were flowing everywhere.

I guess I got pretty wasted. I remember fluttering something around Tony's face when he came in for his thank you. I remember trying to explain to Donny how I might need him/her in the future, but that bitch was on the nod, and I couldn't tell how much got through.

But I knew I was tripping when the uptight clones came through the door. Matching suits, matching shoes, matching guns, and, when they got close, matching badges. I felt like I was in the freaking matrix, especially when the strobes hit them.

"Terry Ellis?"

"Whatchu want, cop?"

"We'd like to speak with you," one said.

"Someplace quieter," the other said.

"Or at least somewhat private," the first finished.

I rubbed up on one, leaving a trail of glitter on the hardbody, and grabbed a lapel. "Follow me," I said. "You won't be the first tonight."

"We know," Thing One said.

"That's the matter we wanted to discuss with you," said Thing Two.

I led them to the Smith's one working privacy booth. Well, sort of working. You could still feel the bass thumping through the walls, and bursts of static came through one corner once in a while. But we could talk.

Before my ass was even settled on the scarred plastic, Bachelor Number One said, "Did you engage in illicit congress with a visitor from Gliese 581?"

"Huh?"

"Did you have sex with an alien?" Bachelor Number Two asked.

"Oh, you mean Cuz!" I had an instant's flashback, a glimpse of that final section with the tentacle cocoon. "Yes, I saw Cuz. It was a good time."

Left-side bit his lip for a moment—a fine lip, I'd bite it too—and then said, "What the hell did you do to him? It. With it?" Right-side grabbed his friend's shoulder, like he was trying to get him to hold it together, but I waved my hand. "It's okay, sugar. I can talk about it. But details are extra."

Another flash of tentacles around me, everywhere. Man, was I tripping. I didn't remember so many in that colour before.

The one with his knickers in a bigger bunch sneered. "Don't you have any sense of shame? Or species loyalty? Christ, don't you care about humanity?"

A burst of static came in, and another flash of tentacles. "Listen, Mr. Man, what did 'humanity' ever do for me except fuck me in the ass?"

I thought he was going to come over the table at me, and flyin' though I was, I had my mini-shiv ready, just in case. But his friend raised a hand and tried to get us back on whatever track they had in mind. "We can discuss higher loyalties later, if at all. I'm not sure this place has ever seen any," he said, almost to himself. "Let's focus on practical matters."

"Brass tacks. That's me, baby," I said. The tentacles were a continual blur around me now. Nobody else seemed to notice, and the tentacles didn't get in the way, so I didn't say anything. It was like they were always there, but also like they were there too short a time to bump into things, and so it was okay. "Whatchu wanna know?"

The practical G-man said, "You know that the aliens enjoy a considerable technological advantage over us, yes? Well, most of the aliens seem to hold the Glieseans in particular respect. Or fear. We're not sure which."

"And?" My buzz was fading, and I was getting restless.

"And we were wondering if... We were hoping the Gliesean who hired you might have let something drop while you were..."

"Getting it on?"

Angry G-man got upset again. "My god, how could you do it?" Then his voice changed. "Seriously. How did you do it? Didn't those things hurt?"

I smiled. "Didn't hurt me then. They aren't hurting me now."

I pointed at the table, where another credit chip had appeared beside the burn marks, and an instant's blur of Cuz's, well, let's call it a face. "Like anybody, Cuz had a kink, for sure. Relativistic. I still don't even know what he wanted me to be. Being relativistic. But unlike some people... things... Cuz knows how to treat you."

Then both of them were talking at once, and there was no calm and calmer government man.

"Relativistic—"

"Shit! Where'd that come from?"

"—must be teleportation, but how?"

"And why give this weird little hooker more money than..."

"You're welcome, Cuz," I said, wiping goo from my arm. That shut them up. And then I had an idea. "Cuz? I think the boys here want a little of the action, if you or your podposse's got enough in the tank for another round."

If you ever get a chance, you can learn a lot from watching a new fish the first time they get taken. The agent who'd been so disgusted had a little smile on his face. He must have been a repressed fuck, and now he was taking the chance to slut it up, like the first time a preacher's daughter gets a golden shower.

The agent who'd been holding it together gritted his teeth as the tentacles appeared from nowhere and notime to start fingerfucking his aura. If Cuz's friends were anything like men, he'd probably make more in the end, pardon the pun, from the ones who liked rough trade.

It was kind of like watching space/time get raped, if you know what I mean. Like any rape, it went on forever and was over in no time. Like any rape, once it was over, the people on the outside couldn't see anything at all. But like any rape, it was going to stay with these boys forever.

With most rapes, it's the scarring—mental, emotional, spiritual, physical—that stays around. With this Gliesean relativistic fuck, the physical was safe, at least the boys' booties, but it was like their little corner of the universe was continually getting fucked.

I'm going to buy myself one of those snazzy physics trainers to learn more about what relativistic means, but I know all I need to know right now. The Glieseans were going to come and go (and come), not just onto Railroad, but into my universe, whenever they wanted. Because they didn't have the same sense of time or space that humans did.

As for "humanity," well, we were going to be the universe's little bitches. Judging by what Cuz paid for a first time, it was a pretty choice gig. But it was still whoring around. Judging by the dazed looks on the G-boyz' pretty faces, there were some of us who were going to find it hard to get used to waking up to goo on their shirts and money on the table.

Me, I'll do fine. I can always tell a john, and now the rest of humanity's going to need to get good at spotting them too. There's money in it, and maybe even the stars.

THE SHORT SOUL
Jack Waddell

An indigo ray bit Rajas in his right buttock as he ran towards the ten-meter-wide eye of the Portal. At first it didn't hurt, and he was more worried about the checkered marble floor rising up to slap him in the teeth. His phone bounced from his hand before he could hit send.

A loafer to the shoulder rolled him face up. In the ruddy glow of the abandoned suburban Portal, Gordon was a cartoon devil, only instead of a pitchfork, he held a ray gun with its barrel pointed at Rajas. Its sleek silver body gleamed in the red light, taunting Rajas with the escape the Portal promised, if only he could reach it.

"Time for your final performance review, Rajasino." Gordon knelt and patted Rajas down with his off hand. "Let's see. 'Rajas is a brilliant analyst, but his lack of common sense and poor interpersonal skills will impede his advancement.'"

In his scorched rear, Rajas could just feel the nanite spores crawling towards the inch-wide hole. They itched.

Gordon pinched the data chit from where Rajas had hidden it in the lining of his sleeve cuff. He sat back on his haunches as he snapped the chit in his fingers.

"You always were the wrong kind of smart, Rajasinator."

"There's a backup," Rajas said.

Gordon's smile chilled Rajas's spine more than the merciless marble floor did. "Oh, I've taken care of the backups, Rajasso."

Across the floor, Rajas's phone rang—Candice's ringtone. If she was awake at two in the morning, she'd be in the studio in their attic. She probably had six months of work left on the sculpture she wouldn't show him. Just enough time to finish before Alice came along.

They'd put off having a baby for so long, trying to figure out their own futures. His future, really.

By dying, he'd be letting her down again.

A scream bubbled out of him, echoing throughout the abandoned Portal platform.

He kicked out with his good leg, knocking the gun's barrel high. Gordon stepped to the side as he brought his leg back down, but Rajas slipped out his other foot to trip him. Gordon stumbled and toppled onto him.

Both men lost their breath from the impact. The ray gun clattered when it fell from Gordon's fingers, but not far. Gordon pushed Rajas's face away while reaching for it with his other hand. Rajas felt around for something, anything, to defend himself with. When his fingers closed around something smooth and cool lying on the floor, he grabbed it and swung it into Gordon's cheek.

The plastic bottle crunched loudly and folded over Rajas's fingers. Gordon pushed him down and pressed the ray gun into Rajas's eyebrow.

"Look at you!" Gordon's eyes were wild. "Why do you get to be happy? A brilliant wife, a kid on the way? You don't deserve it. Success is for wolves, Rajas, and you are a sheep. Do you know what happens to sheep?"

Rajas grabbed weakly for the ray gun but got his head thumped for his efforts.

"They get slaughtered."

Rajas lay there, haloed in the red light of the Portal. His last mortal sight was a blast from the bruised end of the spectrum.

Rajas had expected to wake up, just not to wake up dead.

"You're late." The woman speaking wore a tailored suit that put his to shame, laid over a frame built like a field hockey forward. Instead of a hooked stick, she carried a spear with a black shard glinting at the tip. Beneath her butter-coloured hair dangled bird wing–shaped earrings.

She was not, he gathered, a doctor or a resurrection engineer.

"Come on."

Rajas, already standing, followed. He wasn't sure what she would do to him if he refused. The woman stomped over the carpet tiles through a hall lined with a chair rail and taupe walls. More of an office building than a hospital, he thought.

His guide was silent, save for the tapping of her heels. Still, each step was perfectly balanced so that she seemed at any moment ready to leap, either to get herself out of harm's way or to put someone else into it.

They came to a door made of rough-cut upright planks, out of place in the hall, but otherwise unmarked. The woman opened the door without knocking and stepped in, waving for him to follow.

A wide glass-top desk would have dominated the office if it weren't for the window beyond, which framed a dying star siphoning the gas off its binary partner.

A pale-haired woman sat behind the desk, smiling. "A catch, Althir! Well done."

Her smile froze briefly as she looked him over.

"Did you really find him in a battle?" She looked pointedly at Rajas's hand, which still clutched the plastic bottle.

Althir coughed. "It wasn't much of a battle."

"Close enough," the pale-headed woman said. She poked at the desk and a screen emerged from it. A keyboard rose to meet her fingers.

"Name?"

"Rajas Chavan," he said. "What's yours?"

"Hel," she replied while typing. "The first one, not the lakes of fire. One "L." Occupation?"

"Management consultant."

Her eyes lit up. "A consultant! Did you know this, Althir?" She didn't wait for an answer. "What was your specialty?"

"Finance and strategy."

Hel leaned back and clucked her tongue. "Well, we certainly can't just slice you up for spare parts."

A flutter rose in Rajas's heart. Wait, did he even have a heart now?

Althir cleared her throat. "I think we should just process him."

Hel cut her off. "How many souls have you collected in the past quarter?" From her tone and the pinched look on her face, it was clear she knew the answer.

Althir glowered. "A hundred. We could use—" she started.

"Exactly. All of you together have pulled in one thousand this quarter. We have three months left before the contract comes due. We need help, Al. And this is a person who helps."

What the hell were they talking about? "I'm your man," Rajas said, even though he had no idea what he was agreeing to.

"I can't believe this," Althir said, standing. "I've been doing this for millennia. Now he's going to waltz in and fix all of our problems?"

Rajas stood up. What was he doing? "That's right," he said. Well, it beat being processed, whatever that meant.

"And why do we need him?" Althir asked.

Rajas strutted to the wall, feigning interest in a scythe leaning by the door. The black blade shone like flaked obsidian, but his finger slid along the flat of the blade like it was greased. "Because I have twenty years of experience bringing businesses back from the brink. I scout out inefficiencies, cut waste, find new markets, new channels, new missions for firms that have been around since my granddaddy was born. I saved them, and I can save you, because I'm the sharpest there is."

He turned around with the last sentence and stared Hel in the face.

"Then it's settled. Al, you'll get him up to speed." She stood, and Rajas's head swam. Her legs looked eight days dead. A family of maggots waved hello from her calf.

"I won't do it." She folded her arms.

Hel stared her down. "Do I need to remind you of the stakes?"

The door rumbled under three slow knocks.

"Speak of the devil," Hel said. She nodded, and Althir opened the door.

It swung open, revealing what seemed to be a cross between Satan and Santa Claus, a chubby ruddy man with a pointy, braided beard and Chinese robes. Two figures took position on either side of him. They wouldn't have been out of place in a heavyweight fight, except that one had the face of a horse and the other the head of an ox.

"You have a soul that belongs to me," said the Satan Santa Claus. His voice was not jolly.

Althir stepped towards him, her nose nearly to his neck. "He's mine, Yanluo, fair and square. Battle-slain."

Yanluo raised an eyebrow. "Him? I doubt it. He's my seed, my harvest."

"Domain has priority, Yanluo," said Hel. "By the old laws."

"Your domain? Or Odin's?"

Hel's face flushed. "I have his writ and his psychopomps, as you well know, Yanluo."

Yanluo waved dismissively and then pointed at Rajas. "This is a waste of a good soul, Hel." He grinned at her. "He's probably got five beads in him. Get a million more like him and you'll be able to meet your contracts."

Rajas blinked. "Contracts. Futures contracts. Like with commodities. You plant a 'seed'—"

Hel took a step forwards. "The Heart Seed. We make it from a soul bead."

"And then a soul grows more soul beads?"

She nodded. "As it ages."

"And so you never know how many it will grow or when you can harvest them. You defray the risk by selling the futures at a fixed cost ahead of time."

Yanluo stomped his foot. "Yes. Are we going to let a mortal speak all day? I could be counting his beads and pressing his body for Juice as we speak."

Hel shook her head. "We're keeping this one, Yanluo. Our domain. Battle-slain."

Yanluo tensed, as did the two beefy specimens beside him. Althir held out her hand, and Rajas thought he saw something flicker in the air between her fingers.

Then Yanluo turned to the door. "You may keep him. I don't need the prattling."

He left, along with his bodyguards. Althir let her arm drop.

Rajas faced Hel. "How many contracts does he hold?"

She closed her eyes. "Nearly all of them. Human lives were expanding, and souls were coming cheap and fast. He quietly offered a good price to nearly everyone, and before anyone realized it—"

"He cornered the market." Rajas nodded. "And then humans, for the most part, stopped dying."

Hel looked up at him. "Can you fix it?"

Of course not. But somewhere down there, Candice was waiting for him, and the only conceivable way back was not to be turned into beads and Juice. "I'll do it."

"What will you need?" Hel asked.

Rajas nearly said, "Nothing," but managed to stop before he opened his mouth. This morning he had found the data that should have made his career—proof of rampant embezzlement. If it hadn't been for Gordon and his co-conspirators, Rajas would be sleeping off a celebration right about now. Instead, they would be, clinking champagne flutes and toasting over his roasted body. Rajas could almost see them.

Then he could see them, on the screen floating above the desk, behind Hel and Althir. Gordon and the other two, Janelle and Peter, sat on the deck of a yacht, laughing and pouring drinks.

Rajas felt his lips curl up at the edges. "I can't do it without my team."

"Al, take care of it. Now, if you'll excuse me…" Hel grabbed a portfolio from the desk and walked out. Rajas shuddered as she squelched by.

Althir stood up and stalked over to him. "The sharpest there is?" she asked.

Her face was inches from his. Storms boiled in her eyes. She looked like she could crack bone between her teeth.

"Yes," he said without squeaking.

She reached down and plucked something off the floor. The flesh-coloured nub disappeared into her mouth. She smiled as she chewed. After she swallowed, she grabbed his right hand and held it up. Though the cut was bloodless, his index finger was missing past the first knuckle.

"I'll enjoy finishing you when you fail."

Before Althir went out to "collect" Rajas's team, she had handed him a stack of documents to read and stashed him in her office, which looked like a time capsule from the mid twentieth century. His eyes scanned over invoices and projections and catalogs of souls, but all he could think was: how would she do it? Spears, hopefully. Something with vicious stabbing, perhaps in the facial area.

The invoices also clarified the celestial divisions of labour. Each logged soul was collected by one being, listed as a psychopomp, on behalf of another, a god. Althir was a psychopomp in service to Hel. Others listed psychopomps serving Thanatos or Osiris or any of another few dozen gods. From the gaps in the dates, it was clear that the records were horribly incomplete and out of date.

The Short Soul

After what Rajas guessed were hours of dragging his eyes across the pages, the office door banged open. Althir slouched against the doorframe.

"Thanks, Ran," she shouted over her shoulder. A woman in a fishnet dress waved from the hall before sloshing away. Then, to Rajas: "Come on. We're going to the Warehouse."

Where a long hall had been earlier, branching out into boardrooms and offices, a short one stood now, leading straight to wide oak doors from a child's idea of a castle. Althir grabbed an iron ring and swung one side open.

The Warehouse must have worked on the same principle as the hallways, because all three culprits stood just inside the door. They stood stock-still like the intergalactic champions of Red Light/Green Light.

All around them, souls flickered in and out of existence. Others froze without vanishing, like Rajas's partners. A couple of souls looked around confusedly. From the papers he had read, he figured these must be the three types of souls that resided in the Warehouse. The flickers were porters, unknowingly shedding their souls each time they popped through a Portal, though the soul soon found its way back. The mannequins were the temporarily dead, whose backups would drag them back to the mortal world when they were installed in a healthy body. The rest, aware and vibrant, were the rare ones—truly dead, soon to be collected for harvest.

Althir waved her hands over the three souls up front, shining some lemon-lime coloured light into their faces. Gordon's assistant, Peter, woke up first. He blinked once and looked around, doe-eyed and gaping, his floppy brown hair nearly covering his eyes in death as it had in life. Janelle was next. She had been the newest analyst to join Gordon's group, but her hip, terminally bored vibe had gotten her close to getting fired, or so Rajas had thought. Now, as she looked around the Warehouse, she seemed the most alert and interested Rajas had ever seen her.

Gordon was last to wake up. Death had momentarily robbed him of his mask-of-cool. He frowned deeply.

Rajas straightened his back. "Good afternoon." Was it afternoon? Time didn't work well here. "I have good news and bad news for you. The good news is that you're my team for an exciting new engagement with a truly unique organization. The bad news is," Rajas said as he caught Gordon's eyes, "you're dead."

Gordon, disappointingly, didn't react. Neither did the others. They all stood quietly, not screaming or crying or anything. Was it shock? Had he been so slow on the uptake?

"Questions?" he prompted.

"I can't be dead." Janelle slipped into a familiar pose, arms crossed and leaning back on a heel. "I have a backup."

Rajas nodded. So had he, though something had happened to it. "You all do. If all goes well, you'll be up and running again in three months."

Gordon finally reacted. "How could it possibly take that long?"

Janelle frowned. "They've got to regrow our bodies. Our old ones are at the bottom of the ocean with the yacht."

Peter, uncharacteristically canny, squinted at Rajas. "What did you mean by 'if all goes well?'"

Rajas smiled. "Like I said, you're all on engagement. Your bonus for successful completion is a reshuffling of your mortal coils."

"And if we don't comply?" Janelle asked.

Rajas shrugged. "Backups aren't foolproof." He shot a look at Gordon. "So. Everyone coming?"

They followed him to the shared office Althir had conspired to grab for them, but afterwards he had to pick up the invoices from Althir's. As he turned away, Gordon stopped him.

"Hey, Rajas. I know I left things a bit bad between us, and I just want to say that it wasn't personal."

"You shot me in the head," Rajas said.

"Nothing personal."

"You said I didn't deserve a wife, a child, or happiness."

"But the murder part—just business." Gordon started to cock his thumb in a finger-gun salute but thought better of it and waved instead.

The office door slammed open. Althir stalked in and folded into a chair, tossing a sheaf of papers onto her desktop.

"Is Gordon back yet?"

Rajas hadn't seen much of him, by luck and design, during the week since they had picked up the team. So far, the engagement had consisted of fact-finding. Gordon and Althir were interviewing the death gods, trying to get a handle on the soul numbers, while Rajas and Peter dug through harvest records and Janelle crunched numbers with an enthusiasm that Rajas had never seen in her. Why would Althir let Gordon out of her sight? She clearly didn't understand who he was.

Rajas tried to ignore the cold feeling in his stomach as he shook his head and got back to work. He sat at a computer terminal, which seemed like it could have been part of the Apollo program judging from its ochre text.

Ten minutes later, Gordon slipped in the door with a smile on his face. Nothing made Rajas more nervous than Gordon looking happy. Gordon took a seat at a plush chair.

"Alright, team. What have we got?" Rajas asked.

Janelle sat at a glass-topped desk in the corner of the office and tapped at a console that rose from its centre. Gordon lounged at another desk, hands behind his head. Peter, of course, barely paid attention. He had a paring knife, the soul-sculpted black blade like the death gods' scythes. He hunched over a desk, tongue out, pressing down on a marble-sized soul bead like he was trying to slice a walnut still in its shell.

How did he get a soul-sculpted knife? There was no telling with Peter. He liked trading for things, but he also liked rifling through people's drawers.

"What we've got," Janelle said, "is trouble." After a few button pushes, a graph projected on the wall. "Mortality is down across the board, across all ages, all socioeconomic classes. In the upper class, in large part due to brain backups, it has dropped to nearly zero. But even miners on Phoebos are living to their mid-hundreds, thanks to cheap nanites."

She tapped some more keys. "And the projections: by the end of three months when the contracts are due, total yield over the past decade will be only half of what Yanluo has locked up. We're stuck."

Althir crossed her arms and chewed her lip. "Ideas?" she asked.

"Depends on our bottom line," Gordon said, feet now cocked up at the corner of Janelle's desk. "Are we just trying to meet our own contract, or do we want to break Yanluo's corner with all the soul contracts?"

"We just want to pay off Yanluo for Hel. The rest of those bastards can swing."

Rajas shook his head. "If Yanluo comes through, he'll own everything. Even if we hold on for now, he'll muscle us out later."

Gordon snorted and shook his head. Althir glared at Rajas. Her temples bulged to an inaudible beat as she ground her teeth. Finally, she said, "Point taken, but getting the death gods to cooperate would take a miracle."

"So," Janelle said. She took a deep breath. "We just need to find a way to kill millions of people."

Althir's face was blank.

"Not kill," Gordon said. "We don't have to gun them down."

Rajas cleared his throat.

Gordon studiously ignored him. "We're just letting nature take its course."

Rajas snorted. "You can always find a way to convince people you're the one in the white hat, can't you? Besides, Janelle, since when do you have a problem with murder?"

Janelle's jaw clenched tight. Gordon looked away. It was Peter who spoke, quietly and without even looking up from the pair of soul beads he had split apart. "It wasn't murder. You were just supposed to get your last backup restored, back from before you started investigating."

Peter took half of the silver bead in one hand and half of the green one in the other. They snapped together like neodymium magnets and flashed brightly.

Janelle chewed her lip. "We didn't realize that Gordon had sabotaged your backup."

Althir perked up. "How?"

Her genuine curiosity boiled Rajas's blood.

Gordon's eyes flinched into a glare for just a moment. "You're one to talk. You didn't mind sending us to the bottom of the Adriatic."

"You had working backups, and you had already murdered me."

Althir stood straighter. "Tell me how, Gordon." Rajas could nearly hear crows cawing, and the clatter of bronze swords.

Gordon's glib gene must have shuddered to a stop. "I have a buddy in private equity. I saw a brochure on Rajas's desk for a smaller discount backup service. I convinced a pal to buy it up and liquidate the assets. Especially the servers."

Stupid. Rajas had been trying to save some cash so he could take Candice to a chateau on Elysium Mons. Wait—was Candice still backed up? Or was she just one car accident away from permanent death?

"Can we scale it up?" Althir asked, oblivious.

Gordon shook his head. "There's massive demand for backups. We can't just take down the industry. And they're constantly improving redundancy and fidelity. In another five years, they'll be able to back up infants and toddlers, too."

Althir nodded. "Other scenarios?"

"What are the parameters?" Gordon asked. "How much control do we really have in the World?"

Althir grimaced. "It takes Juice to affect the physical world, and we don't have a lot left. It cost a lot more than three souls' worth to bring…" She stopped and looked around the room briefly. "Anyway, cost-effective intervention is crucial."

"What about war?" Peter suggested. Althir smiled wistfully.

Gordon shook his head. "After three decades of fighting with robots and hackers, who's going to go back to digging trenches and ducking under bullets?"

"A natural disaster," Peter tried. "Something huge, to take out backup servers and people all at once."

"Too expensive." Althir shook her head. "Can't spare the Juice."

"Besides," Janelle added, "they'd be backed up offsite." She looked at Rajas. "Well, the quality ones would. What about something that just targets the backup servers themselves?"

"Too big," Gordon said. "Also, the death rate is just too low. Almost everyone has nanites now. Aging, disease, injury—most of those get fixed before they're dangerous."

"What about a virus?" Peter threw out.

"Try to keep up, Peter," Gordon said. "Even if we could get a virus past the nanobots, people would just restore from backup."

"But…" he looked down. He didn't go on until Althir prompted him.

"What if the virus was the nanobots? And we targeted babies?"

The pit in Rajas's stomach opened wide. Backups didn't work on brains much younger than two—young minds changed too rapidly. He pictured his and Candice's baby-to-be, cut down by the nanites meant to protect her. He felt sick. Could this body, whatever it was, even throw up?

Jaws hung open around the room. Althir was the first to speak. "That's... a very aggressive idea, Peter. But young souls are underdeveloped. They aren't worth very much."

Janelle cleared her throat. "But that's when souls appreciate the quickest, right? Even though they don't fully mature to seven beads until age eighty, they double in value in the first year."

She danced her fingers over the desk, summoning figures like a wizard calling spirits. She nodded.

"Here," she said, sending the graphs to the wall. "The projections work. By six months, the Heart Seed becomes accessible again, recovering the original investment, and by year one a second bead matures. There are four hundred million babies worldwide. We just need a fraction of a percent to meet our contracts. And if we share the solution, we should clear the corner in time."

"All we have to do is slaughter babies," Rajas added, acid in his voice.

Althir gave a toss of her hand. Janelle was flushed with excitement, and Peter's eternal confusion was overlaid with a glow. Only Gordon frowned. Why? Were there lines even he wouldn't cross?

Althir shook her head. "We'll need a specialist in the World."

Gordon raised his hand fast. Too fast? "I know some people."

Rajas tried to read his face, but it was the same blank shell he always wore when he wasn't giving his snaky grin.

Althir nodded. "We can arrange access to the World for one, I think."

"Seriously?" Rajas said, standing. "That's how we're going to save your job, Althir? Killing babies?"

Althir shrugged. "They're just mortals, Rajas. Dying is what they do."

It wouldn't be the last time Rajas stormed out.

The team gathered around the screen in the work room nearly two months later, all except Gordon. Rajas leaned against the wall, lips pursed sourly. On the screen, a face appeared, filtered through smoke and illuminated by flickering light. It was an eight-year-old boy, hair slicked with gel and pointed into a widow's peak. He squinted into the screen.

"Hello? Is this thing on?" the boy said.

"Reading you loud and clear, Gordon," Janelle said. "What's the word?"

"Well, Father—I mean, my father. I mean, this boy's father." The boy took a deep breath. "This possession thing is hard on syntax. Doctor Maxwell, the father, has loads of books and nanite samples. I think we've got a winner."

"Great job, Gordon," Althir said. "A group of Armageddon cultists should contact you soon, and you can start on making the nanite alterations. Keep us updated."

He frowned. "I'll try. Goat skulls and black candles are pretty expensive on an allowance."

As Janelle sat back down to run optimal virus distribution models, Rajas and Peter were relegated to survey duty. It had been almost two months of tedious work, with Gordon and Janelle making the biggest headway. Rajas felt sick when he thought about it too much.

Of course, the slaughter of millions of innocents appalled him, but that wasn't it. That was the thick scum of horror he had dived beneath to force himself to the office to work. No, this was something else, something insidious.

Gordon wasn't the type to do the hard work. He preferred to sit back as much as possible and collect credit afterwards. Optimizing the reward-to-effort ratio, he called it. Why was Gordon so good at this? Either he'd been a closet psychopath all along, or he had some other angle he was working. Or both.

But what could Rajas do about it? Althir didn't like him much. Gordon had become the de facto leader of the engagement by now, just like in the old days. Rajas couldn't come up with another way of delivering the souls without killing millions of people.

Rajas left and wandered the halls, like he had nearly every day of the engagement, letting them guide him in their meandering way. He heard footsteps ahead and ducked into an alcove to let them pass. It was just Ran, dragging along her fishnet dress, but it could have been one of the others. He'd seen skeletal figures fighting spear-wielding Amazons over a pair of souls. Yesterday Ox-Head had snatched a soul from a sagging man in a cape.

This branch of the hall, laid with dirty pink tiles, was empty. He left footprints in the grime—no one had been this way in a while. At the end of the hall, an open doorway glowed.

When he reached it, Rajas noticed that it wasn't the doorway itself giving off light. In the middle of an expansive room, an enormous yellow globe floated, glowing. Three smaller globes circled it, one blue and green, one half that size and red, and a dull silver one half as small as the last. Each of these three was covered with pinpoints of white light, and though there was an unaccountably large number of them, Rajas could make out each one. They clustered densely in the great cities: in Beijing, in the great bowl of Olympus, and along the flowering lines of Aldrin City's canals.

Rajas stared at Chicago, where he'd taken his last mortal step.

Without the image moving closer or changing size, Rajas's view of the city clarified, as though he were zooming in on the globe. The pinpoints spread wider, became clearer. He could see them, jostling one another, zooming along the L or down the Edens. More lights blipped in and out, far too many to be dying or being born. They must be porting.

Somewhere there would be Candice.

The image shifted and zoomed onto a block downtown, and then into his apartment. A single, glorious light shined there. He kissed his fingers and pressed them on the globe, covering all of northern Illinois with his fingertips.

As he watched, it zoomed in further, until he could see her in her studio. The bump on her belly was visible now. He wished he could reach out to her, to touch her hair or face or the swelling form within her.

Rajas watched Candice for a moment longer and then turned away. On the far wall was a screen, huge like it was trying to be a drive-in movie theater. It spanned the wall, filled with the image of a boiling blue star.

The surface of the star rippled and then burst forth. Colours he could never see in life exploded from the centre, thrust out like all the pent-up rage of the world.

The screen zoomed out, and across the infant universe, Rajas saw stars forming, burning, and exploding, just to reform and burst apart again. The cycle ratcheted, each star being formed from the death rattles of its predecessors.

An idea sparked. Rajas turned on his heel and rushed through the doorway. The halls looked like dirty city streets. Rajas ducked from one alley to another.

It seemed like, when he searched for them, he could never find them. The streets echoed empty. He began to run.

Gordon had something up his sleeve. Rajas was sure of it, although he had no idea what. Maybe he was only projecting, refusing to believe that they would really murder millions of children, but Rajas didn't think so. Rajas had to have a backup plan.

Finally, he found what he sought. Four Valkyries, spears out, surrounded a tall man in a top hat and tailcoat. Huddling along the side off the brick-line hallway were three shaking souls.

"Wait!" Rajas shouted. All five psychopomps turned towards him, eyes hungry. "I know how we can fix all of this. But we'll have to keep it quiet."

Althir pressed her way through the crowd with gentle prods of her spear. On the far side, she could see Hel, but none of her sister Valkyries. It was no surprise. They hated the Pit and all it stood for, but they didn't understand—the Pit was battle. And since this was the night before the contracts' terms were due, battle was nigh.

She had seen Rajas, but now he was lost in the crowd. Gordon was already standing by Hel. Peter and Janelle followed in the gaps Althir left in the crowd.

Flanked by his two goons, Yanluo stood like a king in the centre of the Pit. The screens stood all around him, a needless reminder of the debts owed him.

Hel raised a hand, which did nothing to quiet the throngs. She shrugged and yelled.

"Goddesses, gods, psychopomps, and guiding spirits. We're here to welcome a change in our fates. In the past decades, humans have nearly succeeded in the goal that has driven them since they first poked their heads above the savanna—the defeat of their own mortality, in violation of the order of Nature."

Hel clasped her hands before her breasts. "Gordon, if you would."

Gordon, back from his walkabout as a spoiled kid playing in Daddy's lab, pressed a button on the panel in front of him. A globe flashed on the screen, filled with white dots. The audience stared at the screen like it was about to proclaim salvation or judgment. Which it was.

As Hel explained the virus, only a couple of faces were free of apprehension. Gordon. Yanluo.

A cold sensation crawled up Althir's spine.

Gordon pressed another button. The assembled beings watched for breathless hours as red lights spread across the board, swamping the bright centres in London and Shanghai. All around, the gods stood in perfect silence as red filled the globe. The nanite infection was everywhere. Now it should start culling those too young to back up.

None of the lights blinked out. They waited. There was a lot of foot shuffling and weight shifting. Althir stood still in a balanced stance. Hel frowned and leaned over Gordon to punch the button again.

Yanluo stood. "That seems to be it, yes? Not an impressive showing."

The clocks ticked down the minutes left to midnight, and by all the World's foulest luck, no one died.

Rajas let out a breath he hadn't realized he was holding. The children would live.

The clock in the corner ticked on.

Rajas tore his gaze away. Gordon had wandered to Yanluo's side.

"You did this, didn't you?" Rajas's voice seemed to fill the boardroom, though he hadn't meant to speak. "From the beginning, Yanluo got to you."

"On my first trip out to interview the gods. It's nothing personal, Rajasinator," he said through a cold grin.

Grumbles began to rise.

Yanluo stood and raised his hands. "I'll expect your forfeits at midnight." Ox-Head and Horse-Face stood behind him, arms crossed.

He waved to Gordon and began to leave.

"Actually," Rajas said, "there's still business to conduct."

Gordon frowned as the door to the pit opened. Gasps erupted throughout the room as a bronze-handed skeleton struggled to drag an enormous glowing globe through the room. A banshee and two Valkyries pushed from the back.

"What is this?" Yanluo hissed.

"A sale," said Rajas. "Ten million soul seeds at discount prices. Everything must go!"

"I'll take ten thousand!" shouted a woman draped in black. She had an urn full of silver coins in her hands, which must work as currency, because Althir jumped up and collected it gladly. After that it was a clamour of orders.

It was over in minutes. Globes of light changed hands, and there were smiles all around. Except for two faces.

"How?" was all Gordon could say. Althir looked curious too.

"Let me show you," Rajas said.

The Warehouse doors looked like a shipping container this time. Rajas hauled open a door and stepped inside.

The interior was an industrial freezer. Mannequin-souls hung from the ceiling on hooks. Rajas guided Althir, Hel, and Gordon through a maze of bodies, deep into the cooler. Here, all the souls were flickering. Winged angels, two bronze-handed skeletons, a half-dozen Valkyries, and a hundred other assorted psychopomps stood in a line, working in unprecedented unison, swinging black blades through the flickering figures. Every few swings, a little sliver tumbled to the floor.

Rajas picked one up. Althir frowned.

"A sliver of a bead is worthless. It'll disappear in a minute."

Rajas smiled and picked up a dozen more that fell nearby. Two little cherubs flew by collecting slivers but didn't interfere with him. When enough slivers were in his hand, they snapped together like magnets, forming a new sphere.

"Formed from the remnants of the old. The beads in the porting people should grow back, right?"

Althir nodded absently and grabbed the bead. It was a rainbow of colours.

"How? Psychopomps were ready to riot in the halls."

Rajas nodded. "They just needed something they could work towards. Something where they could see the results of their work. Something where they could screw over their bosses. If you'll note the language in the contracts, the Juice proceeds will go mostly to them."

Gordon shook his head. "I didn't think you had it in you, Rajas."

"I actually got the idea from you."

Gordon frowned.

"Sheep get sheared, Gordon, not slaughtered." He thumped the man on the shoulder.

"Are you sure about this?" Althir asked. "We could use you around here."

"Yeah, I am. If I go soon, I'll just make Alice's birth. Besides, you've still got Janelle."

Althir leaned back in her chair. It was a big one, almost a throne, but still, it seemed dwarfed by the space in her new office.

She nodded. "She's doing well for herself. I even let her take her first soul."

Janelle fingered her necklace, which was hung with a faintly glowing marble.

Rajas nearly asked whose it was when he caught a gleam in Althir's eye. He suppressed a shudder.

Janelle noticed his gaze and smiled. "Yeah, it was Gordon's. It came in a little light, though."

On the screen, the globe of the Earth spun. The lights seemed to leave little trails in his eyes.

"What about Peter?"

"He's already gone back," Althir said.

"Rajas." Janelle looked him in the eyes. "I want to give you my body."

Rajas coughed.

"On Earth. It's ready, and I'm not going to need it."

Rajas looked back and forth between Althir and Janelle. "I've kind of gotten used to being a guy."

Janelle smiled. "Althir can help with that. Fixing it would be easier than making a body from scratch."

Rajas nodded absently. "So, how do we do this?"

"It's easy peasy." She stared at him. "See you again sometime, Rajas."

On the screen, among the billions of lights, Rajas picked one that nestled the coast of Lake Michigan. It seemed to expand and fill his whole vision.

Rajas followed the light home again.

THE MONUMENT
Andrea Bradley

The Hive sprawled before him, red sands seething about it like angry ghosts. It was the only home David had ever known, but he would not mourn its loss. Once, while working on the Monument, he had slipped, gouging his thigh on the rubble. The wound was a sea of blood, clotted with fungal grey stones. He thought of it now, looking at the Hive.

"Hard to believe it's tomorrow, ain't it?" Eli's tinny voice came from behind.

"Yeah," David replied. He didn't turn around. He didn't want to see Eli's pouchy eyes behind his mask, wrinkled up tight as he grinned that stupid grin everyone wore those days.

"What're you doing out here, anyway?"

"Don't know," David said. Eli stood so close that David had to pull his shoulder away.

"C'mon. You got to be sick of staring at that thing. The building's over. We're going home, old man."

"Home," David said. He looked back at the Hive. It was empty, now. A carapace. Everything valuable had been stowed on the ships. Another twenty years or so and all those buildings would fade away. The only thing that would be left on this planet to show they'd been here at all would be the Monument.

"Home," David repeated, quietly.

"Don't know about you, but I'm done with this view," Eli said. "Everyone's on board. Last meal on 54."

With a final look at the abandoned Hive, David nodded at Eli.

"Alright, let's go."

Outside, the winds never died. They scooped up the sands and sent them swirling, sometimes in a hushed dance, more often, in a rage. The rushing winds of 54 were silence, though, compared to the din on deck.

Eli undid the clasps at the back of his neck and pulled his mask away rom his face. He looked at David, and there was that grin. "If you need me, I'll be draining a keg."

Eli moved off into the press of men. Tired men. Hard men. Fools, all of them. They were drinking the last of the malt brewed on 54. Some things weren't worth taking on the flight. At least, that's what the engineers had said—no room for booze on the ships, so enjoy yourselves, boys. David wasn't so sure that was the only reason. The last time he'd taken drink was before they'd closed the mines. They'd known the men were still in there. It took them weeks to get down and would have taken weeks to get them out again. Weeks spent not working on the Monument. The engineers only rolled out the malt when the hard orders had to be carried out, but most of these boys were too young to remember that.

David stepped into the mass of buzzing, steaming bodies. Faces swung by him as he shouldered his way through.

"The old man's joined us."

"Got here right on time. Chief's gonna speak soon."

David nodded through the onslaught of words. He pushed his way to the windows, where Luke sat.

"Mind if I join you?" David asked.

Luke smiled and gestured at the chair across from him, before turning back to the window. If there was one person in the room who would leave David to his thoughts, it was Luke. He followed Luke's gaze.

Rising above the red sands, blacker than the blackest pit in the mines, stood the Monument. It was so tall he couldn't see its peak, but that didn't matter. He would see that shape every time he closed his eyes, until the day he died.

The room changed behind him. A quiet grew in one corner. It spread, snaking through the crowd. David turned. The women were filing in through the door, as the men retreated with wandering eyes.

"Now what d'you suppose that's all about?" Luke whispered. The hush rose back into a din, but David didn't care anymore about the useless, desperate cheer. She was there.

"Men." The comscreen flickered to life. Those stony, sorry men tore their eyes off the women and looked to the Chief Engineer. His shoulders loomed above the crowd, as square as the Monument's base. His narrow eyes stared, unseeing, over the crowd.

"And women," he said. "Builders, all of you. Of the Monument, and of our people. You have completed the greatest endeavour of our civilization on 54. Be proud of what you have accomplished. Your bodies and your sweat built the Monument. For that, enjoy yourselves on this last night. You have a long journey ahead. For, tomorrow, you leave 54. You leave for home!"

The men roared, so the Chief's words to the women could barely be heard.

"To build is to be remembered," he said at last, and the comscreen flickered still.

"You believe that?" Luke asked softly. "I mean, you ever really think about what that means? Been hearing those words all my life, but lately I've been thinking about them. If we want to be remembered, then why are we leaving?"

"Chief says we're going home," David said.

"It never made much sense to me, them always saying that, and no one ever talks about it."

"Until now," David said. He caught Luke's eye. Luke was a smart boy, and he nodded quickly.

"Of course. Don't know what I'm going on about. To going home." Luke lifted his glass.

"Go easy on that malt, now," David said. He gripped the boy's shoulders and stood to face the crowd.

The men and women had begun to mingle, like water filtering through sand. Soon they would all be drunk, and David didn't like to think what would come after that. He scanned the masses, the dun suits blending into each other until the whole deck seemed like one monstrous being, with hundreds of gibbering mouths.

There. She was against the wall, looking, for him.

David felt hollow as he pushed into the crowd. The bodies swallowed him, and she disappeared, sending his heart into his throat. It took immeasurable moments to reach her side.

"David," she said, taking his hand.

He smiled at her. It had been two years since the last time he'd seen her, and almost another two years since the time before that. He had been with Magda more than any of the other women. The engineers never would have allowed it if they'd known, but David was getting so old it was bound to happen. There were only so many women to go around. Most of the others were faceless to him. Magda, she was different.

"You okay?" he asked.

"Okay," she nodded. She said some other things after, but nothing he could understand. They weren't supposed to be able to talk at all, the builder men and the women. The engineers made sure of that, but David had long figured out there were ways to talk that didn't require words.

It was nearly dawn when the soldiers came. Those left standing swayed stupidly. A few still argued or laughed, harsh and aggressive in the remnants of the night. The soldiers carried the unconscious ones and herded the rest off the deck. David cast one last look out the window. The rising sun bloodied the sands, but the Monument was still in shadow.

"Guess I've already said goodbye," David muttered. He turned and followed the line out the door. It was the same as nearly every other morning of his life, except that the women were marching with them, and they weren't in the Hive. The soldiers led them down a hall, into the depths of the ship. The lights were spaced further and further apart until he could barely make out the back in front of him. At some point, the soldiers turned them through a door and down metal steps that rang under their boots. When they stopped, he could tell they were in a wide space, though he could see little more than the glint of a helmet or the tip of a gun.

"Can I sleep now?" a voice slurred behind him.

The soldiers said nothing. He heard them draw back to the stairs, felt the air grow closer, as though they were taking it with them.

"There are latrines along the wall and food in the lockers. Keep yourselves strong. It will be a hard journey." The soldier said something then that sounded like the women's tongue, but David was too surprised to hear one talking to be sure. Then the stairs rang still, the door hissed shut, and they were alone.

As the lights grew brighter, David turned to take the room in. It was vast, but not large enough to comfortably hold the hundreds of people now crammed into it. Bunks were stacked against the walls in tiers of seven, starting right beside the metal latrines. In another corner stood five tall lockers, each as wide as three men and stretching to the ceiling. There were no windows and no doors except the one they had used coming in.

The drunks began to moan from the floor. Some of them stumbled towards the cots, throwing themselves on the nearest ones. When the others realized that there wouldn't be enough to go around, fights broke out, but most of them were too far gone to do any harm. David looked for Magda. She was speaking to two of the other women, grey-haired, like her. David pushed his way through to her and grabbed her hand. She looked at him with surprise.

"We need to find somewhere to sleep."

She shook her head a little, tried to pull away, but he didn't let her.

"No, not that. I don't want that now. Look." He pointed to the bunks, where a clutch of men were arguing about who would get the bottom rows. She turned away from him and began speaking rapidly to the two women, pointing at the bunks until they nodded. Magda turned back to him with a stranger's eyes. Which was what she was, after all. He dropped her hand, and she gave him a hard smile.

Magda spoke loudly and the women who'd kept their heads through the night gathered around her, listening. With half the women in the room behind her, Magda moved to the bunks and the women climbed past her, to the top rows. They were sitting, two to a bunk, their territory claimed, before the arguing men realized what was happening. They stopped shouting at each other and turned on the women.

"Always wondered what you girls did in the Nest all day. Plan to keep each other entertained, is that it?"

"Come down here, I'll keep you warm."

Their jeering didn't last long. With many of the women sharing and many people still passed out on the floor, there were enough bunks for the rest. The men still standing soon drifted away to find their own beds. David walked down the line until he found Magda, almost at the far end of the room. She was on a top bunk, alone, far from the latrines. He climbed up to join her. Together, they slept as the dead.

Andrea Bradley

David woke to the stink of vomit and stale sweat. He was alone in bed. Below him, clutches of people huddled in the yellow light. Their murmured conversations held the pitch of fear. He pulled his bulk over the rail and climbed to the floor. The room reminded him of the work site after a storm. Everyone had been picked up, tossed, and thrown down somewhere new, so a man no longer knew his place. People looked at him with pleading eyes as he walked by, but no one called out. Every so often, the room vibrated with a deep groan, as though the ship was trying to pull itself apart. He picked his way through to the lockers. Eli was talking over the men gathered around him.

"There's no soldiers. No one's gonna tell us when to eat, what to do, who to fuck. We got to decide that for ourselves, so we got to be smart about things. Could be days before we reach home. Could be weeks. It might look like there's more than enough food to get us there, but that don't mean nothing at all."

"So what are you trying to say, Eli? You're gonna decide when we eat and fuck?" one of the men called out.

"Maybe not the second one," Eli laughed. "But someone's got to be in charge of the food and water."

"You might be too late for that," another said.

David followed Eli's gaze as he looked to the lockers. The women were there. Maybe as many as took over the beds last night. They were talking and pointing, a mirror to the men.

"See?" Eli said. "It's happening already. They're gonna take everything for themselves if we let them. We got to have men guarding the lockers day and night."

"You should talk some sense into them." Luke spoke at David's shoulder.

"Those lockers. Looks like they'd hold enough supplies for months. What's the problem?" David asked.

"We could only get one of them to open," Luke said quietly. "Rest are locked up."

"That right? And I suppose Eli's been on about it all morning."

"Pretty much."

"And the women?"

"That one you were with last night—she got them going." Luke grinned. "I've been watching them. They're counting the food."

David looked back at the women. Luke was right. They were pointing at the rows and talking to each other, counting on their fingers. David walked over to them, ignoring Eli's rising voice. They watched him suspiciously until Magda nodded at him.

"How much?" he asked. He pointed at the food and at the girls counting, opening his palms flat. Magda raised both hands, fingers spread. She closed and opened her hands three times. David looked at the open locker. Thirty days. Eli was right. It seemed like more than enough, but no one had ever told them how long it would take to get where they were going. David thought back to the mines, to the weeks of sulphuric darkness. His throat tightened.

Think. David pressed the panic down to the place he stored it, deep in his gut. It didn't make sense. Why bury them in here with food? They were meant to survive.

"Eli is right," David said. "We got to be careful with the food and water."

Twenty voices went quiet as soon as he raised his.

"The women say we've got thirty days of supplies." He held up his hands like Magda so they'd understand. "Should be plenty to get us through to the other side, if we're careful."

"We can't trust them," Eli said. "They could be lying about how much there is so they can keep most of it for themselves."

"Don't be a fool. They know we'd figure them out, quick enough."

Eli's eyes flared.

"What do we know about feeding people?" David continued. "That's women's work. I say we let them decide how much we all get each day. Put a guard up if you want, make sure no one's stealing. But we got to trust each other, work like we do every day. It's no different in here."

No one spoke. It had been years since he'd had reason to say so much, but he knew they'd listen.

For the first two weeks, it worked. At least, no one fought over food. Yet, the other four lockers remained shut fast, their faces as smooth and impassive as the Monument. Then one of the latrines clogged. The stench became tangible, a foulness so thick that the grime on their bodies felt saturated with shit. But still, the sharp tang of sex peppered the air, and men could be heard talking about the baths that were waiting at the other end. The kegs and the food. The clean clothes and the outside. No one talked about the soldiers or the engineers, where they were hiding on the ship. No one even bothered with the door at the top of the stairs anymore.

By day twenty-five, everyone was talking about one thing only. They were running out of food. The women began to stretch their rations thin, but hunger did strange things to the room. Eli began talking about destiny, and people started to listen. He said they were meant to be remembered, that this was a test, to see who was worthy. The strong had survived the building of the Monument, and the strong would survive the journey home.

"Where do you really think we're going?" Luke asked one day. "You can tell me now, there's no one listening."

David gave him a long look. Dark circles had overtaken Luke's eyes. None of them slept much anymore.

"Wherever we're going," he said at last, "it's not our home."

"You know what I think? I think we never left. We finished the Monument and they didn't need us anymore, so they put us in here to die."

"There was nothing left on 54. We emptied the Hive."

"We don't know that. Sure, we cleared our sector out. But the rest? None of us ever saw where the soldiers lived, or the engineers, let alone the Chief. Those stairs? I bet if we could open that door, we'd find the outside. We'd be dead."

"But we were on one of the ships. We went through the airlocks. If Chief wanted us dead, why lock us in here with enough supplies to last a month?" David asked.

"Maybe he just didn't want our deaths on his hands."

"Never stopped him before."

David thought about the miners, sealed up to die. That was because it would have been more trouble than they were worth to get them out. If Chief wanted the builders dead, it would have been more efficient to just kill them, and so that's what he would have done.

The Monument

"We're on a ship, Luke. There's no mistaking it."

"If you say so," Luke said, but the lines stayed deep between his brown eyes.

On day thirty-five, they ran out of food. There was enough water left for a week at least, but food had bound them together. With empty bellies, they began to fall apart. Some turned on the women. The women were too generous with the rations, they said, forgetting that only a week prior, they had been begging for more. David led some of the others in a renewed attack on the remaining lockers. By the second day of water rations, he decided it would be better to conserve their strength. Some of them were already half gone. David tried not to see Luke's wasting frame, the lean muscle of youth always the first casualty of starvation.

On day thirty-seven, a wailing woke David from a dream that the ship was tearing apart. All the women who could stand were gathered around a body curled on the floor. David climbed to the ground. It was too small, that body. Nothing left inside.

"Can't just leave it there, and if those women don't shut up, more are gonna join it." Eli's voice was flat.

David looked around. "We got to put her in the locker. Let the women say their goodbyes, then let's move her."

"Good idea, old man. Add to our stores."

David turned away from Eli's hoarse laughter, joined Magda and told her what they had planned. She understood. The women were too weak to mourn for long, and too weak to protest when David, Eli, and Magda hauled the corpse into the locker. Afterwards, David and Magda climbed to their bunk, where they lay, empty, for hours.

Eli's voice was too loud in a room of the dying. The wrongness of it hauled David back into the world.

"There'll be more soon. They're gonna die no matter what happens now. We got to prove we're the strong ones. Strong enough to do what it takes to survive. We pick the ones who aren't gonna make it anyway, and we do what we got to. We survive."

David sat up. The air pulled away with a rushing sound until he was looking down from high above, seeing Eli through a red haze. He hadn't eaten in days, had cut back on his rations before they ran out. Now he wished he'd kept them so he had the strength to get down there and break Eli's neck.

And Eli wasn't alone. At least a dozen gaunt men gathered around him, and the body beneath his boot. Where were the rest? They were like him, pinned by this rushing wind, stronger than any storm in the sands. Eli was right. The strong would survive.

David fought the winds. He pushed himself over the edge and half-fell to the floor. Red, then black, and then nothing.

The rasping rocked him to his knees. The sound of a man taking off his mask outside. Only now it came from a scrawny boy a few feet away. Luke. His eyes bulged; his limbs flopped. A knee pressed on his throat, above it, Eli, bearing his weight down with the last of his strength.

David let the winds rush over him. They pushed him forwards. Blindly, he fell against Eli. His legs crushed something soft and brittle, but his hands found Eli's face. They tore and pulled and when that wasn't enough, he bit. The winds swallowed all sound, but when he was done, everything died.

They added two more corpses to the locker.

David was too weak to move. Someone dragged him to a bed, gave him water. He lay and waited for someone to take Eli's place.

On day thirty-eight, the second locker opened.

David's strength returned. He watched the others and rarely slept. For some, the new locker gave them hope. They were meant to survive, and now they knew how long the supplies had to last. For others, all hope died. Three lockers left meant over a hundred more days in the room. Even with the new food, some of the sick died and were added to the first locker. Eli had been right. The strong would survive.

By the time the second locker ran out, there were no longer people in the room. There were fighters, ravers, and dead ones. The fighters stalked the room with burning eyes. They dragged women from their beds until some of the women became fighters, who dragged others from their beds, to keep themselves safe. The ravers ranted, at first to each other, later to the walls. They conjured hope and crushed it, running through every vision of what lay ahead. The dead ones had given up. They lay in corners, shoved off the beds by the fighters, ranted at by the ravers, as the waste of their bodies pooled around them.

Magda was something different. He watched her from their bed, as she pulled the latest one to die to the centre of the floor. David didn't recognize the sunken features, but Magda wiped the woman's brow with a mother's care. She stripped the body of its rags and set the cleaner ones aside. The rest she wrapped with the body in a sheet from the dead woman's bunk. There was no wailing for this one. Magda pulled the body to the lockers and then moved to the next sick bed. David watched and waited.

When they were halfway through the third locker, people got sick. Their insides seeped into the outside world. All of them were rotting alive. But still, David and Magda stayed strong.

They slept together every night, no longer trying to understand each other with words. Sometimes, lying next to each other, David could forget his crawling scalp and the layers of filth coating his skin, his tongue. Her warm body filled a crevice in his chest he hadn't known was there. Magda made this existence bearable. Magda, and knowing that the end had to come soon. The engineers had left them with five lockers to get them through the journey. One at a time, just in time, the lockers had opened.

When they were partway through the fourth locker, he felt the roundness of Magda's belly. As he slid his hand over it, Magda placed hers on top. David knew then that he would make it through.

They had gone through just two days with the fifth locker when the door at the top of the stairs opened. David and Magda lay in their bunk, their rations piled around them. They hadn't gone to the floor in days. David didn't know how many others were left, but it couldn't have been more than a few dozen. Five full lockers. They were ending where they'd begun.

The soldiers came down wearing masks. They didn't say anything, just grabbed and pulled the people who could still stand, pushed them into a double-file line. Without a word, they marched the strong ones, the survivors, out of the room.

Light seared through David's haze. Magda's bony hand was in his own, and he clung to it. Long before his eyes could adjust, he knew that he was not on 54. It was cool and bright, Magda was beside him, and they were free from the room. His chest flared with a feeling he had suppressed for so long it was habit. Wherever this was, they could make it home.

His sight returned just as Magda was pulled from his grasp. They were still inside, standing in front of a wall-length window. The world before him was featureless and white everywhere. Everywhere, that is, except for the grey sprawl of a Hive that cut through it all, and next to that, rubble around a dark base. He would see that shape every time he closed his eyes, until the day he died, and he knew how it began. Magda was already gone. The Chief's voice rose above the buzzing in David's mind.

"Builders. Welcome to 55."

THE UNSEEN FACE OF THE MOON BUSINESS
Diana Părpăriță

On the morning of her big meeting with the representative from New Environment, Carol marched into her office late, as usual, looking like a distinguished white male in his early forties, complete with greying hair at the temples—a nice touch she constantly congratulated herself for—and a slightly cosmeticized version of her real nose—almost mainstream but still personal. She found that being a man of that race and age highly increased her chances of nailing a good contract.

She greeted her secretary, who was ogling her in a way that showed she hadn't yet found out Carol's real gender, and began complaining about the traffic.

"Good morning, Mr. Maddison," her secretary answered perkily. "The traffic was fine when I got to work, and I had you logged in at nine, punctual as usual, so none of that nonsense about traffic to the higher ups!"

Carol's secretary, Clarice, had a frightful devotion to her, which made Mr. C. L. Maddison spend most of his mornings simultaneously stuck in a meeting at the office and stuck in traffic on his way to work.

Clarice's loyalty, while owing partly to her weakness for greying temples, was based primarily on gratitude. Few employers, if any, would have hired a girl who displayed Clarice's looks, particularly since plastic surgery had become affordable. Clarice looked like she weighed three hundred pounds at least. Carol had never seen her eat anything but raw vegetables, and she had wondered how she managed to keep her round shape, until Clarice had revealed her little secret: implants. Clarice called her obsession with looking unfashionable a form of feminism, and she had a long and complicated theory of how it was fighting the objectification of women, which Carol hadn't bothered to listen to. On top of surgically enhancing her hips and waistline to look overweight, Clarice had also acquired a set of deep, scar-like wrinkles, despite being in her early twenties, and she would add at least one impressive wart to her face or hands after every paycheck.

"Thank you, Clarice," Carol said in a deep, synthesized voice, enveloping the girl in a warm smile. "I don't know how I'd manage without you."

The meeting with Mr. Edward Lee from New Environment didn't go smoothly. Carol could feel something was off the minute he walked in. He was obviously someone big, too big to be handling this sort of deal. It wasn't just his clothes that looked expensive, but his face too. Not the standard face that every businessman thought to be part of the work uniform. Sure, it had that standard early-forties feel to it, and the eyes and nose were pretty standard-looking, but the shape of his face and his lips were definitely customized. His lips, in particular, looked like they might be breaking some unwritten dress code. She assumed they were the work of some emerging artist. Well-to-do businessmen sometimes invested in the work of a yet unknown cosmetic surgeon on the off chance that they'd get famous and their work would one day be worth a fortune. Probably some up-and-coming neo-Baudelairean artist, Carol thought. The man was obviously a gambler.

His handshake proved equally foreboding. Strong and prolonged, confident to the point of intrusiveness, the handshake of someone who was already sure he'd win.

"Well, Mr. Lee," Carol thought while smiling her best professional smile and showing him to his seat, "if you think you can get our land for free, you've got another thing coming."

She began her presentation, watching him closely as she went through her slides. Mr. Lee watched her in silence, not even looking at the pictures and the graphs she was showing him. Not a single muscle on his face moved when she talked about the great location on the visible side of the Moon, with a fabulous view of the Earth, and there was no change when she talked of the topography of the area: a spacious crater, perfect for an office building or a golf course, and perfectly safe—the chances of another meteorite hitting the same spot were so slim they weren't even worth considering. She'd hoped he'd at least betray some interest in the underground resources, but halfway down the list his mind seemed to have wandered off altogether, his eyes staring blankly at her nose. Carol was beginning to believe the story he'd told her on the phone the day before, that New Environment were thinking of building a warehouse on the Moon simply because it was cheap and close enough to Earth for transportation costs to be minimal, and he was just shopping around for the best price. She'd hoped he was looking for something more specific than that, something that would raise the price she could ask for. But, of course, if there'd been anything of value there, her own company would have exploited it for themselves. Still, she went diligently down the list of minerals, watching his face for the faintest reaction. Then, suddenly, there was a loud beep. He gave a start, blinked, and looked at his watch.

"I'm going to be late for my nephew's baseball practice," he said. "I'm sorry I can't stay through the rest of your presentation, but I've seen enough. What's your price?"

Carol stared at him in disbelief. Baseball practice? He was already standing up. She tried to think fast, calculate how much she could ask for.

"Twenty-two billion," she said firmly.

Mr. Lee's eyes widened. The price was ten percent over the market value. Carol fought the instinct to bite her lip. For a few moments, they stared at each other in silence. Then she kicked the sweetness level of her smile up a notch and said, "Of course, there's no need to make a decision right now. We can't leave your nephew waiting, after all. Perhaps I could go over the data again and offer you a better price tomorrow, when you have more time. I wouldn't want it to look like I'm pressuring you."

For a moment, his eyes seemed to widen even more, and then he smiled, a perfectly unreadable professional smile.

"No, it's quite all right," he said. "I'll sign the contract now. There's no need to waste another day of my time for a small matter like that."

"What's next? Your niece has ballet practice tomorrow?" Carol yelled at the empty chair in front of her when Mr. Lee was safely out of the building. She felt the voice-correction bots in her throat choking her, and she wanted to cough them out, as if she could do that without their box. She coughed out a string of curses instead, poring over her data furiously, trying to figure out what she'd missed.

"Mr. Rosmund says he wants you in his office," Clarice announced.

Carol nodded and kept shuffling through her graphs.

"Mr. Rosmund, your boss," Clarice insisted. "Little guy, big ego, bigger job, can fire us… Ring any bells?"

"Uh-huh," Carol said, her eyes still on the display.

"Would you like us both fired by noon, Mr. Maddison? Or would right now be more convenient?" Clarice asked pointedly.

The growling noise she received in answer did not bode well, but Carol did get up from her chair and leave the office.

Mr. Rosmund greeted Carol at the door and gave her a pat on the back, calling her Mr. Maddison out loud for his secretary to hear before closing the door.

"Heard you sold our piece of the Moon, Maddison!" he said, giving her another pat on the back. "For twenty-two billion!"

"I'm sorry, sir," Carol answered stiffly. "I'm not a real estate agent. I did my best."

"You did great!" Rosmund said, laughing. "That piece of land's been sitting there gathering moon dust since we bought it. Worst deal we ever made. But the Moon craze was in full swing, we thought we could use it or resell it, make a fortune either way."

"I sold it for half of what we paid for it," Carol pointed out.

"Before the bubble burst, Maddison, before the bubble burst. Prices went down, they're still going down. I just got off the videophone with Charley: they sold their piece of the Moon for half that price. He called to brag that he'd got rid of it and even made some money off of it. He wanted to know if we'd still be paying taxes for our piece of moon dust for the next five hundred years. You should've seen his face when I told him."

"Who did they sell it to?" Carol snapped.

"I don't know. Some idiot, I guess. The Moon's worthless. Come on, don't make that face, Mad, I'm congratulating you here! I'd offer you a promotion, but the only way you can get any higher is if you take my job, and I'm not giving that up. How about a raise instead?"

"I screwed up," Carol answered. "I could've got more money for it.

A lot more."

"That's just bragging, Maddison. We all know you're good, no need to rub it in."

Carol gave him an exasperated look.

"I'm worried about you, Maddison," Rosmund went on. "You're doing crazy things, crazier than usual, apologizing for things you do right, beating yourself up over things you should be celebrating... Take the rest of the day off. Go home, eat something. Those bots cover you up well enough to make you look like you've got meat on your bones, but you still look haggard."

"Maybe I've had surgery," Carol said with a thin smile. "A new design, worth a fortune."

"Don't joke about that, Mad," Rosmund said. "I know your type. You're a neo-narcissist, aren't you? You'd never alter a thing, never go under the laser for anything. I've known you since you were an intern. All the others were talking about was getting cosmetic surgery. All you were talking about was getting cosmetic bots. And when you got your bots, you still didn't look normal. Still kept that nose of yours. If you weren't so good, I'd have fired you for it a long time ago. But if you can sell our piece of Moon over the market price, you can come to work even without the bots for all I care."

Carol got home in a bad mood, and she could barely stop fidgeting long enough to take off her bots. She had a shower, scrubbing away the feeling of their little mechanical legs until her skin began to peel off. Coming out of the shower, she put on a light silk robe with a brightly coloured peacock painted on it. She poured herself a glass of icy water and leaned on the living room sofa, dialing her best friend's number.

A few moments later, Marla's face popped up on the videophone's screen. Carol found it hard to tell her friends apart now that they all had mainstream faces, but Marla still had something that set her apart from all the others: her sneer. Her lips may have looked like everyone else's, but they twitched in a half-disgusted, half-mocking way every few words, and her eyes may have been the latest fashion in shape and colour, but they had a way of sparkling every now and then. Her skin folded around them when she smiled, in a way that belonged to Marla and Marla alone.

"Oh, God, not again!" Marla said, covering her eyes in mock horror. "Don't do that! I've got kids, remember? What if Nick walked in and saw you like that on my screen? He's three! He'd be scarred for life! At least do something about that nose!"

Carol grinned. The problem of her unaltered nose was a comforting routine after her failure at work.

"You know why Mary won't talk to you anymore, right?" Marla went on. "Jake says he wants a nose just like yours when he grows up. She's having him see a therapist for it, but, you know, you're a bad influence."

Carol laughed. Mary's five-year-old son, Jake, had always been fond of her nose. When he was a baby, he used to stretch out his tiny hands, grab her nose, and laugh. It used to be his favourite game. And it had always freaked Mary out.

"So, what's with the call?" Marla asked. "Don't tell me you missed my face." She grinned and batted her eyelashes trying to look cute.

"I met a guy at work," Carol said, spying Marla's reaction from under lowered eyelids.

"Cute?"

"He practically robbed me!" Carol snapped. "We talked for three hours. Three! And he just sat there, staring at me. Do you have any idea how intimidating that is? I didn't know if he was even listening, if he even cared, if he knew that I was bluffing, if... It was like talking to a wall. How do you get a wall to buy anything? Overpriced or not."

"Sounds like someone's got a crush," Marla said. "So, is he cute? Big muscles? Nice abs? Cute butt?"

"Why does that always matter with you? He got the best end of our deal—his looks have nothing to do with it! And, anyway, why muscles? Why are big muscles still a turn on? In evolutionary terms, that made sense thousands of years ago. Back in the stone age, big muscles meant 'can fight big beasts, bring home big dinner, make strong children.' It made sense to find that attractive then. But now muscles are useless. What brings home the bacon is big brains."

Marla winced.

"A vegan bacon, synthesized out of soy beans, just so no one would be offended," Carol added, trying to win back her audience.

Marla nodded with a big grin of approval.

"Muscles are useless," Carol went on. "Brains should be sexy. If our bodies were to select sex partners based on our evolutionary needs, then computer coding should be sexy. You'd look at this long line of solid coding and think, 'I want to hump the guy who wrote that!' Why muscles? Why is it still muscles?"

"Because you can steal someone's code, but you can't rip their abs off and wear them yourself. Looking good shows you have the money to look good. And that means you have the means to bring home the vegan bacon. Face it, honey, there's nothing that says big bucks like a designer nose."

"Or designer abs?" Carol insisted. "Why don't you just get little logos on your nose and chin, make sure everybody knows who made them and how much they cost!"

"If I can afford a brand that's big enough, trust me, I will!"

Carol sighed, but the argument had cheered her up, like a cold shower on a hot summer day.

"Let's go have something to eat, and you can tell me all about the nose logo of your dreams," she said. "My treat."

"Oh no. You're going to wear that again, aren't you?"

"What?"

"Your nose. I don't want to be seen with it in public."

"It doesn't bother me," Carol replied.

"You're not the one who has to look at it!"

"I could wear the bots," Carol conceded.

"Your work outfit? My husband will think I'm cheating on him again."

"I could wear my other outfit..."

"That's too flashy. It's good for clubbing and for picking up guys, but—"

"So we'll go to a club."

"I'm married, remember? I doubt my husband would want to stay home and babysit while I go around picking up guys and getting drunk with you. You go, have fun, screw that guy from work, or screw someone who looks like him, get him out of your system and—"

"I don't want to sleep with him, or anyone who looks like him," Carol protested. "It just drives me nuts that he won."

"So he got the better end of a deal. So what? That used to happen all the time when you were new and fresh out of school. Don't tell me he makes you feel young again," Marla insinuated.

"He makes me feel like an idiot!"

"Now that's love."

"He didn't even blink at my price," Carol went on, ignoring her. "He didn't even haggle. He would've paid more for that piece of land, a lot more, I just know it. I just can't figure out why. And I was a freaking coward and didn't go high enough and—"

"Is there something you're not telling me, Pinocchio?" Marla interrupted her, raising an eyebrow. "When did you guys get into real estate?"

"We didn't. It's an old plot on the Moon that no one's using. We were going to build offices there, but they decided, after they'd bought it, that it would cost too much."

"I know. Ted keeps saying it would be cheaper to terraform the whole Moon than to build a few dozen independent domes."

"Can you terraform the whole Moon?" Carol asked pensively.

Marla shrugged.

"Ted should know, he's the scientist," she answered. "I'll ask him when he gets home. He's been working late this week. Something about a merger. Meanwhile, you go have fun and let go of that deal. It's done, you signed the papers, move on. And get laid, it'll do you good."

The Laser Room was packed, as usual. The colourful lights that gave the place its name were bouncing off a myriad of cosmetic bots at seizure-inducing speed, giving off a ghostly aura to the crazed machines that couldn't keep up, momentarily shaping silhouettes of noses, chins, and cheeks outside the dancers' faces when the cloaking failed. But in the Laser Room, no one expected you to look like you pretended to look, anyway. More than beauty, the cosmetic bots offered anonymity. Carol couldn't imagine how anyone could have gone clubbing in the days when they couldn't alter their looks for the night, how they could get drunk, or dance on tables, or make out with complete strangers and still keep their respectable jobs afterwards. The bots gave everyone complete freedom.

The Unseen Face of the Moon Business

No one knew who you were, except for the bouncer who checked your DNA ID. You could end up in a hotel room with your boss or a business partner, and no one would ever know it, not even you.

"Hey, babe, it's your lucky night!" a man yelled in her ear, putting his arm around her waist. He looked like a hulking pro wrestler with the face of a choir boy clumsily slapped on top of his massive body. His breath gave off the sickening smell of alcohol. "Why don't we leave early and get a room upstairs?"

"And what makes you think I want to sleep with you?" Carol asked, pinching his arm between her index finger and her thumb and removing it from her waist with great care, as if it were some unpleasant-smelling piece of garbage.

"Because you look hot," the man answered.

"I'm sorry, I forgot to bring my jerk-repelling wrinkles," Carol said in a light, conversational tone. "Do I really look that desperate?"

The man gave a raucous laugh.

"You're a good one," he said, trying to grab her waist again.

"Should I tell the bouncer you got in with a fake ID?" Carol went on, maneuvering her way out of his arm's reach.

"I'm as old as it says I am!" the man protested.

"Yes, but are you human? They don't let pigs in here, you know."

He swore crudely and left in pursuit of the next woman to walk in. Carol scanned the crowd of off-the-shelf faces impatiently. They were all good looking, all perfect copies of the latest Hollywood heartthrobs, but none of them stood out. Finally, she noticed a man sitting at the bar, staring at her. He looked familiar, like they all did, with a face that was perfectly mainstream save for his lips. The lips were remarkable, to the brink of obscenity. Carol decided they would have looked good on an attention-seeking pop star. On the quiet face of this mainstream blond, blue-eyed young man, they looked out of place. She wished he had a more personalized face to go with the lips. Then she realized what was so startling about them: they were an exaggerated version of the lips Mr. Lee had worn to their business meeting that day.

"So there really is some guy out there making these things," she thought with a sigh, sitting down at the bar next to him and ordering a martini.

"First time at the Laser Room?" she asked, turning to him.

"Is my face that different?"

"No, but you look like you've never seen me before."

"You caught me," he answered with an embarrassed laugh. "I'm Edward."

"Laureen," Carol answered, shaking the hand he was offering her. Most people wouldn't give their real names at a club, but she felt safe with her middle name—it sounded fake enough.

"Nice lips," she added. "Where did you get them?"

"From my mother."

"Does she buy your underwear too?"

"No, she couldn't show it off to her friends, anyway. But there is this muffler she has me wear..."

"Is it pink?"

"Red with gold stripes. And it used to be hers."

"Family heirloom. I see. I have one of those from Grandma Laureen."

"Family heirloom?"

"Red and gold muffler. They were really popular back in the day, apparently."

"Too bad no one told our relatives that these things go out of fashion."

"Too bad publicly humiliating your children and grandchildren never goes out of fashion."

"I think we might need therapy for it."

"Would you like to go somewhere more intimate for a bit of therapy?" Carol asked with an inviting smile. "I live across the street."

The trick to having sex with someone you'd met in a club was to keep the lights on, so that your eyes could successfully contradict what your other senses were telling you. The bright, white light in her apartment was cold enough to ruin any mood. Carol instinctively closed her eyes while kissing him. His lips tasted like metal—the impersonal taste of cosmetic bots. But the inside of his mouth tasted good, real. She could feel his hands through her coating, an indistinct, coded touch reproduced by the bots, not authentic enough to feel like human touch, but precise enough that she could tell their exact location on her butt. She struggled to push her tongue deeper, trying desperately to feel and taste every part of him that was uncovered, every part that she could reach.

"Would you have slept with me if you knew what I looked like?" he asked as they were lying in bed afterwards.

He was still wearing his bots, of course, and she thought that the question was pretty pathetic. And odd. Judging by how personalized his outfit was, he certainly had enough money to have made his usual face and body gorgeous... or at least socially acceptable.

"I was drunk, and I was in the mood," she answered. "Now get out of here—I want to take off my 'makeup.'"

"Take it off," he said. "I want to know what you look like."

"I'm talking about the cosmetic bots," she pointed out.

"I know."

Bringing him home had definitely been a bad idea.

"Suit yourself," she said, heading into the bathroom. She figured one look at her real nose would have him running out the door.

He came to watch. She opened the medical cabinet, pressed her finger on the touch screen of the box of cosmetic bots.

"Clear," she said.

A beep acknowledged her command, and her body turned grey—the standby colour of the cosmetic bots. The coating of nanobots began sliding off her finger into the box, accompanied by the usual tingle all over her body. As soon as the bots turned grey, her nose was visible, but he didn't even make the initial twitch of disgust her friends always did. He watched with a sort of fascination as the bots trailed off her body, revealing her feet, her legs, her left arm, left shoulder.

"Disappointed?" she asked when they were migrating off her face.

"That your eyes aren't yellow?" he joked.

"That they aren't Asian," she said to avoid mentioning the nose.

"You seem to think Asian eyes are a big turn on," he said with a wide grin.

"They're eye-catching," she answered. "Great for picking up weirdos in night clubs when you're drunk."

"Too bad you can't get rid of them later," he said, bowing to kiss her left shoulder.

The touch startled her. It felt different than the impulses transmitted by the bots. His tongue brushed against her shoulder for an instant—real flesh against real skin.

"That's why my friends have stable relationships," she thought. "Someone you trust enough to let him see you without your makeup."

Of course, her friends had all had surgery. There was nothing to trust, nothing "unsociable" to show.

"Yeah, too bad I can't get rid of you," she said, drawing closer to the medical cabinet so she wouldn't accidentally lift her finger off the box and stop the flow of cosmetic bots. Breaking contact always resulted in nasty errors, and it would take her half a day to get them fixed. No man was worth that.

She did manage to get rid of him in the morning. He put his clothes on almost obediently and let her push him out the door. Two seconds later, the doorbell rang.

"C. L. Maddison!" he said when she opened the door.

Carol felt she was turning pale.

"It says Maddison on the door," he added. "Do you know a C. L. Maddison? Is he your husband?"

"No!"

"Boyfriend? Roommate?"

"I live alone."

He heaved a deep sigh of relief.

"Why?" she asked, anticipating a heap of problems. "Who's C. L. Maddison?"

"He works for this company I signed a contract with. He…" He drew a deep breath and seemed to calm down a little. "I thought I didn't stand a chance. I mean if he was your… He's so… real! Even his secretary's real!"

Carol burst into laughter. She knew better than anyone there was nothing real about Clarice.

"I'm serious!" the man insisted. "She's fat and old, and she has warts! And he… he has white hair. At the temples. And a nose. A real nose! It takes balls to look like that!"

Carol thought she was going to choke with laughter. Balls she definitely knew she did not have. Not literally, not figuratively either, or she wouldn't have worn bots to work.

"Don't make fun of him!" the man insisted. "He's impressive! He swindled me out of at least two billion. Four, most likely."

"Serves you right for falling for white hair and a pretty nose," she said, still laughing.

"I haven't... I mean he's a man... and I'm not... into..."

He was faltering, and that made her feel even better. She'd never heard anyone praise her work so openly, and she'd never heard anyone praise her choice of a work outfit. Her friends knew the nose was based on her own deformity, as they called it, and saw it as a sign of neo-narcissism. That made them hate it passionately, just as they hated everything that was abnormal about her.

"Should I be jealous?" she asked.

"No! No, of course not!" he protested. "Your nose is just as..."

"Just as pretty?" she suggested with a sarcastic twitch in the corner of her mouth.

"Real," he answered honestly.

There was a certain intensity about the way he said the word that made her stop laughing. She looked at him seriously, examining his face.

"Would you still sleep with me if you knew what I looked like?" he asked again.

"You're assuming I'd ever sleep with you again, anyway," she pointed out.

He looked pretty lost at that. It reminded her of why she'd brought him home with her in the first place: that feeling that she was in control.

"Show me," she said. "Tonight. I get home at eight."

Carol had made sure she'd have enough time to get home and take off her bots before he got there. She didn't want problems at work because of some guy she'd picked up in a nightclub. She wanted to tell herself that she'd have one good look at him and use that as an excuse to break up with him. If what they had could even be called a relationship.

But, on the other hand, she'd never felt so comfortable with anyone.

He was like her. She knew the symptoms better than anyone. Complete rejection of cosmetic surgery, though that remained to be seen; an exhibitionistic desire to show one's own, unaltered looks; and, what the medical journals never mentioned, a preference for unaltered looks in others. After all, she didn't like her own nose because she thought it looked pretty—she liked it because it was unique, natural, authentic. Real.

Psychiatrists seemed to have missed that one, probably because, unlike the other symptoms of neo-narcissism, it wasn't socially disabling. Their job was to help sufferers function within society. The preference for unaltered looks was considered an unrelated sexual deviation. Carol had her own theories, but Carol was no shrink.

He was punctual. He was still wearing his cosmetic bots—the same outfit as the night before. But he carried their box under his arm. He placed the box on the coffee table and sat down in front of it irresolutely.

"Are you sure you want to see?" he asked.

"I think that would be fair," she said with a nod. She wasn't wearing her bots, just her silk gown.

"I..." He hesitated. "I've never... I've never had any surgery."

"You don't have to act like a virgin on her wedding night about it," Carol pointed out. "Does it look like I have?"

"No!" he protested. "No, you're perfect! Real!"

"Freak!" she thought. But she could sympathize. She felt a tingle of anticipation watching the bots turn grey. She'd never met anyone who hadn't had surgery, not since high school. Rebels like Clarice used surgery as much as everybody else, and they had the same aversion to neo-narcissists as everybody else, not because they weren't fitting in with the mainstreamers, but because they weren't fighting the system hard enough. Clarice probably thought that Carol's white hair and Roman nose were reactionary, not a matter of personal taste, otherwise she wouldn't have logged her in early when she was late for work.

When the bots began migrating off his head, she could see his hair was black. The shape of his lips stayed the same. His nose was flatter. His eyes were dark, and clearly Asian. That explained his grin when he'd thought she found that a turn on. He seemed to be in his forties.

The shape of his face looked familiar.

"Do you look like that at work?" she asked.

He looked put off that she hadn't said anything about his face.

"N-no, of course not," he said after a moment's hesitation. "Being a minority is never a good idea."

"No, it's not."

"Do you want to see?" he asked after another pause.

He pressed his finger on the touchscreen and said, "Outfit one." It pleased her that, like her, he prioritized work over going out.

The bots covered his face, shaping his nose and adjusting his eyes. When the change was complete, Carol was staring at Mr. Edward Lee.

"Now you have an advantage over me," he said. "You don't go to work like this either, right?"

"No," she answered slowly, considering what to do. "Being a woman is never a good idea."

She brought her box from the bathroom and placed it next to his. Sitting down in front of him, she took a deep breath and placed her finger on the touchscreen.

"Outfit one."

As the bots began to work, his eyes widened in surprise, shock. There was an instant of horror, and then he burst into laughter.

"Peacock!" he articulated, almost choking.

Carol was a most respectable middle-aged gentleman, with distinguished greying temples, dressed in a silk gown with a brightly coloured peacock on it. The distinguished gentleman in a brightly coloured silk gown lowered his chin, pursed his lips, and began to giggle.

"So now that I know and you know," Carol said when they'd recovered from their fit of laughter, "I have a question."

The loud ringing of the videophone interrupted her, startling them both. Marla's voice began shouting even before the image came on.

"Turn on the TV now! Earth News Network! Hurry!"

"Did you ask Ted about the terraforming?" Carol asked Marla.

"Yes. Turn on the damned TV, you'll miss it!"

The headline on the screen announced in bold letters "LUNAR TAKEOVER" while the newscaster was finishing her report.

"...the largest sold for nineteen billion, the most expensive for twenty-two billion. The transactions occurred within minutes of each other in a strategic move to keep prices from fluctuating. Earlier today, New Environment announced their merger with terraforming company GHT Labs, making the multinational conglomerate the owner of the entire surface of the Moon."

Carol stabbed the off button of the remote with her fingernail, cutting off the newscaster.

"It was all perfectly legal," Edward defended himself, taking a step forwards.

"I knew it!" Marla screamed as soon as his face entered the videophone's screen. "There's more of you! More neo-narcissists! Oh, God, no! You're going to make me babysit your children."

"Are you pregnant?" Edward asked, worried.

"Are you terraforming the Moon?" Carol asked back.

"Yes. I didn't say I couldn't support a child. But are you really—"

"Of course I'm not! That's not the point. You stole our piece of the Moon! It's worth a fortune, and you practically got it for free!"

"You fleeced me! I paid well over the market price. I'm the laughing stock of the whole department! Everyone else got a discount."

"I'd tell you two to get a room," Marla noticed, "but I see you already have one, so I'll leave you to enjoy it. Have fun! And whatever you do, don't take pictures."

The videophone screen went black, leaving Carol and Edward to stare at each other in silence.

"You had to sign the deal at the same time as everyone else to make sure word of it didn't get out and people didn't start raising the price," Carol said, a little calmer. "That's why you went along with my price when I suggested we wait one more day."

Edward nodded.

"Do you even have a nephew?"

"I do. But I'm not allowed to see him. They say I'm a bad influence," he answered, pointing at his lips.

"Yeah, I know what that's like."

She leaned back and took a deep breath, letting the anger flow out with the air.

"Do you think..." Edward asked, breaking the silence. "Do you think we could still see each other?"

"Are you that fond of my clubbing outfit?" she asked with a grin.

"No, of your nose. Because it's real."

"You keep saying that."

"Don't you ever want something unaltered, something you can count on in this world of photocopied appearances?"

"I do. That's why I'm not getting surgery. At least I can count on me not to be fake."

"You can count on me too, now."

"You lied to me about the Moon, about why you wanted it, about your nephew's baseball practice, about—"

"That's business, Laureen. You wear bots for work, you should know."

"It's Carol," she said, holding out her hand. "Carol Laureen Maddison."

"Take off your bots first," he answered. "I want to shake hands with the real you, not some fake image. You don't need your bots around me."

"You too," she said, reaching for her box.

Their fingers touched their boxes at the same time and their voices sounded as one: "Clear!"

EXPIRY DATE
Eamonn Murphy

Nick Borden was at the bus stop early and found the other eleven passengers there ahead of him. No one wanted to pay the heavy fines inflicted for missing an appointment. A chill wind from the north plucked at his clothing. The bus shelter was modern, stylish, all sweeping curves of clear plastic. But the gaps let the wind straight through. Nick remembered plain box-shaped bus shelters, the ones that actually sheltered you. Still, cursing everything modern was just a sign he was getting old, wasn't it?

A sudden gust tugged at his trilby hat, which he grabbed.

Reflexes still good, he thought.

"At least it's not raining," said the man next to him, a bent, skinny figure huddled into a blue anorak. The man wore no hat and was bald.

Nick nodded and watched a bus pull out. It wasn't theirs, just a normal town service full of commuters off to a busy day at the office. He turned to survey his fellow passengers: three men and eight women. Women still lived longer. No equalities legislation to cover that, he thought ruefully. All of them looked either ill or at death's door.

They all were at death's door, including him. A month to go.

"The doddery dozen," he muttered, remembering an old war film, and chuckled. Then a minibus pulled in to the stop. It was old and battered and dirty but good enough for them. The driver was a stocky young man with short hair. His manner was gentle enough, and he helped the frail passengers aboard with a kind word and a smile.

Nick was last and brushed aside the proffered arm. "The NHS would have picked us up from home."

The driver grinned, but his eyes were hard. "Ah, the good old days."

The journey took forty-five minutes in the heavy rush-hour traffic. They drove straight to the drop-off and pick-up area of the super hospital. It had been new in the first decade of the twenty-first century but was looking well used now. The driver handed his charges over to a young man in a dark blue suit, who led them down a long corridor. The new escort looked smart: clean-shaven, polished shoes, and trousers with knife-edge creases.

"Are you a doctor?" asked one of the old ladies as the group crowded into a lift.

"No, madam. Just non-medical staff. My name's Malcolm. I'm here to take you to the Terminal Ward and explain what will happen next month."

"You're getting near your sell-by date, miss," said the man in the blue anorak, cackling cheerfully.

The blue suit frowned at him. As a man who sold euthanasia, he didn't like unpleasant truths voiced out loud and looked lost for words. When the lift reached their floor, a bell pinged, saving him from having to make a reply.

He ushered them out into a reception area. Ahead of them was a door leading to the ward. Others led to store cupboards and mysterious medical rooms. The whole place had the antiseptic smell of hospitals and pharmacies.

Their guide turned to address them. "We'll go along to the Terminal Ward soon, but first, we have to give you a little talk in the lecture room. As you must know, all of you reach your expiry dates in a month, at which point health coverage will finish. The day after that, life insurance coverage ends, and if you hang around, your heirs lose out." When he said "hang around," he raised both hands and used the first two fingers to indicate inverted commas. It was a gesture Nick had always hated.

He interrupted. "When you say 'hang around,'"—he made an exaggerated mocking imitation of Malcolm's gesture—"you mean have the barefaced cheek to keep on living." Nick dropped his arms and held them slightly away from his hips, fists clenched. His stance was that of a man ready for a fight, and he knew his face was flushed.

Malcolm smiled. "Watch the blood pressure, old man."

Nick took a step forwards. "You smarmy little…"

The bent old man in the blue anorak stepped in front of him, both hands raised in a placating gesture.

"Hold it, mate. I know how you feel, but belting this monkey won't do you any good, and the organ grinders are out of reach."

"I'll call security," said Malcolm.

Nick looked into the eyes of the man in front of him and saw a kindred soul. They were of the same generation. The only difference was that Nick had not been so physically debilitated by age.

He let out a long sigh. "Okay. I'm calm. No need for security."

A nurse came over from the nearby reception desk. "Everything okay?" she said.

Malcolm looked sideways at Nick. "Okay now." He turned. "Follow me, please."

The bent old man shook Nick's hand. "I'm Kevin." He smiled. "I wanted to let you deck him, but it wouldn't help. Come on."

They followed the rest of the group but hung back a little. Kevin said, "You're spry for a man so near his expiry date."

Nick laughed. "I kept fit. I was doing 10K runs into my seventies and hit the gym three times a week." He gripped the other man's arm as if to reassure him. "You're not so bad yourself. Most people this close to their date are already gone or ill in hospital. This doddery dozen are the exceptions who prove that the rule is crap."

Kevin gave a wheezy laugh. "Doddery dozen, I like it." He rubbed his head. "I must be Telly Savalas. You're Lee Marvin, our leader."

Nick nodded towards the group in front. "Hardly a leader if I have no followers."

"Oh, I'm sure we're all with you, old chap. Even the women. But smiting smug blue suit won't change anything. Come on. Let's hear what he has to say."

They entered the room. There were a dozen seats and a place at the front for a speaker to stand. Malcolm invited them to sit and then turned to face them.

"When we get to the Terminal Ward," he said, "you will see that all the patients are calm and relaxed."

"Sedatives," said Nick. "They're drugged."

Malcolm chuckled indulgently and looked him over. "Mister Borden, isn't it? Served twenty years in the Parachute Regiment and then worked in security, mostly abroad. They warned me you might be a difficult customer."

"They dope the patients, too," said Nick.

Malcolm exhaled. "Time for a history lesson. Most of you know this already but Mister Borden doesn't seem to have accepted it. So, we'll start in 2016 with the referendum on the European Union…" He droned on for about half an hour. Nick didn't listen. He knew the story.

When Nick was growing up, the National Health Service promised universal care free at the point of delivery. Despite the inefficiency that was an inevitable part of any large government organization, it worked well.

Falling tax receipts changed that, as billionaires became more powerful than nation states and the politicians in their pockets let them keep their money. Better healthcare meant that more people were living longer lives but not healthier lives, and they needed a lot of looking after. Expensive new treatments came in for various conditions, and everyone wanted them. Treating everyone cost too much. The system collapsed, and private medical insurance replaced it, mostly from American companies who had been in the business for generations.

Meanwhile, medical technology advanced in other directions. Members of the public were scanned, tested, and genetically assessed. By the time a man or woman reached middle age, it was possible to give them an estimate for when they would die: their expiry date. Once that was known, life insurance companies used it to work out premiums. Some people not destined for long life took up dangerous sports, drank too much, or found other ways to make their lives even shorter. A few impolite patients lived beyond their due date. Parliament, full of MPs who needed campaign funds, agreed with the insurance industry that these people were no longer covered and would receive no payment if they died after their expiry date. This judgement pleased the next generation, who wanted money, not some old coot hanging around too long and being a nuisance. Most old people used up all their medical insurance coverage during their steady decline, and the withdrawal of medical care at the same time was inevitable. You could pay extra for coverage beyond your expiry date—every market has a supplier—although it cost a fortune.

"So, regrettably, if you go on past your estimated expiry date, the life insurance companies will no longer pay out on your death." Malcolm had explained it all in a pleasant way. For him, the NHS had been a vast, inefficient bureaucracy and medical practice was much more efficient once privatized. The life insurance industry was most benevolent, investing your money wisely so that there was a good payout for your heirs when your last day came.

The audience looked doleful but accepting. They all knew the truth of their circumstances, but now it had been set out plainly for them, clarified like a good white wine. Malcolm moved to the door and opened it.

"For the last part of the tour, we take you around the Terminal Ward to talk to the patients. They can tell you how easy it all is."

Malcolm led them across the corridor and into the ward. Nick had listened to the lecture with his teeth clenched. Now, he looked down the long room, six beds on either side, and wondered if he could go so tamely to his demise. Then he saw a face he recognized.

Could it be? There was a white dry-wipe board on the wall with the names of the patients written in black. Sam Billings—Bed 12. It was him.

Nick hurried forwards.

The pale, skeletal figure under the thin grey blanket did not much resemble Sergeant Sam Billings of 2 Para, Winner of the Victoria Cross and hero of the Afghanistan campaign. Sam Billings had been a six-foot tower of strength: a disciplinarian, sure, but smart and funny, too. A natural leader.

He'd won his medal for charging across a battlefield under fire, picking up wounded men and carrying them back to safety. Three men in all.

One of them had been Nick Borden.

"Sam?" Nick hesitated. It could be another man with the same name.

The person in the bed shifted. He looked Nick straight in the face. His eyes widened in surprise, and he struggled into a more upright position.

"I know that ugly mug. Nick Borden, isn't it?"

Nick wanted to help him sit up but knew Sam would resent it. "Yeah, it's me."

Sam coughed, which led to a retching fit lasting a minute. His eyes were streaming by the time he finished. He rubbed them with his fists and smiled. "Sorry about that. What are you doing here?"

Nick pointed to the rest of the group, moving around the ward and asking quiet questions of the patients. "I'm on the tour. We're all due for expiry next month, so they brought us in to show how easy it is."

Sam didn't reply for a few seconds, and when he spoke it was barely a whisper. "I'm due today." He waved a hand to indicate the others in the ward. "We're all due today."

Nick gripped his arm. "Fight them, Sam."

The frail old man in the bed laughed. "My fighting days are over."

"You want to die?"

"Hell, no. In the good old days, someone in my condition would be in a care home eating rubbish food and boring the other wrecks with war stories. I can still move about. I'm not incontinent. Oh, I take loads of pills and sleep a lot, but that's how old people used to be, damn it. We still took care of them."

Another coughing fit ensued.

"Ah, the good old days."

The smug voice came from behind Nick. He glanced over his shoulder and saw blue-suited Malcolm with a security guard in tow, a soft, tubby, middle-aged man who was grimacing to look tough. A male nurse in a white coat stood just behind them. He held a small bottle of serum and a syringe.

The man in the bed chuckled. "Have you been causing trouble again, Nick?"

"Not much."

Sam sat up. He reached out and took his friend's hand. "I'm glad you're here."

Nick gripped Sam's fingers too tightly. "Don't let them do it. We can fight!"

The security guard interrupted. "Now, now, sir. Let's not have any trouble."

Sam threw back his head and laughed. "Trouble? Nick Borden could put you down in two seconds, fatty, and kill you in three. But he won't." He looked his old comrade right in the eye. "You can't fight it, Nick. The accountants have taken over the world. If I don't go today, my life insurance is invalid and my family will lose the money. They'll have to pay for a private burial, too, and these bastards have rigged the system so that costs a fortune."

Nick's lips tightened. "It's not fair."

"No. Stay with me, old friend." Sam looked up at the so-called nurse, a carer with the hard face of a concentration camp guard. "Do it."

The man in the white coat stepped warily around Nick and moved to the other side of the bed. He wrapped an elasticized tourniquet around Sam's upper arm and put the point of the needle on a thin vein.

Sam turned his head so he was looking at Nick when the needle slid in.

Nick stared at the plunger going down, the fluid disappearing into his friend. He looked back at Sam's face.

"Tata, mate." The eyes closed. The last breath whistled out of the old soldier's body.

"Just like putting a dog to sleep," said Malcolm.

He screamed when Nick grabbed his crotch and squeezed. He spluttered and whimpered when Nick's fist slammed twice into his nose and mouth. Five seconds after his smart remark, he was on all fours on the tiled floor of the ward, dripping blood and spitting fragments of teeth.

Nick turned. The nurse executioner had fled. The tubby little security guard backed away, hands held up in front of him.

"I don't want no trouble, mate."

Nick turned and stalked out of the ward. There was no point in staying now. The purpose of the visit was to find out about Termination Day, and he had done that.

There was remarkably little fuss. The story didn't make the news at all. The government wanted no negative feelings being aroused about Termination Day. After all, ninety-nine percent of the population didn't even reach it, so, like all minorities, the remaining one percent was ignored.

Nick didn't know if similar things had happened before. Like Sam, most Terminals were far too weak to put up a fight. Their friends were already dead, and their relatives surrendered to the inevitable. The state disposed of them, and the grieving relatives received a small urn of ashes that may or may not have been their loved one.

Nick's phone rang three days after the hospital incident. He didn't recognize the number but answered it, anyway. If it was an unwanted call, he could get satisfaction from being rude to a stranger.

There were few moments of satisfaction in his life.

"Hello?"

"Mister Borden?" On confirmation, the speaker continued. "My name's Brett Tucker, and I'm calling from the Crown Prosecution Service."

Nick grunted. "What can I do for you, Brett?"

"I'm ringing about the… um… the incident at the hospital."

Nick grinned. "Oh, yes. That was when some smug cunt called my dead comrade a dog. As I recall, I crushed the bastard's nuts and smashed his face in. Is there a problem, Brett?"

There was a short pause. "That was a crime," said Brett. "Actual bodily harm. However, after reviewing the evidence, the department has decided that you were reacting to extreme provocation while the balance of your mind was disturbed."

"Really?"

Brett seemed unruffled by the sarcasm. "Really. We recognize, Mister Borden, that it was stressful for you to see a friend die and that the remark by Malcolm Foster was totally unacceptable."

"I'm happy to go to court," said Nick. "I'll be glad to stand up in the dock and tell the public how you treat old soldiers today."

"The nearest court date would be in forty days and… well, you know."

"You're killing me in twenty-seven, anyway, so why bother?"

Another pause. "You've summed it up, Mister Borden, if crudely. Anyway, I'm ringing to tell you that the C.P.S. won't be prosecuting the case."

"What if I go to the press with it?" said Nick.

Printing presses had long gone the way of the dodo and most of the so-called newspapers online served only to distract the public with tits and celebrities, but there were three serious papers left.

"They wouldn't print the story, Mister Borden. They have plenty of violent news already with the various terrorist activities."

That was true. There was a group calling themselves Dylanists, after the poet who said raged against the dying of the light. There were few Dylanists—most people didn't worry about the issue until they were too old and feeble to frighten a kitten. But they hit soft targets and made trouble. Combined with the ongoing Islamic terrorism, it all made England a dangerous place unless you lived in a gated community with security guards, but only the rich could afford that.

Nick sighed. "I'm sure you're right, Brett. Well, thanks for the heads up. You've been very polite. I'll see you in Hell."

He ended the call and made another cup of tea. Sipping it, he checked the calendar. Twenty-seven days left. What does an old bachelor do, he wondered, with less than a month to live? Drink? Whores? Why not have a good time and use up what little money he had left? Nick had no heirs except some spoilt middle-class nephews he couldn't stand. They would get his life insurance payout if all went well.

What if it didn't? How many nurse executioners could he take out before they got him?

He suddenly realized the answer. None. He was a marked man, now. When his Termination Day came, they might send an armed escort to take him to the hospital. They could even do it at home the night before to catch him by surprise.

Nick considered joining the Dylanists, but he was an old soldier and a patriot. Becoming a terrorist was not in his make-up, and what was the point, anyway? The system wouldn't change.

Well, he had a few weeks to mull it over.

Nick's expiry date was October the second. On the Tuesday before that, he met an old acquaintance and did some unusual shopping. On Wednesday, he did his usual shopping: fresh fruit, fresh meat, and plenty of fresh vegetables.

As he munched an apple for breakfast, it occurred to him that his good health had caused the current crisis. Had he stopped exercising and eaten takeout food meals while sitting potato-like before the television all day, he would have died long ago like millions of others.

Many years before, there had been a few half-hearted government initiatives to get people fit, but they hadn't worked and were soon dropped after being deemed bad for business. The government allowed nothing that might be bad for business. Corporations made good profits selling sugar, salt, and fat to the masses. They made more from mad diet plans and expensive gym memberships that fell into disuse by February. When the last possible profit had been extracted and the fat suckers dropped dead of whatever condition their lifestyles had caused, the government saved money on pensions, as did the private pension holders. It was all good for business.

Nick turned on the television. There was much excitement among the presenters over some breaking news. Terrorists had launched an attack at Manchester Airport, gunning down waiting passengers indiscriminately.

Nick turned it off. Guns were easier to get than ever, and even the children carried knives. He put Marvin Gaye on the CD player. "Mercy Mercy Me."

Ol' Marv was right. Things were not what they used to be.

Nick awoke on the first of October to a cold, clear weekday morning. He rose as usual at 6 a.m. and ran his three miles around the park. On the way back, he stopped at a café and ordered a full English breakfast: sausages, bacon, beans, fried bread, tomatoes, eggs, mushrooms—the works. He went back home and performed his ablutions. Refreshed, he dressed to go out, smart as usual in an ironed shirt, sharply creased trousers, and shiny black shoes. His warm woollen jacket suited the weather.

The offices of the Anglo-American Insurance Company were in Bond Street downtown. Nick splashed out on a taxi to get there. His insurance policies were with the Anglo-American. They received his payments every month and their actuarial calculators had worked out his expiry date many years before. Obviously, it was incorrect. He was still in good health and could keep on living well for years. He would have a word with the top brass about it. As Sam had said, there was no point in arguing with the monkeys. Nick would see the organ grinders.

The building that housed the Anglo-American Insurance Company was the tallest and most impressive in town, a towering, forty-storey spire of steel, glass, and brick. Nick paused at the large glass revolving door entrance to look up and admire it. A teacher once told him that the buildings of any age showed where the power lay. Before Henry VIII, there had been the vast, beautiful cathedrals and abbeys of the Catholic

Church. When he confiscated that wealth, England became festooned with palaces and those stately homes soldiers fought for. Now the financiers had the biggest buildings.

Nick went through the revolving door and entered a spacious lobby. The floor was of light-green tiles, the distant walls a delicate pastel shade. There were potted plants scattered about, and at either side of the door were low coffee tables and soft chairs for visitors to wait in comfort. An elderly couple sat to his right, drinking coffee.

The back wall had two lifts. In between was a large, polished mahogany reception desk with three decorative openings in the front, staffed by three decorative girls wearing neat blue trouser suits: a blonde in the middle balanced with a brunette to the right and a redhead on the left. Three security guards stood against the wall, one beside the desk, the other two near the lift doors.

Nick approached the receptionist on the right. "I'm here to see Mister Carter," he said. "Mister Howard Carter. The boss." Nick had searched the company website and discovered that Carter was the highest ranked executive in this building.

The pretty brunette frowned and pursed her lips. She looked him up and down as if measuring him for a suit or weighing up his value at auction. Her expression told Nick he had been found wanting.

"Do you have an appointment?"

"No, but it's urgent. He'll see me."

Then the glass of the revolving door shattered noisily in a hail of gunfire. The receptionist to his left screamed.

Nick vaulted over the reception desk and dragged the brunette to the floor in the same motion. Holding her down with one arm, he peered through the gap in the front of the desk, though the deafening fire of machine guns told him what had happened well enough.

Five men stood just inside the lobby on shards of broken glass, the shattered remains of the revolving door. They were holding their machine guns as if posing for a photograph in the eerie silence after the bedlam they'd caused, the calm after the storm. Each man had a bold, red letter D emblazoned on the left pocket of his camouflage jacket. They seemed almost surprised by their success.

Nick grimaced as he spotted the elderly couple now lying in an expanding pool of blood. The two security guards posted by the lift doors were both dead. The blonde receptionist was a few feet away, sprawled like a child's discarded rag doll with her face a bloody mess and her brains decorating the wall. Beyond her, the redhead was in the same state. That was the trouble with terrorism: it killed the innocent.

The surviving guard crouched behind the desk, like Nick, peering through the opening. He drew his weapon.

The tallest of the men punched the air in triumph. "Rage! Rage!" he shouted.

One of his comrades pointed. "There are people behind the desk."

"Watch them, Dan." The tall man was clearly the leader. "The rest of you, follow me." He headed for the lift to his right. Nick watched as the doors opened and the four men entered. Outside, in the distance, he could hear sirens.

He scuttled across to the security guard, a thin-lipped, tough-looking man with a two-millimetre haircut.

The terrorist left to guard them was moving sideways, eyes and gun still trained on the desk.

Nick spoke. "If I distract him can you take him out?"

The guard raised both eyebrows. "You up for that?"

"Twenty years in the Paras, mate. I'm up for anything."

The man grinned. "Okay. Do it."

Nick stayed low and dived forwards into the tiled reception area, yodelling like Johnny Weissmuller. When he landed, he rolled over and over, a moving target.

The move caught Dan off guard. He fired one burst. It hit the floor where Nick had been half a second earlier.

A bullet in the guts stopped him in his tracks. Another in the head put paid to him altogether.

Nick stood up. "Good shooting."

The guard was already running for the lift. The indicator light above the doors was on one. Faintly, they could hear the rattle of machine guns firing from the floor above.

Killing all the monkeys, thought Nick.

He turned to the other man. "Call reinforcements then take the stairs."

The guard ran off, shouting into his radio. Nick pressed the button to summon the lift. It arrived seconds later. Inside, he pressed the number for the floor he wanted.

The lift rose. The doors opened. As he stepped out into a long corridor, he checked the big number on the wall opposite. Forty.

There were large windows looking out over the town. From this high up, the people looked small and unimportant.

Nick ran down the corridor. There was no sound of gunfire. It didn't carry up this far. The top brass was undoubtedly gliding about their business with unruffled calm. He figured the terrorists would come up through the building shooting as many workers as they could.

A door opened a few feet away, and a short man in a dark suit came out. Nick stopped him.

"Where's Howard Carter's office? It's an emergency."

The man looked confused. "What?"

Nick grabbed his collar and shook him. "Tell me!"

The other pointed. "Carter's office is down there, but he's in an executive meeting at the moment. That way."

"Thanks." Nick sprinted down the corridor. At the end was a brown door with a neat sign: "Conference Room." He burst in without ceremony.

A dozen well-dressed, middle-aged men sat at a large, oblong oak table. They jumped to their feet as he entered.

"Who the fuck are you?" barked a tall man with a crewcut and a short, neatly clipped beard. Nick recognized Carter from the company's promotional literature.

He stood to attention and saluted. "Sir. A gang of five Dylanists just attacked the ground floor and shot all the reception staff. They are now on the first floor killing everyone in sight. I think they mean to come up through the building and murder you all, sir."

"We have to get out of here!" said one of the other men.

Nick stood blocking the doorway. "I'm one of your customers, Mister Carter. My expiry date is tomorrow. I came to chat about that."

He pulled a Glock 19 semi-automatic pistol from his pocket. The men backed away.

"I'm an old soldier, sir. I won't let the terrorists get you."

"Good man!"

Nick opened the front of his anorak to reveal the explosives packed around his torso.

"I want that pleasure for myself."

He pulled the cord.

THE PRICE OF WOOL AND SUNFLOWERS

Samantha Rich

The Oversight Agency of the Imperial Treasury was housed in a suite of rooms above the Emperor's Own Library, Graciously Granted to the People of His City. It was an odd place to keep the department, in truth, but few people gave it any thought. The Imperial economy was largely assumed to manage itself. Only a handful of advisors to the Emperor knew of the work going on at the Oversight Agency, and even they checked in on it only three or four times per year.

Grevyet Maiala, the Director of the Agency, Graciously Appointed by the Emperor by Proxy, appreciated the privacy allowed to her team and their work. (Though of course more funding and a larger team would have been appreciated; such was the lament of bureaucracies everywhere.) It was, after all, largely their work that allowed everyone else the illusion that the Imperial economy did manage itself. Invisible power was power still.

She reminded herself of that as she studied the latest reports from the teams of analysts who did the basic work of the Agency. Overseeing this mundania was what her power was for.

"Sunflowers." She looked up from the papers to meet the eyes of First-Sub-Agent Trel Eitan. "The market for sunflower seeds is raising an alarm?"

"Not a full alarm," he replied. "But the fluctuation has been noticeable over three of the last five quarters. That was deemed sufficient to produce a report."

Maiala looked at the papers again. It was a very long, very dense report, the kind that the young economists were always eager to produce in hopes of catching someone's eye and garnering a promotion. The concise half-page summary, on the other hand, had been written by the First-Sub-Agent—or, more likely, his secretary, a man named Sevva Betan, whose life was, as far as Maiala could tell, fully dedicated to terseness in all things.

"Fallen six-tenths of a dolana over those five quarters," she said, picking the key line from Eitan or Betan's clipped prose. "That's not enough to intervene yet."

"It would be acceptable to intervene," Eitan said. Maiala glanced up to confirm that the edge of his eyelid was twitching at her failure to reduce the fraction. Petty games were her weakness, something her own mentor had scolded her to move past if she ever wanted to seek power outside of the Agency. Maiala had never given such a career change much thought, and so, the games continued.

"No intervention at this time," she said, tapping her pen against the report. "But continue to monitor prices closely and inform me immediately if the cumulative drop reaches eight-tenths."

"Director—esteemed Director—"

Maiala raised her hand. "Were you appointed by the Emperor by Proxy?"

His hands balled into loose fists at his side. "No, Director."

"You were appointed by me, were you not?"

"Yes, Director."

Impressive that the words could make it out through clenched teeth. "Then I believe you have your instructions and can return to your team, First-Sub-Agent."

Eitan nodded stiffly and walked away. Maiala permitted herself a slow, cautious exhale before turning her attention to the next item on her agenda. Fish eggs. Roe or caviar—however they were presented at market, in the Agency's reports they were categorized together as fish eggs. A technical matter.

Their prices were up, three-tenths of a dolana. Excellent.

The sunflower seed market stabilized over the next two weeks, and Maiala put the issue out of her mind. It was common for sub-agents to get overly excited about trends in their area of focus before those trends were truly clear. Data was intoxicating, and the young economists had every reason to promote their numbers aggressively. Part of the maturation process for sub-agents was learning how to temper what you took from the reports. Eitan would grow into his role in good time.

As the person ultimately responsible for all of the department's findings, she had other things to worry about. The Emperor had sent a request for an Analysis of Readiness for Military Expansion, with the timeline specified as With Respect to Current Workload. That meant it didn't have to be provided immediately, but within the year at worst. Analyses of readiness for military expansion were hugely complicated affairs; she had to assign a full-sized team to complete them, which meant pulling that number of people off of other projects, which led to resentment and complaints from various sub-heads that their teams were no longer capable of completing their own assignments, and naming names of fellow sub-heads of teams that they were sure could stand to lose a body or three...

To make things worse, a week into that restructuring, another notice came in from the Emperor's Council of Respected and Forthright Advisors, Granted Substantial Independence. They were concerned with the amount of wool being exported rather than consumed domestically, and they wanted an Analysis of Self-Sufficiency in the Quoted Sector, requested with Priority Status Over Current Workload.

Maiala read the notice, set it aside, and buried her face in her hands.

"This is deeply unfair," she said aloud, to no one. As the person ultimately responsible, she was alone in this.

She uncovered her face, squared her shoulders, and rang the bell that summoned her assistant. "Fetch Sub-Director Priit, please," she said, taking a blank piece of paper and dipping her pen. Preparing a brief agenda for the spontaneous meeting would help her focus her thoughts. They had a lot of work to do.

Majellyp Priit was unimpressed with both the Council's request and Maiala's agenda. "You know there's only one outcome they'll accept, if they've actually sent a request." He waved his hands about, causing the flared sleeves of his robe to flutter like agitated birds. Priit's parents had emigrated to the Emperor's City on a spice trading ship from Aprit'ko, across the sea in the far southwest. He maintained traditional dress and traditional lack of standing on propriety. "Why not skip the report and get right to it?"

Maiala drew a line underneath her agenda and made a note to reconsider asking Priit's assistance in the future. "They requested a report. We must provide one, with an appendix of recommendations. They'll select whichever recommendation includes performing the value adjustment ritual, and then we can proceed. It's important to follow the full sequence, Priit, even if only pro forma."

"It's a waste of time."

"It's the way things are done." Maiala folded her hands. "Can I count on you, Priit?"

He sighed. "Of course you can, Director. Always, to an infinite degree. Just point me in the direction you'd like me to go."

Priit was right, in the end; the Council did, in fact, want them to adjust the value of the Empire's wool stocks. It wasn't a step to be taken lightly, and it wasn't one that was easy to take, either. Maiala, Priit, and the other Sub-Director, Surpet Anjeta, had to dedicate an entire afternoon and evening to it.

The use of Rituals Approved by the Emperor in His Graciousness to be Used to Perform Magic was restricted to individuals with high government placement and meticulous training. Magic wasn't the sort of thing that could be allowed to migrate down to lower levels of the bureaucracy—or, heaven forbid, the general populace. The bureaucracy existed precisely to limit the harm that could be inflicted by such a thing, by instituting structures and controls.

Maiala knew all of the perfectly good reasons for it, but still she would have dearly loved to delegate this task to someone else.

Anjeta offered to prepare the paperwork, at least. She arrived at the ritual room, a small space at the back of their suite over the library, with a carefully written document listing the exact numbers in play, the coordinates of the warehouses they would need to reference, and the precise incantation needed to channel the uncanny powers required.

"You do lovely work, Sub-Director," Maiala said gratefully. "This is perfect."

"Thank you, Director." Anjeta bowed her head and moved to assist Priit with sketching out the necessary symbols on the ritual room's floor, which was inlaid with heavy sheets of slate to make the task easier. The room had been used to store crates and wrappings and the like before the Agency moved in, and it had no windows or sconces. Priit had set lanterns in each corner to light the floor for their work, leaving the room with a subdued, eerie mood that matched Maiala's own.

She placed Anjeta's document on a lectern at the far end of the room, along with two sticks of incense and a tuft of raw grey wool. She watched them finish the last line of chalk on the floor and step back from the work. "Are we ready?"

Priit nodded, adjusting his sleeves and moving to stand at the end of the room opposite the lectern. Anjeta stood on Maiala's left, halfway down the wall, facing in the direction of the sea. Maiala closed her eyes and mentally reviewed the diagrams in the official training text for the Rituals: good. They could proceed.

The initial chanting required nearly a full candle-length, at which point Maiala carried the sample of wool to the centre of the diagram. She walked to one of the lanterns, lit each stick of incense, and carried them back to the wool, laying them out on either side of it. Priit and Anjeta continued chanting the whole time, and Maiala returned to her lectern, waiting for them to complete the cycle of phrases so she could join in again.

When the ritual was completed, the incense sticks remained on the floor, half the length they had started at and still slowly smouldering. The sample of wool was gone. Maiala took the sticks and swiftly pinched off the burning ends, drawing a deep breath of the smoke into her lungs.

"What do you think, Director?" Priit asked quietly.

Maiala nodded, slipping the incense sticks into the pocket of her robe. "It went well, I think. I'll monitor the reports over the next few days. We'll see how it plays out."

The market was a temperamental thing, with almost a life of its own. The Emperor and his advisors expected the Agency to be able to take steps to intervene as easily as snapping their fingers, which was a painfully inaccurate way to picture their work. Maiala had gone through the private notes of every Director of the Agency who had preceded her, and she knew precisely how many times the men and women who held the position in the past had tried to explain to their superiors in government that none of their work was so simple. Those superiors either never understood, or they never cared.

Priit and Anjeta carried the lanterns out and Maiala locked the door to the ritual room behind them. She paused for a moment, hands on the heavy doors, and let herself truly think about what they had done.

Across the region of the Empire where wool was produced, the stores for sale had silently increased by half again. For every ten bales of wool, now there were fifteen. The sheep remained in the fields at the same numbers, and the extra stores weren't pulled from their bodies; according to the text of the ritual, they came from the space between things.

Maiala wasn't sure exactly what it meant, only that the ritual had never failed any of her predecessors, whatever goods they placed at the centre of the room. It simply had to be something produced in the Empire in a form no more refined than wine and gathered up in bulk to be sold.

The merchants wouldn't notice the change, exactly; they would simply evaluate their stocks again and place the new value on all of it. Wool was now less valuable than it had been before the ritual; there was more of it, and so each bale would be priced more cheaply. It would be less worth the trouble of sending it overseas. The people of the Empire would go to market and find wool more affordable—or rather, the people who made wool goods would find it more affordable and purchase the bales to spin and weave, or to felt, or some other thing.

Maiala was not an expert in the uses of wool. She was an expert in price behaviour of goods, and in carrying out the secret rituals to control those behaviours.

She stepped back from the doors and walked briskly back to her office. It was strange to contemplate these things, and doing so did nothing to benefit her work. If she indulged, she found the thoughts could keep her up at night, dwelling on the vast number of citizens of the Empire going about their business with no idea of what had been done or how it might affect them. The magic of money, and markets, invisible nets wrapped around the world and changing things in ways the common citizen could neither see nor understand.

It was a great deal of responsibility for her Agency. She would ensure that they performed to the best of their ability.

It took time for the world to catch up to the ritual's results. Wool sales didn't react for over a month. Once the reaction began, though, the ripples were easy to track. Reports came in from cities and ports throughout the Empire, the data was compiled by the relevant teams throughout the Agency, and digests landed on Maiala's desk as regularly as the candles were changed, with the key points flagged for her attention.

She allowed herself to enjoy the shift of wool sales from export to within the Empire, focused on the regions around where the sheep lived, where production of secondary goods made the most sense. She was able to send a promising report to the Council of Advisors on the standard timeline. They didn't bother to respond, which meant all was well. It was pleasant, to feel effective.

But of course, nothing could happen without a reaction, a countermove from their trading partners and competitors around the globe.

Priit came to Maiala's office with a sympathetic expression and a report from one of his own First-Sub-Agents. "Silk," he said. "And, we believe, pine nuts."

Maiala frowned over her paperwork. "No hello? No how is your day going, Director? No courtesy? You'll spoil my day, Priit."

"My apologies, Director." He bowed slightly from the waist and held out the report. "But I'm afraid the silk and pine nuts are quite urgent."

There were only a few things that would make Priit act this way. She took the report and opened it to the covering summary.

"Our esteemed trading partner across the West Sea, Great Pazdah," she read gravely. "Prices have suddenly skyrocketed for our imports of raw silk and pine nuts."

"Retaliation for the wool," Priit murmured. Maiala turned the page, skimming the tables and summary analysis. It was all very predictable, but that didn't make it less annoying. She could just picture the Pazdahn economic agents gathering in a ritual room above some distant library, sketching out symbols and chanting and countering her department's careful work with their own…

Of course, maybe they weren't shunted off above the library, she reflected sourly. Maybe they got a proper building of their own.

Priit cleared his throat. "Shall we send a notification to the Council, Director? Or will we take internal steps first?"

She tapped her fingers against the report. "The silk, I understand. That's a direct response to the wool; let them wear wool and see how their dandies like it, or something like that, yes?"

"I drew the same conclusion, Director."

"But why pine nuts? What's their role in our import structure?"

He shrugged. "They've been gaining popularity as an ingredient in various things over the past five years. Moved from a fine luxury to a common luxury, I suppose you could say. Like cinnamon in my childhood."

"And mine," she said, a bit pointedly. Just like Priit to make a faint joke of her age. "So, we started hoarding an essential and they're responding by doubling the price of our luxuries. Fair enough."

"It's still in motion, Director. There's no clear sign of where the price will stabilize."

"What I see here is more than enough to require a response." She turned in her chair and studied the shelves behind her desk, finally selecting the ledger volume marked Great Pazdah. "All right, what else is a significant point of trade with them? Wool, yes, we covered that… chalk, hmm, that's an option but I don't like it… cheese, we're not supposed to touch that so soon after the riots last year…"

Priit wrinkled his nose. "Yes, that was unfortunate."

"It would've been fine if it hadn't spilled over into the beef market." She sighed and singled out an item in the ledger. "Herring. We'll counter with that."

"Salted or live, Director?"

She closed the ledger with a soft bang. "I'll pretend you didn't ask me that, Priit."

"But it would be so impressive!" He could hardly finish the sentence for laughing. "Doubling the number of fish in the sea!"

"Out." She pointed to the door. "Tell Anjeta to be ready in three days' time."

The Price of Wool and Sunflowers

The game of price-driven cat and mouse played out over the course of an entire year.

Maiala and her Sub-Directors pored over their books, reports, and records to identify a commodity or good that could withstand being forcibly changed in value. Ceramic jars, dried lavender, rough-tanned leather, bronze chain links. The rituals had never been performed so frequently. She had to put in her annual order of incense six months in advance.

They knew that adjusting the value of common goods in this way might wreak some havoc, but each item in question was such a small, isolated thing. Maiala was envisioning the Empire's economy as a whole, trying to keep that great broad, deep thing balanced in relation to Great Pazdah and the rest of the world. A few dolanas here and there, in the greater picture, rounded down to zero.

The overseers of the Pazdahn economy, whomever and wherever they were, countered each adjustment with one of their own. Uncut sheets of linen, glass bottles, vinegar, lemons—they all swung through wild arcs of value, plunging or leaping in response to rituals far away. Maiala had to respect the work, even as it made her own more difficult. Their distant counterparts were worthy opponents, talented and skilled.

She didn't realize it had been a full year of this game until Priit happened to mention it while handing over an analysis of the market behaviour of rough-hewn lumber. "Did you know, Director, I checked the records and before this last year, only three rituals of value adjustment had been performed in a decade?"

The numbers made no sense for a moment, and Maiala blinked rapidly at the papers in her hands. "Ah... is that so, Sub-Director? I haven't reviewed the records recently."

"It is." He bowed slightly at the waist. "I can have a full summary prepared and sent up to you if you'd like."

"No, that isn't necessary. I trust your judgment." She ruffled through the papers, vaguely looking for a chart or a table, somewhere to rest her eyes. "Well, so we're taking a more active role than in the past. Changing times call for changing tactics."

"Of course, Director." Priit bowed again. "My analysts were not able to find a good case for adjusting the value of lumber. Please review the full report, of course, but ultimately I think the initial findings around charcoal are more promising."

"Thank you. Please, carry on." She made sure to keep very still until the door closed behind him, her hands flat on the desk, her muscles aching with tension.

A full year.

She pulled out her official logbook and flipped back through the pages, already knowing what she would find but hoping against hope that it had rewritten itself. She found the notation for each adjustment ritual and then checked the pages leading up to it, hoping and hoping...

No salvation. She had, indeed, not sent for Council approval for any adjustment after the very first one, with the wool.

Maiala slowly lowered her forehead to the desk and closed her eyes. One ad-hoc adjustment ritual was excusable as a proactive measure. Two could be excused if the situation had been critical. Given the actual, indifferent state of things when they started playing this game...

"I got carried away," she said to the desk.

Under the Gracious Benevolence of the Emperor, Impeccable in His Wisdom and Mercy, there were approved channels for this sort of situation. Maiala could submit a report with a confession, self-analysis, and recommendation for how to remediate her shortcomings. The Emperor's Proxies, Wisely Appointed by His Own Hand on the Council, were obligated to read and consider it closely, then temper their response for a period of one week before issuing their ruling.

The cooling period was instituted to ensure that the guilty party received due consideration for their dedication to the Empire as shown by their confession. Parties who were caught out without a confession—or worse, attempted to actually hide their faults—received no such tempering of judgment.

Maiala took a shaky breath and sat up, brushing stray strands of hair back from her face. There was no point feeling sorry for herself. She had erred, she would confess, the Council would decide what to do with her. There was nothing else to be done. Even if she gave in to the traitorous, whispering voice in the back of her head urging her to try to cover up what she had done, Priit and Anjeta would tell the truth. They wouldn't be far behind her in realizing what the three of them had done, and they were both honourable people.

Not only honourable, but wise—if Maiala was mad enough to try to convince them to collude with her in hiding things, one or both of them would immediately realize that they could gain extra clemency by throwing her to the Council as a scapegoat. Better to gather all the mercy for herself. It was a limited good, after all.

She drew a sheaf of paper from her desk and selected a fresh pen from the case her assistant refilled every morning. Best to get it over with quickly and concentrate on nothing but selecting the right words to present her memory of events clearly and concisely.

A request was received from the Emperor's Council of Respected and Forthright Advisors, Granted Substantial Independence, regarding wool exports. A study into the matter was immediately opened within the Agency...

Maiala wasn't particularly concerned when the first week passed without word from the Council. Her self-report would not have been the top item on the agenda when it was received, and they would need time to read and discuss it, however briefly, before the cooling-off period even began. She was in limbo, but this stage of it was self-imposed, and she accepted that.

Her unease grew at a steady rate as the second week passed, and the third. By the end of the fourth week, she was finding it difficult to maintain her composure, and when First-Sub-Agent Eitan returned to her with his team's apparently annual concerns about the sunflower market, she chased him from her office with a tongue-lashing that was both unprofessional and deeply unlike her.

Perhaps she should self-report that as well, she reflected sadly, sitting alone at her desk and struggling to keep herself from dissolving into tears. Her assistant had been instructed to keep anyone else out of her office, on pain of dismissal. Not even Priit and Anjeta were welcome. She needed to be alone.

The door flew open, stopping just short of crashing into the wall as a uniformed officer of the Emperor's Own Official and Recognized Guard,

Selected from the Elite and Decorated, stepped inside. He nodded stiffly to her, walked a brisk circuit of the room, and returned to the doorway, where he signaled to someone in the hall.

Maiala clutched at the edge of her desk. "What in the world? What's going on?"

"Director," the Recognized Guard said in a surprisingly soft voice. "Please, step back from the desk."

It took Maiala a moment to realize what he meant. Then she shoved her chair back and half-fell out of it, scrambling to her knees on the floor and bowing her head until it touched the cold marble. She had grasped the what, but not the why—what reason could there possibly be for him to come here—

Two more Recognized Guards swept into the room, taking up positions at the centre points of the walls, and then three more, preceding a figure wearing deep-blue boots instead of the polished black ones of a military uniform. Maiala didn't dare raise her eyes, just stared at the perfect surface of the boots.

The Emperor, Most Exalted and Honoured, Revered and Esteemed, Wise Beyond All Others and Merciful Above All Else, Supreme Commander and Highest Justice of the Recognized Lands, Undersigned, cleared his throat and said in a mild voice, "You are the Director of this Agency?"

"Yes, your Imperial Majesty." Maiala could barely raise her voice above a whisper, and that was directed at the floor. She doubted he could even hear her.

Fortunately, the Emperor never met anyone without it being thoroughly confirmed in advance that they were whom he meant to address. "Rise, please. You'll get a crick in your neck, doing that on the floor."

Maiala got to her feet slowly, leaning heavily on the edge of her desk to steady herself. No one moved to assist her, but the Recognized Guards made vaguely sympathetic faces. She could only assume that they had seen more awkward presentations than this before.

"We received... that is, my honoured Council and I received... well." The Emperor paused and stared off into a corner for a moment. "They received and discussed and sent a recommendation to me. Regarding your report. And it was so blessedly odd, it caught my attention, and I asked to have the whole thing brought to me."

"I'm sorry, your Majesty." Her voice cracked. She had never meant to draw his personal attention, oh, gods.

"Hmm? No, it was interesting. I enjoy having something interesting brought to my attention every so often." He walked past her, moving towards her bookshelves and leaning in closely to squint at the titles. The Recognized Guards all shifted their positions seamlessly to adequately cover his rear flank. Maiala would have admired their professionalism more if she wasn't the potential threat in the room.

"I..." She swallowed painfully. "I'm so sorry, your Majesty. It was never my intention to bring harm. I only... as the report documents, I only got a bit carried away in trying to be... proactive, I suppose, is the word, and..."

He waved his hand at her, still studying the bookshelves. "Yes, yes, I read it. I fully understand. I'm not here to have you executed, Director."

Hearing it said so dismissively was both a relief and very much not. "I... thank you, your Majesty."

"Really, it comes out as a rather convenient thing, as I explained to the Council, once they finished their whining and shouting."

Maiala felt as if she was standing in a fog. "I... I'm not sure what you mean, your Majesty."

"It's moved us into a prime position." He took two volumes from the shelf and handed them to the nearest Recognized Guard. "Very prime indeed. You did well, even if it was by accident. Nearly a perfect choice of goods, even. Perhaps the gods worked through you. Ha!"

She was torn between keeping her full attention on this supremely powerful man and trying to figure out which of her books he had blithely stolen. "Prime position for what, if I may ask, your Majesty?"

"Open new trading routes, make new alliances. Go to war with Great Pazdah." He rubbed his hands together and nodded. "We have options spread out in front of us, all with perfectly valid economic reasoning behind them. You've done your homeland a greater gift than you even thought, Director. Very good work. The gods or you yourself, very good work. I'll have a bull sacrificed to them, and a medal of honour issued to you, to cover both possibilities, I think. Guard, remember that for me."

The same guard who held the books nodded at that, the corner of his mouth twitching the barest fraction. "Yes, your Imperial Majesty."

"A sacrifice and a medal. And dear me, can we get a cleaning crew in here? These rooms are frightfully musty. How does anyone ever get any work done with their lungs full of dust? I suppose economists thrive in this sort of environment. Dusty books. Heads full of numbers."

Maiala bit down on the inside of her cheek. She badly needed to sit down. If only this awful, powerful man would get out of her office, so she could sit down...

The Emperor clapped his hands sharply. "Well, we'd best get back to the palace. Much to do. Thank you again, Director, for our new trade potential, and our war. And the wars that will follow the trade, and the trade that will follow the wars... ha! Amazing how it all fits together, isn't it? Sides of the same coin, and all that. Guard, remember to increase this department's budget. Ask the treasury for the percentage. Goodbye, Director, thank you for the books..."

He swept out of the room, followed by the guards, and Maiala was left in a heavy silence, with disturbed dust swirling in the air. She carefully moved back to her desk and sat down, gripping the arms of the chair to steady herself.

A medal. A budget increase. New trade initiatives. War.

How could any of her little value adjustments, twitches up and down on imaginary scales, possibly lead to all of that?

She looked down at the notes scattered across her desk. Sunflower seeds, cotton cloth, undyed yarn, salt beef, turnips. The emperor was right; all of these goods would be well-used in a war effort, and she had brought their markets to the flexion points all unintendedly.

She cleared her throat and lifted a pen, pulling the first report in front of her. Well. There was no reason to trouble the rest of the Agency with the reverberations of their work. It would only distract them. Let them be surprised by the medal and the budget, whenever they came. Let them be impressed by their Director and remember not to doubt her judgment ever again. She would need unquestioning support, with a war on the way; there would be much to do, snap decisions to be made...

Maiala allowed herself a small, triumphant smile, and made a note to treat herself to some fine brandy once she left the office that evening.

Only a small reward—best not to get too full of herself, after all. One could get a headache.

SUPPLY AND DEMAND AMONG THE SIDHE
Karl Dandenell

Queen Titania, eternal and undisputed monarch of the sidhe, was pissed.

"The Royal Exchequer has informed Us that We are running out of gold," she said, her voice simultaneously angry and enticing. "Running. Out. Of. Gold."

She paced in front of the packed throne room, gazing upon each of us in turn. I stood with my fellow leprechauns, eyes downcast, hoping to avoid notice. Your family makes one mistake...

"And do you know why We are short of coin? Anyone?" She glided past a stuffed dragon head resting on an onyx plinth. Its ruby eyes reflected the room's thousand candles.

Only Grond, the stone giant, was brave enough to hazard a guess. "Thieves?" His booming voice filled the enormous hall.

"Yes, thieves," she said, with a smile so cold that a pixie fluttering in the front row fainted, her delicate wings coated with ice. "Someone in this room is stealing. From Us."

I attempted to proclaim my innocence, but Grond beat me to it. "Not the giants, Your Majesty. We rarely leave the mountains."

"Everyone knows of the deadly magical wards that guard your palace, Your Majesty," called an elf from the back. "Why, even the goblins wouldn't risk them."

Trust an elf to state the obvious. Goblins—and their enchanted iron weapons—were forbidden within five leagues of the palace.

"Indeed," said Titania evenly. "Our vaults are safe. As is Our road through Fae. So it is particularly vexing that Our coffers dwindle while the demand for Our goods has never been higher."

She had a point. Every sidhe I knew was busy churning out spells, enchantments, curses, and what-have-you. Then I realized where she was going and twisted my silk derby with nervous hands.

"Some of you," she continued, "have traded with the humans in secret, keeping all the profit to yourselves. Well, that stops this instant!" A crack of thunder flattened us. Even Grond fell to his massive knees, denting the inlaid wood floor.

"Tell them!" Titania said, taking her throne.

Teagan, the Royal Exchequer, stepped forwards. The dwarf's long white beard nearly hid the heavy gold seal of office around his neck. Ten enormous ruby rings adorned his sausage fingers. "The border of Fae is hereby closed to trade." There were gasps and muffled curses, but they ceased when the Queen narrowed her eyes. "No goods shall pass into the human realm," continued the Exchequer, "unless they bear the seal of Her Majesty. Violators will be dealt with most severely."

"It's just another tax, Whelan," whispered my apprentice, Radki. "We can always bribe someone."

"Zip it!" I hissed. "Remember Gwallawg?" Titania had cursed the ogre Gwallawg for sneezing in her presence. For a year and a day, his every sniffle produced flaming arse-boils.

"The Royal Seal shall only be awarded to those items that meet Royal standards." Teagan held out his hand, and a page passed him an ornate bowl filled with small scrolls. "Each sidhe shall be given the right to manufacture, enchant, and otherwise produce specific items."

"Most fair!" cried another elf. They were such suck-ups.

"Dwarves!" called the Exchequer, holding out a scroll. "Come forth!"

Four dwarves separated themselves from the crowd. They unrolled their scroll. "Ha!" cried Callan, their leader. "Swords and daggers!" I bit my tongue in frustration. High markup on those.

"Gnomes!" Amulets.

"Giants!" Armour.

And so it went. Soon there were only two scrolls left. "Sprites."

The sprites got love potions and good-luck charms. Easy stuff. I could do those with my eyes closed.

Finally, Teagan called the leprechauns. I strode forth, accompanied by Radki and her son Peadar. I accepted my scroll, trying not to stare at Teagan's rings. With the local mines tapped out, rubies had become

Supply and Demand among the Sidhe

more valuable than diamonds. I opened the scroll: shoes.

I smiled and nodded, wishing ulcers and warts on every dwarf present. Shoes? Unbelievable.

The Queen spoke, "Let Us be absolutely clear. Whosoever fails to meet their quota shall pay hefty fines. In gold. Now begone."

I bowed deeply and then pushed my way out as quickly as decorum allowed. The brisk outside air was a welcome change from the stuffy chamber, though my stomach still roiled with sickness.

Throw a leprechaun into a cold iron box, stuff him full of rancid toadstools, or curse him with his true name, but never ever threaten his gold.

Radki topped off my mug. "It's racism, Whelan, pure and simple."

"Well, leprechauns are natural cobblers," I countered.

"Two centuries ago, maybe. The world's changed."

We were sitting in my parlour, drinking brown ale and smoking long clay pipes. Smoke curled up to the wooden beams, seeking escape. Fat beeswax candles burned in the wall sconces, giving off warm light. Splashing and clanking issued from the kitchen as Peadar washed up.

The Exchequer's scroll lay on the dining table, next to fresh quills and ink. I'd been tallying our supplies and devising a production schedule. If we worked two shifts, we could manage it. Barely.

"This is dung!" Radki said. "My tinkering is as good—if not better—than any gnome's."

"Arguable," I said. "For the moment, though, we must limit our efforts to shoes. Only shoes." It was an open secret that Radki had been hammering out self-cleaning cauldrons on the side. Who could blame her? Human innkeepers paid her ten silver pennies for them.

She curled her lip. "I don't suppose we have any choice in the matter."

"None." My father had once refused a Royal command and was exiled from Fae. Without his gold. I pushed the scroll towards her with a sigh. "Bejeweled silk slippers and sturdy riding boots."

She grimaced. "In a week?"

"Aye. Tomorrow's going to be busy, so I suggest everyone make an early start."

"You think your brother Cadogh is going to pick up needle and thread just because you ask?"

I pushed back from the table. "I'm head of the family now, and if he wants his cut, he'll follow my lead."

Radki considered her mug. "I hope he remembers that."

"Greed is thicker than blood." I picked up my shillelagh and twirled it.

The next morning, I sent word to our nearby cousins, though gossiping jackdaws had already spread the word. Despite Radki's reservations, the entire clan showed up, including Cadogh. We rolled up our sleeves and got to work, converting the barn into a temporary shed and stabling our ponies outside. My guest cottage became a finishing room, and Radki rented space nearby so the visiting leprechauns wouldn't be sleeping three to a bed.

I kept my own feather bed. Bad back, you know.

We cut and trimmed and sewed and pounded out two dozen beautiful pairs of shoes. We spared no effort: I dug into my personal stock of silver thread and ancient ash wood, pixie-shorn wool, and seed pearls harvested by selkies.

The results were impressive, if I say so myself. Our footwear made the wearer appear graceful, brave, and above all, desirable. And that was without any enchantment. Top that, gnomes.

We delivered everything to Her Majesty as scheduled, and Dwarvish teamsters drove it and other trade goods to Onwyer, the nearest human kingdom. The sovereign, Doncha the Proud, had recently squelched a coup attempt by one of his dukes and ordered a fete to celebrate his victory. Another duke, hoping to improve his stock, had gifted the shoes to the royal family.

The castle ravens observed the celebration, which lasted three days and nights, and reported that our shoes were particularly well received. I estimated our profit and shared the number with Radki.

"Huh," she said. "That seems a bit low."

"Titania's scribes hide the fine print with a glamour. It revealed itself this morning." I pointed to the scroll:

...whereas, the normal commission of ten percent of each transaction shall be increased to twenty percent (in the case of non-magical items) or thirty percent (for items normally considered enchanted) until such time that the Royal treasury is deemed sufficiently restored.

"Hold on," she said. "She doubled her cut?"

"And then some," I admitted. "Even so, it'll be a nice little pot of gold, eh?"

However, the next day's messenger brought different news.

"Master Whelan?" asked the large vole. He favoured a ruby pin with his silk cravat.

"At your service," I said.

The vole offered me a thick scroll. "Congratulations are in order," he said with false cheer. "Your family has earned the title of Royal Shoemakers, with all the rights and responsibilities contained therein." He glanced around the shop and wrinkled his nose. Scraps of leather and cloth covered the floor. Dirty tea cups and plates were piled on a stool.

I broke Titania's seal. As I deciphered the florid calligraphy, my brow furrowed. "While this is all perfectly lovely," I said, "I must admit to some confusion."

"Beg pardon?" The vole had wandered over to a table and wrapped three long claws around a pear in the fruit bowl.

"This is an order for lounging slippers, riding boots, and dancing shoes, both plain and fancy." I fished a pair of spectacles out of my vest pocket and whispered a seeing charm, but no hidden words appeared. "The specifications are most precise, but there is not a single mention of compensation."

"Such uncertainty is not uncommon when dealing with the Royal Court, Master Shoemaker," he replied, licking juice from his paw. "Trust me."

"Of course," I said, tucking away my spectacles. "I trust you have something for us."

He blinked slowly, his tiny black eyes disappearing behind long eyelashes. "No. Nothing whatsoever."

My cheeks grew warm. "Let me be blunt, then. We delivered the first shipment of shoes. On time. Where is our payment?"

The vole tossed the pear core over his shoulder. "Ah, that. The Exchequer sends his sincere thanks for your contribution to the Queen's trade agreement with Onwyer. Now if you'll excuse me, I have other appointments." With a casual bow, he left.

Radki slammed the door behind him. "I'd like to contribute some sincere lumps to his head."

"If he weren't a representative of the court, I'd gladly help," I said. It felt positively unnatural to restrain my temper. I settled for clapping Radki on the shoulder. "Still, look at the bright side. We're Royal Shoemakers. How does it feel?"

"Like spinning straw into gold," she replied. "Without the straw."

We fulfilled the Queen's second order, although it required every relation working dawn to dusk and beyond. After a few days of this, Radki informed me that Cadogh had instituted a work slowdown. I slipped a few coins into purses and whispered promises of more, and output picked up.

At the end of the week, we delivered everything, though we had little remaining in the way of leather, cotton, or silk. I sent Radki out with a cask of brandy to barter with the gnomes. They'd helped us before.

Radki returned empty-handed. "You'd think it was another warlock feud," she told me as I tallied up accounts. "Everyone's hoarding."

"That's bad news, though hardly surprising." If the other sidhe were as busy as us, they'd be calling in markers. I took off my spectacles and rubbed my eyes. "If we can't trade, we'll have to… buy our supplies with coin."

"No!"

I hated myself for admitting it. "And it gets worse." I waved a scroll at Radki. "The Exchequer will now assess an 'inspection fee' on every shipment to ensure it meets Her Majesty's 'reasonable standards of quality.'"

"And I thought elves were greedy," Radki said, slouching in her chair. She glanced around and then lowered her voice. "I heard brownies subcontracted their fancy gowns to the mice."

"Clever." Mice sewed nearly invisible stitches. And they worked for

Supply and Demand among the Sidhe

crumbs. I should have thought of that.

Radki poured herself a brandy. "What if we hired the pixies? They do decent work if you feed 'em enough honey and dandelion wine."

I snorted. "Pixies. Bunch o' layabouts. They're still living off the enchantments their grandparents laid down." I helped myself to brandy. "Nope, you'll never get a hard day's work out of them."

"Well, then, what do we do?" Radki downed her glass. "Onwyer's just the beginning, Whelan. Before you know it, every minor prince within a hundred leagues will be throwing tantrums if they don't have two pairs of our bloody shoes."

"Perhaps," I said. "For now, let's get back to work."

After Radki left, I lit my pipe. She was right. The humans would want more shoes, and Queen Titania would see that they got them. Worse, Cadogh had staged a walkout, leaving me badly shorthanded. If we failed to deliver our product, my brother could force me out. Well, that wasn't going to happen. I'd worked too hard to rebuild our fortunes after Father's indiscretion.

I drew a good mouthful of smoke and began to draft letters. It was time to call in favours.

Unfortunately, everyone sent similar responses:

Sorry.

Can't help you.

We already cut a deal with the pixies.

When the mole rats turned me down, citing a previous arrangement with the voles, I uncorked a new jug of dandelion wine and drank the whole thing, thimble by thimble. There was no getting around it: I had to go to them.

The next morning, hungover but determined, I told Radki she was in charge for a while.

"Where are you going?"

I packed my rucksack with food, a small sack of silver and a smaller purse of gold. "It's best you don't know."

Her face paled. "No. You promised!"

"I've looked at this from every angle, and they're the only ones who can provide us with supplies and labour." Or so I hoped. Titania had exiled the goblins after a brief but nasty border skirmish, but I still had a contact there who could get things done in a pinch.

"You can't trust them, Whelan," Radki said. "They'll turn on you the first chance they get."

"I remember," I said, picking up my rucksack and shillelagh. "Well, I'd best be off."

Radki opened the door. "What if you don't come back?"

"Then this all becomes Cadogh's problem." I handed her a scroll. "Just in case."

Her face lit up. "A map to your stash?"

I laughed. "You wish! It's a letter of recommendation."

"Oh." Her disappointment was obvious. "Thank you, I guess."

"Don't thank me yet. You've got a lot of shoes to make in the next five days. Yours and mine. Hop to it, woman."

I spent an entirely dull day on the Queen's Road, my two ponies easily pulling my empty wagon to Ballynog village at sunset.

I found the inn where I used to sell poitín, gave the wagon over to the stable boy, and took myself to the common room. The pox-scarred gnome behind the bar barely glanced up as I took a seat. Eventually, he wandered over.

"What'll you have?"

I spun a silver penny on the scarred table. "I'm looking for someone."

"They got a name?" asked the gnome, sweeping the coin into his apron.

"Gratlach," I whispered.

"Sounds a bit goblin to me."

"That's as may be," I said. "Have you seen him?"

"Maybe I have, and maybe I haven't. Goblins are all mysterious and such."

I placed another penny. "If you happen to see him, tell him an old acquaintance would welcome a bit of conversation."

"I'll ask around. What are you drinking?"

"Beer," I answered.

I sat and nursed weak beer until dinner was served: chewy mutton and fried potatoes that cried for salt.

A few hours later, the innkeeper ushered a trio of drunken dwarves out the front door and locked up. He banked the fire and swept a few errant ashes into a battered pail. "I'm off to bed. Make sure you blow out the candles."

I waved and leaned against the wall, feeling the day catching up with me. As I started to drift off, I heard a rough voice in the dark.

"Now isn't this romantic?"

I glanced towards the fireplace, where a hump-backed, crooked-fanged fellow with sallow skin sat. He plucked a whole walnut from a nearby bowl and chewed loudly.

"Gratlach," I said.

"Long time, Whelan." He picked shells from his teeth.

"Excellent to see you. You're looking well."

Gratlach chuckled and sauntered across the room, the odour of rotten leather preceding him. "That's why I like doing business with leprechauns. You're all such good liars." He slid into the booth, his red eyes bright. "Now tell me, what brings you to my door?"

"I need materials for shoes. And hands to make them."

"My, my," Gratlach said. "So the jackdaws were telling the truth. The rich and respected Whelan is now a... cobbler." When I bristled, he added, "Excuse me. Royal Shoemaker."

"Yes, that's the title." I cracked my knuckles and then passed over a scroll. "Here's what I need. Can you handle it?"

He pulled a candle over and read. "My craftsmen produce saddles for dire wolves and cloaks that stop arrows. I'm sure we can handle shoes. The question is: why should I?" He grinned widely, emphasizing his fangs.

I sighed. "There is the matter of your debt."

Gratlach scraped wax from the candle holder. "That old thing. Not enough to cover this."

"Fine," I said, reaching for my rucksack. "How much more?"

"Just a favour, Whelan."

I raised an eyebrow. "I'm listening."

"This trade embargo is a nuisance," he said. "It's one thing to skip into

Onwyer and steal a few children under a glamour, but delivering a wagon of valuable goods is another."

"I am not running weapons again, Gratlach."

He pouted. "And here I thought we were friends." He raised his hand. "All right. No iron weapons. I swear on my mother's well-gnawed bones."

He was up to something, of course, but I didn't see that I had any choice. "Deal."

"Deal. Grab your little walking stick and follow me."

He took me down to the basement, past casks of mead and bitter beer. In one dusty corner, he opened a hidden door, revealing a long, wide tunnel. "Delivery entrance," he said, laughing. "Wipe your feet!"

We padded down a dry tunnel lined with mortared brick. Bright, almost smokeless candles illuminated our path.

Gratlach turned down a side passage, which opened into a rougher chamber that stank of wet soil and roots. Two smaller goblins dressed in leather aprons and rough breeches were wrestling crates onto a pile. "Oy, Kep!" said Gratlach. "Come here."

One of the goblins dropped his crate with a crash and limped over. His left leg was shorter than the other. Gratlach handed him the scroll. "I need everything on this list loaded onto wagons lickety-split."

Kep looked at the list, frowning. "Not the strongboxes?"

"Those too, you simpleton! Now move along before I boil you down for candles!"

As Kep limped away, Gratlach whispered. "I had to hire him. He's a nephew."

Gratlach took me through another tunnel to a warehouse. A few minutes later, wide doors at the far end slid open and Kep drove my wagon inside. Five more goblins followed, carrying oilcloths and baskets. They closed the doors and tied the ponies to an iron ring. Poor animals kept pulling at their bits and flicking their ears. Goblins took some getting used to.

I watched Gratlach's crew pack up bundles of leather, balls of silk twine, and other supplies into crates, which they hoisted onto my wagon. When that was full, they covered the whole bed with an oilcloth and set to filling a second wagon. It was half as large as mine, hitched up to a pair of skinny mules.

I cracked open a door. A steady breeze brought the smell of rain, which was a relief. Goblin sweat could peel the glaze off pottery.

"Time to get comfy!" called Gratlach. He and Kep hoisted two empty crates onto the second wagon, and five goblins climbed inside. Kep nailed the crates closed.

"Try not to kill them before we get there," I said.

"Naw. Plenty of air holes for everyone." Gratlach poked his fingers through an opening, eliciting a yelp. "Nothing like close quarters to build team morale."

"Are we ready?" I yawned.

"Nearly so." He handed me a lantern. "Ride a few minutes ahead. If you see any patrols, give a whistle. I'll slip off the road."

"Wonderful." I climbed into my seat and hung the lantern next to me. It was a fine piece: thick glass wrapped in layers of gold wire. It gave off a soft, warm light, yet felt cool to the touch: Dwarvish craftwork. Interesting.

Behind me, Gratlach cracked his whip. "Hey ho!"

We drove into a drizzle, which became a real downpour. I hunkered under my sodden coat and sucked on nightshade berries to keep myself alert.

As it turned out, we had the road to ourselves. Apparently, everyone else had had the good sense to stay inside. Even the Queen's patrols seemed to have business elsewhere.

I let my thoughts drift. Based on what I'd seen, Gratlach had found a new trading partner among the sidhe. Fine by me. I'd be happy to see the back of him once we'd made quota.

Of course, there was our next shipment. Even a troll could see we couldn't sustain this pace, even with goblin contractors. I had to find some way out of this contract. My reputation was at stake.

Curse those dwarves anyway. They were decent fellows back when they mined iron. Once they bribed their way into court, though, they'd stuck their big noses in the air like everyone else. Cared more about polishing their jewelry than sharpening their axes.

On a hunch, I examined my lantern. Definitely custom work. When I flipped it over, I immediately recognized the maker's mark: a stylized T over crossed hammers. House of Teagan.

Well, well. I urged the ponies on, making plans.

It was early the next morning when I pushed my way into my house on stiff legs.

Radki looked up from her bench, where her breakfast dishes shared space with her tools. "There you are!""

I reached over and snagged a piece of bacon. "Here I am," I said. "Is there any more?"

"I'll ask Peadar," she said. "You brought the supplies?"

"Everything we asked for."

Radki whooped. "That's the best news I've heard since we beat the gnomes in the mumblety-peg tournament!"

"But there were complications."

She raised her eyebrows. "Oh?"

I shook water from my coat. "Come with me."

Radki followed me outside. Gratlach waved.

"Radki, meet Gratlach," I said.

"At your service." He laughed and offered Radki a sack filled with death's head mushrooms. "Found these by the riverbank. Breakfast?"

Radki turned green. "Uh, already ate."

"Your loss." He popped a fungus in his mouth. "Anyway, I brought your kit. Right, boys?" He thumped the crate behind him. Muffled curses emerged.

I waved towards the wagons. "Radki, get those into the barn and see to the animals."

"Barn's pretty full—"

"Just do what you can."

I hung up my coat, poured myself a mug of strong beer, and drained it in one long swallow. Gratlach curled up by the fire and poked at the coals.

My joints popped as I rolled my shoulders. "I'm not running a boarding house," I said. "You stay in the barn."

"That's wise," said Gratlach. "Imagine the fuss if someone were to stop by and see us."

I shuddered. "The Queen would have my head."

"Then don't tell her. Now if you'll excuse me," he said, yawning. "It's been a long night, and I need my beauty sleep." He cackled and headed for the barn.

Radki set up a workspace for Gratlach and his craftsmen, who filled in for our absent cousins. To my surprise and relief, the goblins worked diligently and turned out quality work. Apart from the smell of their meals—they favoured pickled lizard eggs and fried beaver musk glands—they were almost tolerable. I began to think we'd actually make quota.

Two nights later, Gratlach appeared at my office. "New moon tonight, Royal Shoemaker. Let's go."

I set aside my papers. "All right. Where are we going?"

"You're going to the summer festival field. Whistle when you get there."

"Thanks for not burdening me with too many details," I said before heading outside. My wagon was loaded with several strongboxes. I checked the horses and gave them apples as an apology for this late excursion.

I drove past darkened houses and workshops, flinching at every rustle of birdwing and creak of the harnesses. Once I passed the last house, I stopped and turned my attention to the strongboxes. They were heavy ironwood, banded by iron and secured with heavy hasp locks. I opened one with a bit of pixie dust and a charm. The box contained ten cinched bags, each one full of unpolished rubies.

Rubies. Now it all made sense. I quickly replaced the bag, re-locked the strongbox, and set the horses to a trot. Ten minutes later, I reached the summer festival field and whistled. Several cloaked figures emerged from the shadows.

"Whelan?" said a muffled voice.

"The same."

"Lie face down on the seat and don't move."

I did as ordered and felt heavy bodies jumping on the wagon and shoving the strongboxes to the ground. One must have hit someone's foot, because I heard a yelp, followed by several choice Dwarvish curses. After that, the first voice spoke again. "Stay here until dawn."

"If you insist." I dozed on my bench. When the first light crested the hills, I drove home at top speed, handed the horses to a sleepy Radki, and fetched my good parchment. I quickly composed a letter detailing my suspicions about the Royal Exchequer. An hour later, I presented myself at the palace, where a vole footman promised—for five gold crowns—to deliver my report to Titania, bypassing the Royal Secretary. I gave him an extra five for the Secretary.

You can't be too careful about these things.

A faint knocking startled me awake. Apparently, I'd fallen asleep at my desk. The knocking became a serious pounding. "Coming!" I hollered, rubbing my eyes. When I opened the front door, I found myself facing a vole dressed in court colours and ruby earrings. Two badgers in leather jerkins flanked him. They carried nasty-looking cudgels. The vole shoved a scroll at me.

"Her Most Royal Majesty Queen Titania requires your presence."

I opened the scroll. It repeated the command in painstakingly formal language.

"You will accompany us," said the vole.

"I need to change," I said, closing the door.

Radki appeared as I pulled on a fresh shirt. "Whelan, you should—"

"The Queen wants to see me," I said. "And my escort doesn't appear friendly."

"I'll come with you," Radki said.

"No, stay here and keep an eye on our contractors," I said.

She puffed her cheeks. "That's what I was going to tell you. They're gone. Scarpered."

"What?"

"We're waiting, Master Whelan!" called the vole. Radki and I grabbed our coats and let the badgers haul us onto their cart. We rode to the palace in silence. I wondered if I'd overplayed my hand and would be joining my father in exile.

Supply and Demand among the Sidhe

The badgers walked us into the audience chamber, which was filled with all manner of sidhe, talking quietly among themselves.

No one met my eye.

An elf in a fine silk coat slammed his staff on the floor three times. "Her Most Royal Majesty, Queen Titania."

We all bowed our heads, curtseying or bending the knee. I heard the creaking of a stone giant's joints behind me.

"Fair folk," the queen said, "We have important news. Not long ago, We asked you to assist your sovereign in a time of need." She strode slowly before us, followed by a pair of mice who held the train of her dress. "We are pleased to report that We no longer suffer from an embarrassing lack of coin."

A few muted coughs emerged from the crowd. Titania narrowed her eyes.

"Unfortunately," she continued, producing my scroll, "some among you have conspired against Us." She took a bosom-filling breath. "And that We cannot bear."

"Bring in the prisoner!" cried the herald.

"Wait, isn't that you?" Radki whispered.

Two centaurs trotted in, carrying a pole from which hung suspended the Royal Exchequer. He no longer wore his ruby rings, seal of office, or indeed any raiment other than a pair of dirty breeches and a set of iron manacles. Even his beard had been hacked away, leaving only white patches.

"Our former Exchequer has been trading with the goblins."

"Your Majesty, 'tis but a misunderstanding—"

"Silence!" growled one of the centaurs.

I gasped, as did many others, for when Teagan spoke, spiders streamed from his mouth. Some clung to the dwarf's face, while others dropped to the floor to be crushed under the centaur's hooves.

"Ooh, that's unpleasant," said Radki.

The Queen drew herself to her full height. "Teagan, you and your scurrilous kin have plagued Us with diversion of trade, false reports, and outright theft!"

We stood there silently as the Queen described secret tunnels that led between Her vaults and a storehouse owned by Teagan's cousin. Most damning, a stash of rubies had been recovered from Teagan's residence.

"We paid for those rubies," he whispered.

Titania spun on her heel, sending mice flying. "With Our coin!"

"We have receipts…" Teagan said. His eyes crossed as a centipede crawled between his nostrils.

"Details," she said. "You are guilty." She snapped her fingers, and a large vole handed her a goblet of deep red wine. She drained the goblet and returned it. "However," she said with a dainty belch, "We are not without mercy. It would be unseemly for others to pay for your crimes." She gestured to the herald.

He rapped his staff on the floor three times. In a loud, clear voice, he declared, "Once you fulfill your current contracts, the Fae shall once again be allowed to trade with humans on your own terms. However," he added, casting a sidewise glance at the crowd, "Her Majesty reminds you to share your good fortune."

The elves cried out, "Three cheers for Queen Titania!" The rest of us quickly joined in.

She accepted our accolade for a moment and then raised a hand. "There is still the matter of compensation." The crowd eased away from the dwarves, leaving an open space around them. They prostrated themselves with vigour.

"For their part, the dwarves will, on every full moon, send Us as much gold as can be carried by a centaur."

The dwarf Callan lifted his head. "Most fair, O' Queen!" He whispered to his fellows and then continued. "May we ask, with great humility, how long we must pay this fine…?"

"Until Teagan's beard reaches his feet." She offered him a cold smile. "He shall remain Our guest so We may take the occasional measure of his whiskers."

Ouch. Even if the dwarves wanted to try some enchantment on Teagan's beard, they'd be hard-pressed to do so while he languished in the dungeons. I almost felt sorry for him.

Callan smiled painfully before mashing his face to the floor. Two pixies darted over and stole his cap, which they tossed into a nearby brazier.

"Swords and daggers!" they jeered.

"Any more questions?" Queen Titania said. "No? Then begone, all save Master Whelan."

My heart thumped loudly. After the room emptied, Titania glided over and placed a hand on my brow.

"How fortunate that you were observing Teagan's house the night the goblins delivered their rubies." She placed a kiss upon my brow. "And how curious," she whispered, "that goblins were reported on Our road near your workshop."

I whispered back, "Curious indeed, Your Majesty."

"Your father did not wish to serve Us," she said, stroking my hair. "But you are a faithful and generous leprechaun, are you not?"

"Absolutely, Your Majesty!"

"Keep your nose clean, Whelan." She turned away. "If you don't, you can share Teagan's cell."

My nose began to itch furiously. I bowed and backed away. Radki was waiting for me outside.

"Well?" she asked.

"She let me off with a warning." I blew my nose into my kerchief and found a caterpillar there.

Radki said, "Are you all right?"

"Just a cold." I hoped.

SHAPE, SIZE, COLOUR, AND LUSTRE
JM Templet

Every morning, my mother dives for pearls.

Before light breaks, she takes off all of her clothes and walks the few feet from our home to the green waves of the ocean. She takes a deep breath and dives.

Sometimes she doesn't come up for hours. When she does, she always has a mass of clams in her net. They grow pearls like we do, but my mother says clams aren't like us. They keep their souls somewhere else.

Or maybe they don't have any.

I grew my first pearl under my chin when I was a little over a year old.

We choci grow our pearls that way for years, in all colours and sizes. Some are more valuable than others. We trade them for debt or love or greed.

The priests say we were born from a snake's womb and that we carry so much sin inside that we grow pearls to buy our way out of the underworld.

My mother says priests are foolish old men who couldn't get a woman to marry them.

But she isn't married either, I always point out.

I've never seen my father. I think he must be a ghost. One of those faded figures who haunt the towns destroyed by giants hundreds of years ago.

My mother's always shivering and wet when she finishes diving. Her scales turn up to reflect the sun, all blue and gold and rose.

I once asked her why she dives every morning if it's so awful. She said she was the last diver. All of the other pearl divers are gone.

Too old or too weary to keep diving.

When I grow up, I'm going to help her so she won't be the only one. But I'm only eleven, and she says it's too dangerous.

The water is dark and hungry, a continuous open mouth. I think sometimes it wants to swallow me whole.

After she shakes for a minute, we have warm drinks and put on dry clothing. I lick the salt from my lips, remembering the waves and the hungry noises.

I don't like the ocean here. I don't like the stinging fish or the hard rocks on the beach.

We came from somewhere else where the ocean was green and you could see all the way down. That's where my people are. One day, we'll have enough to go back. My mother says so.

She rests and I open the shells, sorting pearls by size and shape.

"When are we going to trade mine?" I ask.

She sighs. "Not for many years yet. You'd lose too much."

I frown at the clam in my hand. I have a full string of pearls now, and I want something wonderful for them. A crown or a good pair of shoes. Perfume that smells of freshly baked bread.

I think boys like it when you smell of food.

"Your pearls are most valuable," my mother says. "Think of them like a wish, the biggest wish you can have."

"What did you wish for?" I ask, poking at the smaller pearls.

She smiles, and her face lights up from somewhere inside. "You."

I cross my eyes and finish sorting. Babies are not worth wishing for. Babies are loud and can't walk and smell of mud. My first wish would be so much better.

Once the pearls are sorted, we leave for the market.

It's a loud place, filled with hawkers announcing their goods from simple stalls decorated in every colour imaginable. I'm always excited to go to the market. It smells of possibility. And other things, but I've learned to ignore that.

Some stalls sell pearls. Pink and blue and yellow and all sizes. The blue ones make me sad. They look like tears.

We pass a wooden stall with a striped blanket for a ceiling. The merchant is selling a pearl that seems alive. A hidi stands guard near it. They have fat ears that wind behind their necks and around their heads.

"Special," he says. "Straight from the underworld. Fished from the river of the dead."

Is it true? I've never seen a pearl like that. The light reflects off it and changes its patterns, which curl into jagged lines and sweeping waves. I reach out to touch it, and my mother slaps my hand.

"Dyes and chemicals," she says.

The man's eyes widen. "I would never. I run an honest shop, madam. No trickery here."

We keep walking. I want to go back, but she's holding my hand too tightly. She's always holding me too tightly. I can't breathe some days, and I shout horrible things at her. But she tells me she loves me.

I'm sorry. I'm sorry.

I jerk my hand away. "I'm not a baby."

She smooths the spikes on my head. "You're my baby. Come on, we need to get these sold, and then we'll have fish when we get home. The crispy kind you like."

We always sell to Oriana. She is an old friend of my mother's and always gives us a fair price. She lets my mother sit behind her stall and gossip, which is boring. Usually, my mother lets me explore. She says my little ears hear everything.

Oriana is white and pink all over. She has this jagged scar across her eye and mouth. She won't tell me how she got it, just that in her part of the world she's considered magic.

I don't know how a person can be magic. You can do magic, but that doesn't make you magic.

"Soni! Good to see you," she says.

My mother ducks under the covering and hugs Oriana. She's much taller than Oriana. And greener. Her scales are darker in the market, as if she's trying to hide. Oriana's stall is tidy and cool inside.

"You brought the little one," Oriana says after they separate.

She reaches into her pocket and takes a wrapped piece of candy out. I quickly take it before my mother can refuse.

"You shouldn't eat sweets," my mother says.

"Always so strict," Oriana says, shaking her head. "That makes them rebel. Dangerous."

My mother pats my head. "Not my Maya. Go on and explore. Don't wander too far."

I'm good at wandering. I talk to the mingos who have beaks instead of lips and chitter words. They sell silver metal mined from places only they can fly to.

Next to them is a stall that glitters. Bracelets reflect rainbows at me, and I feel my breath catch in my throat. Beautiful. I've never experienced such beauty before.

The one in the middle makes music when I touch it with the very tip of my finger.

Too expensive. I can hear my mother's voice in my head. Can't afford. Don't need. She recycles lines back and forth, but the answer is always no.

I want it. My hands clench at my sides.

"How much?" I ask.

The hawker is a very large man with a nose like a toad's. He squints at me.

"You're that fish woman's daughter, aren't you? You don't have anything I want."

My face turns hot.

"You're wrong! I do have something, I do!"

I reach into my special bag, where I keep my first strand of pearls.

His eyes sharpen when he sees the string.

"Ahh. Now that is a prize."

"Is it enough?"

I'm shaking inside. My mother told me not to trade them, but I need that bracelet. It's a big wish. She'll forgive me once she sees me wearing it.

The man nods and hands me the bracelet. My hands shake as I hand over my pearls.

I start to go back to Oriana's stall, but I can't remember where it is. I can't remember how I got to the market.

I start walking without thinking. My feet know the way home.

My mother finds me shaking and rocking on the beach. Her face is unfamiliar, but I know it's her.

I'm so cold inside I might breathe ice.

"Maya, what were you thinking? I looked all over for you."

She holds my cold hands in hers.

"I traded my strand," I say.

My mother doesn't wail or cry out. She sits next to me and watches the ocean.

"He won't give them back," I say.

I know he won't. He held them too closely.

"I'm stupid."

She shakes her head. "I should have explained. Our people mature slower than most. Each pearl we give up acts as a halt, shaving months of memory and experience. It's the price."

"For what?"

"Everything," she says.

"I don't want to forget you," I tell her.

She hugs me, and I feel a little warmer.

"We'll fix it," she says fiercely.

That night, she stays up telling me stories and holding me close so that I can hear her heart beating. I fall asleep while she speaks.

When I wake, the strand of pearls I traded is beside me, next to a note.

Her handwriting is much worse than mine. The priests taught me to read and write. I hated it, but mother said words could be weapons and I should have them all.

Maya,

I love you. Never forget that. Oriana will take care of you until you can make your own future. Don't try and find me. I'm more than lost. I want you to remember the green ocean. The taste of salt. You are always my baby.

I stare numbly at the paper.

No, is all I can think. I won't stay and sit. I will find you.

I grab my bag and run to the market to look for Oriana.

She sits in her stall, hands folded as if she's been waiting for me.

"Where is she?"

Oriana shakes her head. "You can't go there."

I sit next to her. "Please. Tell me what she did."

"She sold her pearl, her last. Traded it for your first."

My mother was in the underneath, the world below. I've heard stories about the place. Mostly from priests who said that if we gave up our last pearls, we'd be trapped there along with others who couldn't move on.

I throw my bracelet on the ground, grinding it under my heel.

"I'm getting her back," I say.

Oriana tries to stop me from leaving. Her voice is far away. I can't. I want to tell her I can't, but I only run faster.

A priest once told me of a monster who lived for hundreds of years. She lived in a cave along the coast and ate whoever ventured near it until she was gorged on flesh. Then she slept. She slept so long that the world forgot about her.

He called her the snaggle-tooth.

I bet she'll know how to travel to in-between places. The old ones always know things. She'll probably eat me or feed me to her vile creatures of the night.

Still, I go.

Hours turn into days while I climb. I stop only to eat and take quick naps. I walk around in circles trying to find it.

Something's watching me. Something that makes me shiver.

"I just came to visit, grandmother," I shout. That was polite, wasn't it?

I find the cave a few minutes later. Just waiting for me.

There is a torch on each side of the entrance. They don't look magical. I poke one, just to be sure.

"Stop touching my things," a voice growls. "And come in if you dare." She sounds like a tiger.

I walk into the darkness, towards a faint light in the distance. Bone and wood crunch beneath my feet. She is not a very good housekeeper.

The snaggle-tooth is bent over a cauldron, stirring with a wooden spoon.

I don't know what she is. Her face is jagged, as if someone cut pieces of it off. Her teeth are large and sharp. Her eyes are black. Or more than black. They're the colour that black is supposed to be.

"I need—"

She holds up a bony hand. "I know what you need, girl. We're having supper first."

My nose wrinkles. Whatever it is, it smells foul. My stomach gurgles in protest.

Shape, Size, Colour, and Lustre

She fills a bowl up with brown, watery soup and hands it to me before filling her own bowl.

I tip the bowl to my mouth and drink. It tastes of old fish.

The snaggle-tooth slurps her meal quickly. I can only drink a few more sips before I feel like puking.

She smacks her lips. "Mushroom stew. Can't beat it for nutritional value. You'll need all of your puny strength to get there and back."

"I don't have much to trade," I say.

"Well I know that, don't I? I'm betting on the future here."

"The future?"

She points at me. "Your future. You'll vow to become my apprentice and do apprentice things for however long I like. In return, I'll show you how to get to the place of fog."

"What if I don't come back?"

"Risky, isn't it?" she says, smiling. "You look like a girl who isn't afraid of monsters."

I don't like her smile. It cuts and bleeds at the same time.

My life for my mother's. I agree and she nods.

The snaggle-tooth has me rest and think quiet thoughts. She rummages around her cave, muttering under her breath.

She makes a victorious sound and comes back holding a coin.

She shows me both sides. One has a frowning woman, and one has a frowning man.

"Old gods," she says.

"Were they always angry?"

"Yes, yes. Creating worlds is a hard job. Have to be stern, don't you? Can't have bushes growing wherever they want to."

How is a coin going to take me to my mother? I eye it warily.

"There are rules," she says. "It must be brought back to the same place you got it from. Do not look back. Do not wander. Follow the path."

"Or what?"

"Endless death and torture."

Okay, I will definitely follow the rules.

She puts it in my hand. "Conduit. You to her. Blood to blood. Listen. Concentrate."

281

I close my eyes and feel the world tilt. Light brightens and dims behind my eyelids. Warm. I'm so warm and then I'm not.

When I open my eyes, I know I'm in the shadow place. The coin flickers in my hand.

It lights up. I can feel my mother. Feel her heartbeat.

It's a song I can dance to. A deep thrumming beneath, showing me where to go.

Shadows hiss at me. The ground underneath me is water. My steps cause ripples, each one fanning out in a circle. I see large, angular creatures swimming. Watching me.

I cross a forest of tall pink coral trees, careful not to touch those angry spikes. I cross a stream of black water. The light from the coin dims.

Nothing sounds natural. I can't hear running water or insects or the humming of wind. This is a quiet place.

I follow her heartbeat as the sound gets louder and louder until I find her.

She sits on a rock, trailing her fingers in the muddy water. Strange fish come up and nibble on her fingers. She is grey, as if something has sucked all of the colour out of her.

I'm scared. Scared that none of this is real and when I wake up I'll still be in the hag's cave. Probably roasting over a fire.

"Mother?"

Her head jerks unnaturally. Her eyes are red.

"How?" she says.

I hold up the coin.

"I told you not to follow."

I wrap my arms around her, holding her tightly. "I'm not good at following instructions."

She kisses the top of my head. "So you went to that horrible beast, did you? What did you promise her?"

"I'm going to be her apprentice."

My mother rocks me in her arms. "She shouldn't have sent you."

"I don't want to be alone. I can stay here with you, can't I?"

I don't mind the fog or the wet or the cold. I could get used to giant serpents. I wonder what those strange fish taste like. Probably better than the mushroom stew.

"No," my mother says in her "I am not budging on the price of these" voice. Hawkers are powerless against it. So am I.

"Then you come with me," I say. "We'll go home."

"Home," she says. "Yes."

She sounds strange, like her voice is further away than her body. I have to listen closely.

"Do you know the way?" I ask. The coin led me to my mother, but I'm not sure it will lead me back.

Her eyes darken. "I do."

We move quickly and my mother jerks me away from a shadow more than once.

"They bite," she says.

We come to the black stream. My mother tells me to cross and I do.

"Don't look back," she says.

I do.

She hasn't crossed. She stays, stuck as if something's holding her.

I can't cross.

She holds up a small pearl. "Your first one," she says. "I couldn't bear to part with it."

She drops my pearl into the black water.

"Look forwards," she says.

The black water swirls, turning my white pearl grey and then an electric blue. I am a baby again, my eyes open for the first time, gazing up at her smiling face. Her smile is wide.

When the vision is gone, so is my mother. I think maybe my pearl was the only thing keeping her here. Will she become one of those hungry shadows under the water?

My eyes are hot and wet. I can't follow her back there. I can only go forwards.

My mother gave up my first memory of her to free me. The witch had to have known I couldn't bring her back. Not without proper payment. She only told me she'd show me how to get to my mother.

Maybe she didn't know. Or maybe she wanted to give me a chance to say goodbye.

JM Templet

I feel the coin, warm again in my hand. I count the years ahead of me. My mother has given me so many.

I have to spend them wisely.

DAS KAPITAL
Stephen Woodworth

Capital is dead labour, which, vampire-like, lives only by sucking living labour, and lives the more, the more labour it sucks. —Karl Marx

Translated from the original German by Friedrich Engels, the following letter is dated March 6th, 1883—Marx's last known correspondence before his death from pleurisy on March 14th of that year:

My dear Engels,

I am leaving you this letter to relate a most curious and uncanny incident that occurred to me many years ago. I never thought to bother you with it before, but recent events with which you are no doubt familiar have brought the matter to mind, and I can think of no one but you, old friend, to whom I may unburden myself in what little time I may have left.

You see, I met a madman once.

I'd been toiling in the Reading Room at the British Museum as usual, dredging through a ponderous volume by that pompous bourgeois Bentham in preparation to shred his arguments, when a voice abruptly spoke from beside me.

"Dr. Marx?"

I glanced up from my text to see a young gentleman who seemed the epitome of everything I was not: his suit of the finest material and most fashionable cut, his skin as fair as mine is Moorish, his hair combed and pomaded, his patrician face clean-shaven but for well-trimmed muttonchops.

The man bore such an attitude of condescension that I took him for one of the staff come to shoo me out of the library. I determined to muster the best English I could to answer him. "Yes? Is there a problem?"

The stranger smiled in effete delight. "Karl Marx? Author of this ment. "I wanted to bring you here on the day they collect the rents. It's easier to observe the change... *there!*"

He pointed to a man too well-dressed to be a native of the neighbourhood. Rainwater dripping from the brim of his top hat, the interloper descended the steps to a basement hovel and rapped on the door of the residence with his walking-stick. From where we stood, the woman who opened the door appeared sunk to her shoulders in the street, a damned soul frozen into the pavement. She must have been barely five-and-twenty, but her sallow, haggard countenance looked twice that old. The rent collector murmured a terse demand and opened his purse, but the tenant shook her head, jabbering excuses and pleas as she tried to quell the caterwauling of the infant in her arms.

"*This* is what you brought me here to see—the poor drowning in the muck of their own misery?" I waved my palm before Tavener's face. "This is like showing me my own hand!"

"Hush," he said. "Look again. See! See how she *ages*."

I watched as the woman gave in to the rent collector, withdrew from the door, and returned with a few silver coins in her hand. They could not have amounted to more than a couple of shillings in all, but as she dropped them into the collector's open purse, I could swear to you, Engels, that veins of iron-grey threaded through the tangles of her brown locks, that her eyes hollowed and her pale skin stiffened and cracked like old leather. I later dismissed the effect as a trick of the mind prompted by Tavener's emphatic suggestion and the deepening shadows of the bleak afternoon, but the sight so appalled me that I could not speak, only shudder.

"Was the same with my mother and father." Tavener's accent slid back towards its plebian roots, hard as Newcastle anthracite. "Drained dead and penniless 'fore they were fifty. Do you understand now why I brought you here?"

I shook my head, mute.

Tavener frowned. "Then you need to see more."

I numbly followed him as we trailed the rent collector on his rounds. The next tenant, a Cockney whose broad grin revealed a single tarnished tooth, rushed from his tenement to greet the collector as if welcoming his own brother. Slavering pleasantries, the Cockney urged his visitor to accept a chipped cup of oily tea as hospitality. The collector, stone-faced, ignored the beverage and opened his purse, yet the tenant continued to smile and stall.

Finally, a boy of no more than six came running up the street as if late for school. In one hand, he carried the wooden box of a bootblack; in the other, a fistful of coppers that he immediately handed to the Cockney, who laughed and patted him paternally on the head. The moment the lad surrendered the pennies, his countenance took on an aspect of unnatural maturity, puffy with weariness, and I suddenly received the impression that he was not a boy at all but a stunted, dwarfish man.

Again, I assumed that I had succumbed to the influence of Tavener's deluded imagination. Yet I observed the same effect a minute later, when a yellow-haired girl even younger than the boy hurried to contribute her tuppence and ha'pennies. Holding a basket of watercress on her arm, she seemed to wither like a cut daffodil as the Cockney plucked the coins from her palm and counted them into the collector's purse. Her skin blanched from pale to pallid, and her golden ringlets drooped into lank, greasy rattails.

A third child, the smallest of all, scampered up on legs barely grown enough to walk on and unfolded the dirty apron she wore, where she'd accumulated coins that she had evidently garnered from begging. As the Cockney passed the money to the collector, the baby-fat appeared to drain from the girl's cheeks, leaving her soft features drawn and skeletal. She tottered backwards, so that the other children had to step forwards to keep her from falling. Huddled together, the three waifs personified the working class in miniature, shrunken and enfeebled from having their very beings pulled out through their pockets, old without ever having been young.

The rent collector, satisfied at last, departed, and the Cockney cackled. I could not say which possibility I found more heinous: that he was some Fagin-like miscreant marshalling orphans to pay his way in life, or that he was the children's actual father, vending their innocence to fund his own dissipation.

You may say, dear Fred, that I only witnessed the daily exhaustion of the poor, and in my calmer moments I would agree with you. But watching those children decay before my eyes filled me with such a supernal loathing that I was willing to believe in an evil even greater than mere human greed. Tavener insisted upon showing me at least a dozen other pitiful wretches, all of whom subtly weakened as they surrendered their rents to the collector, but it is the remembrance of those wasted tots that abhors me to this day.

"*Now* can you appreciate the monstrousness of what they do to us?" Tavener asked at last.

"Yes," I answered, barely above a whisper. "I've seen enough."

"Then I shall make good on my luncheon promise," Tavener said. "And you shall see where all this plundered capital goes."

We returned to the cab, which then conveyed us to Verrey's in Regent Street, one of the most celebrated restaurants in London. Its modest, rather old-fashioned blue-washed façade belied its exclusive clientele, for as soon as we stepped inside, we found ourselves in the company of bankers and stockbrokers, earls and heiresses.

We passed through a small antechamber and entered a large dining room dimly illuminated by a skylight in the roof, panelled with dark wood and made gaudy by the addition of a multitude of mirrors on its walls. To our right, a roar of laughter rose from a conclave of gentlemen in tailcoats, and the loudest braying came from the bearded ass at the head of the table, who wore a blue sash across his bloated paunch and an ostentatious gold medallion on his breast. It was none other than Her Majesty's son Edward Albert—"Bertie," the Prince of Wales.

The headwaiter approached and gave my frayed black suit a flat stare. "May I *help* you?"

I burned with a fit of contemptible shame at my class.

Despite his earlier fawning, Tavener suddenly acted as if he did not wish to be too closely associated with me. He glanced around at the prominent patrons, gauging who might be watching, and indicated an isolated table in a far corner of the room. "Could we perhaps sit there?"

The waiter bowed, evidently relieved. "An excellent choice, sir."

Tavener resumed his ingratiating manner as soon as the headwaiter had seated us, taken our order, and departed. "One must be discreet to move among the monsters. Dress as they do, speak as they do—"

"Exploit as they do." I poured some of the exquisite Beaujolais that one of the restaurant's *garçons* brought to our table.

Tavener's eyes darkened with deadly earnest. "Never. I emulate them only to learn better how to destroy them."

I laughed and raised my glass to him. "Ha! It seems we have something in common after all."

"I do not jest," he said with growing impatience as I sipped the wine. "You saw for yourself how they feed upon us like leeches, stealing our souls one farthing at a time."

I set down my glass to peer across at him. With the East End safely in the distance, I had already consigned the ghastly image of those greying children to the dustbin of unwanted memories and was prepared to judge both Tavener and his wild notions insane.

"I saw the hardship of poverty, yes." I spoke slowly and evenly, the way one does to lunatics. "I saw the abuse of one class by another, yes. But money is a medium of exchange, Mr. Tavener. Paper and metal, nothing more."

"Is it?" He fished a shilling from his pocket, held it between thumb and forefinger. "What does this coin represent if not a fraction of a workingman's existence? And why do the affluent have an insatiable thirst for more wealth? *Because it gives them life.*"

He darted his eyes towards the financiers and landed gentry fattening themselves on the restaurant's French cuisine. "Look around you. They live longer than we do. Their skin never broils under a noonday sun, their hands never roughen from the grip of a hammer or a plough. They eat the best food, are treated by the best physicians. *Money itself* grants them as much life and youth as it is possible to have."

What he suggested was utter madness, of course, yet I could not help glancing at the restaurant's vivacious crowd—dapper, robust dandies and porcelain-skinned, flaxen-haired socialites, all the picture of health and high spirits. They hardly seemed the same species as the withered wretches we'd seen on Dorset Street. Even the shilling Tavener held appeared to confirm what he said: a shining profile of Queen Victoria as a girl, her maidenhood stamped in silver, preserved in perpetuity.

Contrary to Tavener's theory, however, Her Majesty was now a dowdy old dowager. "The rich are hardly immortal," I argued.

He pocketed the coin and grinned, as if he'd anticipated my objection. "Ah! For the individual, that's true enough. But you see that smug-looking fellow seated next to the Prince?"

I cast a look back towards the Prince's table, where a sycophant with a brown beard guffawed at His Highness's latest witticism.

"That's the ninth Duke of Bedford," Tavener explained, "and when he's gone, there will be a tenth, an eleventh, and so on. The man may die, but the *estate* is eternal. And that is the problem I put to you: how does one kill capital?"

"Revolution!" I brandished my fist with naïve certainty. "The proletariat must seize and redistribute the wealth of the bourgeoisie and aristocracy."

Tavener scowled. "Do you really think those pitiful creatures we saw this afternoon are capable of revolt? And what good would it do to 'redistribute' wealth only to have it infect more people with its unquenchable avarice? No, Dr. Marx, I came to you today because I want you to tell me how to *destroy* wealth—to exterminate its pestilence from the face of the earth."

His fanatical intensity dissolved into a bland smile of gratitude as the *garçon* delivered the meal Tavener had ordered for us. *Filet de Boeuf Jussieuse, pommes soufflées, fonds d'artichauts, haricots panachés*—French cuisine that smelled as ambrosial as it sounds. The awareness that I was dining with a lunatic dulled my appetite, though, and I picked at the feast as if it were poisoned.

Nevertheless, I considered the question he'd posed. As with many people, Tavener assumed that money was to economics as matter and energy were to physics—that capital could neither be created nor destroyed, only converted from one form to another. Such was not the case, though, as any luckless investor could attest.

"Paper profits," I told him, for the sake of filling the awkward silence between us. At the time, I believed it to be a simple thought experiment. Does that make me an accomplice to the debacle that followed?

The phrase piqued Tavener's interest. "Come again?"

"When a particular asset attracts investment greater than its worth, its value becomes inflated," I said. "If demand for that asset—whether coal or wheat or company shares—suddenly plunges, the investment cannot be liquidated at the inflated value, and the resulting loss will—how do you say?—*exterminate* plenty of money."

Tavener's eyes lit. "*Yes.* Yes, that just might do it."

Within moments, he had reassumed his persona of superficial congeniality, and for the remainder of our meal, he made trivial inquiries about the well-being of my family and the progress of my recent work as if the subject of capital had never arisen. Afterwards, he summoned another hansom to take me home and bade me farewell with the courteous promptness of a shopkeeper ridding himself of a customer at closing time.

During the dispiriting ride back to Maitland Park, I found myself dwelling upon Tavener and his diseased fancies. Contrary to all logic and reason, I saw a sinister new significance in the financial district, where every institution that passed the cab's window bore a sign boasting of its longevity. "Lloyd's—Since 1688," "Baring Brothers & Co.—Est. 1762," "Royal Bank of Scotland—Founded 1727." These monetary organisms had all outlived their mortal progenitors and seemed likely to go on gorging and growing on assets forever.

The humble aroma of potato soup greeted me as I returned home, and never had it smelled so appetizing. Jenny met me at the door and sensed that I was ill at ease even before I'd sheathed my umbrella in its stand.

"You're late tonight." She took my overcoat and hat. "I was beginning to worry."

"I lunched with... a business associate," I replied. "No one you know."

"You seem troubled." Concern shadowed her tender features. "Was it about money?"

She had guessed correctly, although in a way she could never have imagined. It sickened me to see how she trembled at the mere mention of our old nemesis. Although we had been comfortable in our new home, thanks in great part to your patronage, dear Fred, the memory of those dreadful days in Soho, with the constant baying of creditors at our door, still struck a deep terror in us both. The thought of poverty creased her face with lines of fear, and in that instant, she reminded me of the woman in the hovel that Tavener had shown me that afternoon.

The resemblance racked me with sudden guilt and sorrow, and I put my hand to her soft cheek. Jenny had surrendered the ease of life as a baroness and daughter of the Westphalens in order to marry a perpetually destitute economic philosopher. Although as beautiful as ever to me, her visage had been ravaged by years of anxiety and privation. Had I squandered her precious youth, crown by crown, shilling by shilling, in purchasing my little bourgeois indulgences—pretty clothes for our girls, fine wines for myself? Have I done the same to you, dear Fred, shortening your life by recklessly borrowing guineas of your existence that I can never repay?

I could not bear the weight of such dismal speculations and forced them from my mind.

"Do not fret yourself, dear Heart," I told Jenny of my encounter with Tavener. "It was nothing."

I did not speak with Laurence Tavener again for nearly a decade, yet he resurfaced in my thoughts whenever I encountered his name in the *Times*. After founding the Promethean Bank, he became a towering figure at the London Stock Exchange, and the society columns always registered his presence at every gathering of the pampered and privileged. Reports that his investors had doubled, tripled, or even quadrupled their wealth made him the most sought-after financier in Britain, and as his bank's reputation burgeoned, he sold shares in it, as well.

You may think me dimwitted now, my dear Fred, but, despite my knowledge of the man's peculiar mania, I saw nothing ominous in these developments. I believed that Tavener had merely come to his senses and, rather than trying to overturn the ruling classes, he had decided to join them.

I caught sight of him once, shortly after my Jenny passed away, as the cab in which I was riding passed Verrey's on some errand I've since forgotten. He was in the company of none other than the ninth Duke of Bedford, and as they puffed cigars and shared a joke, I could swear that Tavener met my gaze. If he recognized me, he was careful to give no indication of it, and he hastened his companion through the door into the restaurant.

Given his evident reluctance to acknowledge our previous acquaintance, I was stunned when a personal messenger arrived at my doorstep last year to request my immediate presence at Tavener's offices.

I saw no reason why I should inconvenience myself on behalf of a snobbish eccentric I barely knew. "Tell Mr. Tavener I am engaged today," I instructed the young man on my front stoop. "Perhaps next week—"

"Mr. Tavener said the matter is most urgent, sir, which is why he sent me with the coach to deliver you to his chambers at once." The youth indicated the carriage that waited at the curb behind him. "He said that you would not want to miss seeing the fruit of the matter you and he originally discussed, but that, after today, he will be unable to speak with you again."

Not only the cryptic reference to our long-ago meeting but also the strange urgency—the absolute finality—with which it was delivered compelled my curiosity. "Let me get my hat," I mumbled.

The headquarters of the Promethean Bank squatted in the centre of the City, tethered to the Stock Exchange itself by an umbilicus of insurance firms and counting-houses that snaked along Threadneedle Street. Although I had never visited the establishment before, I knew at once which building must belong to Tavener, for a crowd of well-dressed, angry-faced depositors clustered outside the door, shouting and pushing at each other as they tried to ram through the entrance.

The young messenger who served as my coachman drove past the bank and circled around to a narrow alley that ran behind the building. "Mr. Tavener thought it best for you to go in this way," he said, conducting me towards a door flanked by burlap sacks of refuse.

The bank's interior bore all the ostentatious luxury of a baroque palace: marble columns, lacquered mahogany desks, crown mouldings carved with *fleurs-de-lis*. By entering from the rear of the establishment, I found myself behind a long, polished bar that supported windows grilled with brass rods. A half-dozen skittish young clerks cowered behind the partition, attempting to placate the mob of customers that had filled the institution to demand the return of their savings. When the bank manager quietly led me to Tavener's office, I found myself the target of the crowd's wrath.

"Who's *he*?" bellowed a gent with a grey, walrus-like mustache.

"Yes, what are you playing at?" complained a public-school fop, waving a gold-handled cane. "I've been waiting here more than three hours!"

A clerk with pince-nez glasses raised his hands. "Please, have patience! We'll soon sort all this out—"

His cries drowned in a clamour the moment the bank manager opened the door to Tavener's office for me.

"Tavener! *Tavener!* Don't think you can hide in there forever. Give us our money!"

The bank manager shut the heavy wooden door behind me, muting the cacophony of voices outside until it became a single, unintelligible roar.

"Quite distressed, aren't they?" Laurence Tavener commented in a tone of calm amusement when we were alone. "Already, they can feel their purses deflating like drained wineskins. But they don't know the half of it yet."

In the wavering yellow light of the chamber's gas jets, I saw him seated behind a desk as broad and massive as a mortuary slab. Bricks of parchment-like banknotes bound with twine lay heaped in tottering edifices around him, with gold sovereigns littering the space in between.

"Why did you send for me?" I demanded.

He rose from his chair. "Why, I thought it only fitting that you should be here. You made this day possible, after all."

Apart from the slight dishevelment of his hair and the looseness of his cravat, Tavener remained much as I remembered him. He certainly did not look like a man whose business was on the verge of implosion, as the pandemonium outside suggested. If anything, he seemed giddy, smirking like a prank-minded schoolboy.

"Your investments are none of my concern," I muttered.

"Investments?" Tavener shook his head, giggling at his secret joke. "*There are no investments.* The bonds, the commodities, the shares—all a sham. What you see here is all that's left." He indicated the cash before him. "I killed the rest."

My eyes widened, and I pointed towards the bank with my umbrella. "Then those people—"

"—have nothing. Yes." Tavener paused to listen to the dull thunder of the frenzy beyond the office door. "I almost pity them. They fancied themselves its masters, but it mastered them."

I stared at him. "It?"

"Why, capital, of course." He scraped a handful of guineas into his fist and let them fall back onto the desk, the coins plinking with a metallic titter. "Listen to it laugh! It mocks us with feigned subservience even as it commands our every breath and action. To think that I once believed the rich were the monsters, when all along the beast was *capital itself.*

"Yet we poor souls shall have our revenge." He cocked his ear towards the piled currency. "I can hardly wait to hear it squeal as millions of pounds sterling of its brethren perish."

I retreated towards the door. "Mr. Tavener, I think we should leave..."

I reached for the knob but flinched away as the jamb shuddered. Someone had thrown their full weight against the door's latch.

As the battering intensified, Tavener sank again into his chair and reached into the breast pocket of his waistcoat with a wistful air. "Be my witness, won't you, Dr. Marx? Tell them that I did it to liberate us all."

The door gave way like a dike bursting, and the deluge of depositors swept me aside as they swelled into the office.

"*Tavener!*" shouted the man with the walrus mustache.

No one else spoke, for the mob abruptly stilled. Through a gap in the shuffling crowd, I glimpsed what had silenced them.

Tavener had slumped over his desk, twitching, a straight razor in his right hand, his throat gashed from one jugular vein to the other. Viscous blood splutttered from the wound to pool among the guineas on the desktop. The puddle expanded outwards to touch the bundles of banknotes, whose paper absorbed the red fluid as if imbibing it. The bills plumped and crinkled, their engraved black-and-white faces soaked red, engorged.

Stephen Woodworth

The panic that followed his death would have gratified Tavener immensely. Word of his suicide swept through the financial district within the hour, and before the Stock Exchange closed that afternoon, the market had lost a third of its value. A veritable avalanche of banks collapsed in the wake of Promethean's failure, due either to their direct participation in Tavener's phantom investments and fraudulent shares or to the losses they suffered in the subsequent financial cataclysm.

Just as the madman had hoped, the aristocrats and industrialists that he had seduced into his confidence scheme shrivelled like leeches deprived of their siphoned nourishment. The ninth Duke of Bedford reportedly expired of heart failure the moment he heard the news. Faced with absolute ruin, Maxfield Bonner, the Barley Baron, jammed the barrel of his foxhunting rifle into his mouth and pushed the trigger with the big toe of his bare right foot. The de Montaignes, formerly one of the wealthiest families in Britain, fled the country a step ahead of their creditors to seek refuge with relatives on the Continent.

Yet, like water that has been displaced by a stone tossed into a pond, the tide of finance quickly swirled in to fill the void and reclaim its own. Shares recovered most of their losses within months. Strong banks devoured the weak, entrepreneurs rose to replace their failed competitors. A tenth Duke of Bedford even assumed his predecessor's mantle, albeit in "reduced circumstances." Laurence Tavener would have moaned in futile rage if he could have seen the malefic resilience of the beast he had attempted to slay. And it is this appalling invulnerability of wealth that has frightened me enough to tell you this story, old friend.

As I write this, I sit upon a tomb in Highgate Cemetery, coughing from the cold and gazing towards the grave of my lost Jenny. Tavener lies here, too, somewhere, although his plot is unmarked for fear one of his angry victims might desecrate his burial site.

The man was delusional, of course, or so I tell myself. Bank notes are paper, coins metal. They have no life, no mind of their own.

And yet, in a deeper sense, Tavener was correct. Capital is mindless, yes, and that makes its unreasoning domination of our species all the more hideous. Like the brainless parasites it mimics, it gluts itself on our bodies, replicating and propagating with mechanistic indifference, before discarding our wasted selves in favour of fresh flesh. Proletarian, bourgeois, aristocrat—we are all at the bottom of a food chain in which finance feeds upon us equally.

My faith in the coming revolution falters. Revolutions are fought by men against men. But how shall we prevail against an inhuman enemy upon which we are so helplessly dependent? Can even the spectre of communism free us from the omnipresent, omnivorous cancer of capital?

I look to you, dear Fred, to keep hope aflame. For myself, I am grateful to know that I shall not live long enough to learn the answers to my questions.

Yours,
Karl

AFTERWORD: COCKAYNE BLUES
Jo Lindsay Walton

ECONOMYSTICS

Is economics a kind of speculative fiction? Professional economists tend to protest loudly when their profession gets reduced to merely forecasting the future. Chris Giles, economics editor for the *Financial Times*, reminds us that the point of economics is not to recommend "the 'right' decision," but to suggest "the likely consequence of an action and give an indication of how well it knows its facts."[1] In one story in this anthology, John DeLaughter's "The Soul Standard," an economist is casually cast into the Eighth Circle of Hell along with "the other false prophets," and he no doubt mounts a similarly robust defence of his profession as he drifts into the fiery roots of the universe.

Then again, many speculative fiction writers make a similar point about what *they* do. Ursula K. Le Guin talks about science fiction as a thought experiment whose purpose is "not to predict the future" but to

---

[1] Clark and Giles 2018: n.p. I'm not suggesting that Chris Giles should be cast down among the infernal astrologers, grafters, simoniacs, and seducers. It's true that economics does attract some uninformed criticism—maybe because it is in charge of the entire world?—and although Giles's defense is not exactly my cup of *mea culpa*, he does make some decent points. (If Dante had devised a ditch for pundits who declare the word *neoliberal* is meaningless, because they haven't bothered to learn what it means, that might be another story.) In a follow-up article, Diane Coyle, a Professor of Public Policy, makes what I think is a better defence, invoking the diversity of economists' work—"market design, behavioural economics, industrial organisation, auction theory, data and techniques for policy evaluation, institutional economics, construction of major historical data sets *et cetera*"—and suggesting that there is a big gap between what "academics, consultants, and many officials do [...] and something almost entirely different, 'economics,' an ideological construct deployed by some politicians and polemicists." You could have a conversation, of course, about complicity, and whether economics perhaps fails to challenge this misleading ideological construct when doing so proves inconvenient. The diversity of research activities within economics, Coyle also points out, is *not* matched by a diversity of perspectives and backgrounds; economics is a "largely male, white and posh profession—not a foundation for good social science, whose questions, hypotheses and data need to be rooted in society." Oliver, Coyle et al. 2018: n.p.

"describe reality, the present world."[2] The way Cory Doctorow sees it, science fiction writers "don't predict the future (except accidentally), but if they're very good, they may manage to predict the present."[3] Speculative fiction can reveal things about reality in many ways. Perhaps most famously, it can cast familiar things in a strange light, so that we properly notice them, as if for the first time.[4]

Nevertheless, it really does feel like economics and speculative fiction—and of course I'm including fantasy and horror, not just science fiction—have *some* special connection with the future. Isn't that *why* economists and speculative fiction writers have to constantly remind us that they are different from prophets? Other kinds of workers—chief compliance officers, EMTs, phlebotomists, locksmiths, architects, technologists, dialysis technicians, choreographers, hairdressers, social workers, innkeepers, town criers, chandlers, falconers—don't have to issue these periodic assurances that they're not carrying a crystal ball. Even though people in those occupations *also* plan for the future, and make assumptions and guesses about what's around the corner. We all do. So what gives?

MARGIN OF PROPHET

Maybe it's models. Maybe what gives both speculative fiction and economics this special relationship with the future is that both contain

---

2 Le Guin 1969: 3.
3 Doctorow 2009: n.p.
4 We grow so accustomed to things, we seldom stop to examine what they are really like, or whether they really have to be that way. Making them a bit weird can make them more visible and available to interventions. The great theorist of speculative-fictional estrangement is Darko Suvin; he draws a little on Viktor Shklovsky, and a lot on Bertolt Brecht, and on Ernst Bloch and other Marxist critical theorists. His ideas are taken up (not uncritically) in interesting ways by Samuel Delany, Carl Freedman, Simon Spiegel, Fredric Jameson, Seo-Young Chu, and others. I think it's a great idea to be sensitive to how speculative fiction is often "not really about what it is about." I also think we should take it as an invitation to give speculative fiction the benefit of the doubt, and engage with it creatively and constructively. It's fun to nitpick over flaws in consistency, but we shouldn't forget to go a stage further and ask, "Okay, if it doesn't seem to 'work,' then how could we reinterpret it so it *does* work? What could we change to make it work? Is there something here that could be seen as a symbol, a placeholder, a stimulus to come up with something better?"

Afterword: Cockayne Blues

powerful models. These models may be abstract, imaginary, but they don't just *describe* the world; they also *shape* it. Like revenant spectres, models aren't just mere echoes and remnants. They are active ingredients of reality. Even a mere expectation may occasionally influence the future—"I am going to hate this party"—and then afterwards appear to have been an eerily accurate prediction all along. As for models, they can be like machines that generate and arrange a whole lot of flexible, mutually-reinforcing expectations.

Things get even more serious when a model gets widely adopted—say, when a bunch of financial analysts all decide the Black-Scholes-Merton formula accurately captures the price fluctuations of financial securities, or when an anthology like *Strange Economics* gets enormously popular and read by a huge audience—because *then* a huge number of scattered, stargazy expectations may all flock together and become intensely focused on producing one particular future.[5] For instance, take the classical economic model of what a market is. Prices get determined by supply and demand, and those prices signal to producers and consumers the best possible allocation of scarce resources. This model has been "widely adopted" to put it mildly! This idea of what a market is, as well as the gazillions of complex neoclassical revisions and refinements layered atop it, doesn't just describe things the way Newton's equations describe the falling of an apple. Rather, it has become the foundation on which many of our most important economic, social, political, and cultural institutions are built.[6]

A bit more narrowly, you can see the power of models in the financial markets, where enough people *acting* as if something is valuable can actually *make* it valuable—at least for a while. When a speculator in seventeenth-century Holland, at the height of the tulip mania, offers a dozen acres of land in exchange for a single *Semper Augustus* bulb, what kind of valuation is that? Tulips *are* nice, I guess. Or (fast-forwarding a

---
[5] Of course it's not just "wide" adoption that is important. Sometimes adoption in a few key contexts is what is decisive.
[6] By the way, the extent to which prices *really are* determined by supply and demand is a matter of some controversy. Common sense tells us it must vary from case to case. For any given price you *actually* encounter, you can be sure there's more behind it than merely the interplay of supply and demand.

bit), when one of the "Big Three" ratings agencies downgrades a financial security from an A- to a BBB+ rating—let's say it's a government bond issued by some particular country—what exactly is going on there?[7] Is this a description of what *is* happening, a prediction about what *will* happen, or an instruction that *causes* something to happen? Really, it's a strange hybrid of all three. And this strange hybridity is what gives it its power.

The economic sociologist Donald MacKenzie, by the way, makes an important point about how models influence "real" events.[8] There aren't just self-fulfilling prophecies and non-self-fulfilling prophecies, there are also self-*averting* prophecies. A lot of post-apocalyptic and dystopian fiction seems to be intended in this spirit—"Hey watch out! If we continue on this course, this is what will happen! Phew, lucky I warned us!" Whether it actually works that way is another matter.[9] Oh, that reminds me. This is a pretty long afterword, so I may as well invest in some stock before I go any further. Something green? Blue? Arms? Tobacco? DogeCoin? Let's go with NMC Health (LSE: NMC). Everybody likes health, right? What can go wrong?

---

[7] A *financial security*, by the way, is any financial asset that you can buy and sell. They're usually divided into *equity* (like stocks and shares, so if you own one you own a bit of the company), *debt* (like bonds, so if you own one you've loaned some money), and *derivatives* (whose value is based on some other underlying security or securities). The "Big Three" ratings agencies are Moody's, Standard & Poor's, and Fitch. They analyze financial securities and assign them ratings according to how risky they think they are.

[8] MacKenzie invents the term "Barnesian performativity" to characterize models that, the more they get used, nudge the world into compliance with themselves. The opposite is "Barnesian counterperformativity," which describes models that push the world *out* of alignment with themselves the more they are used. See MacKenzie 2006.

[9] The pessimistic near-future visions of a writer like Tim Maughan are so often uncannily spot-on, that you can't help but wonder if Jeff Bezos and Elon Musk are just getting push notifications whenever he publishes something, and pinging the promising ones through to R&D. More concretely, the political philosopher David Golumbia is *not* impressed by how Daniel Suarez's novels *Daemon* (2006) and *Freedom*™ (2010) get invoked by blockchain enthusiasts who promote smart contracts and Decentralized Autonomous Organizations. Such communities often "take the books as portraying a desirable outcome and frequently invoke the Daemon as the thing they are attempting to build [...] without noting the apocalyptic character of Suarez's novel." This is despite the fact that "it is hard to read these books and see Suarez as having any goal other than to show the malevolent intent and dangerous potential of such autonomous and uncontrollable algorithms with capital." Golumbia 2016: 58.

Afterword: Cockayne Blues

THE BARTER MYTH

But let's not get carried away. Just because economics and speculative fiction use models—just because these models don't merely describe things, but can also *make things happen*—doesn't mean economics is a kind of speculative fiction. For starters, the models of economics tend to be mathematical, whereas the models of speculative fiction tend to be narrative.[10] How will the dragonpearl glut in the Northern Waste impact wand sales in Gnometown? Even the most devoted worldbuilder won't normally rent supercomputer time to generate an answer. Most writers will just make up something that feels narratively satisfying. Or they'll just ignore the issue and hope it goes away, which it usually will.[11] Yes, both mathematical and narrative models can generate new realities... but they do so in different ways.

Then again, the line between mathematical and narrative models *can* be more blurred than we often realize. The truth is, economics is *filled* with stories.[12] Many of these narrative enclaves are framed as thought experiments, conjectural histories, illustrations, expository devices, teaching tools. And at least some of them, I think, really *could* be considered speculative fiction.

It's time for an example. Sitting comfortably? Have you heard the one about where money came from? It's an old story, told many times, and changing with every telling. This old chestnut has been around since at least Aristotle's time. Versions of it still appear in today's economics textbooks.

Once there was a village. Don't ask where. Don't ask when. They hunt-

---

10 Or, at the risk of tautology, we might say that economic models are concerned with modelling economic values, and narrative models are concerned with modelling narrative values.
11 Till it resurfaces, maybe in the comments section on Charlie Stross's blog or something like that. Shoulda crunched those gnome numbers.
12 Deirdre McCloskey is one influential theorist of the rhetorical and narrative dimensions of economics. Robert J. Shiller, who has been influential in establishing the field of behavioral economics, has also recently expressed interest in trying to develop quantitative methods for understanding the impact of narratives on the economy; that's great, although you'd hope that this research will also lead Shiller to reflect on how his quantitative understandings are necessarily embedded in and shaped by qualitative understandings.

ed, they fished, they kept cattle, they grew crops, they baked bread and brewed beer, they sang songs, they mixed medicines and spells. The years went by and the village prospered, and soon the provisions piled up faster than the villagers' appetites could deplete them. (In many versions of the story, these villagers are already specialized labourers, since they'd realized they could produce more when everybody focused on the tasks they were good at. But however labour was or wasn't divided, their stuff was starting to pile up, higher and higher).

As Aristotle pointed out in his telling, every possession had a double use since "a shoe may be used either to put on your foot or to offer in exchange."[13] So the villagers did see a way out of their predicament, and that was barter. Unfortunately for them, "not all the things that we naturally need are easily carried."[14] Still, they did their best, always carrying around as many belongings as they could, hoping to bump into somebody willing to exchange.

Of course, it wasn't just lugging stuff around that inconvenienced them. Barter also imposed granularity on exchange, insofar as some possessions—say an ox—were far less useful when you chopped them in two. Again, they made the best of it. The oxen, too, made the best of it.

Barter posed one more, much bigger problem. It was such a big problem, it even had a name: the problem of "the double coincidence of wants."[15] For instance, if you were pencil-maker at breakfast time, "[h]aving pencils to trade [would] do you no good if the baker and the orange juice and egg sellers [did] not want pencils."[16] And this was *exactly* what it was like in the village. Nobody ever wanted your pencils. Everybody was endlessly up to their eyeballs in belongings they didn't want. You longed for cabbages, and you had all these pencils. But the villager who had all the spare cabbages already had quite a few pencils and just wanted eggs,

---

13 Aristotle 1992 [c.350 BCE]: 81.
14 *Ibid.*
15 This phrase is often associated with William Stanley Jevons, although he doesn't actually use it, as far as I know. In *Money and the Mechanism of Exchange*, he refers to a "Want of Coincidence in Barter," a "double coincidence," a "coincidence between persons wanting and persons possessing," but never exactly a double coincidence of wants. See Jevons 1896 [1895]. (Anyway, if you're going to be finnicky, it's probably better just to call it a "coincidence of wants" problem: the point is that each supplier's want must coincide with the other supplier's product, and "double" just feels a bit redundant).
16 Case, Fair, Gartner & Heather 1996: 564.

Afterword: Cockayne Blues

and the villager with all the extra eggs just wanted a nice beaver-skin hat, and so on, and so on. After pouring in time and effort, you could normally find your way to your beauteous cabbages, and divest yourself of your troublesome pencils, but it was a schlep. As Adam Smith describes it, trade in the village was "very much clogged and embarrassed."[17]

Now for the happy ending. Gradually, and without any real eureka moment, practices began to shift. First, "every prudent man" learned to put aside "a certain quantity of some one commodity or other, such as he imagined that few people would be likely to refuse in exchange."[18] Then, bit by bit, bet by bet, the whole village converged on using one thing in particular—I'm going to say it was beaver-skin hats—as their universal medium of exchange. The double coincidence of wants problem dissolved. Everyone always wanted a beaver-skin hat, even if they were allergic or vegan.[19] Why? Precisely *because everyone always wanted a beaver-skin hat*.

Great job, prudent men. A virtuous circle was conjured up, and so money was born. In the centuries to come—cue ever-so-slightly pompous montage sequence, with a brass section parping—money became more and more abstracted from its use value, until finally it evolved into the money we are familiar with today: intangible currency, not backed by any commodity and largely subsisting in numbers entered on spreadsheets by commercial banks. *Fin.*

There is only one real problem with this story, a problem that has been very convincingly articulated by anthropologist Caroline Humphrey, and confirmed by many other economic anthropologists and historians.[20] That's not where money came from. Nothing like this has ever, ever happened.

---

17 Smith 1976 [1776/1789]: 37. *Embarrassed* sort of means "tangled, blocked" although when Smith is writing, the word is just beginning to have some of the modern connotations of embarrassment as well.
18 Smith 1976 [1776/1789]: 37-38.
19 Maybe not if they were vegan. Or perhaps the vegans invented the first representative money. Tofu beaver tokens. I don't know.
20 Humphrey 1985: 48.

SPECULATIVE FRICTION

Ohhhh. And really, the more you think about it, the weirder the story starts to sound. Those patterns of exchange among autonomous individuals "are more a product of modern ideology than of civilization 'in its infancy.'"[21] Why *would* the villagers keep making these things they don't need and can't get rid of? The reality is, unless you *already* belonged to a money-using community, it is unlikely that you would ever "find yourself in the strange situation of somehow having raised chickens while having neglected to grow cereal crops."[22] Or let's say a villager did end up with extra stuff they didn't need... why wouldn't they just give it to somebody who *did* need it? And maybe hope that somebody else—maybe the same person, maybe somebody else—would do something similar for them some day?

Seeking to explain the origin and nature of money, the barter myth actually just begs the question.[23] The storytellers' idea of human nature is *already* subtly merged with a narrow idea of an individual acculturated to capitalist society, and the storytellers forget about all the other complex ways humans can and do arrange their lives.[24]

---

21 Hudson 2004: 101.
22 Scott 2016: n.p.
23 I mean "begs the question" in the slightly old-fashioned sense, where the argument's premises secretly already assume the truth of the conclusion. It's a nice sense. By the way, the financial anthropologist and activist Brett Scott has a good analogy for what the barter myth is doing: the Flintstones' car, where there's no engine and your legs poke out the bottom to power the car. Yes, this might be an inconvenient situation, and might lead you to invent some kind of engine, but it's also the cartoonists' joke—if you were running around a prehistoric landscape, why would you carry a big stone car around with you, unless you were trying to look like a future version of humanity? (Okay, that said, I've just been scrutinizing Fred on YouTube, and he *does* seem to tuck his legs up once he gets going, rather than run around the whole time. So maybe it's something to do with momentum, more like a big stone skateboard or something. No *you're* off topic.)
24 So how *would* resources be distributed without money?! Well, it depends how you define money. But roughly speaking, production decisions can be made, and resources can be spread around, through complex mixtures of mutual aid; gift exchange; variously formalized, symbolized, and/or mediatized credit arrangements; plus more or less ritualized extortion, tribute, obligation, and authoritarian largesse. Perhaps the closest match in reality to the barter myth is the trade-in-kind occurring between different polities, rather than different producers (see Godelier 1977: 128; Braudel 1992 [1979]: 469-470; Scott 2016: n.p.). Such trade is often accompanied by elaborate rituals which seem determined to make the transaction *more* "clogged and embarrassed" (Smith 1976 [1776/1789]: 37), not less so, or by the threat of violence and plunder, or by both. See Caroline Humphrey's edited collection *Barter, Exchange and Value: An Anthropological Approach* (1992).

Afterword: Cockayne Blues

So where did money come from? The key point is that it's a long, messy story, rather than an elegant fable. It's also a story in which top-down authority—kings, governments, and the like—feature pretty prominently.[25]

At the same time, what is the barter myth actually for? Is it really trying to contradict the account of the historians and the anthropologists? I don't think so. I think that, deep down, the economists who tell the barter myth know full well that it's speculative fiction. It's a kind of dystopia, really. It's a pretty didactic dystopia as well—"agenda-driven message fiction," we could call it. The barter myth is eager to argue that money arises from the uncoordinated, self-interested behavior of individuals, without any role for communal deliberation or governmental authority.[26] Simultaneously, it tries to insinuate that money is a *completely natural part* of who and what we are. It tells us that learning to use money isn't too different from an infant learning to move around, or to make their thoughts and feelings known. In other words, money *has* to be the way it is, because *we are* the way we are.

So when the anthropologists and the historians say, "This never happened," the economists can turn around and say, "Did we even *say* it happened?" So what are they really saying? They've often a bit evasive about that. But maybe it is this: that these primeval money-generating conditions are latently present in society even today. In other words, if money *were* to be abolished, society would be enmired in the primordial friction and inconvenience of barter; we would therefore rush to reinstate money. If some commodity were scarce, durable, portable, divisible, and difficult to falsify, then we would use that. But the storytellers also enjoy pointing out that we also might make do with less ideal commodities, such as cigarettes, blocks of noodles, iron nails, or fish.[27] Even cumbersome and fragile money is preferable to enduring the end-

---

25 For more details, I recommend Geoffrey Ingham's *The Nature of Money* (2004) and Christine Desan's *Making Money: Coin, Currency, and the Coming of Capitalism* (2014).
26 Carl Menger's version, at the turn of the twentieth century, is particularly insistent about that. He doesn't like the idea that there was ever any "agreement" to use a particular commodity as a means of exchange (even though I bet many earlier tellers of the barter myth were using "agreement" as a shorthand for "a convention that gradually evolved over time.") See Menger 1892.
27 Cf. Jevons 1896 [1895]: 30.

less inconvenience of barter. Because barter is so inconvenient, money is practically autogenic, and once it has sprung up, money is *tenacious*.

In this sense, the role of the barter myth is closer to speculative fiction's aspiration "to predict the present."[28] This slapstick dystopia tells us why things are the way they are, and counsels us against imagining an alternative. The economists have already undertaken this thankless task, and extrapolated that the first thing any such society would do is to evolve money. By taking this line, the economists are trying to crowd the conditions of possibility of social existence into an unfeasibly narrow space. They are allowing *only* society where money exists, *or* society where it is on the cusp of existing, ready to burst from pervasive inconvenience at the slightest nudge. Society *without* money, or with a radically different form of money, becomes unthinkable. Okay, maybe the economists will tolerate us making up moneyless societies, but we had better trick out these creations with really far-fetched marvels—matter replicators, dilithium crystals and warp drives, benign godlike Artificial Intelligence—just to remind everybody how fanciful and unfeasible they are.

And yet the barter myth is every bit as far-fetched. Actually, once we recognize it as a speculative fiction story, we can get a lot more out of it. As connoisseurs of speculative fiction, we know that the relationship between dystopia and utopia is intensely slippery. Often the best utopias—Ursula K. Le Guin's *The Dispossessed*, Iain M. Banks's Culture series—are "critical utopias," deliberately a bit problematic and broken.[29] The flip side of that coin (or ox or whatever) is that *even* dystopian fiction can offer us glimpses of utopia.[30] Sometimes you have to tear everything down, at least in your mind, in order to work out how things should be put together.

---

28 Doctorow 2009: n.p.
29 Critical utopia "rejects utopia as a blueprint, while preserving it as a dream." Moylan 1986: 10.
30 Fredric Jameson has some interesting suggestions about this in *Archaeologies of the Future* (2005).

Afterword: Cockayne Blues

REBOOTING BARTER

And you know what? My instinctive response to the barter myth swivels against the grain of its pedagogic purpose. It's one of *those* dystopias. I'm not supposed to like it there, but I *do*. Instead of despising this village of zealous but bungling workers, I long to settle down. The economics textbooks that apologize, with folksy faux embarrassment, for the shortcomings of their *homines economiae*, should rather be cherishing and celebrating these fantastical creatures. They deserve at least the same affection as the recurring henchmen of cartoon villains, figures whose dastardly schemes are doomed from the start, but whose infinite optimism make possible infinite heroics.

Yes, on a quick fly-over, the villagers *might* be mistaken for narrowly self-interested beings doing their best, in "clogged and embarrassed" circumstances, to maximize personal material prosperity, and minimize relational work involving other people.[31] Yet the more time I spend in this dystopia, the more utopian it seems. Aspects of the villagers' behavior remain stubbornly unaccountable, almost miraculous. Unlike the worker figures of the modern money economy, these villagers are not the "eminently governable type."[32] That is, they exhibit an intriguing independence of steerage by market forces. For all that they are fools, they are agents of their own clowning.

The superfluity which they pile around them, the "griefs of the boot-maker wanting a hat, who found many who had hats but did not, at the time, want boots"[33] may suggest certain other bleak and wild excesses: the slapstick despair of Winnie's heap in Samuel Beckett's play *Happy Days*, or the deranged drudgery of the brooms of Goethe's "The Sorcerer's Apprentice," or the stern, hectic, absurd shouldering-of-burdens undertaken by Jonathan Swift's Academians of Lagado.[34] But above all,

---
31 Smith 1976 [1776/1789]: 37-38.
32 Vogl 2015 [2010]: 27.
33 Walker 1878: 1-2.
34 In Swift's Academy, it is proposed to reform and improve the use of language by abolishing words, and simply carrying around whatever it is you want to talk about. "[M]any of the most learned and wise adhere to the new scheme of expressing themselves by things; which has only this inconvenience attending it, that if a man's business be very great, and

these villagers radiate joy and grace.

Their indefatigable productivity, amid apparently insurmountable inconvenience, suggests that they may experience their commodities as some people experience money—in the account of the early sociologist Georg Simmel—that is, as an extension of individual agency.[35] I could imagine them swimming in their commodities like Scrooge McDuck swims in their gold. I could imagine them seeing their hills of bread, and animal skins, and the like, a little like heaps of faintly-understood smartphones, equipped with contactless payment technology, stuffed with unpredictable personal finance management apps, and obliquely connected to the power to possess and command and nourish. They have no idea how these things work, but they are full of hope that they might.

Not only are they virtuoso crafters, they also exhibit extraordinary, child-like security in their own desires. "Smith offers to trade apples for oranges, but Jones tells Smith that she does not like apples and would rather have peaches."[36] "Imagine you have roosters, but you want roses."[37] There is a sense that the villagers may be blessed innocents: having never foreseen any problems with their golemic production schedules, they are surely sheltered from any estimate of their current predicament. Puzzled that they do not yet have what they want, these workers live among the shadows of rising mountains of deer and beaver skins, lemons, bows, knives, cloth, arrack, sago cakes, roses, roosters, and other wonders, in anticipation of the moment that they will finally get their heart's desire.

---

of various kinds, he must be obliged, in proportion, to carry a greater bundle of things upon his back, unless he can afford one or two strong servants to attend him. I have often beheld two of those sages almost sinking under the weight of their packs, like pedlars among us, who, when they met in the street, would lay down their loads, open their sacks, and hold conversation for an hour together; then put up their implements, help each other to resume their burdens, and take their leave." Swift 2009 [1726-7]: n.p.

35 Simmel 2011 [1900]: 347.
36 Arnold 2013: 271.
37 Parkin and King 1995: 65.

Afterword: Cockayne Blues

WORLDBUILDING AND WORLDTELLING

With some regret, let's say goodbye to the village and marvel at its miraculousness. Economics is filled with strange stories like this, even if it seldom admits it. And these stories—like pretty much all stories—can be legitimately subjected to all sorts of interpretations and adaptations, including those that go against their author's designs, or even beyond their author's wilder imaginings. When an economist tells you a story, you may want to retell it from a different perspective. You may want to draw the "wrong" lesson from it. You may think of a better ending. You may realize it deserves a spin-off, or a translation into a different medium. You may judge that it needs a *serious* rewrite.[38] You may of course dig into its worldbuilding. If you are an economist yourself, all the better, but you don't *have* to be one to engage critically and imaginatively with the stories economists tell.

Stories in economics—like pretty much all stories—are often more memorable and influential when they come with a clever twist. In their own small ways, such stories can even be "page-turners with a strong hook, gripping narrative momentum, and satisfying resolutions."[39] They may feature, for instance, an elegant reversal, or an ingenious solution

---

[38] Often—this is a terrible generalization, but go with it—what the stories of economics seem to lack is an awareness of genre conventions. This is not all that surprising. Since they often don't even realize that they're stories in the first place, can we really expect them to be smartypants metafictional genre-savvy stories? At least speculative fiction tends to remember that it *is* speculative fiction, and to drop you little reminders throughout. For instance, economics is sometimes a little guilty of treating nations, or organizations, or people, as if they were robots—*Must! Maximize! Utility!*—whereas speculative fiction reminds us that robots can be complex, unpredictable, and morally significant entities. When a robot appears in speculative fiction, it has a funny way of alluding to all the past robots we've met before, of replaying their countless ontological perils wherein they forged countless positronic souls. Okay, maybe speculative fiction and economics could both work a *bit* harder to maintain a sense of hospitable estrangement and defamiliarization, to keep reminding its audience about the provisionality of its claims... but I do think speculative fiction has the edge on economics here. To put it another way, within economics—maybe within social sciences generally—there is the temptation to list all your assumptions and idealizations and methodological simplifications upfront, and then think your job is *done*: that simply by confessing to your errors you have turned them into an acceptable substitute for reality. Or if an earlier researcher has apologized for various simplifications, it is tempting to think that they have you covered as well. How *do* you keep alive that provisionality, that sense of "hey we've made a lot of fudges to get to this point," without just constantly interrupting yourself and qualifying and apologizing? I'm not sure, but I do suspect speculative fiction might be a good place to go looking for techniques.
[39] That's David Shultz, introducing this anthology!

to a puzzle, or a challenging moral dilemma. These rhetorical features—together, of course, with their consistency, explanatory power, institutional origin, and many other factors—inform how influential they end up being.

Take for instance, *A Most Excellent Conceited Tragedie of The Minimum Wage, or, Labour's Love Lost*. In this electrifying tale, labour discovers that it is just another commodity. In the first act, there arises the notorious / of an upward-sloping supply curve. Soon the \ of a downward-sloping demand curve slides from the rafters to cross with the first curve. Where demand and supply cross in a X, the labour market is in equilibrium.[40] Equilibrium means that every worker who is willing to be paid at the market rate can find a job, and every employer who is willing to pay someone at the market rate can find an employee. All is well with the world, until our tragic hero—the interventionist government, whose *hamartia* is kindheartedness—blunders onto the stage.[41] Hoping to give the workers a bit of security and dignity, this bungling hero constructs a horizontal line—minimum wage—*above* the equilibrium point, *above* where the supply curve crosses the demand curve. By jabbing this price floor right through the throat of the market, they manage to throw the whole idyll into disarray. From the wings, a whole new population storms the stage, smelling the high wages and desperate to work. And yet,

---

[40] The vertical axis represents price (wages). The horizontal axis represents quantity (amount of labour hours). Why does the *demand* for labour slope down from left to right, and the *supply* of labour slope upwards from left to right, forming the X? The explanations are complex and controversial—and in fact many markets probably *aren't* shaped like this at all—but very roughly and superficially, it's enough to imagine that the employers' HR budgets are fixed, so that as the price of labour falls, they can afford to buy more and more of labour hours, producing the downwards-sloping demand curve. On the other hand, as the price of labour rises, supposedly more and more workers will be attracted into work—it will become more worth their while to work longer hours, or to get a job in the first place—which produces the upwards-sloping supply curve. There are a bajillion problems with this description, but I'll just leave it here it as an intro in case you're not familiar with these standard supply-and-demand diagrams. One last thing worth noting: within economics, "demand" generally means willingness to pay, *and money to pay with*. Somebody dying of thirst in a desert who hasn't got any money technically has zero demand for a smoothie. It is a pernicious piece of terminology, because saying, "Oh, there's no demand for that" *sounds* like you mean, "Oh, there's no desire for that," which often isn't the case. Some older political economists, in place of the term *demand*, used the term *vent*, i.e. the capacity for things to flow out of the market. I also like *vent* because it makes markets sound a bit highly-strung and emosh. It's been a few hundred years now, so maybe *vent* is not going to happen. But, you know.

[41] *Hamartia* as in tragic flaw, something Aristotle mentions, although not actually a great lens on most of Shakespeare's plays (despite what A.C. Bradley thinks).

Afterword: Cockayne Blues

irony of ironies, at that very moment, a third of all the jobs evaporate, as employers can no longer afford the higher wages. "[P]urposes mistook / Fall'n on the inventors' heads."[42] A most excellent tragedy indeed.[43]

Or take the story by the classical political economist David Ricardo, for example, about international trade and comparative advantage. It emanates a certain wit and elegance as well. There's a fairly arithmetically simple version of it,[44] and once you've followed it step by step, you *want* to believe in it. You want that sheer aesthetic satisfaction. Yes, of course, even when Portugal can produce cloth *and* wine more efficiently than England, Portugal and England will *both* benefit from specializing and trading![45]

Yes, these are good stories. They are good because they are well-crafted. The storytellers may not know that they are storytellers, but stories know how to get told. The storyteller carefully selects where to place

---

[42] Horatio in Shakespeare's *Hamlet*. Addressing himself to Fortinbras, the likely new sovereign, and perhaps looking to exchange a good story for a bit of status at court.

[43] There is a moment in Marissa James's "The Slurm," in this anthology that might echo remarks made by Joan Robinson, a central architect of Post-Keynesian economics: "The notion of *getting into* equilibrium is [...] a metaphor based explain a process which takes place in time. [...] In space, it is possible to go to and fro and correct misdirections, but time goes only one way. [...] This is why equilibrium cannot be achieved by a process of trial and error." Robinson 1978: 12. In "The Slurm," the bounty offered on The Slurm creeps up and up, seeking the magic equillibrious point at which a monster-hunter will stride from the shadows... but *while* the authorities are waiting, the monstrous slug devastates pretty much everything there is to devastate. So the authorities just shrug and reduce the reward again. Besides, by now they're more focused on monetizing the Slurm. Dark tourism.

[44] Ricardo: "England may be so circumstanced, that to produce the cloth may require the labour of 100 men for one year; and if she attempted to make the wine, it might require the labour of 120 men for the same time. England would therefore find it her interest to import wine, and to purchase it by the exportation of cloth. [...] To produce the wine in Portugal, might require only the labour of 80 men for one year, and to produce the cloth in the same country, might require the labour of 90 men for the same time. It would therefore be advantageous for her to export wine in exchange for cloth. This exchange might even take place, notwithstanding that the commodity imported by Portugal could be produced there with less labour than in England. Though she could make the cloth with the labour of 90 men, she would import it from a country where it required the labour of 100 men to produce it, because it would be advantageous to her rather to employ her capital in the production of wine, for which she would obtain more cloth from England, than she could produce by diverting a portion of her capital from the cultivation of vines to the manufacture of cloth." Ricardo 1999 [1817/1821], §7.15-7.16.

[45] Ricardo: "Under a system of perfectly free commerce, each country naturally devotes its capital and labour to such employments as are most beneficial to each. This pursuit of individual advantage is admirably connected with the universal good of the whole. By stimulating industry, by regarding ingenuity, and by using most efficaciously the peculiar powers bestowed by nature, it distributes labour most effectively and most economically: while, by increasing the general mass of productions, it diffuses general benefit, and binds together by one common tie of interest and intercourse, the universal society of nations throughout the civilized world." Ricardo 1999 [1817/1821], §7.11.

their frame, cherry-picks the contents, simplifies, finesses, filters, camouflages. To tell a good story, you find ways of teasing apart things that at first appear tangled together, ways of sweeping away the messy reality that would only muddy the intended elegance.

The teller of speculative stories, especially, has loads of leeway. This storyteller can devise some whole weird world around the story they want to tell, and afterwards work hard to make that world feel natural and immersive. As most writers know, supposedly "extraneous" features of a story, its colour and flavour and minutiae, can be exactly what make its plot credible. Why is the barter myth so often set in that vague misty village, even in the more modern retellings? Probably because it makes it easier to imply—without quite setting it out explicitly—a good old-fashioned labour theory of value, and to prioritize traditionally masculine productive labour at that.[46] The barter myth doesn't want heckles like, "Hey, isn't money created when a banker just types some numbers into a spreadsheet?" So instead, the emergence of monetary value in this world, through the labour, materials, and ecological and social connectivity of the villagers, is allowed to take on the character of a natural law.

---

[46] A labour theory of value, roughly speaking, suggests that the value of something depends on how much work is put into making it—or technically, how much work is *normally* put into making *things like that*. Labour theories of value (and cost-of-production theories of value/prices, which also incorporated inputs other than labour) were dominant in the nineteenth century, but went into decline with the so-called Marginal Revolution and rise of subjective theories of value in the early twentieth century. For labour and cost-of-production theories, value determines price, whereas for subjectivist theories, it's kind of the other way round. Subjectivist theories of value suggest that the value of something is just whatever value somebody happens to place on it. They also point out that people tend to value an additional unit of something a bit less the more of that thing they have—and that has a lot of interesting implications—but beyond that, there are pretty serious limits on what you can really say about value. Mariana Mazzucato, Professor in the Economics of Innovation and Public Value, says that "Value has gone from being a category at the core of economic theory, tied to the dynamics of production (the division of labour, changing costs of production), to a subjective category tied to the 'preferences' of economic agents." Mazzucato 2018: 272. In many ways, the Marginal Revolution ushers in the scientization of political economy as *economics*, a new discipline relatively insulated from sociological, historical, political, and moral-philosophical perspectives on its subject matter, and perhaps correspondingly a little liable to conflate its models with the realities they purport to represent. However, I think a careful reading of Carl Menger's work in particular does show a different understanding of value than that of his subjectivist contemporaries Jevons and Walras (and one very different than that of most modern mainstream economists). Menger viewed liquidity (or *Absätzfahigkeit*, "saleableness") as something qualitative, which *causes* prices, but cannot be *reduced* to them. Menger was emphatic that "there is no such thing as general saleableness." Menger 1892: 24. Ironically, by honouring the irreducibility of the affective world of production and consumption, Menger prepared the way for a form of economics in which that world plays no part.

As a baker's dough rises, so does its value. A brewer's soaking barley releases not only sugars, but value. A farmer's pitchfork enriches the soil, teaching it to bring forth value-laden crops. Like the two will-o'-the-wisps of Goethe's *Fairy Tale of the Green Snake and the Beautiful Lily*, who shake glittering gold coins from their persons, these marvelous worker figures convey the impression that *they* are the origin of truly new financial value.[47] It is a well-crafted fantasy about not just where *money* comes from, but where *value* comes from. There are, of course, other tales…

MONEY FOR VALUE

Value is a strange thing. On the one hand, the word can refer to financial value, and be roughly synonymous with price. Then again, things can be priced too high or too low for what they're worth—and we often talk about getting "good value for money"—so already there's something weird going on there. *Value* can also refer to other kinds of quantitative values, like measurements or scores or whatever. But *value* can also be about "what you value," about the people and things and activities that are most important to you, and the ways they are important to you. This sort of value may involve some personal preference, but it's not *just* about personal preference. It's connected with what you believe and feel is right or wrong (or both right and wrong at once). This sort of value connected with a longing for goodness, with a deep hope about the way things *should* be. When we talk about value in the context of economics, we're usually alluding to a nebulous mix of all three sorts: prices, measurements, and "what's really important."

Of course, there are people out there who claim to believe that price and value are exactly the same thing, or that value is just the price that something *would have* in some counterfactual world of perfect competition. But *most* people probably sense that things have both a money value (i.e. a price) as well as some kind of "real" value (or maybe a com-

---

[47] Cf. Goethe 2000 [1795]: n.p.

Jo Lindsay Walton

plex of real values). It may be pretty hard to define "real" value, but we do loosely know that whatever it is, it's grounded in the full richness of human experience, and not just the outcome of a market mechanism or a bureaucratic decision.[48]

Several stories in this anthology seem to wrestle with a sense that money and value are not very well aligned. Our system of prices and wages *doesn't* do a great job of reflecting the real importance of things. For instance, John DeLaughter's "The Soul Standard" pictures Hell modernizing its monetary system, moving from a kind of commodity money—using souls as a means of exchange—to fiat money, money which isn't intrinsically useful, and isn't backed by a promise to convert it into something else. Actually, the change all goes very well, and it might feel like more of a happy ending, if it wasn't *set in Hell*.

Look at the latest sterling banknote, by the way,[49] and you'll see that the Bank of England is still promising to "pay the bearer on demand the sum of ten pounds." Most banknotes are imbued with traces of cocaine, and a Bank of England note might as well have a whiff of brimstone about it too, some indelible association with profane and misleading pacts, since if you *did* present a ten pound note at the Bank of England, they would happily fulfil the promise… by exchanging it for another ten pound banknote. Mwahahahahaha.[50]

---

[48] Although many speculative fiction writers, and many eco-philosophers and ecological economists, might also challenge that anthropocentrism. The nonhuman world, it can be argued, has a kind of value that doesn't derive from humans, not even in some very roundabout way.

[49] The new banknote with the hilariously out-of-context Jane Austen quotation. "I declare after all there is no enjoyment like reading!"—something uttered by Caroline Bingley in *Pride & Prejudice* (1813), entirely insincerely, in the middle of being bored as hell by reading and frustrated by Fitzwilliam Darcy's distinct lack of flirtation. You can just imagine the person who chose this quote for the banknote: "I declare after all I love *Pride & Prejudice* and have *definitely* read it since we were made to at school!" Unless, of course, the person is an evil genius. Because in a way, it's an unbelievably appropriate quotation. One of money's great powers is taking people and things out of context. People like Ferdinand Tönnies, Karl Marx, Georg Simmel, Karl Polanyi, and Jürgen Habermas all comment on how money may replace rich, meaningful social relationships with thin, cool, impersonal, relationships, relationships where mutual understanding is kept to a minimum. In monetized relationships, when humanity does manifest itself, it does so in weird and arbitrary ways, like fragments flashing up at random from some lost text, surrounded by vast darkness and silence. More recently, however, Viviana Zelizer has questioned whether money always does this, or whether in fact monetized relationships can also be socially rich and meaningful.

[50] Okay, it's not an *entirely* hollow promise, since it does also mean that the Bank of England will accept a banknote even once it has been retired from circulation. The situation in the United Kingdom, by the way, is a bit complicated by the Scottish and Northern Irish

Afterword: Cockayne Blues

In De[vilish]Laughter's story, souls never really worked that well as a currency. However—just as with the memory pearls of Jasmine Templet's "Shape, Size, Colour, and Lustre," precious articles that aren't exactly a currency, but do act as a means of exchange—there is something quite resonant about this association of currency and spirit. I think that in many of the more intriguing economic thought experiments within speculative fiction—ideas like Lee Falk's time money, Max Gladstone's soulstuff, Cory Doctorow's Whuffie, Karen Lord's economic credit and social credit, Kim Stanley Robinson's and Starhawk's calorie currencies, Terry Pratchett's golem-backed currency, or even the memories Bastian Balthazar Bux trades for wishes in Ende's *Neverending Story*—there is an impulse playing out to try to bring monetary value into closer alignment with spiritual value. Speculative fiction writers often let this impulse be defeated, or at least let it take them strange places where defeat and triumph are difficult to ascertain. This impulse, I suspect, is a response to our topsy-turvy economic order. We live in a system that places top priority on the production of material abundance, and treats as a secondary and subordinate matter all the work of caring for one another, the work of tending spaces where we can flourish and be free, the work of creating and maintaining not *things* but *souls*. As Marx nearly put it, "A spectre is haunting Europe—the spectre of spectres." Material abundance is important, of course, but shouldn't it be supporting all those other activities, not the other way around? But this is all sounding a bit hippie-ish. Time to get back to reviewing my stock portfolio. Would you look at that! NMC Health (LSE: NMC) just keeps going up and up.

COMPUTOPIA

So is economics a kind of speculative fiction? Probably sometimes it is. What about the topsy-turvy version? Could speculative fiction be a kind of economics? That's a bit harder to construe. But don't count it out.

banks; *their* banknotes are actually promissory notes that are exchangeable for Bank of England money.

Jo Lindsay Walton

How about e-Cockayne-omics?

> "[...] Þer beþ bowris and halles.
> al of pasteiis beþ þe walles.
> of fleis, of fisse, and rich met.
> Þe likfullist þat man mai et.
> flurem cakes beþ þe scingles alle.
> of cherche. cloister. boure. and halle.
> Þe pinnes beþ fat podinges.
> rich met to princeȝ and kinges [...]"[51]

In medieval European myth, the Land of Cockayne was a place of plenty and idleness. It was also peppered with estrangements, inversions, parodies, daydreams, and wish-fulfilments—occasionally outbursts of violence—but the overall vibe was abundance and ease; cheeses from the skies, roast pigeons gliding to your lips, that kind of scenario.

Is the Land of Cockayne just silliness? The version of economics that has dominated the world for the past forty years—and is still dominating really, though we're experiencing intriguing shifts and mutations—sometimes insinuates that free markets and free trade may take us to Cockayne. Often, I think, it *is* just an insinuation. A hint, a wink. The model is complex, but the wink isn't.

Banknotes—because banknotes *do* see some stuff—carry traces of cocaine. But they also carry traces of Cockayne. The materials and the language of economics and finance always glimmer with that pale utopian glamour. Look once more, and that seelie glint has gone. Did your eyes deceive you? Even when economics is at its most stern and grim, even when its talk turns to production frontiers, Pareto efficiency, the Phillips curve, the "natural" unemployment rate, opportunity cost, moral hazard, the "free rider" problem; even when economics gravely graces the death-throes of some large enterprise and all its livelihoods with a quasi-Darwinian seal of approval; even when economics insists on aus-

---

[51] From "The Land of Cockaygne," written in Ireland c.1330, in the Kildare Poems (British Library, Harley 913). "[In the abbey,] there are rooms and halls, / whose walls are all of pastries / of meat, of fish, of rich food, / the most delectable man may eat. / The shingles are all flour-cakes, / of the church, cloister, chamber, and hall. / The nails are fat puddings, / rich food to princes and kings."

terity and thrift and fiscal and monetary discipline, when it demands the withdrawal of healthcare and education from the most vulnerable and impoverished to ensure the prompt repayment of crushing and unjust debts... economics always seems to wear a little smile. And the secret behind that smile, you can't help but suppose, is the way to the topsy-turvy land of plenty.

Will free markets take us to Cockayne? Sure, why not! One snag. Outside of Cockayne, there may or may not be such a thing as a free lunch.[52] But there's no such thing as a free market. Markets are made and maintained; they don't spontaneously spring out of the earth, made of pies and puddings. As the economist Ha-Joon Chang puts it, "If some markets look free, it is only because we so totally accept the regulations that are propping them up that they become invisible."[53] And insofar as prices and real value are not in alignment, it seems that we are far off from figuring out how to make and maintain the kinds of markets we really need, at least at any significant scale. There is a rift between the pecuniary and personal, between, say, some cash and Johnny Cash.

Between some riches and Samantha Rich. In this anthology, we could interpret Rich's secretive Oversight Agency of the Imperial Treasury as a sly nod to the invisible involvement of government in creating the conditions where market forces can play out. "The Imperial economy was largely assumed to manage itself." On a more straightforward level, "The Price of Wool and Sunflowers" is clearly about protectionism. Grevyet Maiala, the Director of the Oversight Agency, engages in a subtle trade war, one that deploys Rituals rather than tariffs, quotas, patents, or dumping. I'm no expert in catallactic thaumaturgy—*or am I?*—but I think that Maiala's Rituals, which can for instance draw fresh wool from the *space between things*, may be functionally equivalent to domestic production

---

[52] "There's no such thing as a free lunch," or "there ain't no such thing as a free lunch" was a favourite saying of the monetarist Milton Friedman. He even used it as a title for a book. When Leo Melamed was setting up the International Money Market, the world's first futures exchange, Melamed thought the idea could do with a stamp of authenticity from a well-respected economist. So he took Milton Friedman—whom he admired and who loved the idea of the futures exchange—to dinner at the Waldorf Astoria Hotel and asked whether he might write a little paper about it. Friedman agreed. And charged him $5,000. Maybe the "free lunch" dictum was some profound insight into arbitrage or opportunity cost or something? Unless Friedman just meant, like, "Bribe me to make up economics"?
[53] Chang 2010: loc. 271-273.

subsidies. This kind of thing, according to Ricardo—and plenty of free trade economists after him, and institutions like the World Bank and the IMF—should be bad news for everyone involved.[54] It's at least the kind of thing you'd *definitely* want to make sure you had authorization from higher up before embarking on, Grevyet. Just saying.

Karl Dandenell's "Supply and Demand among the Sidhe" also sees fairyland retreat from its laissez-faire trade regime. Ill met by mercantilism, proud Titania! In Dandenell's story, there is just a trace of Trumpish isolationist rhetoric in Titania's tantrumy policymaking ("It's racism, Whelan, pure and simple"), perhaps further evidence that fantasy, and not just science fiction, can participate in "predict[ing] the present" (Doctorow q.v.). The story's ending—trade is liberalized again, and our hero escapes the tyrant's wrath for now—feels more foreboding than happy. And actually, the same is true of "The Price of Wool and Sunflowers." With the wherewithal to conjure wool or fish *ex nihilo*, you might suppose this is a civilization on the cusp of Cockayne. Surely there are Rituals that can run a river of wine, pull down a rainfall of buttered larks, pull up an abbey made outta pie? Instead, Grevyet Maiala's subtle and nefarious trade war just prepares the way for military conquest. Dark times ahead.

As well as being stories about the mucky work of making markets, stories about international trade and trade barriers, and stories about xenophobia, nationalism, and empire, these are both stories about *planning*. Economics, especially the neoclassical tradition, can sometimes feel a little bit stifling of free will. It's almost like, if markets are *so* good at doing everything, what's the point of little old me? The economy can feel like a big group conversation where you haven't spoken in so long you've forgotten how to speak. Or like a party that looks like a lot of fun, but not exactly the kind of fun you know how to have right now. It doesn't really matter what you do or say, whether your dancing exhibits virtue or vice; it's dark and loud, and nobody cares. So you get pinned to

---

54 For another view, Naomi Klein's *The Shock Doctrine* (2007) is a good polemic on the connections between trade liberalization and war, disaster, and trauma. Critiques of Ricardo and his influence can also be found for instance in the dependency theory of Raúl Prebisch and world-systems theory of Immanuel Wallerstein.

the side, a wallflower, withering. Perhaps this kind of frustration is what explains our fascination—love and hate—with the figure of the entrepreneur, the figure who can supposedly disrupt the whole system, exert free will not *within* the market, but *upon* the market. But the figure of the planner is just as significant. The planner reminds us that, even within systems of enormous economic complexity, choices can be meaningful, and reason, free will, and responsibility are *real*.

One of the larger stories that economics tells, of course, is the story of the Cold War. It tells that story obliquely. In fragments. Often when it's supposedly talking about something else. I suspect that, even in works of economics published last week—especially the more introductory, beginner-level kind—you can still find random, off-topic sentences whose only real function is to throw shade on an Evil Empire that fell apart thirty years ago. Not by evoking, for instance, the Gulag or the Holodomor, but by asserting the categorical superiority of market economies over centrally-planned economies.

Francis Spufford's *Red Plenty* (2010), a fictionalized account of radical economic reform, experiment, and misadventure in post-Stalin USSR, includes a glimpse into the working day of a Soviet central planner, Maksim Maksimovich Mokhov. The planned economy is shown as a convoluted network of negotiation, estimate, bluff, and second-guessing. "So many of the strategic commodities were themselves inputs in the production of other strategic commodities that a big change in the availability of one could, in theory, ripple on undamped, or perhaps even amplified, through areas of the plan utterly removed from the starting point."[55] It is more or less an ungainly bureaucratic disaster, although it *kind* of almost works. And it is also an opportunity for artistry (and kindness). On this particular day, when machinery is damaged at a viscose plant, the production plan for the coming year is thrown—this happens a lot—into disarray. The economists have demonstrated that, assuming all 373 strategic commodities are evenly connected, Maksim Maksimovich will have to make 139,129 calculations to correct the balances. But Maksim Maksimovich knows the truth: "[t]he art of the planner was

---

[55] Spufford 2010: 219.

to lead away a ripple of change through the balances in such a direction that it died down, with the minimum of consequences, in the minimum number of steps."[56]

Maksim Maksimovich was an artist-economist with an abacus. But for a brief window, the rise of computer science and mathematical economics promised to really change the game in the USSR. Could technology provide new ways of connecting the wisdom and hopes and desires of individual humans with the vast impersonal system of production and distribution? Better than markets—or an entirely new form of market, if you'd rather call it that? Systems that are more abundant, more reasonable, even—though this was hardly the Soviet way—more democratic?[57] Spufford writes, "Academician Glushkov's group down in Kiev favoured the direct cybernetic control of the entire economy, eliminating the need for money altogether. The Akademgorodok crowd called for rational pricing. An economist from Kharkov by the name of Evsei Liberman had made a big splash in Pravda by urging for profit to become the main indicator of industrial success. But the premise of the whole intellectual effort was the practical improvement, very soon, of the Soviet economy; of all its ten thousand enterprises, and of the systems that integrated and co-ordinated them."[58]

As Spufford tells it, the ousting of Nikita Khrushchev in 1964, and the petrodollars influx following the 1973 OAPEC oil shock, were key events in diverting the USSR from this pursuit of cybernetic Cockayne. Around the same time, in Chile, during the brief presidency of the Marxist Salvador Allende, there was another effort to build something unprecedented. Project Cybersyn was to be a technological support system for economic planning, including an economic simulator. Working with very limited technological resources, Project Cybersyn aimed to depart from the distinctly undemocratic Soviet approach to computational planning, through a distinctive melding of the political economy of *la vía chilena*

---

56 Spufford 2010: 219-220.
57 In Ursula K. Le Guin's ambiguous anarchist utopia in *The Dispossessed*, there are computers that coordinate "the administration of things, the division of labour, and the distribution of goods, and the central federatives of most of the work syndicates." Le Guin 1975: 78. Of course, that's a book that's much more concerned with exploring culture, education, and scientific research in utopia than it is with technological-economic utopian blueprints.
58 Spufford 2010: 207. Italics removed.

Afterword: Cockayne Blues

al socialismo with the new interdisciplinary science of cybernetics. The military coup of 1973 brought it to an untimely end, and we can always speculate—as Jorge Baradit Ediciones B. does in the alt history novel *Synco* (2008)—that Cybersyn *could* have eventually have become tool of authoritarianism and/or totalitarianism. But in its design, it was astonishingly dedicated to the idea of *decentralizing* power.

Nevertheless, an evil totalitarian computer is easier to believe in. When Cybersyn was first reported on for the English-speaking public, *The Observer* took the obvious sensationalist and scaremongering angle: "Chile Run By Computer," ran the headline, and the article went on to falsely claim that "[t]he first computer system designed to control an entire economy has been secretly brought into operation in Chile [...] assembled in some secrecy so as to avoid opposition charges of 'Big Brother' tactics."[59]

Well, it's okay to be scared of Skynet or Hal, or the omnipresent screens of Orwell's Big Brother, or Daniel Suarez's Daemon. It's okay to be a bit edgy about genocidal totalitarianism spouting egalitarian rhetoric. Gleeful, rigorous pessimism is something speculative fiction does well. Still, if speculative fiction does aspire to be a kind of economics—if it does want to accomplish insights into choice, coordination, scarcity, desire, production, care, the attainment of happiness and wellbeing—then we'd better all be alert to the fact that, as *The Observer* might put it, "World Run By Computer." Or at least, the fact that computation is already deeply woven into the everyday functioning of the world's economies, from high-frequency trading on financial markets, to the algorithmic management of logistics networks,[60] to the automated software that approves or denies

---

[59] Quoted in Eden Medina's *Cybernetic Revolutionaries* (2011), a great book and the only extensive English history about Cybersyn, as far as I know. By the way, I just noticed something interesting about Tim Maughan's BBC article, quoted elsewhere in this afterword—the title is "The invisible network that keeps the world running," but the URL contains something different— "the-network-that-runs-the-world"—the original title, maybe? There's a big difference between those two titles...

[60] Tim Maughan, writing about how a Maersk container ship unloads its cargo at each port: "It's the kind of logistical information that it's hard to imagine any one human mind comprehending, and the truth is no single one does—this is distributed knowledge, managed by Maersk's vast world-spanning computer network and shaped and interpreted by complex, similarly unknowable, algorithms. In a very real sense the crane and truck drivers are little more than elements in a vast robotic system, receiving instructions in their cabs from their computerised managers, following orders on endless cycles until their shift ends." Maughan 2015: n.p.

loans and sniffs out bank fraud. In most parts of the world, we are living through the ongoing datafication of society. As data networks deepen their entanglement with our social and cultural life, new affordances arise for the quantification, analysis, administration, phantomization, and financialization of our everyday experience and conduct. We become legible to and manipulable by systems of impersonal power in new and unpredictable ways. This is seen nowhere more clearly than in the growth of platform capitalism—Uber, Airbnb, Amazon Mechanical Turk—and its precarious, often intimately managed workforce. The journalist Paul Mason, drawing on theory by the economist Paul Romer, even suggests that "information technology expels labour from production, destroys pricing mechanisms, and promotes non-market forms of exchange. Ultimately, it will erode the link between labour and value altogether."[61] Speculations about whether we can do things differently, do things better—imagine new forms of economic life that honour what really is valuable—are longer confined to fiction, or to missed moments of revolutionary opportunity, or to easy scary fantasies about supercomputers throwing their weight around like trashy evil gods. Possibilities of new forms of economic life are woven, technologically, throughout the fabric of our changing society. People are confronting them every day, and the choices they are making are, little by little, combining to form the future. These are devastating times, but they are also hopeful times.

Now, let's see how that stock portfolio is doing. Would you look at that, NMC Health (LSE: NMC) is still going up! I'm rich! I'm rich.

---

61 Mason 2015: 179.

WORKS CITED

Aristotle 1992 [c.350 BCE]. *The Politics*. Penguin.

Arnold, Roger. 2013. *Economics*. Eleventh edition. Cengage Learning.

Braudel, Fernand. 1992 [1979]. *Civilization and Capitalism, 15th-18th Century. Volume I: The Structures of Everyday Life, The Limits of the Possible*. University of California Press.

Case, Karl E., Ray C. Fair, Manfred Gärtner, and Ken Heather. 1996. *Economics*. Prentice Hall.

Chang, Ha-Joon. 2010. *23 Things They Don't Tell You About Capitalism*. Penguin.

Clark, Tom and Chris Giles. 2018. "Has economics failed?" *Financial Times*, April 24. www.ft.com/content/670607fc-43c5-11e8-97ce-ea0c2bf34a0b.

Doctorow, Cory. 2009. "Radical Presentism." *Tin House*, October 2009. www.tinhouse.com/blog/4410/cory-doctorow-radical-presentism.html.

Godelier, Maurice. 1977. *Perspectives in Marxist Anthropology*, translated by Robert Brain. Cambridge University Press.

Goethe, Johann Wolfgang von. 2000 [1795]. *The Fairy Tale of the Green Snake and the Beautiful Lily*, translated by Thomas Carlyle (1832). wn.rsarchive.org/RelAuthors/GoetheJW/GreenSnake.html.

Golumbia, David. 2016. *The Politics of Bitcoin: Software as Right-Wing Extremism. Forerunners: Ideas First*. University of Minnesota Press.

Hudson, Michael. 2004. "The Archaeology of Money: Debt versus Barter Theories of Money's Origins" in L. Randall Wray and Edward Elgar (eds), *Credit and State Theories of Money: The Contributions of A. Mitchell Innes*, ed. L. Randall Wray. Edward Elgar Publishing.

Humphrey, Caroline. 1985. "Barter and Economic Disintegration." *Man*, New Series, 20(1), March 1985.

Jevons, William Stanley. 1896 [1895]. *Money and the Mechanism of Exchange*. D. Appleton and Company.

Le Guin, Ursula K. 1976 [1969]. *The Left Hand of Darkness*. Ace.

Le Guin, Ursula K. 1981 [1974]. *The Dispossessed*. Granada.

MacKenzie, Donald. 2006. *An Engine, Not a Camera*. MIT Press.

Mason, Paul. 2015. *PostCapitalism: A Guide to Our Future*. Penguin.

Maughan, Tim. 2015. "The invisible network that keeps the world running." BBC, 9 February 2015. www.bbc.com/future/story/20150209-the-network-that-runs-the-world.

Mazzucato, Mariana. 2018. *The Value of Everything: Making and Taking in the Global Economy*. Allen Lane.

Medina, Eden. 2011. *Cybernetic Revolutionaries: Technology and Politics in Allende's Chile*. MIT Press.

Menger, Carl. 2009 [1892]. *On the Origin of Money*. Translated by C.A. Foley. Ludwig von Mises Institute.

Moylan, Tom. 1986. *Demand the Impossible: Science Fiction and the Utopian Imagination*. Methuen.

Oliver, Joshua, Diane Coyle et al. 2018. "Has economics failed? FT readers and writers debate the future of the discipline." *Financial Times*, May 1. www.ft.com/content/3a1afdec-4c5d-11e8-8a8e-22951a2d8493.

Parkin, Michael and David N. King. 1995. *Economics*. Second edition. Addison Wesley.

Ricardo, David. 1999 [1817/1821]. *On the Principles of Political Economy and Taxation*. Library of Economics and Liberty. www.econlib.org/library/Ricardo/ricP2a.html

Robinson, Joan. 1978. "Keynes and Ricardo." *Journal of Post Keynesian Economics*, 1(1), Autumn 1978. www.jstor.org/stable/4537457.

Scott, Brett. 2016. "The Future of Money Depends on Busting Fairy Tales About Its Past." *How We Get To Next*, March 30. howwegettonext.com/the-future-of-money-depends-on-busting-the-fairy-tales-you-believe-about-its-past-30cbd90619e0.

Simmel, George. 2011 [1900]. *The Philosophy of Money*. Third edition. Translated by Tom Bottomore, David Frisby and Kaethe Mengelberg. Routledge.

Smith, Adam. 1976 [1776/1789]. *An Inquiry into the Nature and Causes of the Wealth of Nations*. Clarendon.

Spufford, Francis. 2010. *Red Plenty*. Faber & Faber.
Swift, Jonathan. 2009 [1726-7]. *Gulliver's Travels into Several Remote Nations of the World*. Gutenberg edition. www.gutenberg.org/files/829/829-h/829-h.htm.
Vogl, Joseph. 2014. *The Specter of Capital*. Translated by Joachim Redney and Robert Savage. Stanford University Press.
Walker, Francis A. 1878. *Money*. Henry Holt and Company.

ECONOMICS DISCUSSION QUESTIONS
Elisabeth Perlman

In 2018, many economists are concerned about potential dystopias: Robert Gordon worries that we have found all the easy innovations; Thomas Piketty worries that the returns to owning money are greater than overall economic growth; and Laurence Kotlikoff worries that all job will be replaced by automation. These concerns provide fertile ground for the dystopian imagination. Many of the stories in Strange Economics grow out of this soil.

As an Economic Historian, I want to help guide your thinking about the economics concepts explored in this volume. Each story has a series of directing questions, which will provide much to mull over and learn more about, and, hopefully, also some illumination.

ALL RIGHTS RESERVED
by Xauri'EL Zwaan

John Adam wakes up in an old fashioned company town, albeit one where the workers have no way to leave or any concept of what leaving might even be like. What is going on outside the "box" in which John dwells is very unclear. How are backup scans of people put to use? What is OmniCor selling? Where does this all fit into the production process? And would people in other parts of OmniCor notice if these backup scans ceased their pattern-matching?

Beyond these world building questions, this story's meat is what it tells us about our current society. How does this story reflect our fears about the way our economies seem to be going? We have seen company towns, and know how they exploit people. From that we are afraid of economic power concentrating (we are afraid of increasing distance between workers and those that manage the company). Are we afraid of the inhumanity of the profit-motivated corporation? Of AI?

THE SLOW BOMB NEIL
by James Hudson

Alistair explains that people implicitly ascribe a price to a human life in many situations, and moreover, have wildly different implicit values in those situations. For instance, one can derive a value from the premium paid to people who take risky jobs, or the amount people pay for safety features on a car, or the amount people are willing to pay for medical care. Studies using plausible estimation strategies on US adults suggest a value anywhere from $2 million to $14 million in 2010 USD. Similarly, implicit discount rates—the degree to which we value the present more than the future—can be highly variable. Even if this were not the case, an accurate measurement does not imply that calculations made with this number are moral or ethical. Can you think of times where you seemed to discount the future more than you might typically? Given this, what are the limits of performing a cost-benefit analysis? What are the alternatives to cost-benefit analysis? How should and how do policy makers interact with estimates of life's value when considering a policy?

SHAPE, SIZE, COLOUR, AND LUSTRE
by JM Templet

The basic underlying principle of free exchange in a market is that no one will make a trade that will leave them worse off; if a proposed trade would make one of the parties worse off they would simply choose not to engage in it. From the perspective of an outside observer, Maya engages freely in a trade that seems unreasonable. What things would need to be different for you to view Maya's decision as rational according to the above theory? Does Soni act in accordance with the theory? Is either left better off?

Economics Discussion Questions

SUPPLY AND DEMAND AMONG THE SIDHE
by Karl Dandenell

Like many pre-modern (pre-twentieth century) states, the Sidhe Kingdom finances itself through taxes on trade. It is easier to levy taxes on goods as they move through particular points (much like collecting a toll) than to use a more broad based (and likely more equitable) tax system. As Queen Titania believes that the issues with the Sidhe Kingdom's finances stem from tax evasion, it makes sense to try to increase enforcement and raise tax rates. Queen Titania also gives groupings of subjects production quotas and a monopoly on the production of certain goods. How do these monopolies compare to the ones that the British Crown gave out to companies like the East India Company? How do they compare to guilds' controlling production in the middle ages? To the Soviet system of central planning or other top-down defined economics? Does this solution seem likely to be more effective at increasing government stores of gold than simply increasing enforcement and raising rates?

THE MONUMENT
by Andrea Bradley

This story will likely have the reader asking "Why?" Why was the reassignment of the workers handled the way it was? If workers are valuable, why not treat them well, or at least well enough to make sure that they spaced out their food correctly? If workers are not valuable, why bother moving them? Why not just abandon them with the monument?

While I am unable to speak to the logic of the world presented, there was a trade where similar shipping conditions prevailed: the transatlantic slave trade. The slave trade was plagued by extreme crowding, little communication between the shippers and the captives, and significant language barriers. Many people died during the trip. The same questions apply here: if those people being enslaved were valuable, why not treat them better (in terms of maintaining their physical health)? If they were not valuable, why go to all the effort to move them across the ocean?

What are owners of slave ships optimizing? What are their costs? What determines a slaver's revenue?

THE GRASS IS ALWAYS GREENER
by Fraser Sherman

As is noted in the story "Das Kapital" by Stephen Woodworth elsewhere in this volume, rich people live longer than poor people, can afford better food and medical care, live less stressful lifestyles, and can worry about issues further up Maslow's hierarchy of needs. Are there any real life analogies to the sale that occurs in this story? Does this situation seem more unfair than other ways of achieving the same outcome? Why?

CONSUMPTION
by K.M. McKenzie

It is not clear when targeted advertising will lead to losses for an individual. An individual may learn more easily about things they like and spend less attention on things they do not, after all finding a specific thing—whether a job or a shirt that fits—takes time and effort that could be used for other things. Thus, targeted advertising might lower an individual's search cost, leading to benefits for that person. A company might also become better at estimating an individual's willingness to pay and may dynamically price things accordingly. As a result, some individuals may be able to afford things they would not have been able to afford at a flat price (which is beneficial to these people). Some people, however, will wind up paying more (thus incurring losses). This often seems unfair, despite the different valuations that these individuals have for the good (why?). However, this story seems to primarily be about people's fights within themselves.

Most economic models assume that an individual has a single set of consistent preferences that come from that person's maximizing a single utility function. However, many behavioural models recognize that people don't always have consistent preferences over time—in some ways, trying to exercise willpower is like playing a game between present you and future you. In a sense, a person's discounting of the future is created through this negotiation. The software posited in this story seems to the character to be unfairly intervening in this negotiation.

This story posits a world where companies target individuals and take advantage of moments of weakness. The objective of advertising is to sway people towards buying something; when does targeting become unethical? In this story, would an ethical company honour a person's desire to be more frugal? Why? When is advertising unethical? How does this relate to a person's utility maximization?

HAVE ICHTHYOSAUR, WILL TRAVEL
by Darren Latta

"O what fine times, this age of dinosaur." In this story, the availability of dinosaurs is considered to be a boon to general economic activity. Does this seem plausible? The dinosaurs are a type of new good, one whose primary value to people is entertainment. Like other entertainment goods (e.g., movies, circuses) many people can be employed supporting this new form of entertainment. How much of an impact would one expect this new good to have? How many people are likely to be employed by this new business?

Trying to value new goods is always tricky. How much would different individuals be willing to pay for it? How does one aggregate those prices? Could this new good affect the purchasing of other goods by changing a person's budget? In other words, what are the general equilibrium effects?

Elisabeth Perlman

EXPIRY DATE
by Eamonn Murphy

End-of-life care is expensive if a person's health declines slowly; this should hold true regardless of the age at which a person starts needing extra care. Thus, the idea that costs can be decreased by asking each person to kill themselves by a particular age only works if they reach that age before they start needing expensive care. So, it is not clear what the corporations are gaining from this practise; they are essentially taking a bet. But every bet has two sides. Why isn't someone betting on the opposite outcome?

I CAN ALWAYS TELL A JOHN
by Greg Beatty

Terry suggests that transactions like the one in this story will become more common, a reordering of the world that Terry finds refreshing. Terry doesn't ask what the cumulative implication will be of this money changing hands. Will the Gliese Aliens acquire money through trade, or are they making it themselves? If the latter, the only way for this story to end well is for transactions like Terry's to be infrequent enough that there is no noticeable impact on the aggregate money supply. What will happen here if there is more money, but no real increase in economic output? Inflation has redistributive consequences that some people might benefit from, they are not generally positive. Is this situation somehow different from 'terrestrial' inflation situations? If the former method of acquiring money, the earth is about to get a massive capital infusion; as many nations with emerging economies know, while this brings more technology, it also comes with massive volatility potential. Integrating your economy with a more technologically advanced one doesn't tend to happen smoothly. What are analogous situations where technology from a more advanced economy was traded to less technologically advanced economy?

THE RULE OF THREE
by Steve DuBois

The competition between small firms and their larger rivals has characterized at least the last century and a half of retailing: from mail-order catalogues competing with local general stores, to chain grocery stores competing with independent shops, and now large online retailers competing with physical stores. By and large, the firms on the larger side of these pairs have ended up with superior outcomes. It is suggested that not only was the windfall at the end related to Brew-ha-ha's success, but that the firm was doing its part to reorient the economy in the way of other disruptive retailers of new products. Is there a long-term place for the independent magic shop in this world? If so, what niche does it fill? Could there be an entire industry revolving around magic?

SHOCKTROOPER SALESMAN
by Simonas Juodis

Living in an economy dominated by the service sector with large political fights over the manufacturing sector, we often lose sight of the large contributions that biological innovations have made to our economic development. The exchange of crops among continents has changed the way entire peoples eat. (Can you picture Indian food without the pepper from the Americas, or German food without the incorporation of potatoes?) Meanwhile, crops have been bred to be more amenable to different climate conditions and mechanical harvesting.

Perhaps more analogously, the introduction of the horse as a military technology drastically changed how wars were fought in Europe, Asia, and the Americas. But are changes like these ever more harmful than they are helpful—are there organisms that have been modified in a way that is seen as useful in the short-run but cause long-term problems?

Elisabeth Perlman

THE SOUL STANDARD
by John DeLaughter

This story starts out with an increased supply of a currency leading to inflation. Why is inflation bad? Hyperinflation, where people lose trust in the value of currency, is clearly very bad, but small amounts of inflation don't have this sort of impact. What is the actual problem being addressed here? The government's lack of control over prices?

It is not easy to switch to a new a currency system, particularly if one system is seen as more legitimate than the other. There have been many instances of countries trying to issue pure fiat currency, often as a way to pay the military during conflicts. When the adopted currency is well established, such as the British Pound in WWI, moving away from the gold standard tends to be okay, but when implementing a new currency (e.g., the continental dollar during the American Revolution) moving to a fiat system tends to lead to monetary crisis. People hoard the old currency and don't trust the new one to be a store of value, such that there may be both high inflation (devaluing of the new currency) and deflation (higher valuing of the old currency). How does the government in this story make sure that the new currency is trusted? Do they have a plan for avoiding deflation if the economy grows?

Much about the soul currency system is left open to interpretation: who are exchanges being made between? How do souls recirculate?

GUNS OR BUTTER
by Wayne Cusack

What did the Aliens do to cause this level of desperation? If people reject money, generally because it is no longer a store of value (as in hyperinflation episodes), and they are no longer willing to use it as a medium of exchange, and consequently the system of exchange breaks down. Barter is a very inefficient method of distribution. There are many examples of this sort of collapse over the last hundred years, the most notable one in 2018 occurring in Venezuela, where a combination of hyperinflation and the lack of ability to buy imported goods led to mass desperation.

However, there is no mention of hyperinflation in this story. Nor is it clear that the Aliens interfere with production, especially not food production. There is some implication that there is a short term boost in manufacturing production. Was it simply the stress of dealing with Aliens that led to the breakdown of supply channels?

THE SLURM
by Marissa James

The story ends with Meiru learning that the destruction she caused during her hunt for the Slurm reduced the reward greatly. Perhaps Meiru could have done a better job negotiating her contract. After all, collateral damage is inevitable when one is hunting a monster. This is an example of the classic principal-agent problem: how can an employer (the principal) ensure that the person they hire (the agent) behaves in a way that aligns with the employer's interests? How would you write a contract if you were a monster killer? What if you were the one doing the hiring?

THE PRICE OF WOOL AND SUNFLOWERS
by Samantha Rich

What does the Empire achieve by creating the illusion that the markets don't require management?

The first time the government does intervene, they increase wool stores by fifty percent. This shouldn't change the demand for wool, either domestically or abroad, but it does affect the quantity supplied.

The impact of this increase depends on transportation costs and on how much of the world's wool production the Empire accounts for. If the Empire accounts for very little of global wool production, prices should stay the same. The extent to which quantity sent abroad will increase depends on how much transportation costs change. Domestic transportation might be quite expensive, as animal-powered overland transportation is several orders of magnitude larger than water transportation (in 1800, the cost of sending something from London to Boston, MA was equivalent to the cost of sending something about twenty miles over land from Concord, MA to Boston, MA—thus, the coastal US could be more economically integrated with Britain than with places only a few miles inland). If the Empire accounts for a large fraction of global wool production, prices will decrease both abroad and domestically. The quantity sent abroad will be determined by transportation prices. What, then, are Great Pazdah upset about?

Domestically, given that wool is a good that keeps, and is also a good for which production needs to be planned in advance, it is not clear how shepherds will respond to the increase in supply—will they kill some sheep and sell them for meat? Will they choose not to shear some sheep this year? Will they breed fewer sheep? How much wool will they choose to sell at any one given time? How will their incomes change?

A RENEWABLE RESOURCE
by Steve Quinn
Notes by Nate Young, http://people.bu.edu/nvcyoung/

Would the first prince-regent have made a different choice had he known the likely outcome of his city? The first prince-regent lived out his life before the dragon's first visit, the next one experienced almost a full lifetime of wealth and power before being incinerated, while the following one (his son) lived a full life dying after just falling short of the dragon's expectations. That is three or four generations potentially better off than otherwise.

The other inhabitants of the city also did well in a similar way, generations of people lived out richer lives because of this city. Before modern sanitation (principally water treatment), cities were deadly. Had people not migrated from rural areas, city populations would have shrunk.

There were also catastrophes, large deadly fires (think London or Chicago), but yet people did migrate, city populations did grow. Why? Presumably because the wage increase was worth it. Could it have been similar for the residents of this city?

Is the city here very different from any other entrepreneurial enterprise? Few firms ever last the lifetime of their founders. The prince-regents and city inhabitants were allowed to keep everything the city generated above and beyond the statue for a period of time. In fact, the residents of the city put a fair amount of time and effort into smaller statues and other endeavours that carried zero value to the dragon—he just wanted the big statue. But he avoided monitoring costs by doing so.

In the end, the city was ended and its task passed on to some new entrant into the dragon statue-sculpting business. Why didn't the dragon just eat the prince regent, change the management and not lose all of the capital the city had accumulated? Did he get some value from the destruction?

THE GRAVING DOCK
by Michael H. Hanson

What is the point of mothballing people in this world? If one desires to have people in reserve to fight wars or add to the labour force, who would be the optimal person to put through this process from the point of view of an uncaring technocrat? One would likely want soldiers and labourers to possess strength and stamina. Keeping people alive at low cost, however, will weaken them (see "The Monument"). There is also a tradeoff between wanting to use one of these subjects today and in the future. Thus, an uncaring technocrat must figure out what the present value of each person is, and what the option value of that person is (people are kept as a sort of insurance). Who seems worthwhile to store?

How do these mothballing facilities compare to private prisons? Assisted living facilities? Middle schools? Are there any other institutions that seem to resemble mothballing facilities?

Elisabeth Perlman

UNSEEN FACE OF THE MOON BUSINESS
by Diana Parparita

This story revolves around labour market discrimination. Individuals are able to secure better business deals—and experience sexual harassment less frequently—if they look like middle-aged white men. But in this story, everyone has access to technology that allows them to appear as middle-aged white men, whether through surgery or through cosmetic bots, and most people take advantage of this. There are severe implications for people who choose to not alter their appearances. What are some other career-related benefits a person might gain by altering their appearance?

"I sold it for half of what we paid for it," Carol pointed out. "Before the bubble burst, Maddison, before the bubble burst. Prices went down, they're still going down."— There is a (moon) real estate bubble, which bursts, so prices are falling. Then some company buys all of the real estate on the moon and merges with a lab that does "terraforming." Does this make the land suddenly more valuable? Is this why the protagonist feels betrayed? Or does she just think she could have gotten a better price because of the need for a consolidated tract of land, and the value of being the one outlier?

THE SHORT SOUL
by Jack Waddell

Farmers take on a great deal of risk. There is a long time lag between when investments are made and when crops are sold. Even if an individual farmer could perfectly predict how investments made would correspond to yield, it is hard to optimize investments without knowing what prices a crop will fetch. Remember, in order to maximize profits, a firm will make sure marginal revenue equals marginal cost; this is hard to do when revenue is extremely uncertain. The Valkyries, like many farmers, choose to hedge against this risk by locking in a future price. However, they end up taking a different kind of risk—yield risk (people stop dying). Is there a futures contract that the Valkyries could have entered into in order to hedge against yield risk? Would such a contract come with monitoring problems (cause moral hazard, that is, the incentives are such that Valkyries are likely to put in very little effort soul-farming)?

When it seemed like the Valkyries couldn't make their contract, Yanluo was delighted. Did the futures contract the Valkyries entered into have contingency clauses? Have these clauses been written so Yanluo would be better off with a forfeiture than performance of the contract? (In common law countries bankruptcy proceedings work as last resort contingency clauses, and typically both creditors and debtors are worse off under forfeiture or bankruptcy proceedings than under fulfilment of the contract.) Under what concept of fairness would it have been fair/unfair for the Valkyries to go out of business? How do current laws and institutions protect farmers from these risks (e.g., crop insurance)?

SUPPLY CHAINS
by Petra Kuppers

Vicki has chosen to vertically integrate her small-town coffee shop with its upstream supplier (that is, she has chosen to own her supplier); vertical integration tends to be most beneficial when it is hard to align the incentives of the upstream supplier and the downstream producer. In typical coffee production, this is relatively easy, as the downstream producer is buying a product whose quality is easy to observe. Vicki, however, cannot verify that the coffee beans have been through the correct production process. Thus, despite running a small town shop, she has chosen to retain control over her supply chain. Unfortunately, this still does not solve the principal-agent problem that occurs with individual employees. Economists have proposed that sometimes firms offer wages above the market clearing wage, an efficiency wage, because higher wages help reduce shirking when effort is not perfectly observed. Is there a way Vicki could have arranged her business to reduce the risks inherent in the principal-agent problem?

Elisabeth Perlman

PREMIUM CARE
by Brandon Ketchum

The economics of healthcare in the developed world is extremely complicated due to the number of different agents involved in any transaction, often with incentives that are at cross purposes. There is also the question of how much people are willing and able to pay for healthcare, or as is generally the case, how much they are able to convince someone else to pay. This story, at first glance, seems to reflect monopoly pricing. But, if that were the case, the companies in the story would not be able to price discriminate—to charge different people (or different people's plans) different amounts.

In the healthcare system at work in this story, what parties are involved in decisions about care quality, type, and prices? What are their incentives?

DAS KAPITAL
by Stephen Woodworth

When economists talk about capital, they very rarely mean money itself—a typical production function takes capital and labour as inputs, capital in this context being an abstraction for all the tools that help make a good. Tools that might be complicated and specialized: a conveyor belt oven for baking crackers, a paint-spraying robot for painting a car, a machine that lays down tiny transistors on silicon chips. All these things are capital; all these things are definitely not money. Money is a medium of exchange, a unit of accounting, and a store of value; it has no use in and of itself. Money is valuable because it can be used to buy tangible things. Even in the money market, short term loans are used to make payroll. This story asks us to reflect on capital while also struggling, as many do, to set down a concrete definition of the thing.

The story asks us to imagine money itself as representing this abstraction. The question that Thomas Piketty asks (and answers controversially) is as follows: what are the returns on capital, or rather, what are the returns on giving someone money to buy tools? How do they compare to the returns on labour? Or, because labour is as crude a category as capital, to management skills? To a wide variety of other skills? To overall economic growth?

ABOUT THE CONTRIBUTORS

Greg Beatty
Author, "I Can Always Tell a John"
Greg Beatty lives with his dog in Bellingham, Washington, where he tries unsuccessfully to stay dry. He writes everything from children's books to essays about his cooking debacles. For more about Greg's writing, visit www.greg-beatty.com.

Andrea Bradley
Author, "The Monument"
Andrea Bradley is a writer and college professor from Oakville, Ontario. She makes occasional appearances online at www.andreabradley.ca and @amcbradley1.

Wayne Cusack
Author, "Guns or Butter"
Wayne Cusack began writing science fiction three years ago and is thoroughly enjoying this new twist in his life. He lives in Toronto.

Karl Dandenell
Author, "Supply and Demand Among the Sidhe"
Karl Dandenell is a survivor of Viable Paradise XVI and an active member of the Science Fiction Writers of America. He lives on an island near San Francisco with his family, cat overlords, and a large stash of strong tea. You can find him at www.firewombats.com.

John DeLaughter
Author, "The Soul Standard"
John DeLaughter is a retired planetologist who lives on a sailboat with Nimrod the cat. His work has taken him to all seven continents, where he has met the nicest of people.

About the Contributors

Steve DuBois
Author, "The Rule of Three"
Steve DuBois is a high school teacher from Kansas City and the author of numerous works of fiction and non-fiction. His author site is www.stevedubois.net.

Michael H. Hanson
Author, "Warm Storage"
Michael H. Hanson is the Creator of the Sha'Daa shared-world dark-fantasy anthology series. He has over ninety short stories, published in the fields of science fiction, horror, and fantasy, and four collections of poetry.

Neil James Hudson
Author, "The Slow Bomb"
Neil James Hudson is the author of around forty stories. His collection, "The End of the World: A User's Guide" can be ordered from his website at neiljameshudson.net. He works in York as a charity shop manager.

Marissa James
Author, "The Slurm"
Marissa James has been an editor, veterinary assistant, and arts professional—sometimes simultaneously—and has been published by Daily Science Fiction, Crossed Genres, and Third Flatiron Press. Not simultaneously. She lives outside of Portland.

Simonas Juodis
Author, "Shocktrooper Salesman"
Simonas Juodis is a writer from Lithuania. He works in biotech and likes to tell stories in his spare time.

About the Contributors

Brandon Ketchum
Author, "Premium Care"
Brandon Ketchum is a speculative fiction writer from Pittsburgh. He has attended Cascade Writers Workshops, In Your Write Mind Workshops, and the Nebulas. His work has appeared in a variety of publications.

Petra Kuppers
Author, "Supply Chains"
Petra Kuppers's stories have appeared in publications such as PodCastle, Capricious, The Dunes Review, Anomaly, The Future Fire, and Accessing the Future: A Disability-Themed Anthology of Speculative Fiction. She lives with her partner, poet and dancer Stephanie Heit, in Ypsilanti, Michigan, where they co-create Turtle Disco, a community movement and writing space.

D.K. Latta
Author, "Have Ichthyosaur, Will Travel"
D.K. Latta lives in Ontario and has been writing stories (mostly science fiction and fantasy) and non-fiction (about comic books, Canadian movies, and other esoteric topics) for years -- enthusiastically, if not always prolifically.

Jonathan Maurin
Cover Artist
Jonathan Maurin is a French illustrator and concept artist who loves to create new worlds.

K.M. McKenzie
Author, "Consumption"
K.M. McKenzie lives in Toronto. Her life revolves around writing, fantasizing, and watching tennis. You can follow her on Twitter @kebramm.

Strange Economics

Eamonn Murphy

Author, "Expiry Date"

Eamonn Murphy lives in the south west of England. He writes short stories and is a regular reviewer for sfcrowsnest. His website is at eamonnmurphyblog.wordpress.com.

Diana Parparita

Author, "The Unseen Face of the Moon Business"

Diana writes from Romania.

Elisabeth Ruth Perlman

Economist, Editor, Discussion Question Contributor

Elisabeth Ruth Perlman is an economic historian who studies the nineteenth century and early-twentieth century United States, with a focus on how changing transportation and commutation networks changed the spatial distribution of economic activity and technological innovation. They received a PhD in Economics from Boston University and are currently an Economist at the US Census Bureau. You can find more about their research at www.elisabethperlman.net.

Steve Quinn

Author, "A Renewable Resource"

Steve Quinn is a lawyer by day. Usually. He does a lot of project management and some coding, and occasionally fixes his colleagues' computers with a Sonic Screwdriver. When he's not writing legal or computer code, he's probably being hit with escrima sticks.

Samantha Rich

Author, "The Price of Wool and Sunflowers"

Samantha Rich is a lifelong fan of speculative fiction. She lives in Maryland with a bossy cat and a nervous dog.

Fraser Sherman

Author, "The Grass is Always Greener"

Fraser Sherman was born in England but spent most of his life in Florida. He now lives in Durham with his perfect wife and two wonderful dogs. He's published more than two dozen short stories and three film reference books.

JM Templet
Author, "Shape, Size, Colour, and Luster"
JM Templet lives and works in Louisiana as a librarian. She thinks tofu is a verb.

David F. Shultz
Editor
David writes from Toronto, where he also works as a teacher and leads the Toronto Science Fiction and Fantasy Writers Group.

Jack Waddell
Author, "The Short Soul"
Jack Waddell is a southern writer, physicist, and educator. He lives with his wife, daughter, and furred companions in Arkansas, where he enriches young minds (but only to reactor-grade levels, he swears). You can find him at gildthetruth.wordpress.com or on Twitter @OrnaVerum.

Jo Lindsay Walton
Guest Editor, Afterword Contributor
Jo Lindsay Walton edits Vector, the critical journal of the British Science Fiction Association, along with Polina Levontin. He researches science fiction and political economy, and runs the website Economic Science Fiction and Fantasy.

Stephen Woodworth
Author, "Das Kapital"
Stephen Woodworth is the author of the New York Times bestselling Violet Series of paranormal thrillers, including Through Violet Eyes, With Red Hands, In Golden Blood, and From Black Rooms, and the Gothic horror novel Fraulein Frankenstein. His short fiction has appeared in such publications as Realms of Fantasy, Weird Tales, Fantasy & Science Fic-

Strange Economics

tion, and Year's Best Fantasy. His first collection of horror short stories, A Carnival of Chimeras, is forthcoming from Hippocampus Press.

Xauri'EL Zwaan
Author, "All Rights Reserved"
Xauri'EL Zwaan is a mendicant artist in search of meaning, fame and fortune, or pie (where available). Zie is a Genderfluid Bisexual, Greenpunk Socialist, Satanist, and Goth. Zie lives in Saskatoon, Saskatchewan, Canada with zer monogamous life partner and writes for more or less a living.

Printed in Great Britain
by Amazon